Strategic Multiverse Operations

LIGHTNING | ORIGINS
[DEFINITIVE EDITION]
Antonio Reyes Jr.

ISBN: 978-1-09832-180-2 (Paperback)
ISBN: 978-1-09832-181-9 (eBook)

Any references to historical events, real people, or real places are used fictitiously. Names, characters, and places are products of the author's imagination.

Table Of Contents

Welcome

This Science Fiction Techno Thriller contains concepts of Military Action,

Romance, Drama and Faith

Keep an open mind as you dive into this multiverse of infinite possibilities

I hope you enjoy reading Origins as much as I have enjoyed writing it

Welcome to the multiverse and Strategic Multiverse Operations

Definitive Edition Notes

This Definitive Edition of Lightning | Origins is now in a smaller form factor

book template, has a more professionally designed interior, and Lightning

Archival Records Excerpts positioned in key locations through out the book

giving more insight into the Lightning Multiverse. This is the Definitive

Experience of Lightning | Origins

In the early twenty second century, man-kind had begun its expansion into space. As newly discovered worlds were colonized, a sense of independence was formed between each of these colonies. Although official government for these worlds were established by the UEG, United Earth Government, many colonists mistrusted Earths intentions. In fear of the UEG's power and possible corruption, some colonists started an extremist rebellion against earth to gain full independence from Earth's influence.

For fifty years between 2188 and 2238 this conflict over the independence of the colonies had been waged. In that time, the leaders of the UEG, the Continental Council, had ordered to cease all space expansion operations until the situation with the current colonies have been dealt with. This order from the council created the border of the unreached worlds. The UEM, United Earth Military, had engaged these extremist rebel forces led by Garza Liankos on the planetary colonies near these borders. This conflict is known as The Colonial Wars. This war's conclusion is the Origins of Organization Lightning.

Lightning Archival Records
Brief History Of FTL (Faster Than Light) Technology
In Universe IIII
By Timothy "Hawk" Doyle

Between the years 2082 and 2100 A.D., A Space Engineer by the

name of Doctor Danial Stone officially began to experiment with FTL

technology hoping to bring fourth a new era of space travel for

mankind. The first FTL drive was completed and successfully tested

on January 1st 2100 A.D. just in time for the new 22nd century.

Prologue: Discovery

"Control, this is Endeavor requesting permission to engage FTL drive within fascinate of Luna. Destination, Mars." Naval Lieutenant Douglas said through the communications channel wearing a green flight suit with a flight helmet as he sat in the pilot's seat prepping the Endeavor for launch. The Endeavor was a small Class A Cargo freighter designed for local system transportation and cargo delivery with a crew of seventeen personnel.

"Roger that Endeavor, launch when ready. Hope you make it back before poker tonight." Air Force Colonel Moss responded with a chuckle as he stood wearing his service uniform with silver clovers on his shoulders representing the rank of Lieutenant Colonel. He sipped on his coffee and walked through the flight control center looking at a large monitor watching ships leaving and entering the base. The control center had many controllers sitting at their stations in multiple rows conducting tasks in front of their computers.

Lieutenant Douglas on board the Endeavor laughed. "Roger that control, Endeavor out."

"So, what's the task of the day sir?" Lieutenant Junior Grade Nelson asked Douglas from behind while entering the cockpit also wearing his green flight suit and gear with little enthusiasm.

"As usual, an easy supply run to the training outpost on Mars. Making sure that the soon to be deployed units out there are getting fed."

Nelson sighed in disappointment. "Sir, I'll be honest. I signed on to be a pilot to fight the Rebels in orbit around the colonies, not to do supply runs on the home front."

Douglas was getting annoyed. "Nelson, I told you a million times, this war is no joke."

"I don't think it's a joke sir, I just want to fulfill my duty to earth like so many others out there on the colonies. Been waiting for my combat flight school to get approved for months now and I still haven't heard anything."

"What do you think we're doing right now?" Douglas said looking at Nelson. "Serving Earth by serving our fellow soldiers. Take pride in that at least. Trust me, don't go looking for trouble." Douglas got back on communications looking away from Nelson. "Control, Endeavor. Ready to engage FTL in five, four, three," During the count down, the engines of the ship revved up louder and louder while Douglas slowly moved up the FTL control throttle. "Two, one." When the throttle reached full, he pressed a button at the top of the throttle that said "Launch FTL". Suddenly there was a bright flash of light as Douglas and Nelson jerked back in their seats from the sudden burst of speed. As the G-Force stabilizers kicked in, their body's quickly relaxed. "What's our status?" Douglas asked Nelson.

"Maintaining speed at FTL Three under the FTL Four solar regulations, our flight path is clear, hull is stable, should reach Mars in three hours."

"Good. So, how's the family?" Douglas asked while turning his seat towards Nelson.

"Well, Jenna is expecting again." He responded while finishing up his launch report on his console.

"Really? Congrats! That's number two right?"

"Yea, Me and her are hoping it's a girl this time." He turned his seat to face Douglas.

"A girl? First you want to fight the Rebels and now you want a girl? You like danger don't you?"

"Why do you say that?" Nelson said laughing.

"Girls are the hardest to raise, not to mention the most expensive. First her puppy dog eyes begging for stuff all the time, then prom, and don't forget about wedd-" Suddenly a collision alarm sounded. Douglas was worried. "I thought you said our flight path was clear?"

Nelson responded nervously. "It was..." They both quickly turned back to their consoles trying to figure out what was happening. Their fingers danced along the ship controls quickly scanning for any possible ships, debris, or even a rogue satellite. "I double checked there's nothing else out there."

Douglas thought for a moment than had an idea, although he thought it was impossible, he suggested it anyway. "Scan for any spacial anomalies."

"Anomalies? In the solar system?"

8

"Do it!" Douglas ordered.

"Aye!" Nelson began his scan. Less than a second later the scanners picked up something. "Oh my god..." he said in shock looking at his station's monitor.

"What is it?" Douglas asked in fear.

"Switching it to the main monitor." The main monitor at the front of the cockpit showed a thermal scan of what was in front of the ship. It seemed to be a large red cloudy object that couldn't be seen with the naked eye.

"What the hell is that?"

"I have no idea." Suddenly the ship began to violently shake in every direction. Douglas and Nelson held on to the sides of the cockpit for dear life while still trying to pilot the ship. The seventeen crew members on board were becoming worried at what was causing the ship to shake so violently.

"All stop! Now!" Douglas ordered.

"I already did! We're not stopping!"

"What!?"

"It's like, it's pulling us in or something! I can't stop it!"

"OH SHIT!!!" Douglas screamed as he suddenly felt an extreme force pulling him and Nelson forward so violently, their body's tore to shreds along with the rest of the cockpit and the ship.

"Sir!" One of the controllers in the flight control center back on the Luna base shouted.

"Lieutenant?" Colonel Moss asked in concern.

"I just lost contact with the Endeavor!"

"What?" Colonel Moss became worried as he walked towards the Lieutenant and his station.

"Right here sir," He points to a spot on the solar system star chart on his console zoomed in on an area between Earth and Mars closer towards Earth.

"Send drones and alert Search and Rescue." Colonel Moss firmly ordered.

"Yes sir." The Lieutenant responded as he conducted what the Colonel ordered.

Continental Council Chamber – Earth
October 16th, 2233
0800 Standard Earth Time

A full day later, the Endeavor incident was presented to the Continental Council of Earth with great concern. "This meeting is now in session." A man with gray hair said while sitting in his seat behind and in the center of a very large semi-circular desk in a very large and dimly lit room with a second floor balcony in front of the desk. On the face of the desk was a name plate lined up with the man that said Soller. Along the rear of the desk were six other people, three to Soller's left, and three more to his right with name plates lined up where they were sitting, all wearing professional business attire. At each end of the desk were armed guards in military uniform. In front of the semi-circular desk, almost in the middle of the semi-circle, was an Army Four-star General named Madson in an all-black dress blue uniform. Next to him on his right was Colonel Moss in an all blue uniform. Councilor Soller continued to speak. "Colonel Moss, please give us your verbal report on the incident."

"Yes councilor." Moss began, "On October 15th 2233 at 0901, the Endeavor mysteriously disappeared in a region of the solar system between Earth and Mars's orbits. Drones were deployed to search for survivors however there was no confirmation of wreckage or body's at the site."

A female councilor to Soller's left near the end of the table with the name plate reading "Grant" spoke. "How is it possible for there to be no signs of wreckage?"

Moss looked at General Madson for an okay to say something. The General nodded in agreement, then colonel Moss continued. "We couldn't get any confirmation on a wreck because... our drones were disappearing within range of that location as well." The council was surprised at what they heard.

"What do you believe this to be Colonel?" A dark skinned male Councilor with the name plate reading "Stratus" on Soller's right near the end of the table asked in concern

"Councilors," General Madson Spoke. "If I may?"

"Please General." Councilor Lock who was also on Soller's right just before Stratus said with an English accent.

"Thank You, our top scientist believed it to be some kind of spacial anomaly we have never encountered before."

"A spacial anomaly?" Councilor Greaves, who was on Soller's right just before Lock, asked with a Spanish accent. "We've been traveling between planets in the solar system for years, why haven't we found this anomaly sooner? Why shouldn't we believe this to be some kind of terrorist attack from the Rebels?"

"According to our scientists, this anomaly only exists in that one specific spot in space. Just so happens that Luna and Mars were in perfect orbital positions for the Endeavor to set course directly into it."

The council members looked at each other agreeing that this made sense. Then councilor Yang, who was on Soller's left just before Grant, with an Asian accent spoke with dissatisfaction. "So you're telling us we have some random anomaly in our own backyard pulling disappearing acts on our ships?"

"I'm afraid so councilor." Madson said.

Suddenly a mysterious man clothed in all black, wearing a hoodie, a mask and tinted glasses slowly walked into the middle of the council chamber from out of the shadows with his hands up and his elbows at a ninety-degree angle. "If I may councilors!?" The whole room looked at the mysterious man as he approached the council. Immediately, the guards drew their side arms along with Colonel Moss and General Manson. The guards yelled "GET BACK!!!" and other harsh warnings.

"SECURITY!" Colonel Moss yelled out loud. "We have an intruder in the council chamber!"

"WO, WO! Take it easy!" The mysterious man said. "I'm just here to talk about your little anomaly issue!"

General Madson spoke with anger in his voice to the guards. "Put this man under arrest!"

The mysterious man continued as the guards approached him. "That Anomaly is a Universal Rift. If you let me, I can show you how to use it for your benefit." He finished just as the guards were about to put cuffs on him.

"Stop!" Councilor Soller ordered. The guards looked at the Councilor halting their arrest. "Are you a scientist?" He asked.

"No sir, however I know more about how these Rifts work than any scientist in your universe."

"Our universe?" Councilor Sven who was on Soller's left just before Yang, said with a Russian accent in intrigue. "What are you getting at?"

"Council, if you'd allow me, I can show you everything I know. Let me approach the sight under your observation and I can get the remains of the endeavor back."

Soller had doubts. "I heard enough, get this mad man out of here." The guards continued their arrest just as the mysterious man suddenly disappeared. Everyone in the room gasped in shock wondering what happened.

"Councilors!" The mysterious man said while slowly floating down from the balcony with his hands still up drawing the attention of the council. Everyone in the room reacted to his voice in surprise. "As you can see, I am no ordinary man." Everyone was in shock as the man tried his best not to present himself as a threat while he softly landed back on the floor in front of the council. "I am offering you a chance at something great for all of humanity. All I ask is that you give me a chance to show you."

Councilor Sollers was now fully interested but also somewhat afraid. "Alright than... we'll give you a shot... what is your name?"

"Forgive me councilors as I must keep my identity hidden for now until I have the full support of this council and its subordinates." He glanced at General Madson as he gave the mysterious man a stern look. The man than looked back at the council. He slowly removed his tinted glasses revealing his eyes. "But for now you may call me," His left eye was blue and his right green. "Rifter."

Chapter I: Slinger

At the top of a plateau surrounded by a vast forest, a man stood near the edge looking towards the horizon as Croza's sun slowly began to crest over it. At a distance he can hear gunfire and explosions from an intense firefight. As the forest met the horizon he sighed in awe at the beautiful sight ignoring the ugliness of the war waging nearby. His Clothes and advanced combat gear consisted of a multi-camouflage combat shirt and pants with integrated knee and elbow pads, fire retardant high grip gloves with his pointer and middle fingers exposed on both hands, a vest like plate carrier connected to shoulder Kevlar plates with magazine filled pouches and other miscellaneous tactical gear, an advanced operator's helmet on his head with small dents, scratches and a name tape on the back reading "Slinger" with some of his dark brown hair exposed below the helmet, and his AR30 Assault Rifle slung on his back with a single point sling and a belt clip.

He pulled his wallet out from the back right pocket of his pants and opened it, exposing his UEM Identification Card on the left side of his wallet with a picture of himself on the left of the card and his name on the right reading "Sergeant First Class Raymond Reynolds". He looked down towards the wallet looking at a picture of a beautiful woman on the right of the wallet with brunette hair in a ponytail smiling back at him. "If you were here right now, you would probably brag about how you could kill every single one of these rebels from this position." He spoke to the picture, then looked back towards the horizon. "Then enjoy the view..." He took in the sight a little longer. "I think I'll send a picture of this to her." He unlatched what looked like a small military grade smart phone called a Taclet from its case strapped to his left forearm. He was about to open the camera app when suddenly the communications app notified him of an outgoing transmission from someone on his team.

"Command, this is White, we need MEDEVAC for these civilians immediately." Captain Lucas "White" Walker, said with a calm voice over the encoded communications channel. Deciding not to take the picture, Raymond quickly latched his Taclet back to his forearm case with his expression turning serious remembering that this battle was still far from over, especially with the predicament his team was in now. He turned around watching Lucas releasing his SDT, Sub-Dermal Transponder, with his left hand ending the transmission. He wore matching gear to Raymond with light brown hair slightly exposed below his helmet and his own AR30 Assault Rifle in his hands with his finger off the trigger in a similar configuration to Raymond's AR30. Comparable to the older model M4 and M16 platforms, it was modified for green side scenarios with an adjustable stock, an ambidextrous safety switch with safe, semi and auto settings, a digital hybrid sight capable of switching between one times to ten times digital magnification with compact ultra resolution, a standard thirty round magazine, and a twenty inch barrel with a matching shroud lined with tactical rails covering the whole barrel up to just before the compensator modified muzzle break. The bottom half of the barrel had an angled fore grip connected to the rails, and the top half had a PEQ30 infrared laser and range finder.

A professional sounding female voice responded back to Lucas over the channel. *"That's a negative White. We can't risk another drop ship. Still too many hostiles in the area, Over."*

Lucas held down the SDT with his left hand again and responded. "Roger that command, out." Then released it. The SDT was surgically placed under his skin behind his jaw and below his lower ear lobe just before the back of his neck.

"So that's it?" Raymond said to his commanding officer and friend with anger in his voice after monitoring the previous transmission. "These people get caught in the cross fire and we're not gonna help them?"

Emotionless, Lucas responded. "Raymond, we have a job to do."

"I know Lucas but, this isn't right." Raymond said in concern,

"Commands priority is finishing this fight against the rebels. These people had their chance to leave, this is a war zone. It's not our fault if they didn't heed our warning."

"But they're still people. They are here, and they need our help." With desperation in his voice. "Ask command for permission to CASEVAC via ground vehicle at least."

Lucas was growing annoyed as he thought to himself for a moment, than agreed. "Ok. I'll try." He looked back to his own Taclet with the communications app open making sure the encoded frequencies were still active knowing the encryption keys would change soon. He then pressed and held down his SDT and began speaking to command again through the encoded comm channel. "Command, this is White. Requesting permission to CASEVAC the civilians out of the battle space via ground vehicle, Over," He released the SDT.

"Negative White, we need you and your team to hold that position to support the advancing element."

Holding down the SDT, "What is the advancing elements ETA Command? Over." than released.

"Fifty-Eight Mikes, over."

Still monitoring communications, Raymond had shock in his voice while still trying to maintain his composure. "A whole hour?!"

With an annoyed expression, Lucas responded to Command. "Roger that Command, out."

"These people aren't gonna last thirty minutes." With frustration in Raymond's voice.

"I know Raymond, there's nothing else we can do." Lucas says to him regretfully then begins to walk away.

Raymond looks down thinking for a moment. He looks back with a determined look and smiles at his companion with an idea. "There is one."

Lucas stops, closes his eyes with a sigh of annoyance and says "What?" with an annoyed tone than turns around while opening his eyes.

"I can take them back by myself in the ATAV."

In surprise, "By yourself?! Are you nuts?! The enemy is still out there!"

"The All-Terrain Armored Vehicle only needs one driver, the Auto Targeting System can handle any hostiles that get in the way. The ATAV with the ATS is all I need to drive back to the nearest outpost in the rear line, the nearest one is less than fifteen minutes away, even less if I'm punching it." He said confidently.

Lucas knew it could work but it was too risky for Raymond.

However, knowing Raymond, he could handle himself very well, but

Lucas still had convictions. Trying to convince Raymond, "We need you here with the rest of the team."

"You guys and the platoon of Croza militia can handle this position just fine without me. Please Lucas, don't hold me back from doing the right thing."

Lucas thought it over one more time. With a sigh, he responds. "This is stupid, and reckless. If you mess up, you and those civilians will die. You get that right?"

"Yes," Raymond responded with a serious tone. "But If I do nothing, they'll die for sure. At least this way they have a chance."

Lucas calmly nodded his head noticing the seriousness in Raymond's eyes. "You go as fast as you can, and don't stop. Understood?"

Raymond smiled. "Gotcha." He walked past Lucas down the hill away from the edge of the plateau towards the ATAV where the wounded civilians were being treated.

Lucas turned towards him as he walked. "We'll provide over watch as you move away from this position but if you move out of our FOV, you're on your own."

"Got it." Raymond acknowledged. He looked up for a moment while he was still near the top of the hill. Through the dense forest and dim sunlight, He could barely see the outpost he planned to move to at a guess estimate of two Kilometers away dead ahead. There should be no reason for his travel path to move outside of his team's Field of View.

Lucas, watching Raymond from afar with a worried expression, whispers, "God's speed crazy." He then looked down at his Taclet and began to privately text his fellow teammate Jake of the situation while saying to himself, "Looks like we're hitching a ride with the militia."

While Raymond continued walking down the hill, it was as if everything around him began to move in slow motion. Croza's sun began to rise even higher above the horizon behind him as he took off his advanced operators helmet, looked towards the sky and took a deep breath through his nose. The smell of carbon, smoke, and grass flooded his nostrils as he also felt the cool breeze through his dark brown hair that had grew out a little further than the military standard cut. On exhale he closed his eyes in mid step focusing, meditating himself into battle mind, preparing for a fight. He opened his eyes while putting his helmet back on leaving the chin strap unbuckled. His situational awareness was on point as he heard what sounded like a friendly F-93 Multi Environment Fighter behind him in the distance providing air support. With each step closer to the vehicle, he felt his boots bristle against the grass. He looked around and saw trees in greater detail with their branches and leaves defined. He heard the distant gunfire even more clearly to the point where he could recognize the sound signatures of each weapon that was fired as other teams in the battle space engaged the enemy. He pulled on the hose of his camel back and took a sip of water. It tasted warm.

His perception of time became normal again as he grabbed a disc shaped case out of his combat shirt's left shoulder pocket with his right hand. He opened the case which contained military grade face paint. It had green, brown, and black paint separated by small triangles. However, black was the only one that seemed to have been used before. Raymond swiped his left pointer and middle fingers across the black paint, then wiped the paint onto the left side of his face near his eyes from the nose, all the way back to his thin haired side burn, switched the disk of paint to his other hand, and did the same on the opposite side of his face. A black stripe covered his eye lids from ear to ear as he opened his eyes and checked the application of paint with a small mirror on the back of the disk case lid. He saw it was perfect as his killer instinct began to rive in motivation. He closed the disk case, put it back in his pocket, then buckled the chin strap on his helmet.

Raymond looked left and saw a team sized element of four Croza Militia soldiers securing the perimeter in that direction. He looked right and saw another team of militia doing the same. He then looked forward and saw four ATAVs in a circle facing outward from each other with their ATSs active. As he walked towards the ATAV on his left with his Assault pack on the ground next to it on the driver's side, he met with his teammate and friend Petty Officer First Class Jake "Rophe" Morgan. He was a dark skinned muscular man also clothed in combat gear with his AR30 clipped to his back while his sleeves rolled up to his biceps wearing rubber medical gloves on his hands, covered in blood. Raymond stopped in front of him as Jake removed the gloves trying not get blood on his own skin.

"Well don't you look like a killa." Jake jokingly commented to Raymond about his face paint with a smile.

"I thought the occasion called for it." Raymond responded with a chuckle.

"Na man, looks good. After she left I thought I'd never see that paint job again."

"Thanks man, how are they holding up?"

"Not too good but they're prepped and ready for transport in the back of the ATAV." Jake said while rubbing his hands together in hand sanitizer. "One of the militia men claimed he knew them and decided to go back with you to make sure they made it safely so at least you'll have company. Try not to get into too much trouble okay?"

"Understood."

Jake sighed "You know this is strike three right? The Colonel is gonna have your ass after this."

"I know, but I'd rather get kicked out with a clean conscience than stay in feeling guilty."

"Yea, I figured you'd say that." with a clean right hand, Jake grasps Raymond's left shoulder "Good luck brotha."

Raymond grasps Jake's left shoulder "You too Jake." He let go of his shoulder and made a fist with his right hand. "Unity?" Raymond said with pride, reciting the first half of the United Special Operations Division motto.

"Is Victory." Jake responded proudly completing the motto while giving Raymond a fist bump.

They both smiled and nodded in acknowledgment, then walked around each other. Raymond picked up his Assault pack weighing around thirty pounds with food, equipment and other gear as he pulled on the handle of the ATAV's driver seat door. The heavily armored hydraulic assisted door hissed as Raymond opened it. He unclipped his AR30 from his back and moved it to the front of his body, climbed inside the vehicle, and sat down in the driver's seat feeling his damp camouflaged combat pants press up against the back of his thighs. He shifted his plate carrier on his upper body slightly so he can feel more comfortable sitting in the seat. "Dang vest..." He said to himself as he felt the plates shift slightly rubbing against his thin laird multi-camouflage combat shirt, compressing against his skin.

The door hissed again as he closed and combat locked it from the inside. He then placed his assault pack to the right of the driver seat between himself and the front passenger's seat. The steering wheel and other controls were in front of him. He switched the ATS into moving fire mode as the M320 Light Machine Gun on the roof gunner position swept from left to right checking for new targets than re-centered back to the twelve o'clock position. A man from the rear of the ATAV grunted, as he crawled into the front passenger seat. He looked like he was in his forty's with gray hair and blue eyes with basic combat gear wearing old Khaki combat pants, T-shirt and chest rig filled with magazines and an older model M16. "What can I do to help?" he asked.

Raymond looked at him and assumed he was the militia man Jake had mentioned. He looked more closely at his equipment with little confidence seeing the older model weapon. He thought for a moment, then unclipped his AR30 from his single point sling connected to his plate carrier. He grabbed the barrel of the weapon from the top, closer to the magazine well. He than pulled back on a spring action lever connected to the inner gas tube with his thumb, disconnecting the front half of the gas tube from the rear half in the upper receiver, while pulling on a small trigger underneath the barrel unlocking it from the upper receiver barrel threads. He twisted the barrel towards himself, separating the barrel from the upper receiver. He than looked down at his assault pack, unzipped it, placed the old twenty-inch barrel inside and pulled out what looked like a 14.5 inch barrel for his AR30 with a vertical fore grip on the bottom rail and a PEQ30 on the top rail. "Here, take this." he said while quickly conducting the same procedure in reverse, connecting the 14.5 inch barrel to the upper receiver making his AR30 the perfect size for manipulating in and out of a vehicle, but still long enough to be effective in field environments. "Shoot back at anything that shoots at us."

The militia man nervously smiled. "Gee thanks but what if they're friendlies that just mistaken us for the Rebels?"

"In the direction we're going pal, trust me, there are no friendlies."

The militia man suddenly seemed nervous due to Raymond's grim words.

Feeling guilty for scaring him, Raymond continued. "At least for the first kilometer." He said with a smile.

"Right..." The militia man responded nervously as he grabbed Raymond's AR30 while placing his old M16 to the side. He then settled into the front passenger seat while Raymond called command on his SDT.

"Command, this is Slinger. I am breaking off from my team and heading to this grid, check mail." Raymond punched in the numbers of the position he was planning to go on his Taclet.

"Negative Slinger, you do not have authorization to move to that outpost at this time. Stay with your team."

"I wasn't asking permission command. I am Oscar Mike to that position with the wounded civilians. Out."

Suddenly what sounded like a very angry man came in on the channel. "S*linger, what the hell are y-!*" Raymond muted the volume on that channel through his Taclet comms app, cutting him off.

Raymond looked at his partner next to him and asked, "You ready?"

"Yeah"

"Let's do this." Raymond put the vehicle in gear and drove down the hill at top speed.

"HEY!" A young male militia sergeant yelled out to Raymond as he drove by. "The fuck is he doing?!"

"The right thing." Technical Sergeant Katherine "Cat Eye" Luma said while standing up just as she finished setting up an over watch position with a range finder and binoculars in the prone position in the direction Raymond's vehicle was traveling. She was also clothed in combat gear taking off her advanced operators helmet and replacing it with a camouflage baseball cap with a United Earth Government flag patch Velcro to the front with shoulder length blond hair running out the back of the cap in a ponytail with her AR30 on the ground next to her equipment with the ejection port facing up and dust cover closed.

"You gotta be shitting me!" The young militia sergeant said. "Your boy is gonna get himself killed!"

"He's our boy, and we'll take care of him!" She snipped while looking straight at the man. "Unlike you."

"The fuck is that supposed to mean?" He asked in anger.

"Wasn't it one of your guys who accidentally shot those civi's in the first place? If you trained your soldiers in better trigger discipline like a real sergeant should, our boy wouldn't have to do what he's doing now."

"You little bi-"

"That's enough!" Lucas interrupted firmly. "Kat, focus on helping Raymond."

"Roger," She respectfully acknowledged as she laid down in the prone while looking into her binoculars.

"And you, get back to your platoon."

The militia sergeant paused in anger. "Yea, sure." He said with an attitude while he walked away with unresolved anger in his step.

"Asshole…" Katherine whispered as she began to recon the path in front of Raymond's vehicle. She called Raymond on the communications app tapping twice on her SDT with her left hand, switching communications to automatic. "Slinger, this is Cat Eye. I have eyes on you traveling south east to the friendly outpost, over."

Raymond responded by also tapping twice on his SDT. "Roger that Cat Eye, what do you see ahead of me?"

"I see a large open area you'll have to pass through before you reach the outpost. However, I also have a visual on multiple hostiles positioned there. I would say to skirt the wood line but I'm assuming you're in a hurry."

"Affirmative Cat Eye, think you can hit that open area with Mortars before I get there?"

"Sure, if you slow down a little."

"Negative Cat Eye, I can't slow down. How far away is it from my position?"

"About half a Click."

"Roger, just send it anyway. I'll figure something out to avoid the kill radius."

"Uh, okay, roger that." she replied surprised at his decision. "Looks like this is gonna be danger close..." she said to herself in concern as she switched her communications to fires net on her communications app and began calling for fire on that area.

The militia man next to Raymond said to him with relief, "At least someone is helping us."

"Yea well, it's the only help we're gonna-" suddenly there was a loud crack sound in the air at the exact moment a large crack on the front window formed.

"CRAP!" Raymond yelled in fear as he turned the wheel to the right around the incoming gun fire.

He turned his head left as he saw Rebels dressed in dark woodland camouflage firing at him and his vehicle from the brush. At that same time, the ATS had snapped towards the Rebels and returned fire. The rebels were torn to shreds as more of them came from the right.

"HANG ON!" Raymond yelled at the top of his lungs as he turned the wheel left, back on course. "FIRE THAT WEAPON!" Raymond yelled at the militia man next to him just as he slid open the heavy ballistic window with force, stuck the AR30 out the window and began to fire at anything he saw moving. 5.56 caliber rounds tore through the air at full auto out of the AR30 striking the rebels dead on. By the time the ATS reacted to the threat, they were already down. Raymond managed to get the vehicle back on course and noticed how well the militia man had handled the hostile rebels. With a surprised expression he saw how quickly he pulled a fresh magazine out of his rig, then reflexively reloading his weapon. "Not bad for a militia guy." Raymond complimented.

"I picked up some things here and there." He responded as he fired his weapon killing more rebels faster than the ATS can react.

"Yea, I can tell." Raymond responded with confusion.

The vehicle started taking fire from all directions; however, it was further away from the last group. "Gotcha." Raymond said as he pressed the Mark Position button on his Taclet. "Cat Eye, Slinger. I have hostiles on my marked position, Check mail!"

"Roger Slinger, good mail. I'll set up a fire mission on that area once your clear. What's your status? Sounds like you took some fire."

With the M320 and the AR30 from the militia man firing in the back ground "I'm okay, we're just taking pot shots now, nothing serious. ATS is responding to threats effectively. You set up the fire mission for that open area yet!?"

"Roger, you are danger close so we are digitally adjusting fire and are about to real world fire for effect now."

"Roger that, I'm gonna skirt the edge of the wood line until the fire mission is done, Slinger out." Raymond slowly turned the wheel right towards a group of rebels firing towards him. The ATS took out one at a time in a sweeping motion while the militia men with Raymond's AR30 fired at targets the ATS didn't react to fast enough.

Back at the top of the hill with Kathrine, "Mongol, this is Cat Eye, fire for effect on Alpha Bravo 0051, over"

Over the channel. *"Roger that Cat Eye, fire for effect on Alpha Bravo 0051, out."*

Raymond continued to follow a straight path bulldozing through enemy fire like the ATAV was invincible. The ATS continued to fire nonstop killing many of the rebel targets in the way. "Ha-ha! Like fish in a barrel!" Raymond said in a cocky fashion.

"Black on ammo!" the civilian yelled while bringing the AR30 back in the window. He then quickly leaned over towards Raymond, "Excuse me." and grabbed a magazine from Raymond's plate carrier.

"Wo, hey!" Raymond reacted in surprise. The militia man reloaded and stuck the barrel of his weapon back out while yelling "UP!" than immediately began firing again.

Raymond was once again surprised at the militia man's reflexive initiative. He knew he had definitely done this before. "Sure, help yourself why don'tcha." He sarcastically commented out loud.

"Cat Eye, Mongol, shot, over"

Katherine Responded "Shot, Out" Katherine switched channels. "Slinger, Cat Eye. The shot was just sent, be ready to move."

While swerving back and forth trying to avoid trees and gunfire "Roger Cat Eye." He quickly turns his head towards the others in the vehicle "Hang on guys, we're breaking right!" Raymond sharply turned right going a little further back into the wood line. As he turned the vehicle, he heard a loud familiar crack in the distance to his left. He turned his head and saw a Rocket Propelled Grenade headed towards him "RPG!!!" he floored the gas in an attempt to dodge it. The rocket impacted against the side of the ATS knocking it out of commission. The explosion was not powerful enough to severely damage the ATAV but created a nasty dent in the roof. For a

moment, Raymond lost control but gained it back. The civilians in the back cursed in shock. The militia man helping Raymond asked "The hell was that?!"

"An RPG, we're lucky to be alive, must have been one of their crappy homemade ones." Raymond noticed that the ATS was not shooting anymore. "Oh great..."

"What's wrong?"

"Our gun is down, we gotta get out of this area now."

"*Splash, over*" Mongol said over the radio to Katherine.

Raymond began to hear a loud whistling coming from the open area. "Get down!" Raymond said out loud while slamming on the ATAV's brake and pushed down than covered the militia man next to him from any possible shrapnel from the coming explosion. Suddenly multiple loud explosions erupted and covered the whole field in smoke and flashes.

"Splash, out." Katherine responded to Mongol as she observed the power of high explosive mortars impacting the enemy's position in a sheath of death and destruction from above.

The mortar strike lasted for ten seconds as the whole field was covered with smoke and flashes from the explosions and debris. The rebels in the tree line took cover in fear. Raymond waited five seconds after the last explosion just to be sure that was the last round, He quickly got off the militia man, turned the wheel towards the open area and slammed on the gas while yelling "Here we go!"

He gunned the ATAV into the open field just as the rebels got back on their feet and started shooting at the vehicle again. Once Raymond's vehicle was out of sight in the smoke the rebels stopped firing knowing they had lost him.

All Raymond could see was smoke as he continued to drive to the friendly outpost with a way point marker guiding him on his Taclat he posted on the dashboard of the vehicle. By now he was at top speed and already half way through the field, far out of range from the Rebels who were firing at him earlier.

"Cat Eye, Slinger, I'm clear of that previously marked area. You can begin a fire mission there to cover your flank."

"Roger that Slinger, setting it up now." In concern "Are you okay?..."

Raymond was about to respond but then noticed the smoke clearing. He began to see craters on the ground from where the rounds impacted, weapons and gear destroyed and body's blown to pieces and mangled beyond recognition.

"Just Peachy Cat Eye..." He replied somberly and sarcastically.

"Roger..." Katherine responded respectfully.

"We're almost there, hopefully no one else gets in the way."

"Understood. What do you think Watchmen is gonna say about all this?"

"It is what it is now, I'll take full responsibility like I always do."

"Of course. See you soon."

"Roger Cat Eye, Slinger out"

Moments later, just as Raymond made it to the other side of the field, another vole of mortars hit the North West end of the field where he had initially taken fire. While driving through the woods everything seemed quiet. As Raymond got closer to the outpost he saw a few friendly militia and UEM platoons on patrol. As long as Raymond's vehicle transmitted a friendly IFF signal, the friendly patrols didn't have any reason to stop him. Raymond looked at the soldiers as he drove by. Some young, some old, some worn out from battle, some motivated for more. These guys were grunts like him except he was a whole other breed of warrior.

Raymond had thought back to when he first joined the Army at the age of sixteen as part of the UEM's Early Enlistment Split Training Program and signed up to be a USOD operator. Basic training was easy for him as he quickly returned to school at the end of that summer to finish his senior year. That next summer, he went to infantry school which he also found easy. The real challenge began after completing infantry school and was sent to Special Forces Selection, his first step in joining the USOD. It was boarder line torture as he went through hell at a chance to be one of the best the UEM had to offer. After what he thought was just barely passing selection, he began his Q-Course training to be a Weapons Sergeant. After completing his training, he reunited with his best friend Lucas "White" Walker as he was assigned to Charlie team of the 3rd USOD

Commanded by Colonel Jefferson "Watchmen" Vial.

Raymond and his team have been together for over two years and have seen their fair share of combat against the rebels in this conflict scaling multiple planets. This conflict has gone on for so long, even Raymond couldn't believe that this would be the final battle to put an end to it all, according to the mission brief him and his team received. In that brief, they were informed that the leader of this rebellion, Garza Liankos, was on the surface of this world making his final stand. As Raymond thought about this, he whispererd to himself sadly "As long as mankind exists, there will always be battles..."

"What did you say?" The militia man next to him asked

"What? Oh, sorry, um. I said as long as mankind exists, there will always be battles."

"Ah, I see. I can understand that. Maybe mankind should focus their efforts somewhere else for once. Distract themselves from conflict and look into discovering new worlds and things of that nature."

"Haha, why do you think we're out here on the border of the unreached worlds? We tried that already and it failed. War is always gonna be a factor no matter how much we try to distract ourselves."

"Maybe in this universe yes. But what about other universes?"

"Other universes?" with a chuckle "what are you talking about man?"

"I'm just saying, if there was a whole other universe from this one out there where there is no war, needless death and hate, would you want to live there?"

Raymond gave the militia man a strange look. "Although that does sound a little crazy..." He looked back to the road slowly. "Yea, Of course. I may be a war fighter but it doesn't mean I would choose war over peace. If anything, I would rather fight a war knowing there will be true long lasting peace at the end. Long enough so that I will already be dead when the next war happens. Heck, I'd rather just not have war at all even after I'm long gone."

"I see. Thanks for your answer, I'll see you again soon."

"See me again? What are you-" Raymond said as he turned his head toward the militia man then immediately hit the brakes when he saw the man was gone. Surprised and confused, he looked out the windows and mirrors but couldn't see the man. The only thing left of him was his M16 and the AR30 that he borrowed from Raymond.

"What the hell?..." Raymond said to himself grabbing his AR30 and reconnecting it to his single point sling while wondering if that militia man was actually there or was just a crazy figment of his imagination. He shook his head forcing the thought to the side, getting back on task and continued driving as he still couldn't believe the man could just vanish before his very eyes like that.

Minutes later, Raymond reached the outposts front gate. A group of men all wearing multi-camouflage uniforms were waiting for him. Some of them medics that came to the vehicle to pick up the wounded civilians. A few others stood next to a man in a combat uniform with no helmet, short black hair and gray streaks along the side who seemed really angry towards Raymond. He climbed out of the ATAV, faced the angry man and greeted him.

"Watchman-" Raymond immediately corrected himself remembering that calling Colonel Vial by his call sign when face to face in a safe zone was disrespectful, "I mean, Colonel Vial."

"Sgt. Reynolds!" He responded furiously. "I gave your team orders to secure that hill for the advancing elements and you had the audacity to abandon that position!?"

"Sir, that area was secure, if anything, on my way back I secured it even more when I spotted enemy forces massing for an attack near the base of the hill on our flank. Sgt. Luma called in a fire mission and finished them off."

"That doesn't excuse you from abandoning your post!"

"I abandoned my post to save civilian lives!"

"Your job is to fight this battle with utmost tactical precision! Not save lives!"

"No Sir! As a soldier, it is my duty to protect civilians! That's what this is all about in the first place isn't it? To end this war before more civilians get hurt?! Not helping them would contradict everything we're doing here!"

"Don't talk to me about your philosophical believes like some damn idealist!" Colonel Vial turned towards his right. "Sergeant Burnes!" Sgt. Burnes ran up to the Colonel promptly. "Take Sgt. Reynolds here to the brig. Then prep to Transport him to the

Recluses."

"Yes sir." Sgt. Burnes moved behind Raymond and escorted him to the brig.

"And take that damn paint off his face," Colonel Vial continued as he turned around and began to walk back to his shuttle. "It's not even in regs anymore!".

Raymond quickly responded back to Colonel Vial's comment. "You never said that when she wore it." Colonel Vial paused, then slowly turned half way towards Raymond angrily. He wanted to punch Raymond in the face for that quip, but decided to hold his composure and continued towards the shuttle. As Raymond walked to the brig, many things were going through his mind. However, one thing that kept coming up in his thoughts was how that militia man suddenly disappeared and wondered where he could have gone.

Chapter 2: Rifter

Back on the Recluses, the Star Carrier shaped like an oval cylinder with many weapons and docking bays lining it's hull, Raymond waited to be questioned about his actions by Colonel Vial and other members of USOD's command staff while still wearing combat gear with no helmet or face paint. He sat in his chair in an interrogation room in front of his Commanding Officer Captain Walker also still in his combat gear with no helmet exposing his light brown hair also a little longer than the military standard cut. The walls in the room were gray metal like the rest of the ships interior with a two-way mirror in front of Raymond, behind Lucas. The silence was deafening until Raymond spoke up. "...Any word on those civilians we saved?" he asked with a smile.

Lucas slowly looked at him with a stern expression and responded. "...They'll live." He then looked away.

"Oh, well that's good." Still smiling.

"I can't believe I let you talk me into this shit... again."

"You knew it was the right thing to do."

"As always, you put our careers at risk every time. Not to mention the tactical advantage we had over the enemy this time around."

"I said you didn't need me, you took contact and you still held the hill."

"Yea, this time because we got lucky, what about the next time?" Lucas was becoming increasingly annoyed with Raymond's calm demeanor.

"Then you do it again." Raymond responded carelessly.

"NO!" Lucas slammed the table with his right hand in a fist. Raymond flinched in surprise. "You don't get it do you?!" Raymond never saw Lucas act like this towards him before. Lucas paused to calm himself than continued with a calmer demeanor. "What's gonna happen when we're not so lucky? We will need everyone in order to survive, including you. We can't just have one of us running around like a fucking hero. We made a mistake. I made a mistake, and I will accept that responsibly and consider it to be a lesson learned. I suggest you do the same." Lucas walked out of the room turning his back on his friend as the automatic door slid right than closed after Lucas exited. Raymond relaxed and thought for a moment. He realized that Lucas was right.

After being alone for a moment he heard voices outside his door. They seemed to be muffled due to the minor sound proofing of the room. Raymond grew curious. He got up, walked to the door and leaned closer to listen in. It sounded like two men arguing. Just as his ear was about to touch the door, it slid open. He immediately snapped his posture back as if he was just standing there doing nothing. The two men arguing can be heard perfectly clear for a moment with Raymond recognizing Colonel Vial's voice as one of the men arguing, and the other voice being somewhat recognizable but couldn't remember who it could be. At that same moment, a beautiful woman walked through the doors surprising Raymond as he began to stand up straighter trying to act casual so she wouldn't suspect him of eavesdropping. The door immediately closed behind her, muffling the two men arguing again. She was slender with glasses, long brunette hair in a black professional looking suite with a long tight skirt giving Raymond an odd look. With an Australian accent, she asked, "What were you doing?" She asked while giving a smirk.

"Uh… nothing, thought I heard someone talking so I was about to see what was up."

"You mean eavesdropping."

Nervously "What? No! Really! I-"

"For a Tier Four operator, you sure have a strange demeanor," She said while scanning him from head to toe. "And you're a terrible liar."

"I only lie well if it's really important." He said calmly with a smirk.

"Mmm… I guess I can understand that." She responded with a smile while walking around Raymond. He had never seen this woman before and started to feel nervous as to why she was there. "Take a seat please." The woman said. Raymond sat down in the chair facing away from the two-way mirror trying to keep to the opposite end of the table from where the woman was standing as she looked down at the tablet in her hand. "Sergeant First Class Raymond "Gunslinger"

Reynolds?" She asked.

"Yes. And you ar-?"

"Age 22?"

"Uh...?" Raymond wondered what was happening.

"Answer the question please." She asked politely.

"Uh, yea, I'm 22."

"Born on Earth, New York, New York, in 2216?

"Yea, are those my personnel files?"

"Yes, fell victim to a church bombing at age 12 in 2228?"

Raymond became aggravated. "I'm done answering obvious questions until you tell me what's going on. I thought I was supposed to be talking to Colonel Vial and the rest of the command staff?"

"Oh, you mean that rude colonel? We took care of him, you belong to us now."

In frustration "First of all, I never belonged to anybody in the first place. Second, who's us?"

"Me and my employer of course. I've confirmed that you are actually Raymond Reynolds, and you seem to be growing inpatient so, I'll have him come in to meet you now." Raymond had a sense of anxiety wondering who could have completely over ruled Colonel Vial's authority. She keyed in something into her tablet. A second later the door opened again. A very familiar man wearing black business slacks, leather shoes, and a jacket with a white button down shirt underneath with the top button open with short gray hair on his head and different colored eyes, right eye green, left eye blue, walked into the room smiling while looking at Raymond and sat down in the chair opposite from him. His posture was perfect as his fingers and hands overlapped on the table. "I do believe you recognize me." The man said to Raymond.

"You... You're that militia guy that disappeared!" Raymond was surprised.

"Yes, allow me to introduce myself. My name is Gehnarne, call sign, Rifter. This is my lovely assistant Gia, and I just want to thank you for saving the lives of those men who I am not actually affiliated with at all."

Raymond was Confused. "Why the hell did you lie about claiming to know them, and what was that disappearing act about?"

"Trust me when I tell you that I will explain everything in due time, as for why I lied at least, it was so I can get close to you and test to see if you were the right man for the job."

Raymond looked directly into his green eye curious to whether it was some new style of body augmentation or his natural eye color while also wondering who Gehnarne was and what he wanted. "What job?"

"I'm glad you asked!" He smiled as he got up and started pacing in the room while talking. "Let's start from the beginning. Earth government's plan was to attack the final Rebel strong hold on Croza and finally put an end to this war."

"Yea, that was in the brief that me and my team had received before deploying to Croza"

"Of course, However, knowing how close the rebels were to the unreached worlds, there is a very likely possibility that some Rebel elements could be on the unreached worlds preparing to strike back once they think we have withdrew from the frontier, assuming from our side that there is no more fight. The war will be over so there will be no reason to have our forces continue an advance."

Raymond pieced together what Gehnarne would say next and spoke. "If they do continue to advance, it would lead into exploration of these unreached worlds which the military is not suited for. Plus, knowing how much resources have been spent fighting this war, UEG will just have us either stay where we are in colonial space or withdraw completely. Hopefully the council chooses the former."

Gehnarne continued. "Yes, Also, we have been fighting this war for so long, we don't even have any official organization for exploration anymore. Everything has been folded into the military for the past fifty years this war has been waged."

"That's the cost of victory." Raymond said sarcastically.

"Now, too great of a cost. We need an organization like that and it doesn't exist... Until now." Gehnarne took a seat in front of Raymond. "The council of seven has granted me full authorization to use whatever resources I need to create a para military organization that not only can handle combat operations against remnants of rebel forces, but can also effectively explore other worlds and with my personal help, other universes."

"You mentioned that in the ATAV, what do you mean other universes?" Raymond was very interested.

"Other universes! You know, the theory of the Multiverse? Your familiar with it aren't you?"

Raymond took a moment to think than answered confidently. "Yea, mostly from articles and science fiction novels." Gehnarne sat back in his chair with his right leg crossing over his left leg and his arms folded in a relaxing manner gesturing Raymond to continue. Gia mildly giggled. Raymond looked at Gehnarne with confusion for a moment, then understood what he wanted him to do judging from his body language. Raymond sighed than continued. "Okay, I'll explain what I know. The Multiverse Theory is the concept of our universe being one of many in existence. Level one of this theory states that there are other parallel universes overlapping our own meaning there are infinite amounts of me doing the same thing I am doing now or, going out far enough, could be doing something completely different making these universes theoretically impossible to reach. Level two states that other universes are just another reachable part of space that would take billions of years at light speed to reach beyond our current universal bubble that we live in. Level three-"

Gehnarne interrupted after realizing that Raymond indeed knew what the theory consisted of. "Level three, multiple layers of three-dimensional space, four, different historical outcomes due to different possible choices in the flow of time, and five," Gehnarne looked at Gia and gave her a smile as if he was admiring something about her. "... Math, the one thing I was never that good at." Gia smiled back at Gehnarne blushing as he looked back at Raymond. "One, Two, Three, and Four are the most important but the math part does help in the concept of navigation."

"Wait a second," Raymond chuckled in disbelief. "Are you telling me you plan on navigating and reaching these other universes?"

"Yes, and I already have."

"What!?" Raymond mildly laughed in disbelief. "That's impossible!"

"Oh it's very possible my friend." Gehnarne stated proudly. "I can prove it to you." Gehnarne turns and nods at his assistant. She quickly sets up her tablet with a built in stand, places it on the table and begins showing Raymond a video.

Gia explains. "This footage was taken with a helmet camera as Gehnarne was doing his first human test with the UTS System."

Raymond Asked "UTS?"

"Universal Teleportation System."

"Uh huh," Raymond said sarcastically, still not believing Gehnarne. "and who was this human test subject exactly?

"Muah of course!" Gehnarne mildly bowed in his seat.

Raymond looked at Gehnarne in annoyance at how giddy his personality was. "Figures..." Then looked back at the screen.

Raymond watched as he saw Gehnarne in the video from first person giving a thumbs up to Gia who was in some kind of overhead control room. Gia pressed a button. A Blue wave of electricity began to encircle Gehnarne. The image became brighter and brighter. For a split second the image went black than came back up. As Gehenarne in the video looked around and saw buildings, the Gehnarne in the room with Raymond spoke. "Now this is supposed to be earth in a Level four universe of our current level two. Let's just call it universe 1112. Digit one is the number of our discovered level One universe which is number one, which is where we are right now, digit two is the number of our discovered level two universes which is also number one, where we are still located, digit three is the number of our discovered level three universe, which is again one, which we are once again still located, and the fourth and final digit is the number of our discovered level four universes which is now two because the universe in this video is our second discovered level four universe. We are in level four one because this is our first discovered level four universe. Which means, our current dimensional code is 1111. This universe's code in the video is universe 1112. Understand?"

Raymond seemed a little confused "Yea... a little..."

"Don't worry, you'll get the hang of it." Gehnarne laughed.

"Right," Raymond responded sarcastically again, still not believing Gehnarne. "So where on earth is this supposed to be anyway?"

"This is supposed to be New York City. Do you see anything strange in the video?"

Raymond observed. "No... it looks pretty much the same... maybe a little dirtier than usual but nothing that really sticks out."

Gehnarne responded impatiently "Come on, you can't see it? look closer."

Raymond looked in more detail for a moment than immediately paused the video. "No… there's no way..." He saw what he was supposed to see.

"I couldn't believe it either when I saw it with my own eyes." Gehnarne added. "The twin towers. They were still standing."

Raymond was in shock. He than put the tablet face down, shook his head while closing his eyes, opened them again upon stopping his head, than lifted the tablet back up to make sure he saw the towers correctly. "...How is this possible?"

"With what I just told you, the UTS. It brought me to a level four universe where 9/11 never happened because someone either made the choice not to do it or someone stopped it before it could happen, who knows. This universe was created due to a choice deviation compared to our own history."

Raymond was in such denial, he stood up from his seat. Not trusting Gehnarne, Raymond responded. "For all I know, you could have fabricated this! This could be some kind of advanced editing!"

"Why would I go through all of this trouble not only to deceive you but your chain of command, your council, and your government?" Gehnarne pointed to the tablet. "These are the facts right here in this video. This is real."

Raymond knew what Gehnarne said made sense. He calmed down and slowly took his seat again while saying. "Tell me… was this universe at peace?"

Gehnarne hesitated to tell the truth. "On the contrary… no"

"But why? The war on terror never happened so there shouldn't have been any follow up conflicts right?"

"That universe was a living hell. The crime rates were disgusting. Rape, murder, robbery almost every second of the day in your local area, globally. And I don't mean local as in the same city, I mean your local neighborhood. That place was lawless like Sodom and Gomorrah."

Raymond was very disappointed. "I see… so why did you go there of all places?"

"I uh... didn't choose to. That was just an experimental algorithm that Gia had placed into the UTS system and was converted into dimensional coordinate data. But, I did make first contact with the people there."

"Really?"

"Yes, I got in contact with the highest authorities that universe had, if there were any left. I figured that should be Standard Operating Procedure when we continue to do this again in the future. The leaders of that universe told me we can help them gain order in their universe by finding a man named Izzy Gerard, call sign "Digit", and deliver the plans to a device he was working on to them. Getting this device will not only help the people of that universe but us as well. When I found him we immediately began to work on the device however, one day he and the device disappeared. He sent me a message and told me where he was. Turns out gangs had found him, leaving him with no choice but to run to a safe house he made for himself and where the device was also hidden. I told him I would send someone to get him. That message was sent today. That someone I am sending, is you."

"Why me? You could have chosen anyone else."

"There are many reasons why I chose you. Your young in mind and body, you have a ton of combat experience for your age, you're a Tier four operator despite how reckless you are, and, the most important thing, you always seem to want to help people. Yes, it's obvious enough you get carried away with it at times but the point is that you have a good heart. The core of our organization will be to help people and make sure we're fighting on the good side of a fight. To help bring true peace to a universe in chaos. This place, universe 1112, is the start. All we have to do is find Izzy and give the leaders of that universe the device."

"How do you know the leaders of that universe aren't as corrupt as the animals who created that chaos in the first place?"

"I talked to them. I got pretty good vibes of their intentions. Besides, once you go there yourself, you will see that giving those leaders this device is the only way to save their world from what is currently total anarchy. It's the right thing to do."

Raymond began to believe him "Okay, let's just say I do this mission, will I be going alone?"

"Of course not," with an attitude "You go there alone, you won't last five minutes. You'll need a team of your choice at your disposal."

Raymond was surprised. "My choice huh? Alright than, I want USOD's Charlie team. They're good people and I've worked with them for a while, they're like family. We can flow together very well on a mission like this."

"You got it."

"All right." Raymond smiled. "As for QRF-"

"No."

"What?" Raymond immediately frowned.

"No Quick Reaction Force."

Raymond highly disagreed "Are you crazy? What if crap hit's the fan down there? What are we supposed to do?"

"Fight for your life I guess. I can't send too many people at once for security reasons and system integrity. You must understand, this technology is still being tested, it's unstable. One four-man team and that's it. Too many people could over load the system. Also, too many power fluctuations could draw unwanted attention."

Raymond was surprised "You mean rebel spy's?"

"Exactly. We can't take that risk, not now. You and your team go and that's it, you've been on ops like this before haven't you? Ones that were so top secret that you couldn't get support?"

Raymond thought back at a terrible moment in his life "Yea… and it didn't end well."

"I'm sorry but it has to be like this." Gehnarne paused and thought for a moment. "Think of this as another test. A test to see if either of us are worthy of such an organization with the power to visit other universes and planets. The very key to humanity's future. To pass this test is simple, just survive. Okay?"

Despite the extremely bad feeling Raymond had towards this mission, he said "Okay, I'll do it. But make sure my friends get the full brief on the mission details, they deserve to know that they could be volunteering for a suicide mission."

"Here I thought you were an optimist." Gehnarne commented.

"I usually am." Raymond nervously responded.

"Oh ye of little faith." Gehnarne said while holding out his hand with a smile expecting a handshake. Raymond didn't want to disrespect him so he stood up, reached out and shook Gehnarne's hand. "Welcome to SMO, Strategic Multiverse Operations."

Raymond chuckled. "Did the council give you guys that lame name?"

Gehnarne mildly laughed. "I actually had something better in mind however, we are still fringe. We have to prove ourselves to the council first before we can have a more official name and recognition." Gehnarne and Raymond let go of each other's hands. "Now, let's get you out of this dreadful room."

"That would be greatly appreciated" Raymond smiled.

Meanwhile, on the other side of the two-way mirror, Colonel Vial and Lucas watched the whole interaction between Raymond and Gehnarne with crossed arms. "I don't trust this guy." Lucas said.

"I don't trust him either." Colonel Vial responded. "But he works directly for the council so, not much we can do to stop him from doing what he wants. While you're working with him, I want you to keep an eye on him, Understood?" Colonel Vial said while dropping his arms and looking at Lucas.

"Yes sir." Lucas responded facing the colonel.

"Good." Colonel Vial turned to his left and walked towards the door exiting the room through the sliding doors.

Once alone, Lucas turned back towards the window with a frown remembering what Raymond said about Gehnarne simply disappearing in front of him in the ATAV. "Who the hell are you Mr. Gehnarne?"

Chapter 3: Digit

The next day, Raymond, Lucas, Katherine, and Jake walked down the hall of deck three inside the Recluses to reach the Universal Teleportation System that Gehnarne had set up in bay 349, down the hall. They were all dressed in civilian attire with heavy duty backpacks on their backs. They also had body armor under their cloths and weapons tucked in their jackets. Raymond seemed nervous but tried to stay positive. "Thanks for accepting this mission guys, I know I wouldn't be able to do this without you." Raymond said to break the ice. He was wearing worn jeans with black and white sneakers, and a blue shirt under a black hoodie with a brown backwards baseball cap and a black shemagh around his neck.

"Well," Lucas responded in a repulsive manner while wearing all brown with cargo pants, boots, a leather jacket and baseball cap facing forward." Since they took you off our roster, all of our missions are suspended until we get a fourth, except this one since you will obviously be our fourth."

"Oh… Sorry." Raymond apologized.

"Don't worry about it," Katherine said. "It just sucks to be on this baby sitting op."

"You're not babysitting me, like Lucas said, I'm your fourth. I'll be pulling my weight like I always do." Raymond reassured Katherine.

"Not you, this Izzy guy. He's a civilian, probably doesn't even know how to fight."

Raymond disagreed. "I don't know, Gehnarne did say this universe we're going to seemed pretty rough. Maybe this guy knows how to handle himself."

"Doubt it"

Jake cut in "I still can't grasp the concept of us going to another universe. I didn't think we even had the technology to do that, it's mind blowing."

"Me neither" Raymond agreed. "Crazy that it just happens to come out of nowhere like this. Gehnarne and his people must have had their plans on complete lock down, however, I wouldn't be surprised if the old man caught wind of it somehow, right Lucas?"

Lucas knew who Raymond was talking about and grew annoyed that he brought him up. "Can we not talk about the old man please?"

"Oh, sorry Lucas." Raymond switched topics. "So what's your load out?" He asked.

"Well, I figured this is gonna be an urban environment so that's why we're in civis, blend in with the locals right? Encase we're in contact, which I doubt, we'll be ready with our own compliment of weapons. We all modified our AR30's for CQB." Lucas pulled open his jacket and showed it to Raymond. Lucas had his AR30 in a concealment holster strapped to his torso inside the jacket on his left and filled magazine holsters, under the weapon. The barrel was seven inches long with a standard thirty-round magazine. It was such a compact set up it couldn't be seen as long as Lucas wore the jacket. Perfect for a Close Quarters Battle environment. On the right side of his torso, he had his M76 pistol holstered between two filled magazine holsters.

"Extra ammo and barrel configurations?" Raymond asked.

"In the bags." Lucas responded as he closed his jacket. "You do have the same or similar load out right?"

"Of course I do, I learned from the best." Raymond said proudly.

Lucas chuckled, and responded with pride. "Damn right you did." Katherine and Jake softly laughed.

For a small moment, Raymond felt like it was the good old days with his team again. However, someone was missing. Raymond distracted himself from the thought of that missing person with another question for Lucas. "So why do you doubt we'll take contact?"

"Honestly, I just find it hard to believe that there is a world out there completely taken over by pure anarchy. Maybe this Gehnarne guy is over exaggerating."

"He went there first, he would know"

"True." Lucas acknowledged.

"Here we are." Jake stated as the team turned right into the doors of bay 349. The doors slid open as the team marched through them like they owned the room, then closed behind them once everyone was inside. They saw the UTS right in the middle of the room humming with energy waiting to be used. Gehnarne and his assistant Gia were in the second floor control room when they saw the team come in. They immediately went down stairs to greet them.

"Charlie team, welcome! Glad you can make it." Gehnarne seemed very excited. "Before you go, here are some last minute mission details, follow me." He led them to a small table near a small control panel next to the UTS. "These are your new Taclet's ready to sync up with your Sub-Dermal Transponders.

Gia continued for Gehnarne as the team grabbed their gear. "We've updated the Taclets with an application that controls the UTS. We also updated the communications app's algorithms so we can talk to each other between our two universes."

"So we can control the UTS ourselves? We don't have to go back to the same spot we came from or contact you for transport?" Lucas asked.

"That's right, your all in full control of the UTS."

"That's a relief" Raymond said.

"How is it possible for our Taclets to communicate with you and control the UTS even though we are in completely different planes of existence?" Kathrine asked.

Gia looked towards Gehnarne as he hesitantly explained. "Sorry but uh... that's classified, but don't worry, we tested the system and it works, trust me"

"Classified? … Okay." Katherine said sarcastically.

"Also," Gia continued, "we have been granted access to that universes aerial reconnaissance network. We should be able to see everything around your AO."

"Lastly," Gehnarne finished. "When you make contact with Digit, make sure you use this challenge password to confirm his identity. Password is 'Who are the Rifters', the response is, 'The Nexiose', understood?" As Gehnarne gave them this information, Gia expressed concern but tried her best to hide it.

As Raymond noticed Gia's lightly cringed expression, he was about to ask about it when Lucas cut him off. "That's a weird challenge password, why not just use something a bit more simple like different combinations of beer brands or something?" After asking that question, Raymond shook his head while looking down in embarrassment towards Lucas forgetting about his question to Gia.

Gia sighed. "Because not all universes have the same brands of beer mister Walker."

"Oh..." Lucas felt a ping of embarrassment himself. "Shit, that makes sense."

"Indeed."

"Comms Check" Katherine said over the channel holding down her SDT than releasing.

"Check." The whole team responded one at a time starting with Lucas, Jake, then Raymond.

"Lima Charlie." Katherine responded to the positive radio check.

"All right everyone, step onto the platform when you're ready, and good luck" Gehnarne said.

"Thanks." Raymond responded as him and the team stepped onto the platform while Gehnarne and Gia walked away from the team and continued up the stairs to the control room.

"So who's that pretty smart ass with the accent working for that guy anyway?" Lucas asked Raymond quietly.

Raymond became annoyed. "Her name is Gia, and don't you start Lucas."

"Don't start what?"

Katherine jumped in with a giggle "You know very well what."

Than Jake commented. "Always trying to be the playa Lucas."

He sighed. "Whatever..."

Once everyone was on the platform, they faced the control room and looked at Ghenarne. "Okay team, I'm about to start powering up the system." Gehnarne said over the intercom. He flipped a switch starting the teleport ignition sequence. The teleport began to hum louder. After a moment, blue waves of electricity began to circle around the team in a spherical shape as the team began to levitate off the platform leaving the whole team surprised. "Wo, Hey! Is this normal!?" Lucas asked as the teleport got louder.

Gehnarne quickly responded "Yes it's quite normal, just stand still or your body will start to spin around on its own. Next thing you know, you'll land on whatever side of your body is facing the ground". Raymond grew excited as he continued to levitate towards the center of what was now a blue orb of electricity surrounding the team. The rest of the team stood perfectly still with worried expressions. Gia punched in what looked like coordinates into the computer. Gehnarne came over to the keyboard and held his finger over the enter key as he got back on the intercom. "Ok here we go, any of you guys want to give me a cheesy execution command like from one of those old school sci-fi shows?" he said with joy.

"Is he serious?" Lucas said out loud extremely annoyed.

"Strike us in!" Raymond said with a smile of excitement.

"What!?" Lucas immediately turned to Raymond with a puzzled expression.

"Roger that!" Gehnarne said with motivation, lifted his finger higher off the enter key. "Striking in three, two, one!" Then with force he quickly tapped the enter key with his right pointer finger. Suddenly there was a loud almost thunder like sound and the team was gone.

Universe 1112-Earth
August 3rd, 2238
0632 Standard Earth Time

In the new universe, there was a loud thunder like sound and the team instantly appeared in an ally way between two buildings with openings to the streets behind and in front of them. The team felt like they had fell one meter off the ground with some force pushing them downward making them land on one knee and one hand on the ground. The team was silent for a moment as it was raining in the city they had landed in. "Strike us in?" Lucas asked Raymond in disgust.

"It was the only thing I could come up with."

Lucas rolled his. "Status?" The team began to stand up.

"Rophe, up"

"Cat Eye, up"

"Slinger, up"

"White, up. Teams up command." Lucas spoke through the channel.

"*Roger that White.*" Gia said over the channel. "*I'm sending you a way point to the objective area now. The objective is 430 meters from your current position. Go down that ally, turn left, and go down the street. Should look like an old public housing building.*"

"Check." Lucas acknowledged while looking at the map on his Taclet showing the way point. "Way point received, we are Oscar Mike." Talking to the team. "Alright guys, blend in, move together and keep comms on auto, roger?"

43

The whole team responded with a "Roger." while they all double tapped their SDT's, switching comms to automatic, as they began to walk down the ally. When they reached the end, they looked around and started to piece together where they were.

"Wo," Katherine said. "I think we're on Wall Street."

"What makes you say that?" Jake asked. Katherine pointed to her right guiding the rest of the team where to look. "Oh man..." Jake said. They all saw what looked like the charging bull and a statue of a little girl in front of it. The bull was rusted and had graphite sprayed all over it. The little girl was still brass clean with no graphite vandalizing it and had candles circling the statue almost as if someone was recently worshiping it.

"That's not creepy at all." Raymond commented sarcastically with a concerned expression and jittery voice.

"Keep moving guys." Lucas said. The team stayed on the move and didn't stop anywhere. As they walked in a diamond formation keeping a five to ten-meter distance from each other, they heard all kinds of noises. Gun fire, people screaming in the distance, even heard the crack of stray bullets here and there. It kept them all on edge. They were 100 meters away from the objective, right around the corner when Raymond, who was positioned at the rear of the formation, noticed someone following them. With a professionally serious voice, he reported it to Lucas. "We got a tail."

"Check." Lucas responded, who was at the front of the formation.

Katherine, on the right of the formation, saw another one. "Got eyes on another, directly to my three o'clock."

Jake, the left of the formation, "Another, nine o'clock."

"They're boxing us in." Raymond advised.

"I know." Lucas said. "I got two more at our twelve."

"Crap..." Raymond said nervously.

"Stay focused, we're almost there." The team began to walk faster. As the men trailing them got close, their details became more noticeable. They all wore different colored and designed bandannas over their faces, black hoodies and jeans of different shades. "Command, besides the ones we see, are there any other possible contacts in our fascinate?"

"Negative white, I'm detecting many different signatures but none

of them are in range of you."

"Roger. Team, prepare to engage targets within your area of security. I got the red and the black bandannas at our twelve. Execute on my command."

The team in unison all with deadly professional voices responded with a "Roger".

Suddenly the man with the black bandanna in front of the team spoke up "Hello friend."

The team stopped with Lucas responding with a solid expression. "Hello, can I help you?" Each member of the team faced they're assigned targets slowly and casually.

"Yes, you can actually. You see, this is our place, you wanna pass, you have to pay a toll."

Lucas and his team was always taught to deescalate a situation first before taking lethal action to not only avoid unnecessary deaths but to also avoid the unnecessary use of resources. "I see, what would you take as payment?"

The masked anarchists laughed as they were surprised he asked. "Wow! You are the first person to actually ask that question, most people would have ran by now."

Lucas continued Calmly "Do you want money? We can give you money if that's what you want?"

The gang looked at each other confused. The thug with the red bandanna with a female voice spoke. "Uh, no asshole, money has no value here, we want your shit."

"You mean our stuff? Like our bags and cloths and things?"

With an attitude "The fuck else we talking about? While you're at it, we'll take that bitch off your hands to." Katherine started to boil with anger but kept it in check.

"And if we say no?" Lucas said this purposefully trying to get a threat level assessment.

The man in black bandanna nodded at the other members of his group. They began to draw weapons. Black banana pulled out a pistol holding it down by his side, red pulled out a machete, dog mouth near Raymond, a chain, Tiger stripped near Katherine, a knife, and Blue near Jake, a bat.

"Then you're fucked." Black said.

Lucas chuckled lightly "Look buddy, your barking up the wrong tree, just leave us alone and you'll never see us again, you have my word."

Red responded with an attitude. "Your word don't mean shit! Give us your shit or we're gonna fuck up your shit, you can have MY word on that!"

Lucas knew if his team was gonna do something, it had to be now. Action beats reaction every time. Things were quiet for a moment than Lucas made a long sigh while casually saying, "...Execute."

"Wha-" Black tried to speak as he was interrupted suddenly by the team drawing their weapons at lightning speed. Lucas fired a controlled pair, and one to the head at the black bandanna man eliminating the immediate threat first since he had a gun, then shifted fire to the red bandanna woman and fired five rounds tearing through the woman's center of mass. Katherine, Raymond, and Jake all fired controlled pairs and one to the head at their assigned targets. All the thugs dropped to the floor like rag dolls. After that, the team head checked right, then left visually checking their surroundings then looked back at their targets making sure they were down. When Lucas looked back at his second target with the red bandanna, he saw her trying to reach for her buddy's gun. Lucas immediately put another controlled pair into her head as her body immediately went numb.

"Status!" Lucas barked

"Slinger, up!

"Cat, up!

"Rophe, up!

"To the objective, ninety meters, Double time!" Lucas pulled his AR30 into the up position holding by the pistol grip with one hand while sprinting. The rest of the team followed holding their weapons the same way trying to maintain formation. They didn't stop until they reached the building where the objective was located. "Stack up, left side, go soft." The team acknowledged with a "Roger" as they approached the door. Raymond was the first in the stack with his weapon down, Katherine second with weapon up facing the right of the stack, Jake last with weapon facing the rear of the stack. Lucas moved to the right of the door prepping to open it by hand. He looked at Raymond and nodded. Raymond nodded back and tapped Katherine's leg, then Katherine tapped Jake's leg. Jake, tapped back, then Kathrine tapped Raymond again. Raymond gave a second nod to Lucas. Lucas opened the door quickly. The team moved through the door way together. Raymond visually cleared the right corner with his weapon up, then shifted his weapon towards the center while still moving to the right corner, taking the path of least resistance. Katherine moved left and visually cleared the left corner with her weapon up, also shifting her weapon towards the center while still moving to the left corner. Jake visually cleared the center of the room with his weapon up while moving along the same path Raymond took stopping five meters away from Raymond, then finally Lucas came through visually clearing the center of the room again with his weapon up. He then dropped his weapon to the low ready while turning around so not to flag his buddy's. Once clear, he brought his weapon back up, posting security on the door they all just came through at an angle. This was their Standard Operating Procedure in room clearing.

"Clear." Raymond said as he looked around the room seeing a perfectly squared lobby with an elevator to his left and stairs directly in front of him. The lobby smelled like urine and had strange stains along the walls.

"Good execution." Lucas complimented. "Command, anyone following us?"

"*Negative white, no contacts.*"

"Okay." Lucas stood back up normally, reloaded and holstered his weapon than relaxed. "Weapons down guys, let's try not draw any more attention."

"Right." Raymond agreed. The team reloaded and holstered their weapons as well. Lucas checked the nearby elevator but it didn't seem to work. The team began walking towards the stairs. "Command, which floor is objective Digit on?" Raymond asked while looking up the stairwell. He guessed that the building was thirty stories high.

"*The top floor Slinger.*"

Sarcastically "Great… here comes my leg day." The team chuckled at Raymond's mild joke as they began to relax. Thirty stories of stairs later, the team felt their calf's and thigh muscles burning. When the team made it to the top floor, Raymond looked around. He saw three doors. One to his left that said Thirty A, to his front that said thirty B, and to his right that said thirty C

"Digit should be in apartment Thirty C." Gia informed.

Raymond looked towards the door that said Thirty C on it. "Got it." The team moved toward the door and stood near it casually maintaining 360-degree security. Raymond knocked on the door with no response. A moment later a nearby speaker started talking to them. *"Who are you?"*

Raymond looked around for the speaker and found it above the door and responded. "Is this Digit?"

"Identify yourselves." The voice in the speaker demanded.

Raymond remembered the challenge password that was briefed to him and his team earlier on the Recluses. "Who are the Rifters?"

"The Nexiose." Izzy responded. *"Come on in."*

Lucas sighed, "I still think that's the weirdest challenge password we've ever used."

"Yea, like yours was any better," Raymond commented.

"How was I supposed to know that beer brands were different in this universe?" Interrupting their banter, the door behind them labeled thirty A opened instead of the door in front of them, thirty C. The team turned around and felt a little concerned and confused. They walked through the opened door and saw Izzy standing there in the room wearing a brown trench coat with black cargo pants. On his right was a work bench with something on it covered with a white plastic tarp. Despite a rundown apartment building, this particular apartment was very clean, organized and freshly painted white. "Welcome, I'm glad you can make it!" The door closed behind them as they walked through. "Sorry about the confusion, I had to switch up rooms encase anything happened. My name is Izzy Gerard. Good to finally meet you Raymond.

Raymond was surprised. "You know who I am?"

"Of course, Gehnarne's told me all about you and your potential! You being here must mean he finally decided to recruit you. Is this your team?"

"Yes, this is Lucas, our team lead." Lucas nodded his head. "Jake, our medic, and Kathrine, our communications expert."

Izzy was immediately entranced by Katherine's beauty. Her short blond hair and blue eyes had him stunned. He froze for a moment than snapped himself out of it. He went to each member of the team shaking their hand. "It's a pleasure to meet all of you." When he got to Katherine he couldn't help but shake her hand and say "It's especially a pleasure to meet you miss." Katherine was a little surprised and almost blushed. She thought Izzy was handsome with evenly cut short brown hair, a short stubble beard, brown eyes and what would seem to be a lean but not too muscular of a body judging from how the trench coat fit on him. "Good to finally meet you all, now let's get back to business shale we?" Izzy walked back to the other side of the room. All the men on the team looked at Katherine with a concerned expression like they were asking permission to give Izzy a beat down. Katherine immediately blushed and waved her hand at them gesturing to leave him alone like she was okay with it. Izzy grabbed his backpack and placed it on the table next to the object covered by the plastic tarp.

"So what's this device that Gehnarne was talking about?" Raymond asked.

"It's right here." Izzy grabbed the plastic tarp and pulled it off of the covered object. "May I present to you, the Flow System." On the table there lay a pair of gauntlets with wires protruding out of them and what looked like silver discs on the back of each gauntlet, and a module like tablet thicker than most tablets that seemed to be the main source of control for the system. "Currently in the prototype stage, this system will revolutionize the way we fight in combat." Izzy said proudly.

"Wait, this thing is a type of weapon?" Raymond asked.

"Yes and no. You see, this thing alone isn't a weapon. Once you put it on, it makes you the weapon. When activated, this system will surround your body in a magnetic gravity field, separating you from the gravity in your current environment allowing you to make more dynamic use of your body. The gravity field can propel the user's body forward faster, making them run and physically move faster all together, and in culmination with certain physical movements, it can focus the gravity field forward allowing the user to gain almost super human abilities like punching harder and faster or other aggressive movements."

"Wow, this sounds cool!" Raymond said feeling gitty about what he just heard.

"Impressive." Lucas said. "Have you tested it?"

"Yes but..." Izzy thought for a moment. "It takes some getting used to."

"What do you mean?"

"Well, first time I tried it I experienced an unfortunate side effect

"Like what?" Jake asked.

"I passed out"

"What?" Raymond was concerned

"What made you pass out?" Katherine questioned.

Izzy took a moment to think of how to explain. "You see, from what I can gather, it has something to do with our body's susceptibility to the new gravity field. Trying it for the first time, our body isn't used to it and throws everything out of whack. When I passed out, I couldn't even remember turning it on. Next thing you know I woke up six hours later with one hell of a headache. I immediately turned it off and tried to figure out what happened."

"Did you try it again?" Raymond asked.

"Yes but this time I took the proper precussion's. I set the system to an auto off setting after ten minutes of use, just encase I passed out again. I felt extremely light headed but I got used to it. By the time ten minutes was over, I felt just fine."

"Interesting" Jake said out loud."

"Were there any other side effects?" Katherine asked.

"None that I can tell at this time." Izzy seemed a bit worried. "The system is still in the testing phase so I haven't seen all of its side effects just yet."

"This thing sounds too dangerous to me." Lucas commented.

"I assure you, it won't harm the body permanently if that's what your worried about."

"We'll see, let's Get this thing and any valuables packed and ready to move, we're leaving."

"You don't have to tell me twice, I can't wait to leave this dump." Izzy said excitedly. He moved back to the table and started packing up the Flow System in his bag. Lucas turned around to face his team.

He was smiling at them thinking everything went okay. They smiled back, including Raymond. "So, are we going to teleport out of here or are we taking the rift?" Izzy asked. Suddenly Lucas and his team's expressions melted from a smile to confusion.

"What?" Lucas asked while turning around.

"The Universal Rift? Are we going through the rift or are we just gonna teleport out?

"What Rift?" confusion turned into suspicion.

Izzy paused as there was a moment of awkward silence. "Aw shit, he didn't tell you..." Izzy seemed very concerned.

"Assuming he, as in Gehnarne, no he didn't say a word about a Rift." Lucas answered with a hint of aggression in his voice.

"Okay listen, I assumed you knew judging from that challenge password we used but if he didn't tell you about the Rift, it was for a good reason, trust me." Izzy said trying to calm Lucas down.

"I didn't trust this Gehnarne from the start," Lucas spoke as he aggressively walked towards Izzy, "and now you're giving me a legitimate reason not to trust you either so start talking, what the hell is this Rift?" He asked with aggression in his voice almost within arms reach of Izzy.

"Lucas," Raymond cut him off, "Take an easy-"

"*Charlie team, this is command,*" Gia interrupted, "*we are detecting a large group of possible hostiles in your area.*"

Izzy looked at Lucas with discontent while Lucas continued to grill Izzy for a couple of seconds. He than looked at his team and nodded. They immediately knew what to do as they drew their weapons while spreading out to different possible entries into the room. "How many?" Lucas asked as he walked away from Izzy.

"*We have eyes on ten hostiles with masks, looking similar to the group of people you ran into earlier, moving into your building. Nine more entered the building next door. We also see three hostiles on the roof of that next door building with so... ind.... Device.... Whi... d.... ead... e?...-*" The channel's audio became nothing but static and communications with command was lost.

"Command do you read me? Over."

Static

"Command, this is white, do you copy? Over."

Static.

"Shit..."

"Didn't command mention something about a device on the roof of that other building?" Izzy asked.

"Yea, I think so." Lucas responded.

"Our comms are disrupted." Katherine said. "That must have been some kind of jamming device."

"Can we still teleport out of here?" Lucas asked

Katherine checked the UTS app. "Negative, it's down to."

"Oh man..." Raymond whispered to himself.

"Now what?" Jake asked.

"It's okay." Izzy interrupted than swung his back pack onto his back. "I have a plan." He said while smiling. He walked through the team to the front door. He pulled off a piece of the ceiling tile next to the door exposing what looked like some kind of bomb.

"Wo!" Raymond was surprised.

"You had this place rigged the whole time?" Lucas was shocked

"Yep, just encase this safe house was ever compromised." He pulled on a wire connected to the bomb carefully than attached it to the front of the door. "Whoever opens this door blows the whole apartment."

"Nice." Jake was impressed as he smiled.

Izzy pulled out a tablet and activated a security camera just outside the front entrance to the apartment building showing the last of a group of thugs running through the building's front door. "Okay, the front entrance looks clear. Knowing these thugs, they don't know anything about securing a perimeter around the objective. We should be able to walk right out of here."

"How do we get back down there with those guys coming up the stairs?" Raymond asked.

"We go down the elevator shaft, by the time we get down there, all those thugs will already be up here, they won't even see us leaving, this wall over here." Izzy walked to his left and pulled a large piece of dry wall to the side exposing the entrance to the elevator shaft. "This wall was made on top of the shaft. All I had to do was blow a hole in it and presto, an immediate exit."

"Not bad." Katherine gave Izzy credit.

"Not bad at all," Lucas agreed. "Okay team, hook up." He said with a sense of motivation.

The thugs were already on the twenty eighth floor. Charlie team with Izzy had already started repelling down the elevator shaft. The thugs ran up the stairs with so much noise that they couldn't hear the sound of rope friction coming down the inside of the walls. The thugs were now on the twenty ninth floor when the team had just reached the bottom of the shaft. They quietly opened the elevator shaft door and walked out with weapons up. "They're almost at the top floor" Izzy whispered to Lucas.

"Let's go." Lucas ordered leading the way to the building front door when he saw a thug facing away from the doorway, guarding it. As soon as Lucas saw him, he immediately through up his left hand in a fist giving a "Freeze!" hand signal to his team behind him, halting them where they stood. Lucas slowly approached the guard as he lowered his weapon and pulled out a knife from his belt sheaf. Once close enough, he aggressively grabbed the thug's mouth, surprising him as the thug's gasp was muffled, than immediately became a muffled death gargle as Lucas slit his throat deep enough so he wouldn't be able to scream for help. "Go!" Lucas said in an aggressive whisper as the team ran by him while he confirmed his kill. After making sure the thug wouldn't be a problem, he wiped his blade on his pants, cleaning off the blood, sheaved the knife than ran off to regroup with his team.

The thugs reached the thirtieth floor and tried to open thirty C. It was locked so they kicked it open. There was nothing in the room. They checked thirty B next, nothing. Then they reached thirty A. They kicked the door open.

A loud explosion erupted on the thirtieth floor blowing out the windows and fire blazing through. Five surviving anarchists ran back down the stairway with burns and wounds with only two of them at a safe enough distance from the explosion to only suffer from disorientation. After several minutes of running down the stairway in fear, the anarchists ran outside the front door of the building immediately being met with gunfire from Charlie team taking cover behind old burnt cars parked on the edge of the street in front of the building. The anarchists were torn apart in the kill zone as they staggered and fell dead on the wet floor. A minute after initiating the ambush, the team confirmed their targets. "Clear!" Lucas announced just as he heard grunting from one surviving anarchist. He walked up to the anarchist noticing he was only shot in the leg and left arm. Lucas stepped on his leg, causing the male anarchist to scream in pain. "Who sent you!?" Lucas demanded.

"Fuck you!" The anarchist screamed back.

"You're wasting your time," Izzy spoke getting Lucas's attention while Izzy walked towards him. "A simple thug like him doesn't know anything."

Unnoticed to Lucas, the anarchist immediately tried to pull something out from behind his back. Izzy saw this and reflexively pulled out a kind of suppressed pistol from under his coat lifting and firing it at a fast rate of fire at the anarchist's head. He put ten rounds into his skull, more than enough to kill the anarchist, than stopped. Lucas and Charlie team looked at Izzy in surprise at how vicious he looked in killing the man while practically saving Lucas's life as they noticed a pistol half way drawn out of the male anarchist's belt. At that moment, Charlie team gained respect for Izzy.

"*What the Fuck is going on down there*?!" The anarchist leader said over the radio to one of his men in the entrance to the building where the jamming device was located on the roof.

"I don't know, I think the whole fucking building just blew out, they're all dead!"

"*Calm down man, you stay there and hold that area you hear me!?*"

"Fuck that! They practically brought down a whole fucking building with that explosion!" The anarchist overreacted. "Who knows what the fuck else they can-" Suddenly there was a loud explosion blowing the front door open. The anarchists inside were stunned. Raymond stepped through the door moving through the path of least resistance to the right corner while visually checking the right corner of the room with his weapon up, then shifted fire left to engaged his most immediate threat while still moving towards the right corner putting five rounds center mass into his target as the thug dropped to the floor. Katherine came in second immediately moving to the left corner, visually checking the left corner of the room with her weapon up than shifted fire right to engage her most immediate threat also while moving towards the left corner. Jake came in third engaging two targets down the middle of the room while moving through the same path Raymond took and stopped five meters away from Raymond. After killing her target, Katherine shifted fire a bit more to the right to engage a target around the corner from Raymond in his blind spot. Last, Lucas came in, double checked the middle which had two downed targets thanks to Jake, moved left down the same path as Katherine while keeping his weapon towards the center of the room and stopped five meters away from Katherine.

Lucas. "Status!"

Raymond. "Slinger! Up!"

Katherine. "Cat! Up!"

Jake. "Rophe! Up!"

Lucas "White! Up! Room Clear!" The team lowered their weapons into a low ready. "Digit, get in here!" Izzy walked in through the blown out door. The team began moving towards the stairs with Raymond on point. He had his weapon up and was scanning for targets as he moved. While moving, Izzy noticed a working elevator.

"Hey guys!" He said while taking off his back pack than his trench coat revealing a black compression shirt. "Why don't we use the elevator?" The shirt compressed against his body revealing his lean physique. Katherine glanced at Izzy for a split second than did a double take in surprise at how physically fit he looked. She than immediately looked forward again trying not to get distracted. She lightly blushed hoping that Izzy didn't notice her checking him out.

"Are you kidding?" Lucas responded to Izzy. "That thing is a death trap. As soon as we reach the top, they'll just light us up while still inside."

"That's not what I meant." Izzy pulled out a flash bang grenade from his trench coat's pocket. "How about we get a little dynamic?" Izzy smiled. Lucas smiled back understanding what he meant.

The Anarchist leader started talking to his men in the top floor hallway just before the entrance to the roof. "*I can't get the guys downstairs on the radio. I think those bastards got em. Be ready*"

"I hear ya." The anarchist responded.

"Yo, look at this!" One of the other anarchists pointed to the elevator as little lights on the control panel began to flash. "I think they're comin up."

"Holy shit! Okay, as soon as that door opens shoot em." The six anarchists on that level pointed their guns at the door waiting anxiously for it to open. The elevator beeped with each floor. Twenty-seven, twenty-eight, twenty-nine, thirty. The door opened and the anarchists opened fired into the elevator for five seconds than stopped. "The fuck?" They noticed that there was no one inside. Izzy, while wearing his backpack, was standing by on the roof of the elevator in front of the opened emergency exit on the ceiling of the elevator. He threw an already primed flash bang grenade into the elevator. The moment it touched the floor, there was an explosion that went off right in front of the thugs instantly blinding them. As they blindly staggered, Lucas and Raymond barged through the stairway door down the hall from the anarchists moving to opposite walls. Raymond took the left wall, Lucas, the right wall and immediately engaged the thugs while moving down the hallway. The thugs staggered in pain and fell to the floor dead. Katherine was behind Lucas with her weapon just over his shoulder. Jake was behind Raymond doing the same thing. They moved down the hall way in unison maintaining their formation and reached the small stair case inside a small piece of alcove.

"Clear Right." Raymond said. "I see a door, probably leads to the roof."

"Alright, Stack up." The team moved to the door in a center stack formation. Raymond and Jake stacked left, Lucas and Katherine stacked right. Izzy jumped down into the elevator through the emergency hatch and regrouped with the team while checking the thugs to make sure they were dead.

"Camera up." Lucas said. Kathrine moved in front of the door with what looked like a camera on a bendable wire. She looked at the camera feed on her Taclet while moving the camera back and forth.

"Oh shit..." Katherine said in worry.

"What's wrong?" Lucas asked.

"I got eyes on a model B30 Communications Jamming Device, three hostiles, and what looks to be three model T-ATS turrets."

"No way." Raymond said. "How the hell did a group of street thugs get their hands on tech like that? That stuff is from our universe."

"I know." Katherine responded. "That's what worries me. That B30 CJD is invulnerable to EMP so we'll have to destroy it directly, the problem is those turrets though. They are also invulnerable to EMP and have infrared sensors so smoke won't block their scanning. Nothing we have is gonna protect us from those turrets unless we destroy them directly."

"We gotta find another way around." Lucas said.

"Maybe not." Izzy interrupted as he turned around the corner to see the team. "How much cover is out there?"

"We got some heavy duty looking vents lined up horizontally on the left and some smoke stacks but nothing we can get to right away that's useful." Katherine said in detail

"That might work."

"What might work?" Jake asked.

"We can use the flow system." Izzy suggested excitedly. "One of you put it on and-"

"No way." Lucas interrupted. "You said that thing is still in the testing phase."

"Just hear me out, if one of you put it on, you can move fast enough to get around those turrets before they can line up a shot. From there, we move in, take out the jamming device and the last of the hostiles and that's it. I know your tech, Gehnarne showed me, those turrets can only move so fast and they automatically engage the closest threat right?

"Yea, he's right." Kathrine confirmed.

"We can do this." Izzy pushed

"But not by using that thing," Lucas protested. "I won't let one of my guys put themselves at risk unnecessarily. We'll find another way around."

"There is no other way around." Raymond spoke up. "That's the roof. The only other way back up is from the outside. That means repelling back up, out in the open while they get reinforcements. We can't take that much time or the chance of getting shot out there on repel. We have to move now with whatever is available to us."

Lucas knew he was right. "Okay... I'll-"

"No, I'll do it."

"What?"

"I'm not officially part of the team anymore remember? so it would make sense for me to do it?"

"Why not let Izzy do it?" Jake suggested.

"Because he's the VIP, last thing we need is to put him at the front to be shot at directly, I'll put on the flow system." Raymond solidified.

Lucas wanted to stop him but, he knew there was no time. They had to move now. "Make it so. Izzy, set him up. Everyone, back away from the door." The team moved back into the hallway. Jake posted security on the roof top door while Katherine and Lucas posted security down the opposite ends of the hall way. Raymond was behind the perimeter taking off his jacket and exchanged it with Izzy for pieces of the flow system. "While Raymond is getting ready, I'm gonna get a plan together." Lucas stated. "I'll tell you guys as I figure it out."

The team acknowledged with a "Roger."

Meanwhile, outside on the roof. The last of the anarchists waited nervously for the team to come through the door. They were positioned behind the turrets Katherine had mentioned, guarding the jamming device behind them. It was half their height with a small rotating satellite dish on top of it. "Yo," one of the anarchist said. "The fuck are we waiting for. Let's just get em." He asked the leader.

"We're safer near the turrets. We let them come after us, we'll have an easier time fighting them."

"Than what the fuck is taking them so long! This waiting is killing me!"

"Chill man!" The leader yelled making the other anarchist calm down a bit. "They'll come. Just be ready."

Back in the hallway, Raymond was ready to go. "Wo… this is pretty cool." He was wearing the gauntlets on his hands with the control console MOLLE webbed to his plate carrier. "Wouldn't my plates get in the way with movement?"

"Not at all." Izzy advised. "Whatever is inside the gravity field will have the same weight as everything else in the gravity field. Those plates will weigh about just as much as your gauntlets."

"Nice." Raymond nodded his head in approval as he reached

towards his jacket on the floor and grabbed his face paint disc case. He began to apply the black face paint in the same ritualistic way he did on Croza.

"The heck are you doing?" Izzy asked with a confused expression.

"I don't know about your universe but in mine, warriors wore face paint like this for thousands of years to intimidate their enemies. At first I thought this was stupid until a friend of mine gave this to me. She taught me that this face paint can have a psychological effect on the user as well."

"Really? In what way?"

"It could help the user feel like someone else on the battlefield." He finished applying the paint than looked at the small mirror making sure it was perfect. "Someone else who lives for the thrill of battle." He said with a voice of vicious resolve as his killer instinct begged for him to tear his enemies apart.

"You ready?" Lucas asked.

"Yea." Raymond answered.

"So are we." Lucas dropped security, turned around held out his hand to help Raymond to his feet. Raymond grabbed it as Lucas pulled him up and said. "Be careful."

"I will. Okay, so how do I turn this thing on?" He asked Izzy.

"Just tap the wrist pieces on the gauntlets together twice. You'll hear two beeps than the gravity field will surround your body almost instantly."

"Okay… here it go's." Raymond tapped the two wrist pieces together. Two beeps sounded on the control console. Suddenly the discs on the gauntlets spun up while a strange quick flash of light sparked around his body with a deep bass hum like sound. "WOOO!!!… oooohhh!..."

"Are you ok?" Lucas asked

"uuuuhhhh… yea… I think…?" Raymond had a very disoriented look on his face as his body felt completely off balance and was slowly getting sick to his stomach.

"Turn it off!" With concern in Lucas's voice.

"No no… I'm good, really."

"You sure?" Still concerned.

"Yea… I can fight it." Raymond seemed to be a bit more normal.

"Interesting..." Izzy said. "I guess everyone's reaction to first time exposure of the gravity field is different."

"If you say so..." Lucas had a bad feeling about this. "All right guys, on my mark, we execute the plan. Roger?"

"Roger." The team Acknowledge.

Outside, the thugs were growing more nervous as they watched the door waiting for their enemy to come through. Finally, a loud explosion blew open the wall on the right side of the door where a part of the hallway would be. "The fuck was that?!" one of the anarchists said. Suddenly Raymond burst through the smoke running at almost inhuman speeds along the right edge of the roof. The turrets reacted and fired however; he was running just fast enough for the turrets to lag behind in targeting him. When he reached the horizontal vent that Katherine had mentioned, he dove into cover behind the vent landing on the outside of his forearms with the turret fire almost catching up to him.

While still sliding on his forearms, he flipped his hands down and pushed himself off the floor focusing the force of the push on his left side throwing him into the air in a spinning fashion. The turrets were still firing trying to keep up with him. The thugs were so confused by what was happening, they couldn't get a shot out fast enough. While in midair spin, Raymond drew his M76 pistol set to full auto, loaded with armor piercing twenty-around magazine and fired three to five round controlled burst's into each turret's power core disabling them. The armor piercing rounds tore through the turret's armor like butter. As Raymond was about to land, he pistol whipped the anarchist leader next to him in the face with so much force that his neck snapped while the body spun around off his feet and fell to the ground. Raymond landed on both of his feet and left hand. "HOLY SHIT!!!" The last two anarchists were shocked. They lifted their weapons just as Raymond slid into cover on his right. He was already half way in cover by the time they began to fire. Just as the anarchists were about to shift fire towards Raymond's cover, the rest of the team began firing at them and the jamming device. The anarchists dropped dead on the floor as the jamming device was pelted with bullets eventually sparking than shutting down.

"CEASE FIRE!" Lucas yelled as the team immediately ceased fire.

"Slinger! Are you okay!?"

"Friendly... coming out!" Raymond stood up and started walking towards his team as he slowly tapped the gauntlets wrists together three times powering down the flow system. The system made a fast down like noise while the disc's stopped spinning. The team started to smile after realizing what he had done. It was truly amazing to them. Izzy was even prouder knowing that the device worked successfully.

Lucas walked up to Raymond with joy. "Slinger! You crazy son of bitch! That was amaz-..." Lucas's emotions shifted from excitement to concern once he saw Raymond more closely. "oh no..."

Raymond felt extremely light headed and felt his right chest closer to his shoulder wet with blood and in a lot of pain. He was hit. "I... guess I... took one for... the team today huh?... ugh" Raymond fell forward uncontrollably.

"RAY!!!" Lucas ran forward and caught him before he could hit the ground. "MEDIC!!!"

"Moving!" Jake ran desperately to help Raymond.

"KAT! Get command on comms now! Get us out of here!" Lucas ordered.

"Got it!" with desperation in her voice, Kathrine immediately looked at her Taclet.

"Oh no..." Scared for Raymond's life, Izzy felt guilty that he helped put Raymond in danger using the Flow System. He thought it would be terrible for him to die now when they were just getting started.

Lightning Archival Records
Segment Of Speach To The People Of Earth
From Rebel Controlled Colonies
Universe IIII-Broadcasted on April 9th, 2228
Possibly By Garza Liankos Himself

My brothers and sisters of Earth, rise up against the council

for you were the first victims of this oppressive government.

By whatever means necessary, show them that you will sacrifice

everything to free your extended human family of

the colonies and yourselves.

Only when the blood of the innocent from there own home world

begin to fall on their hands is when they will finally begin to take our

demands seriously-

Due To Extremist Views
This Broadcast Had Been Terminated
From Public Broadcasting
Unless Authorized To Licensed News Media

Chapter 4: Past Memories

Memory Fragment From Raymond "Gunslinger" Reynolds
1001101010011101001010101101
ERROR: Fragment Undefined

Raymond started to wake up. His vision was blurry at first but cleared up quickly. As his vision cleared, he looked around and realized where he was. He was in his old childhood bedroom at his family's apartment. His Holovision, computer, posters of super heroes and VR game characters were exactly how they were when he was a child. Raymond looked at himself and realized he was about twelve years old again. "What's happening?" he thought to himself. "Am I dead?" Raymond's younger body was moving automatically. He had no conscious control over it. He got out of bed, got dressed in his old childhood cloths and went down stairs. His Mother and Father were waiting for him at the exit to the apartment.

"Come on Ray, we're gonna be late!" His long brown haired mother said while smiling at him wearing a beautiful blue one peace dress with a long skirt.

"Mom?..." He said to himself.

"You heard your mother, let's go kid!" His dark brown haired father said while also smiling wearing a black suit with a blue neck tie, matching the blue dress of his beautiful wife.

"Dad?..." Raymond felt like he was on the verge of tears but couldn't cry for some odd reason. He felt like something unseen was physically blocking his tears from flowing out from his eyes. His body moved forward to his parents. They walked outside to a car. As they were moving towards the car, a childlike voice called out to him

"Ray!" Raymond turned right and saw his best friend Lucas as a child. During this time, Raymond could remember that Lucas was fourteen years old. "Hey man! Off to church?"

"Of course," a childlike voice came out of Raymond. But he felt like someone was talking for him. "Aren't you going too?"

"No, I told my dad I didn't want to go anymore because of paintball practice. I really wanted to get better for my team. He wasn't too happy about that though."

"Oh, sorry."

"It's okay. I just wanted to do my own thing on Sundays for now on you know? Plus, I really love paintball! You should come with me some time; it would be fun!"

"Sure, that would be great!"

"Raymond, you can play with Lucas later okay we're gonna be late." Raymond's mom said.

"Okay mom. Seeya later Lucas."

"Seeya Ray." At that moment, Raymond just realize something. Lucas hadn't called him Ray since they were kids.

Raymond entered the car. As they were about to drive away he looked through the driver's side mirror back at Lucas. However, he saw Lucas as an adult in full combat gear holding an AR30 looking back at him in the mirror with a deadly expression, then turned around. Raymond got scared and turned around to see Lucas with his own eyes. He still looked like a kid walking back into his apartment building. The car started to drive away as Raymond sat back in his seat and looked up at the rear view mirror in the front seat area. In shock he saw himself as an adult in combat gear still wearing the Flow System with blood on his shirt from where he remembers getting shot.

"Son?" Raymond looked at his father. "Are you ok?"

"I'm fine." He wasn't fine. After what seemed like several minutes of driving, the car stopped in the parking lot nearest to the church. From there they got out and walked another three minutes to the church building. They walked into the church and saw all of their friends. Some new, some familiar, some they knew for so long they were like family. Raymond felt happy there like a void of fellowship was being filled.

Raymond and his family walked into the sanctuary. It was filled with even more people. They found seats two rows before the front of the pulpit and stayed standing along with the rest of the congregation. The Pastor of the church, Pastor David Walker, Lucas's father, walked up to the pulpit and opened a bible wearing his best casual clothes with a business jacket and a black leather glove on his left hand. "Please stay standing as we turn to Mathew 5:43. I'll be reading from the New International Version." Pastor Walker said happily.

"Mom, what about praise and worship?" Raymond asked quietly.

"Not today honey." Raymond was confused. They always do praise and worship at church before the pastor preaches his message. It was strange.

"But what about children's church?" He asked again.

"Son, pay attention." His father kindly said to him.

Pastor Walker began to read the bible. "Jesus says in Mathew 5:43 through 44, "You have heard that it was said, 'You Shall Love Your Neighbor and hate your enemy'. But I say to you, love your enemies and pray for those who persecute you." Pastor Walker closed his bible and happily said "You may be seated." The congregation sat in their seats. "So, Jesus himself said "Love Thy Enemy". Clear and simple right? But what about when it comes to war? With the war against the rebels on the colonies, a lot of people have been asking me, isn't it wrong for us to be at war? Doesn't it even say in the Ten Commandments that "Thou shall not murder"? Let's do some research here." Pastor Walker looked up and down at his notes and read them out loud to the congregation as he explained. "The Hebrew word used for that commandment literally means "The intentional premeditated killing of another person with malice." A synonym for malice is hate or hatred. Which means that God isn't necessarily against war, but against hatred, to kill in malice." He begins to look back at the congregation away from his notes as he paces back and forth facing the congregation. "To kill out of hate is to murder. Even to hate someone without ever even laying a finger on them is murder. Let's be honest, war is horrible, it should never be glorified. A large majority of you should know, most of you have served... so have I." He said as he briefly looked down at his left hand covered with a black leather glove.

As Pastor Walker preached, Raymond starred at the Pastors left hand remembering there was a cybernetic prosthetic under the glove. Lucas told him he lost his arm in the war but wasn't exactly sure of how. "But, we can't deny that if it's the last resort, war is sometimes a necessary thing. In a world filled with hate and people who wish to simply destroy our way of life, war is inevitable. Sometimes the only way to stop such terrible people from killing and destroying the innocent is by going to war. As Christians, and I would think in other faiths as well, we should not desire war. But if there are no more words to be had with an enemy whose soul dedication is to kill us, than so be it. As long as we fight not out of a spirit of hatred but of mercy towards our enemy when the chance is presented and love to protect those we care for and other innocents, then we should do what we must. For some of you, what you must do is pray for godly wisdom for our leaders, for safety of our military, a quick resolution to the conflict, and for minimum casualties among civilians on both sides. For another amount of you, what you must do, or what you feel you're being called to do, is fight." Pastor Walker suddenly froze in place. Raymond looked around and noticed that everything was now frozen in time.

"Mom?" He tugged on her skirt. She didn't move.

"Dad?!" Raymond's father didn't move either. He became afraid as he looked back at Pastor Walker.

The Pastor was now clothed in combat gear similar to what adult Raymond and his team used on their missions. The Pastor was also missing his cybernetic arm and had a tourniquet wrapped tightly just above a wound dripping with blood where his real arm was severed. The rest of his gear seemed to have been covered in dirt and blood as he held what looked like a German Long Sword in his right hand that Raymond recognized as his own GLS1, a sword he had recently purchased for himself as a part of his German Long Sword training. Pastor Walker began to speak as he unsteadily lifted the sword towards Raymond and pointed the tip at him with the blade oriented vertically. Pastor Walker struggled as he spoke. "Free will is like a double edge sword." He flicked his wrist left turning the blade of the sword horizontally showing both sides of the blade perfectly. The left edge of the blade was clean with the razor sharp edge glistening. The opposite edge was stained in blood that looked hardened into the steel. "Which side will you choose?" Pastor Walker finished his statement as he looked at Raymond with a thousand-yard stare. Raymond was petrified. Suddenly there was a loud explosion and everything went black.

As Raymond's eye's opened, he realized he was laying supine on the floor. He looked around and saw that the sanctuary was completely destroyed. He turned right and saw his mother torn to pieces by heavy shrapnel from the explosion. "MOM!!!" he cried. She didn't move. He turned left and saw his father's lifeless body staring at him. "DAD!!!" Raymond began to weep. In the distance he heard others screaming and crying for help. But no one would arrive. Raymond's lower body started to feel strange. It began to hurt really badly. He looked down and saw the most horrendous sight he's ever seen. He saw his entire lower body gone as if it was mangled off from the explosion. His spine and organs where hanging out. "AAAAAAAHHHHHHH!!!!!!" he screamed at the top of his lungs in excruciating pain.

Fragment Redefined
Universe IIII-The Recluses
August 3rd, 2238
1903 Standard Earth Time

Raymond woke up as his adult self in a hospital bed. "AAHH!!!!" He sat up straight with the most horrified expression on his face. A cold sweat was felt dripping down his body and tears flowed out of his eyes like backed up water as there was nothing in the way to block them anymore. He frantically checked his lower body, everything was there. He saw himself still dressed in the civilian cloths he wore in the last mission except with no shirt, revealing his lean physique with no wound on his shoulder. Jake Probably tore through the old shirt to check his wound from earlier he thought to himself. He felt his face and realized his face paint had been removed. Besides that, he was physically fine. He realized what he had experienced was just a nightmare. "Oh my god..." He said in disbelief. "Lord, what was that?" he began to pray. "What was the point of that?" Than he began to weep. He was about to continue praying when he stopped himself and signed in dissatisfaction. "The heck am I doing?... no one's listening..."

The door in front of Raymond opened as he jumped in fear. Lucas walked through wearing a camouflage uniform with one of Raymond's shirts in his hand. "Raymond! Glad you're up." He saw Raymond was highly disturbed at the moment. "Wo, You okay?"

Raymond wiped his tears, found his composure and chose to be honest with his best friend. "No... I had one of those nightmares. You know, like the ones I had as a kid after... after those monsters killed our family."

"Oh man... you haven't had one of those since basic right?" He said while walking up to Raymond and handing him his shirt.

"Yea, It was a little different though." He took the shirt from Lucas

"What do you mean?" Lucas asked as he began to lean against the wall to Raymond's right, hearing him out.

"When that incident happened, I was in the basement of the church for Sunday school. I wasn't with my parents. In the dream, I was next to them when they died. It was weird. Do you know what your dad was supposed to preach about that day?"

"Dude, I was at Paintball practice with my other friends remember?"

"Oh... right. Sorry."

"You need me to get someone?"

"No, I just need a minute to adjust. So what happened to me? Where are we?"

"Well, you were hit but not as bad as we thought you were, it was very superficial. We took a fragment of a 5.56 out of you, must have been from one of the turrets."

"A fragment?"

Lucas explained. "The other pieces chipped off into your plate. It was very awkward how it impacted the plate and your body. Izzy was saying that the ballistics must have been effected by the gravity field from the Flow System. He might be able to tell you more about it."

"I see."

"As for where we are, we are back on the Recluses with a course set back to Earth. We'll be there in a few of days."

Lucas was puzzled. "Earth? Why are we going back there?"

"Well, this is the complicated part... the war is over."

"What?! what happened?"

"Garza Liankos is dead, by the hands of Reaper team."

"Reaper, Tier One?... No way... it's really over." In disbelief.

"According to our chain of command, yes. It's finally over."

"Oh man..." Raymond was happy to see the end of this conflict but was also a bit disappointed. "It's great that it's finally over but... I always thought it would be me or you to finish that monster off."

"Same... but, it is what it is. Our team was only Tier Four so I'm not too surprised they gave a mission that important to Reaper team,

Our parents have been avenged."

"Yea... doesn't feel any different..." Raymond said mournfully

"Tell me about it..." Lucas said while looking away from Raymond.

"So what does this have to do with us going back to earth?" Raymond asked.

Lucas looked back at Raymond. "Well, now that Garza is dead, the council's plan is to send back one ship at a time in shifts to get some leave, re-arm, then head back to the front. Then the next ship comes back to earth once we've returned to the front."

"How long of leave do we get?" Raymond was a little excited.

"We? You're not with us anymore remember? You can stay on earth as long as you want. This is just your free ticket home."

"Oh."

"At that point, it's just up to your new boss, Gehnarne..." Lucas said cynically. "I still don't trust him. Especially after that Rift thing."

"Did you ask him about it?"

"I did, he said he'll only talk to you. I swear, I was this close decking this guy..."

"Relax Lucas."

"Yea... I just hate it when information like that is kept from us. That's how people get killed."

"I know."

"Well, make sure you ask him about it next time you-" The door suddenly slid open and Gehnarne walked through.

"Raymond! Good to see your all right!" He smiled. Both Raymond and Lucas looked at him with displeased expressions. "...Wow... is it just me or is it kinda cold in here?"

"I gotta go." Lucas said with an emotionless voice. "See ya Raymond."

"Bye Lucas." Lucas walked through the sliding door not paying any mind towards Gehnarne, then the door closed.

"Man, he needs to lighten up a bit." Gehnarne said. "So, how are you feeli-?"

"What Rift?" Raymond demanded.

Gehnarne knew this would happen. He turned around calmly and looked quite serious. "Okay Raymond, I'll tell you. But before I do, I want you to understand that I couldn't tell you or your friends at first for a reason. I wasn't trying to sabotage you guys, I just couldn't afford this kind of info to get out in the open yet. Especially with the war going on."

"Well the war is over now so spill it, what is this Universal Rift?" Raymond was growing impatient

"Wow, news travels fast around here." He said while grabbing a nearby seat and sat in front of Raymond. "All right, let me explain. Remember when I told you how we found the universe Izzy was from?"

"Yea, Gia just punched some algorithm into the teleport computer right?"

"No, I wasn't being entirely truthful, there's more to it than that. It was a calculated algorithm converted into coordinates. Gia would know more about how that works. We sent those coordinates through a signal we sent to a beacon just outside of universe 1112's Rift."

"A beacon? How does that work?" Raymond was very curious

"Well, first we find a Universal Rift leading to another universe. The Rift that leads to Izzy's Universe is in orbit around Croza's third moon. We found that one a few months ago when deployments to Croza had increased."

Raymond had remembered something about Croza's third moon. "Is that why there is a permanent no fly zone around that moon?"

"Yes. We had set up a facility on the surface to study the rift, plus when we find a Rift they are in a chaotic state making them very dangerous to fly towards. We set up a Beacon that helps stabilize the Rift to be used for safe travel to the universe on the other side. Than we go through the Rift. Once we're on the other side, we set up another beacon so the two beacons can talk to each other through the Rift so information can be sent between the two different universes. That's how we sent you and your team to Izzy. We put in the coordinates to the beacon here in this universe. That beacon sent your bio data to the beacon on the other side in Izzy's universe."

"That's interesting... and kinda scary."

"You better believe it. If we had made any mistake in entering in your coordinate data, you and your team could have been sent into the middle of nowhere in the vacuum of space."

The thought of that made Raymond shiver. "So assuming that our communications work through the beacons, is that why you told Kathrine that the details of how our new comms systems worked was classified.?"

"Exactly."

"Okay, so knowing that, why is it that we ended up on Earth and not Croza in Izzy's universe? I would think we would have been there since this Rift is located next to our universe's version of Croza?"

Gehnarne explained. "Because, we programmed the beacon on the other side of Croza's rift to communicate with another beacon we set up back at Izzy's version of Earth. You see, every system of planets, in every universe, has a Universal Rift. We just needed the technology to find and use them safely."

"One rift per system? How is that even a thing?"

"Actually it's one to two per system and to be honest... we don't know. For thousands of years it's been that way."

"Thousands of years? Your acting like we've always known these existed."

"Your people didn't but mines did. The UEG found their first rift near Earth five years ago due to a freighter accident. That Rift leads to universe 1211 which I have visited many times already for testing and recruiting."

The freighter incident sounded familiar to Raymond. "Wait a minute... that freighter incident... you don't mean the Endeavor?"

"Yup."

Raymond was shocked. "We were told that was a terrorist attack."

"A cover story."

"Man..." Raymond chuckled knowing there was always something fishy about that incident. He let that sink in as he thought back to something Gehnarne had said earlier that he still didn't understand. "So, what did you mean by when you said your people knew about the existence of these rifts earlier?"

"I knew you'd get back to that." Gehnarne stood up and took a deep breath, preparing himself for what he was about to tell Raymond. "What I'm about to tell you doesn't leave this room. That stuff about the Rifts and the Endeavor you can talk to your friends about in the USOD. But this is classified at the highest level, and is very personal to me as well. So not only could you be sharing classified info but it will also be a personal insult to me. Understand?"

Raymond was concerned but he had to hear the truth. "Understood."

"All right." Gehnarne sat back down. "I am not from this universe. I am from another universe where my people were known by many different names in many different universes. The most commonly used name was 'Rifters'".

"Rifters?...You mean like your call sign and... the challenge password-"

"Nexiose." Raymond was surpised as Gehnarne continued. "That's what my people call ourselves. We were a massive government that had united all of the populated worlds of our own universe under one banner, one mission. To explore other universes. We traveled from universe to universe finding people to trade, establish relations, and help with their problems. But one day, we found a rift that we should have never ventured into."

Raymond was becoming more interested. "What happened?"

"I was 253 when it happened-"

"253?! How old are you?!"

"Ugh... 921." Gehnarne said with an annoyed voice.

"WHAT?! So what's 253 equivalent too in human years?"

"Twelve." Gehnarne responded in aggravation.

"Oh..." Raymond felt a ping of guilt. "Sorry... I-"

"It's alright." Gehnarne cut him off. "Anyway, there were reports that our government had found a new rift. With every new rift we find, we made a celebration of it, practically a Holiday. Everyone would watch as the first ship would take the honor of traveling through the new Rift for the first time. However... this celebration turned into horror. When the ship went through, everything seemed normal. About an hour later, the ship came back. Normally a ship would come back almost a week later to report back on their findings. An hour later was not normal at all. When the ship came through, it was almost completely mangled. Eighty-three percent of the crew and her captain where killed. Even worse, something followed them. Something of pure evil. We all felt it. The ship was finished off right in front of us all by that thing. Then, it came after us. This event in my people's history is simply known as the Darkness. At the brink of total inhalation, my government chose me and many others to be sent to other universes to carry on the legends of our people. I don't know how many of us their were or where they are now, for all I know I could be the last of my kind... Despite that however, I know my mission and must do whatever is necessary to make sure it is carried out."

Raymond grew nervous "Does this thing know your here?"

Gehnarne promptly responded "No, no. It's trapped in my home universe. After we left, our people locked out all the rifts, leaving them in their original chaotic states so no other universe would suffer the same fate as ours."

"How is that possible?"

"My people controlled the rifts on our own will alone. We evolved as a species that way. As long as I can remember, it was always like that. We called it, the power of the Nexiose. It granted us many powerful abilities. As for the civilizations we helped to ascend, they controlled the Rifts through technology like what we're doing now with your government. Those who controlled the rifts through technology launched an emergency lock down and destroyed all the beacons leading to other universes including the ones leading to my home universe, just to be safe. In doing so however, they broke contact with all the other universes in existence bringing them back to square one. As you can guess, hundreds of years have passed. Over that time, my people's existence either drifted into legend or were completely forgotten in some universes."

"I see... so when you said you sensed this thing's evil?"

"We actually felt it... nothing but darkness down to the very soul... I'll never forget that feeling of dread...."

Raymond was shocked. "wo... okay, this feels heavy..." Raymond noticed Gehnarne's somber expression and tried to lighten the topic a little. "With power like that to sense evil and control rifts, I can imagine you doing other things too like... disappearing out of a vehicle in the middle of the forest?" Raymond jokingly suggested with a chuckle.

Gehnarne chuckled at Raymond's clever suggestion seeing that he was trying to cheer him up. "Yes, I thought you might bring that up again. The ID Maneuver. Instant Displacement. I instantly displaced myself just about ten meters in the tree line to the right of your vehicle. I stayed low so you couldn't see me. ID has its limits though."

"That's cool." Raymond said with a smile.

Gehnarne chuckled, "Yea, it kinda is. Listen, I know all this sounds extreme but it's the truth. And your apart of this now. A part of my mission."

"And what exactly is your mission?" Raymond had to ask.

Gehnarne stood up and took pride in his answer. "We are the Rifters. Our mission, is to help the people of our new home universe to ascend technologically, morally, and peacefully, in order to show and help them understand the ways of our people, The Nexiose, and to encourage the concept of not only space exploration of their own universe but of other universes as well."

Raymond's eyes were wide open to how serious Gehnarne was. It was like he had just recited a creed of his people right in front of him. "Okay, I understand. So now what?"

"We carry on with our plans. We have the Flow System, you tried it right? How was it for you?"

"It was awesome but despite how well my first time went, I still feel like it will take some getting used to."

"Well, you better get used to it fast, we have more work to do. Our first task now is to head back to Earth. It will take us five days to get there at FTL Six. In the mean time I suggest you train with the flow system, learn the ins and outs of how it works and how you can effectively use it in combat."

"Right, then?"

"Then once we reach earth, I will get in contact with the council and see if they have our new ship ready for us."

"New ship? I thought we were going to operate out of the Recluses?"

"No, the Recluses will be our QRF encase we run into any trouble beyond the border. The real ship we'll be operating on is still being prepped back on earth."

"Do we have a crew?"

"Yes, of course. We have four departments and could possibly make more if necessary. Ship crew, science team, combat group, and now an R&D department headed by Izzy."

"Nice." Raymond was getting excited. "Who's the Captain?"

"Me of course." Gehnarne smiled with pride. "And you will be the head of the combat group."

"What!? Me!?" Raymond figuratively felt something heavy on his shoulders.

"Is something wrong?" Gehnarne was concerned.

"Isn't that something for an officer to be in charge of? I mean, it doesn't sound like the kind of position an NCO like me would take up."

"In the military you probably wouldn't but our organization won't be limited by those concepts. I see your potential. I know you can do this. Besides, your Special Forces. You can learn anything you want at any given time. Just pick up a book and read."

Raymond made an annoyed face as he thought about how he hated studying. "Yea sure, so how long will we be on earth anyway?"

"More than a week. In that time, you should be able to learn all you can about your new job's responsibility's and training with the Flow system, and if you have some free time, recruiting for our organization. We already have the minimum of people we need but we can always use more. You never know what can happen out there."

"Okay, can I recruit people I know?"

"Of course! The more chemistry you have with people the better."

"All right then, I know a few people who might be interested. What's next after we get the ship and leave earth?"

"I did plan that far ahead but I'll tell you more once we have the ship. Right now I need you to focus on your current tasks okay?"

"All right. In that case, I'm feeling a lot better so, I'll head down to Izzy and pick up the Flow System and start training." Raymond said as he stood up from the hospital bed.

"So soon?"

"Yea, my shoulder is fine and I'm actually excited to find out what I can really do with the flow system with enough training."

"Sounds good, don't forget to train your mind to." Gehnarne said as he and Raymond walked out the door together.

"Trust me, I won't." Raymond said in a way that he knew what would happen if he didn't, disaster.

Gehnarne and Raymond walked out of sickbay together where they parted ways with Gehnarne walking down the hall away from Raymond. "See you later Raymond."

"Seeya Gehnarne." Raymond responded as he accessed a terminal on the wall near the sick bay door in the dark colored metal hallway with white LED lights lining the sides of the ceiling. He looked up Izzy's location than began to walk to his quarters. He was staying at the officer's level guest quarters which was a decent walk from sick bay allowing Raymond to take his time. As he walked through the decks of the Recluses he said hello to familiar faces and even stopped by his team mates quarters just to let them know he was okay. He briefly talked to Jake and Kathrine about what he had done on the roof of the building from their previous mission and how worried they were that he was hurt. After a few moments of conversation, he moved on with a kiss to Kathrine's cheek and a hug, than gave Jake a hug however, being the big guy Jake is, Raymond thought he was going to be crushed with his immense strength. As he continued walking to Izzy's quarters, he took in the atmosphere knowing that in a few days he wouldn't see this ship again for a long time.

After reaching Izzy's quarters, he pressed the doorbell with Izzy answering it. "Raymond! Good to see your all right!" Izzy gave him a hug leaving Raymond awkwardly surprised.

"Uh… yea, good to see you too."

Izzy let go. "So what are you doing here? Shouldn't you be recovering?"

"Nah, It wasn't that bad. I figured we can get straight into training."

"Training? You mean the Flow System?"

"Yea, you have it right?"

"Yes I do, come on in, I'll get it for ya." Walking into the room, it looked like a small studio apartment with a sofa that can be pulled out into a bed. "Here it is." The Flow System was on the floor in the corner in an organized fashion.

Raymond was excited. "Was there any damage from the firefight?" He asked while moving closer to the Flow System.

"Not really. There were some scratches on the gauntlets but

nothing that could hinder the performance of the system. I think those scratches came from you sliding on that roof, pretty impressive move by the way."

"Thanks." Raymond said with pride as he held the gauntlets in his hands and inspected them.

"I did some testing based on the ballistic feedback from when you were hit in that last fight. Turns out the gravity field alters the trajectory of the rounds as they get closer to your body however, not by much so don't depend on it. If it's a straight shot, center mass, it's gonna hit somewhere on your body. If it's close to a limb it might still deflect but the chances are fifty percent. If it's a sub sonic round the chances of deflection will increase by twenty-five percent. The chances of deflection also increase as you move faster so if your ever under fire in the open, running as fast as you can to the nearest cover helps even before you make it to cover.

"Nice." Raymond said with motivation. "I'll keep that in mind, you really designed some interesting piece of technology here Izzy."

"Actually, I didn't design it."

"You didn't? Than who did?"

"Well, Gehnarne notified me about telling you his secret so I'll let you in on another secret. This Flow System is actually a Nexiose weapon."

"Really?" Raymond was intrigued.

"Yes, you see Gehnarne told me that the Nexiose power allows him and others like him to fight in extremely dynamic ways. Those who worked with the Rifters that didn't have that power made the Flow System so they can keep up with the Rifters in combat situations. He's the one who gave me the design of the flow system when he got in contact with me in my universe however, he also mention that the design of this system was made just before The Darkness began so the design wasn't exactly completed, I had to add a little of my own interpretation to the design based on experience and practicality."

"I see... wow... another element of duality between pure evolutionary power and technology like with the beacons huh?"

"Exactly. Also before I forget, I've reconfigured the system to work with an app I created for your Taclet so you won't have to use that control module anymore. The app is simply named FS, you can download it from the recluses servers."

"Thanks. Did you give the leaders of your universe the plans for this system yet?"

"No not yet. I promised them a finished product. As you know, this is only a prototype so, it's not ready for them or us yet for official use or even mass production… not that we plan on making a mass production model anytime soon."

"I see."

"As I see you use it more, I'll take notes on how the final product should be."

"So what? I'm your Guinea Pig now?" Raymond said sarcastically.

"You could say that." Izzy chuckled. "So go ahead and give her a spin whenever you want, just make sure you give me feedback. Where are you going to train anyway?"

"The hanger should be a big enough place as long as people don't distract me."

"Sounds good. I'll check in on you from time to time." Izzy threw Raymond a carrying bag for the flow system.

Raymond took the system and stuffed it gently in the bag. "Thanks Izzy, I'll see you later."

"See ya."

Raymond left Izzy's quarters and walked straight to the hanger. During the walk, he downloaded the FS App on his Taclet like Izzy recommended.

Entering the hanger, he saw a group of United Earth Marines doing PT. They sounded a bit unnecessarily loud as if they were trying to show off. He ignored them and did his own thing. He found a secluded spot in the corner of the hanger behind an F-93 Fighter and put on the flow system. He took his time making sure it was on correctly, then he double tapped the gauntlets wrists together. Two beeps sounded as the discs on his gloves spun, and with a flash and bass like hum, the system turned on. He felt a little light headed however, not as bad compared to the last time he used it. "I should have Izzy turn that beeping off." He suggested to himself as he began to focus and went into a fighting stance.

He threw a jab and immediately felt the difference in speed and power. He laughed in amazement. He threw another jab. Then another. Than a one, two combo. Then a 1, 2, 3, 4 combo. Then at inhuman speeds he started throwing punches, jabs, elbows, uppercuts, back hands and crosses at such fast speeds, it was creating bass like thumbs with each strike in the hanger. After five seconds of a striking barrage, he kicked with his right leg. "Ha!!!" bass thumb, spun around to his left, then kicked with his left leg. "Ha!!!" bass thumb. He lowered his body to the ground with his left hand touching the floor and his right hand open in front of him as a guard, built up force in his legs "HRAA!!!" and jumped into the air spinning twice while kicking both times creating bass thumbs, then made a downward floor slamming kick landing him on his feet with his right leg stretched out across the floor and his right hand up in a guard position. He stopped and breathed out calmly with a smile of pride. It suddenly grew quiet... too quiet. He had the strange feeling someone was watching him causing him to reflexively look left. The group of Marines that were doing PT nearby saw him with shocked expressions on their faces, some with their jaws hanging open. "Uh... Hi guys." They were silent. "Uh... nothing to see here... Just training... just like you marines." They all turned around and walked away while whispering to each other unable to believe what they saw while Raymond mildly laughed in amusement.

As the Marines walked away, Raymond noticed that someone in that crowd was still standing there. It was Colonel Vial. "Colonel!" Raymond quickly turned off the flow system and snapped straight to attention.

With his usual stern expression. "At ease Reynolds." Raymond relaxed and his posture went back too normal. "So, this is the new toy that Gehnarne had you and Charlie pick up."

"Yes sir."

He inspected the system as Raymond wore it. "I'll be honest, when I received orders from the council to hand you over to that outsider, I was pissed. I mean, who does this civilian think he is just barging in our house telling me what to do. Do you know how that feels?"

"Not really sir..."

"Mmm, of course you wouldn't." Colonel Vial was silent for a moment while looking at Raymond than spoke. "Good luck on that new assignment with Gehnarne, you'll probably have more freedom to do what you want without getting into trouble I'm sure." Raymond felt a bit misunderstood as Colonel Vial turned around and began to walk away.

"Sir,"

"Yes?" He turned around.

"Sir I..." Raymond tried to find the right words without disrespecting the Colonel like he did back on Croza. "I just wanted to say sorry," Colonel Vial raised an eye brow in curiosity. "I know it seemed like I had no respect for you, but on the contrary I do have great respect for you. It's just weird that things kept going south, I couldn't just let innocent people die. Those Rebels were already massacring innocent people as it was, so what would have made us any different from them if we just ignore the very people we're trying to help? I do know there were times I got carried away, hell even Gehnarne said the same thing. But the point is that, I never did those things for myself or out of wanting freedom, I just couldn't let those people die if there was any possible way to save them, even if those ways had the smallest chance."

Colonel Vial thought for a moment as his attitude changed. "I see... I don't like that Gehnarne guy. But he is right about one thing. You do get carried away. And one of these days, it's gonna bite you in the ass." Raymond seemed discouraged from the colonel's comment. "But, I can't help but feel your like this for a purpose." Raymond looked back at him in surprise. "With that, don't change who you are unless it's for the better, just control that urge a bit more that's all. Take that as one last piece of advice from me, and in return I have a favor to ask of you."

Raymond found it surreal that Colonel Vial was asking him for a favor. "Uh, sure sir, what do you need?"

"As you know, we are all going to earth. While there I assume you plan to see... her correct?" Colonel Vial began to walk close to Raymond.

Raymond knew exactly who he was talking about. "Yes sir."

Colonel Vial stopped in front of Raymond. "I would say to keep your distance from her, for her own sake, but I know you'll just go anyway so when you do see her." He slightly leaned forward to make sure Raymond could hear him clearly as Colonel Vial expression changed from stern to compassionate. "Tell her that her father misses her... and that he loves her. Can you do that for me son?"

Raymond hadn't seen this side of Colonel Vial in a long time and knew it was genuine. He smiled and responded, "Of course sir."

He smiled back. "Thank you." He turned around and walked away. Raymond stood there for a moment and wondered how different things could have been between him and the Colonel if she was still there. Raymond pushed the thought out of his mind and focused back on task, continuing to train.

Lightning Archival Records
Brief History Of The Fall (The Fall Of Governemt)
In Universe 1112
By Izzy "Digit" Gerard

As the Anarchist movement grew in strength and support, the governments of the world in my home universe struggled to maintain control. Once a highly aggressive computer virus hit the internet, it caused an economic collapsed on a global scale putting a final nail in the coffin for resource management and cooperation between the governments of the world as they now struggled to maintain their own economies. In the end, they all failed bringing an end to official world governments. There are still those around who we turn to for leadership to help restore government one day, however, our world will never be the same again.

Chapter 5: Shore Leave

Raymond had set up a training schedule for himself. 0600, Wake up, 0630, PT for an hour to an hour and a half. 0800, Hygien, 0830, Breakfast, 0900, Leadership Training. He had talked to Lucas for guidance in what to learn for his new role, he was actually happy to help. He taught Raymond some of the basics in being in an officer type position just by letting Raymond follow him around and observe as he lectured. He was even directed to specific study materials for the tasks that where expected of him in that kind of position. Raymond knew he didn't have to be on point with everything knowing the nature of Gehnarnes organization, but he tried his best anyway. The more he knew, the better. 1200 to 1230 was lunch, then back to leadership training. After another two hours of Leadership training, he would train with the flow system at 1430 for an hour to an hour and a half. At 1600 he would call it a day, take a shower, and eat dinner at 1730. After dinner, free time. He would spend that free time with his friends Jake, Katherine, and Lucas. Even though he wasn't officially on the team anymore, they were still the only family he had. Lucas saw how serious he was taking his training and was proud of him. Even though he still didn't trust Gehnarne, he knew that this new thing was better for Raymond. By 2200 hours, he would be in bed and ready for the next day. He continued this routine for five days until the Recluses reached dry dock in orbit around Earth.

Raymond looked out the window of the Recluses dressed in civilian clothes along with the rest of his friends ready for shore leave. "Earth… it's been a while." He said wearing black jeans, and a black polo shirt with black casual shoes and a leather jacket.

"Sure has." Lucas said while wearing light blue jeans with a black shirt and black sneakers. "Feels good to be back."

"Definitely" Jake said wearing tan cargo pants with a white shirt and white sneakers. "Can't wait to see my parents and family again."

"Can't wait to hit up the club." Katherine interrupted while wearing tight jeans with a blue shirt and white sneakers. "Might even hit up this guy I've been talking to on social media."

"Really?" Jake asked. "Does he have any female friends interested in a handsome black man?" Jake said in a confident way.

"No." Katherine looked at Jake annoyingly.

"Come on, I'm sure he knows a few ladies."

"I said no. So, what do you plan to do Lucas?"

Lucas Responded. "Well, I was gonna see some sights in New York. Feels like forever since I've seen the freedom tower or the statue of liberty."

"I thought you New Yorkers didn't see your own monuments?" Jake said chuckling.

"Hey, if this deployment has taught me anything, it's not to take anything for granted."

"True." Katherine said. "So what about you Raymond? You seemed dressed for a specific meet and great" She said with a suggestive giggle.

Raymond spoke with hesitation. "Well... you guys might not like this but... I'm gonna see an old friend of ours."

"Old friend?" Katherine thought than gasped with her response. "Wait, you don't mean her?"

"Yea... her."

"What!?" The whole team was shocked.

Katherine responded. "Raymond, I love her like a sister and all but maybe she isn't ready to talk or see you or even us yet. Maybe you should leave her alone and give her more time."

Raymond explained. "You never know unless you try. Besides, Gehnarne wants me to recruit people for our organization. She's one of two people that I had in mind to recruit."

"Why do I get the feeling I know who the second recruit is?" Lucas said with suspicion.

Raymond knew immediately of who Lucas was talking about. "What makes you so sure I'm recruiting Yab-...ooooohhh..." Raymond groaned realizing the name had slipped.

Lucas brought his right hand's palm to his face while slowly shaking his head back and forth with a no gesture as he groaned, "Because you just told me..."

"I-" Raymond paused than continued. "Okay, I guess it was pretty obvious at that point. Anyway, Lucas, you and Yabin are gonna have to talk eventually, you can't just avoid him forever." Raymond said.

"Fine, whatever. Just don't expect me to be friendly with him off the bat. Hell, I'll probably be more friendly to Gehnarne than the old man at this point."

"Speaking of Gehnarne," Jake whispered to Lucas while nodding towards Gehnarne.

Gehnarne walked towards Charlie team wearing his usual casual business attire. His assistant Gia and Izzy were with him as well, also dressed in civilian clothes. "Charlie team! Good to see you again. Isn't it great being back at your home world?" Gehnarne said while Izzy waved at Kathrine with a smile. Katherine saw him and immediately blushed while smiling and waving back. Jake saw this and immediately became jealous.

"Of course." Lucas responded to Gehnarne. "It's been too long for all of us. Need something?"

"Well, I just came to give you guys some good news." Gehnarne said

"What news?" Jake asked

Gehnarne looked at Gia letting her talk. "You guys have been selected to be the starting team for the combat group in our new organization. You are now re-designated as Alpha team of SMO."

Gehnarne interrupted "Isn't that great!? The council just approved it."

"Really?" Lucas was surprised. "We're still headed back to the front right?"

Gia continued. "Yes of course but that also means an extra two days leave." The whole team was happy about that. "And, not only will you be headed back to the front, but you will be going beyond it."

"The unreached worlds?" Lucas said with a serious tone.

"Exactly." Gehnarne said. "Enjoy your leave Alpha. But once your back, be ready for anything."

"Of course." Lucas said "We'll see you guys around, we gotta catch the shuttle planet side." The team grabbed their bags and began to walk away.

"Enjoy your leave." Gehnarne said in farewell.

"We will, Thanks." Raymond said as him and the team walked into the shuttle, took their seats, and buckled up. "Can't wait to breath in that fresh earth atmosphere." He said giddily.

"Me too." Katherine agreed.

The shuttle detached from the docking port of the Dry Dock station where the Recluses was docked and descended down to earth towards the North American continent. The sun seemed to be setting already in that region of the world. The whole shuttle was surrounded by a barrier powered by a generator on the shuttle. The shuttle was designed to easily break through earth's atmosphere with little turbulence. Once the shuttle was through the atmosphere, it went through clouds than came out the other side. From the windows in the passenger compartment, you can see land stretching far and wide. The shuttle was scheduled to land in New York by 1900 hours than to New Jersey where Katherine and Jake were from. Raymond looked out the windows and saw the freedom tower and other buildings. "It's definitely been too long." Raymond said to himself. The shuttle landed on the roof of the Port Authority Terminal. There was a landing platform for incoming shuttles from the dry dock stations in orbit. Once the shuttle touched down, the door opened and let its passengers off.

"Have fun guys." Katherine said to Lucas and Raymond as they walked out the shuttle.

"We will, you too." They responded. They walked off the shuttle with their luggage and moved towards the elevator leading to the street level while the shuttle door closed and steadily lifted off again. They stepped into the elevator and pressed the button for the street level. "So, where are you gonna stay?" Lucas asked Raymond.

"A hotel."

"A hotel?" Lucas questioned. "You're not gonna go back to your family's apartment?" Lucas was puzzled.

Raymond paused than answered. "I want to enjoy my leave. Going back there will be... a bad idea."

Lucas was concerned but knew that this was an issue that Raymond had to deal with himself. "As you wish."

"What about you?" Raymond asked.

"I'm going home. We've always been neighbors so if you do decide to go back home, hit me up okay."

"Sure." Raymond knew he would never go back home but agreed to see him anyway to keep the conversation away from the past.

"Here's our stop." The elevator doors slid open into a large lobby. Lucas and Raymond walked through the Lobby to the exit and went outside to the side walk. They looked around and took in the view. The city felt alive with electric cars driving along the streets and hover cars levitating above them as horns honked, people walking around with some talking on their smart phones, and lights on the signs glistening. The pair felt at home again. "Beautiful..." Lucas said out loud.

"Yea... Well, I gotta go Lucas, i'll see you later. Want me to say hi to the old man for you?"

Lucas simply responded, "No." with no emotion.

"Suit yourself." Raymond responded.

"Whatever man, have fun and enjoy yourself." They hugged each other than parted ways.

"See ya!" Raymond said while walking the opposite direction towards the Greenwich village district of Manhattan. He walked East on forty second street for thirty minutes than turned south on fifth avenue taking in the unique sites of Manhattan and fresh air of earth's atmosphere. "Feels good to be back..." Raymond spoke to himself.

He continued walking till he heard a loud commotion coming from Washington Square park from a block away. In concern, he began to walk faster. When he reached the Washington Square Arch, he saw a large group of protesters speaking against the perceived occupation of the colony's during the Colonial Wars. The protesters shouted many different quotes such as, "LEAVE THE COLONIES BE!, LEAVE THE COLONIES BE!" or "It's their home! NOT OURS! It's their home! NOT OURS!". Raymond looked at the protest in sorrow realizing that the obliviousness of earths populace still hasn't changed. Although he was pro council, there were some decisions that were made by the council that he disagreed with. However, whatever intentions the council had in getting involved in the Colonial Wars, he knew that innocent civilians were being murdered by the Rebels on the colonies and if they weren't dealt with, the people back on earth would suffer next, the same way his parents did. It had to be stopped, despite what the large percentage of civilians from Earth felt about not getting involved. Raymond looked at the crowd of protesters and said to himself, "The next generation of peace will not be obtained through words." Than he continued to walk past the protesters, "But through action."

Another half hour later, Raymond made it to the hotel he had made a reservation for, four days prior to his arrival. He checked in, secured his stuff in his room, than left in the evening to visit a beloved friend. He arrived at a popular lounge located near the hotel. He nervously checked his watch with it reading 2200 hours. "Okay, let's get in there... be cool." He said trying to calm himself. The entrance was the same size as your typical apartment door way with a sign above it that read "The Velvet Star" glowing with red neon lights. As Raymond got closer to the entrance he saw a familiar face and casually said "Hey!" to a big muscular bouncer just outside the lounge entrance.

The bouncer turned around. "Yea, what do you-... SLINGER!?" The bouncer was shocked and happy to see Raymond.

"Crow! Good to see you buddy! How are ya?" He asked as they clasped hands together and hugged.

"Doing awesome now that your back. How's the front looking?" They backed away from each other after the hug.

"Well, not that any of these people would care but, we won the war. It's over."

"No way..." with a surprised expression. "Really? Garza is dead?"

"Yea."

"Wow..." Crows expression turned sad. "I guess my brothers were finally avenged then huh?"

"Definitely."

"Thanks for telling me."

"Of course, you deserved to know. Hey, I would love to catch up but I'm actually here for something important."

"What's that?"

Going back into a nervous posture. "I need to talk to the old man... and her..."

"Her?!... Sheena?" With a suggestive expression.

"Yea..." while looking down trying not to look embarrassed.

"Well isn't that sweet." While chuckling. "Picking up where you left off?"

Raymond laughed nervously. "Yea, something like that."

"I'll let you through, don't worry about entry fee." Crow started unbuckling the red rope to let him through.

"You sure?"

"Yea I'm sure, I owe you my life last I checked."

Raymond chuckled in flattery. "Thanks man, I appreciate it."

"Your welcome. If you need anything, let me know."

"Sure. It was good to see you again."

"Like wise."

Raymond was about to walk away, then he just remembered something. "Hey Crow."

"What's up?"

"I just joined this new para military organization and they need people. I was wondering if you wanted to join?"

Crow paused for a moment than responded "Sorry but..." Crow lifted his right pant leg revealing his cybernetic leg. "I just can't man." he let go of the pant leg. "Some guys can still go back into it despite these kinds of injuries but me... I'm not one of those guys... I'm done with that stuff, sorry."

"It's all right man, I understand."

"Thanks for asking though, at least some people think I still got it." They both mildly laughed.

"Okay bud, if you change your mind, you know how to contact me, okay."

"Of course, see ya later and have fun." Crow smiled in appreciation.

Raymond smiled and nodded his head then turned around. Nervously he said to himself. "I'll try..."

He walked through the doors into a dimly lit room. He immediately saw a bar to his right with a large assortment of different alcoholic drink bottles behind it with a few dozen people sitting in front of the bar on stools. On his left he saw tables with chairs where people were in conversation and eating meals. In front of him on the other side of the room was a small floor level stage with a microphone on a stand and a guitar just off the right of the stage also on a stand. He moved to the other side of the bar closest to the stage, then took a seat facing the stage.

"Raymond "The Gunslinger" Reynolds" A man behind Raymond said out loud.

Recognizing the voice, Raymond immediately turned around in the seat and saw a slender man about the same height as Raymond with short gray hair and brown eyes with a smile. He wore a white dress shirt with no tie and black slacks with black shoes. "I told you to stop calling me that old man." Raymond said with a smile as he moved towards the man for a hug. "Good to see you again Yabin."

"Good to see you to!" They hugged then let go. "So how are you?"

"Doing great, just on leave, here to see an old friend of ours."

"I figured as much, why would you be here for an old coot like me?" They both laughed.

"You're not that old."

"Well, I'm old enough. Can I get you something?"

"Sure, just a beer."

"Gotcha." Yabin grabbed a bottle, popped the cap open with a bottle opener and handed it to Raymond. "Here you go, It's on me."

"Thanks Yabin."

"Your welcome." Yabin smiled. "So..." He paused than continued. "How's Lucas doin?"

Raymond paused unsure of what to say, than simply responded, "H-He's... Okay." While smiling at Yabin nervously.

"Still hates me huh?" bluntly.

With a cringed expression. "Yea, pretty much."

"Mmm... Of course he does, what else is new?" Yabin said sarcastically.

"Ah, don't worry about it so much Yabin." Raymond said feeling bad while taking a swig of his beer than looked back at Yabin changing topics. "Hey, are you still in touch with your..." Raymond lowered his voiced and moved closer to Yabin as he looked back and forth checking their surroundings. "...Contacts?"

"Yea I am, Why?"

"Well, I've been reassigned to a new organization headed by a guy named-"

"Gehnarne AKA Rifter?"

Raymond was shocked. "Dang old man! You still got it."

"Of course! You never know when the Intelligence community can come in handy, even after retirement."

"Right." They laughed. "I was wondering if you could look into something for me?"

"What do need?" Yabin was curious.

"Has your network detected any illegal shipments of military grade hard ware?"

"Anything specific?"

"Three or more Model T-ATS turrets and-"

"A model B30 Communications Jamming Device?"

Raymond was surprised again. "I swear, you give me chills every time you do that."

Yabin chuckled. "Yea, yea I got wind of a shipment of those."

"Who did it come from?"

"Some big time mercenary organization named Carnivore. They purchased the stuff from the military legally but sold it illegally to a group of unknowns at an unknown location."

"Unknown? That's a first for you."

"Yea I know, it's like the stuff completely disappeared from our universe if you catch my drift." Yabin said suggestively.

"Had a feeling you'd know something about the multiverse stuff we've gotten ourselves into."

"Yea, so I assume you know what happened to that jamming device and those turrets?"

"We ran into them on our first mission to another universe. Some street gang had them, I think they were hired to take out our VIP."

"I see, makes sense. Have someone else do the dirty work to attract less attention."

"Yea but they weren't prepared for the ace we had up our sleeve." Raymond thought for a second as he paused with the beer bottle to his lips. "Carnivore... Now that I think about it, didn't the council hire Carnivore for some ops in the past? I think I remember reading about them somewhere in old combat logs in the USOD."

"Yea, but almost five years ago they officially broke off all contracts with UEG. Now they're just a band of high tech mercs."

"Five years ago...?" Raymond remembered what Gehnarne told him about the Endeavor five years ago. "Could they be connected...?" He thought to himself. Asking Yabin, "Does anyone know where they are now?"

"No one knows. Last anyone heard they took their small fleet beyond the borders of the unreached worlds. All we got on them now are some of their financial transactions which means they are still active out there, but doing what, I have no idea."

"I see... whatever it is they are doing they clearly have access to multi universal travel, and here I thought we were the only ones with access to that kind of technology. Yabin, can you continue to monitor their transactions and keep me and my organization updated?"

"Well if it involves me leaving my lounge than no, but if you're okay with me working at home I can do it for ya."

"That's perfect, once I get set up, I'll give you more official contact information."

"Okay, thanks, and one word of advice for you Raymond."

"What's that Yabin?"

"Rattle the cage enough times and the bird will eventually escape."

Raymond was puzzled. "Your point?"

"What I mean is, if you keep beating the guys that are under Carnivore's pay role, like those thugs or whoever else could be with them-"

Raymond figured it out. "Carnivore will eventually reveal themselves to us."

"Exactly." Yabin finished. "That's usually when things get more dangerous... Be careful."

The lights in the room dimmed. "You better turn around, or you'll miss the first performance."

"Thanks." He said to Yabin as he turned back towards the stage and took a swig of his beer.

An announcement was made. "Ladies and gentlemen, welcome to the Velvet Star's open mic night, where we find rising artists to show case their talent to the public! Tonight's first performance will be from the lovely Sheena Vial. Please welcome her to the stage." The people in the lounge started to clap their hands as the door to the left started to open. A beautiful woman about the same age as Raymond walked out the doorway wearing a black dress with the top wrapping around her neck with a skirt just over her knees, black stockings, medium length black heeled shoes, a short red jacket over her dress, Crimson colored lipstick, finely contrasted make up and shoulder cut brunette hair with red highlights at the ends. She respectfully smiled at the audience as she walked on stage however, she seemed a bit shy and nervous. The spot light focused on her as she picked up her guitar, sat in her seat and adjusted the microphone. Raymond looked at her in shock almost choking on his beer. He immediately took out his wallet and looked at the old picture he had of her. Same face, but new style. He couldn't believe it was the same woman. Despite the different look, he felt an old familiar feeling he hadn't experienced in a long time. A sense of warmth in his chest and longing to be with her. He saw Sheena as the most beautiful woman he had ever met and looked even more beautiful now. He put his wallet away as old memories of her and him together flooded his thoughts while he tried to focus on the present with her on stage.

"Hello." Sheena nervously greeted. "This song is called "Saved Me"." The song started with her softly playing the guitar at a C note. She sang the lyrics softly trying not to sound nervous as the audience listened to the first verse. "I once walked on water... Moving towards you... Thought I was ready... Set to pursue. Than the waves distracted me, I fell drowning to the dark depths." Her nervousness slowly disappeared as her voice started to sound more naturally beautiful. "I tried to swim up, wasn't strong enough. Thought I was done, I gave up." Suddenly her voice grew louder with confidence. "Then I saw your hand, reaching for me, I grabbed, you pulled me free." She fluctuated her voice to a louder tone and higher pitch as she began the chorus. "You drew me out, from the darkness deep in my soul. You saw my pain, my wounds and you have healed me. I saw death, you brought me back to life. Oh you, have saved me. Oh you, have saved me."

The audience seemed to enjoy the music as Raymond also enjoyed it. He always loved her incredibly beautiful singing voice however, the theme behind the song sounded very familiar. Listening closely, Raymond knew what the song was about but didn't realize that Sheena was into faith. He figured it probably started after she left the USOD, after her terrible experience. He started to remember the good old days again and the time he spent with her, wishing he had gone back to earth in her time of need.

"Oh you... have saved... me..." The song and her voice softly came to an end as the people around the lounge started to clap. Sheena stood up and took a bow as she couldn't help but notice the familiar face by the bar. Raymond noticed that she was aware of him while she kept her composure despite being surprised. She than stood straight up with a smile looking directly at Raymond and exited the stage to her right through the door while the announcer spoke. "Thank you Ladies and Gentlemen. Please continue to enjoy your evening as we bring our next artist up to the stage please welcome..." Everything around Raymond had faded as he got up, leaving the bar behind and walked towards the door Sheena had walked through. He slowly moved left and right walking around tables in the middle of the lounge. Finally reaching the door, he opened it and saw a dimly lit short hallway. He went in and closed the door behind him.

He saw four different doors down the hall, two on each side. He walked down the hall a little and saw the door on his right with a sign reading "Sheena". He faced that door, took a deep breath and politely knocked three times. "Come in!" Sheena politely said through the door. Raymond opened it, entering what looked like a dressing room with a big flashy mirror and a makeup stand. Raymond faced Sheena as she faced away from him towards the mirror. She had already taken her short red jacket off exposing her elegant arms and shoulders as her black dress covered her back and the top elegantly wrapped around her neck. "Hello Raymond..." She said to him through the Mirror with a smile, turned around to face Raymond, then ran to him with a hug. As she hugged him, her fore head just grazed the bottom of his chin.

Raymond felt very warm inside as he embraced her. "It's good to see you Sheena. I missed you." He said with enthusiasm, glad that she was happy to see him.

"I missed you too!" She backed away from him, still holding his hands smiling.

"Wow... Your hair looks," Raymond said as Sheena held her breath waiting to hear what he would say. "Amazing! You look truly amazing."

Sheena immediately smiled and blushed. "Thanks." What are you doing here? I thought the invasion of Croza was still happening?"

"It happened all right, and we won." He said with pride.

"That's great! And Garza?"

"Dead."

"Good, It's finally over..." She said with relief in her voice as she let go of Raymond's hands.

"I feel ya, I just wish it was me that did it."

"Our team didn't do it?"

"No, Reaper team did."

"I see," Sheena rolled her eyes. "Of course they would send the Tier One heroes of the USOD and not our little band of misfits."

Raymond laughed at her comment. "Yea," He looked around the room. "Nice dressing room you got here."

Sheena laughed. "Yabin just lets me use this one whenever I perform here."

"Those USOD connections at work huh?"

"Yup." They both laughed.

"USOD connection or not, you were always an amazing singer, you deserve it."

Sheena blushed again. "Thanks."

"I really liked your song by the way, but I must say, I'm actually kinda surprised by it."

"Why so surprised?"

"The theme of your song. It was inspired by the story of Peter walking on water towards Jesus wasn't it?"

Sheena was pleased he understood. "Yes! That's exactly it. I actually forgot that you were a man of faith once."

"Yea... once." Raymond expressed displeasure in the topic.

"Oh, I'm sorry, I didn't mean to make you feel weird about that."

"No, it's fine. So..." Raymond felt awkward asking this. "How long have you been... well, saved for, or... whatever?"

Sheena chuckled at how he awkwardly asked that question. "A few months now. I left the USOD almost a year ago and was encouraged by my mother to try going to church. As you know my situation... I was desperate so, figured what else did I have to lose right? So I went. I wasn't saved immediately on my first visit but... I was intrigued by everything that was preached about love and kindness and-" Sheena noticed Raymond's expression growing more awkward. "I'm sorry, I'm sure you really don't want to talk about this, you know where I'm getting at anyway," Sheena giggled in embarrassment.

Raymond smiled at her. "Hey, if that's something new in your life that makes you feel better and happy, then I'm happy for you."

Sheena felt relieved. "Thanks for understanding Raymond."

Trying to shift away from talking about faith, Raymond changed topics. "By the way, your father said he misses you, and loves you."

Sheena was surprised to hear that, "And yet... he's not here to tell me himself?"

Raymond shrugged. "You know the Colonel, he's a busy man."

"I know... I just wish he could have come by to hear me sing at least... see how much I've changed."

"Well since Garza is dead the war is technically over so maybe he might just come by sometime?"

"You and I both know that's only partially true. We still have to worry about retaliation efforts, new leadership and other nonsense like that."

"I know, that's kinda why I'm here actually."

Sheena looked at him with concern. "What do you mean?"

"I've been invited into a new outfit tasked to explore the unreached worlds."

"Explore? Since when does the military do that?"

"We don't, that's why it's a new outfit tasked specifically for exploration and combat ops against possible rebel remnants beyond the border."

"I see... so what does this have to do with me?" Sheena crossed her arms.

"This new organization needs people and I was wondering if you would be interested."

Sheena looked a bit annoyed. "You came here to ask me that? Raymond, you know my condition. I can't... I won't be psychologically fit for something like this."

"You don't have to do anything combat related, I was thinking you could just help out around the ship and the crew."

"And just sit back and watch you guys do the hard work? I can't Raymond, I'm sorry. Military stuff like this isn't me anymore. I just can't."

Raymond felt bad for asking. "Okay... sorry. I didn't mean to make you think I only came here to ask you that, I actually really did come here to see you again... I really did miss you."

She smiled. "I know you didn't just come here for a job offer." She slowly came back towards him. "I missed you too... very much." They looked into each other's eyes and couldn't help but get lost in each other for a moment.

Raymond snapped out of it realizing how awkward that was. "Oh! Sorry." He laughed.

Sheena laughed as well. "Don't be." Suddenly Sheena heard a familiar song playing in the concert area she could just hear through the walls. A slow song that was perfect for a slow dance. "What a beautiful song huh?"

"Yea... it is." Raymond caught himself as he took that for a sign. "Oh!-Uh, care to dance?"

Sheena giggled. "Why not." She placed her arms over Raymond's shoulders as he placed his hands on her waist with Raymond taking the lead as they both slowly and steadily rocked back and forth around the room to the rhythm of the slow song. "So how's the rest of the team?"

"They're great. Katherine is still the party girl as always."

Sheena laughed. "She was always like a little sister, I swear."

"Jake is still the calm teddy bear you hold him up to be but I'm pretty sure you're still the only one who's allowed to describe him in that way though."

"Well you guys always gotta maintain that tough persona but me and him both know how cute he can be." They both laughed. "Has Kat finally stopped playing hard to get with Jake? I would think by now she would have noticed how he feels about her, unless she's really that blind."

"Blind as a bat unfortunately."

"Oh..." Sheena seemed a little sad. "Hope she snaps out of it soon and gives the poor guy a chance. At least just one date or something."

"Maybe some people just aren't meant to be together Sheena." Raymond suggested

"Raymond, you of all people should know that you never really know till you try, I mean, look at us. We hated each other when we first met." Sheena giggled thinking back at their past.

"True" Raymond chuckled as he also remembered.

"How is Lucas?" Sheena asked.

"Still the big brother. Trying to make sure we're okay and leading us from the front."

"I'm surprised he hasn't made Major yet."

"He did but… he turned it down."

"Really?"

"Yea. He just loves being team lead. A lot of Captains are like that in USOD."

"I see. He Still angry at Yabin?"

"Yup."

"He still hasn't gotten over that?... wow." Sheena sighed. "I wish I can see them all again." She said while resting the left side of her head on his chest, feeling and hearing his calm heartbeat.

"We're all on leave for a week so your welcome to look them up."

"Really?" Sheena looked back at Raymond. "That's great. It would be fun to have the whole team together again."

"Same." The song was still going but the couple had stopped moving as they gazed into each other's eyes again. This time, nothing was snapping them out of it. They both edged closer and closer. They closed their eyes as their lips touched softly in love. After a beautiful moment of this unexpected kiss, Sheena began to slowly back away. "I uh... I gotta start getting ready to leave now..." She said somberly.

Raymond looked at her as she avoided eye contact. He knew there was something wrong. "Oh… um... sorry. Need me to help you, or walk you home?"

"No… it's okay. I'll be fine." She let go of Raymond and slowly moved away from him.

Raymond didn't want her to leave alone but he thought about what Kathrine had said about giving her time, it would be best to just let her go for now. "Okay..." Raymond somberly responded. "I'll start leaving then."

"Alright." Sheena said while looking down away from Raymond.

Raymond began walking towards the door as he noticed Sheena's open purse on a chair next to the doorway on the left. He had an idea. He reached into his pocket and took out the disc case of face paint remembering that face paint originally belonged to her. In a respectful surprise, he wanted to give it back to her, so he threw it in her purse hoping she would find it after he left. He then opened the door and turned around just before walking through it. "Listen, I know you already said you're not interested in the offer but, encase you change your mind, I'll be at the hotel down the street. I'm staying in room 595 okay?"

"Okay." She said while facing away from Raymond.

"Hope to see you again this week some time if you're up for it." Raymond suggested.

"Of course." Sheena said while turning around slightly to face Raymond. "Make sure to invite the whole team okay?"

"All right." Raymond walked through the door. Just before closing it, he turned around again. "It was good seeing you again."

Sheena worked up the courage to look at him directly before he left. "Same" She smiled.

"Bye."

"Bye."

Raymond closed the door leaving Sheena behind as she put on her short red jacket and began to pack her things in her purse to go home. While packing she started to remember all the great times her and Charlie team had together, in and out of the field. Especially the times she spent with Raymond. She started to feel sad knowing she had left them. Struggling to fight off her feelings of weakness and depression, she packed not noticing the face paint case Raymond had threw in her purse earlier. She walked out of the dressing room with her purse on her shoulder, then went down the hall. She then went through the hallway door back into the lounge. There were still live performances on stage as she moved through the crowed and exited through the loung's front door running into Crow. "Hey Crow. What's up?"

"Hey Sheena. Did Raymond talk to you?"

"Yea, he did."

"Sooo..." Crow made a suggestive look.

"Soooo what?" Sheena was curious.

"You two... well... you know... back together?"

"Crow?!" Sheena was annoyed.

"What!? I'm just curious! He always did care about you." Crow responded with a mild laugh.

"I don't know... I guess we'll see how things go I guess..." Sheena said calmly.

"All right girl, take your time okay?"

"I will. Thanks Crow." She gave Crow a friendly hug.

"Any time." He hugged her back, than parted ways. "Have a goodnight, be safe going home."

"You too." Sheena walked down the sidewalk to the right of the bar entrance, the opposite direction from the hotel Raymond was staying in. As she walked, she continued to reminisce on the past slowly falling deeper into depression as she began to remember the details in her life that had started her pain.

Chapter 6: Crimson

In the middle of a dirt wasteland with barely any signs of life sat a small building near the edge of a hill with a flat roof. On the top of the roof looking out towards the wasteland from a prone position was a woman laying on top of a sleeping mat for a comfortable shooting position behind an M-130 sniper rifle equipped with a twenty inch 7.62 caliber barrel with a ten-round magazine, a one to twenty times adjustable scope that could switch between standard, thermal, and night vision, a range finder, and a wind direction and speed detector. A perfect setup for any sniper working without a spotter. She was wearing full multi-camouflage combat gear with her plate carrier off to the side from where she was prone. She also wore a Boonie cap on her head with her hair in a ponytail. Her brunette hair mildly blew with the wind as she looked through the scope of her weapon with a black stripe of paint on her face from ear to ear. "White, this is Crimson, what's your status? Over." Staff Sargent Sheena "Crimson" Vial asked with a professionally deadly voice in concern after hearing static on the channel with her SDT set to auto.

"Crimson, White. So far so good. The platoon of militia is taking point, we're gonna straggle behind a little to let them do their own thing. How's your over watch position? Over."

"Nice and quiet. Just watching your backs, as usual."

"Roger that, keep your eyes peeled."

"Check." Sheena was confident and composed as she looked through the sight of her M130 sniper rifle with both eyes open. She grew bored and decided to entertain herself a little. "Slinger, Crimson. Private channel." She said playfully while opening a private channel on the communications app and sending Raymond an invite with a text showing an emoji with a winking eye and a tongue sticking out.

The whole team stopped and slowly looked at Raymond. They gave him a smile and tried to hold back their laughs. They all had a feeling something was going on between Sheena and Raymond. This confirmed it. Raymond looked back at them in embarrassment as they continued on patrol. He tapped "Accept" on the private channel invite on his Taclets communications app than responded with a mild chuckle, *"what's up crimson?."*

"Hey Slinger." She smiled. "You feeling okay down there?"

"Yea, just enjoying the sights while hunting bad guys. You know, cool stuff."

Sheena laughed. "And watching from the scope of a sniper rifle isn't cool?"

"Eh... it's overrated"

Sheena laughed again. "Sure it is." She said sarcastically. "Excited about tonight after this patrol is over?"

"Yea, back on the Recluses with you, can't wait."

"Yea, me neither. What would you like for dinner? I can cook your favorite if you want?"

"Eh, you can surprise me, I'll try whatever you cook." He said with a smile.

Sheena was happy. "Okay, I think I'll try to make something new tonight."

"Sounds great. Looking forward t-" Static.

Sheena became concerned. "Slinger?... Slinger you there?" Suddenly, there was a loud explosion from a distance in front of Sheena, ahead of Charlie team. "The fuck?!" Sheena cursed in surprise.

"CONTACT! THREE O'CLOCK! TWO HUNDRED METERS!" Sheena heard from Lucas on the open channel as she heard gun fire from a distance and over the channel. She immediately shifted her body and weapon to the right and saw muzzle flashes from Charlie team, taking cover inside a small trench near a small house, and more muzzle flashes from the enemy that had engaged them in the direction that Lucas called out.

"The militia platoon is cut off from us," Raymond reported on the channel. *"They got hit hard with an IED!"*

Switching back to the open channel on her comms app, Sheena said, "Roger, I have eyes on the enemy." Sheena switched to thermals to get a better view on the enemy's position and numbers. "I count five hostiles on the berm six hundred meters from my position. Engagi... wait... what?" She noticed that the thermal silhouette's seemed smaller than a normal person. She zoomed in closer than switched back to standard view. She gasped. "Oh God," in the scope she saw five children. "No... not kids."

"Say again crimson? Over." Lucas asked.

"I say again, those are children firing on you, some kind of rebel child soldier unit."

Lucas's heart sank. He heard reports of other teams running into small units like this before but his team never did, until now. Even though he didn't like it, he knew what needed to be done. *"Good copy Crimson."* He paused. *"Weapons free."*

"What!? I can't do that!"

"Those are enemy combatants Crimson!"

"GRENADE!" Jake screamed in the background as there was an explosion like sound through the radio.

"You good!?" Lucas asked Jake while still transmitting to Sheena.

"I'm okay!"

"Crimson, they already have the tactical advantage, we are cut off from the militia platoon, you're the only person who can help us, now open fire!"

Sheena shifted her body slightly and adjusted the weapon on target. Her cross-hairs were lined up directly on the forehead of one of the child soldiers, a girl maybe ten to twelve years old. She tried to pull the trigger but froze. "I… I can't..."

"Crimson, Fire your weapon or we will die!" Sheena heard more gun fire over the radio. *"That's an order!"*

"I..." still frozen.

"Crimson! Private channel!" Slinger yelled over the radio.

Sheena snapped out of it and quickly switched to the private channel. "Slinger!?"

"Crimson! Listen, I know this sucks, I wouldn't want to do this either, but at the end of the day, it's us, or them. Kids or not, they are enemy combatants." There were Loud cracking sounds just over Raymond's head as the enemy began to fire near him. *"You have to shoot!"*

"We're being flanked!" Katherine said in the back ground on the radio and returned fire.

"Don't think! Just do!" Raymond said.

"O… Okay." Sheena responded. "Engaging."

"Do what you always do! Show them what happens when they pick a fight with the Morri-" Static. The private channel suddenly cut off.

"Slinger?!"… No response. She feared for Raymond's life making her desperate. Sheena gained a steady position, focused back on her first child target down the sight, took a deep breath and exhaled as she slowly started to squeeze the trigger. While steadily squeezing, she remembered what Raymond was about to say before he got cut off. The Morrigan or Battle crow, also known as the phantom queen or great queen in Irish mythology. That was what the rebels notoriously called her, The Morrigan of planet Kalista where she had killed one hundred ninety-three of her one hundred ninety-five total kills. For a while now she was excited to make it all the way up to two hundred kills, making her the most-deadliest sniper of the colonial wars. However, now knowing she will reach two hundred with five dead children, she started to regret ever being excited about that. "I am... The Morrigan..." She whispered to herself while crying as she pulled the trigger. The rifle fired with a slight recoil. Almost a full second had passed when the round impacted into the skull of the child creating a pink mist behind her head. Sheena gasp in sorrow as she shifted left and fired another round killing another child soldier. She shifted again, then shot, shift, shot, Shift, shot, killing the last child soldier. She scanned the area. No contacts. "White… Crimson…" She paused. "Are you clear?..." For a moment there was silence on the radio. "White… do you copy?..." After a long pause. "Whi-"

"This is white. Crimson, we're clear. Nice shooting."

Sheena sighed in relief. "Is everyone okay?" She was worried.

"Roger, we're all okay. Cateye, call a MEDEVAC for these militia guys, they're in bad shape."

"*On it.*" Katherine said over the open channel.

"*Crimson...*" Lucas continued talking to Sheena over the channel. *"I know that was hard... I'm sorry you had to do that... are you okay?"*

"Yea… I'll be alright."

"Roger that. Regroup with us at the evac site." Lucas ordered.

"Roger… Oscar Mike..."

As Sheena began backing away from the sniper rifle, she couldn't hold it in anymore. She collapses back on her stomach as she broke down in tears and cried. She could never forgive herself for what she did. Enemy or not, she felt those children didn't deserve this.

The Recluses
September 19th, 2237
2211 Standard Earth Time

That night, when the team got back to the Recluses, Raymond went to visit Sheena in her quarters. "Sheena?" Raymond knocked on her door. "You there?" With no response, he began to worry. "You hadn't said much after the... incident. So, I thought I should check up on you." Still waiting at the door. "Can I come in?"

After a momentary silence, "Come in..." The door slid open at her command. Raymond walked through the door, entering a dark room. He couldn't see her.

"Where are you?"

"Over here..." Raymond heard a voice to his right. He turned and saw a figure in the dark. His eyes were starting to adjust. He was sure it was Sheena sitting on her cushioned chair where she would normally read her books and write her music. She was leaning forward with her elbows on her knees, head down, and feet flat on the floor. Raymond walked towards her, grabbed another chair and sat in front of her leaning forward.

"Are you okay?" Raymond had never seen her like this before. She was usually very bright, happy and kinda full of herself. He even got to see her loving side as they got closer over the past few months. This dark and depressing atmosphere was not like her at all.

"No..." She responded.

"What's wrong?" Raymond asked.

"I made two hundred today..."

"You used to be proud of that."

"Not anymore..."

"Because you feel it's tainted now? Those kids?"

"Yes..." She responded as she began to cry.

"I'm so sorry..." Raymond felt bad. He wanted to help her. "Do you need me to get someone? Like the Chaplain or your father?"

"No!" She shook her head as she looked up at Raymond. Her eyes were red with her face covered in tears. Her black face paint was mostly gone with little smudges left behind down her cheeks. Raymond had never seen Sheena cry before. His heart sank as he looked into her eyes expressing the feeling of someone broken who was looking to be fixed. He didn't know what to do or say however, Sheena continued to talk before he could say anything.

"I… I just want you!" She lunged at Raymond and hugged him tight. "I was so scared you had been killed! I didn't want to kill them but if I didn't, you and everyone else would have died, and it would have been my fault! Either way, it's my fault no matter who died!" Despite being in shock, Raymond was still able to hold her close. "It's all my fault..." She began to sob even louder.

"No..." Raymond responded trying his best not cry himself. "It's Garza's fault." He backed away from Sheena a little and looked into her eyes as he held her shoulders. "Those kids should have never been there in the first place, he put them to fight. Remember, he was kidnapping children for his army as well, he forced your hand in this. This is not your fault Sheena." Sheena looked into his eyes seeing hope in them and stared for a moment. He was completely aught off guard when she suddenly lunged at Raymond kissing him. Her eyes were closed as his were wide open for a moment due to the shock since he had never actually kissed her before till now. The shock went away as he closed his eyes and accepted the kiss. He stayed with her that night to make sure her depression didn't go too far but respected her enough to not take advantage of her. As he helped her wipe the face paint smudges off her cheeks, she agreed to talk to a chaplain and her father, Colonel Vial, the next morning about how she felt. Raymond watched her throughout the night in her chair as she slept in her bed.

Unfortunately, as weeks went by, the experience with the children stuck with Sheena. She showed multiple symptoms of PTSD. It even went as far as her having nightmares about the dead children from the ambush in her room wanting to kill her. It was at that point she wanted psychiatric help. She chose to be medically discharged for psychiatric reasons and went back to earth. Raymond wanted to take care of her however, he felt obligated to stay in the fight leaving him with no choice but to let her go. Sheena understood. Even though she was out of the fight, she had faith that Raymond and her friends will end this war soon and in some way, put an end to her suffering. Before leaving, she gave Raymond her black face paint remembering his compliments on how cool she looked when wearing it and told him the secret behind it's psychological effect on the user. Raymond promised to cherish it, use it, and give it back to her when they see each other again.

Earth
August 8th, 2238
2347 Standard Earth Time

It began to rain softly as Sheena was still walking home from the lounge. She smiled as her memory came to a close saying to herself "I'm glad I got to see him again..." She started to cry a little but stopped herself. "No, I've cried enough." Sheena started thinking aggressively. "I feel better now, I can help, why did I turn him down?" She started getting angry at herself. "Am I scared or something? Afraid that I can't do it anymore?" Then she stopped walking. "Or is it because of him?" She became somber. "Do I not feel good enough for him anymore? Because I'm broken?..." She began to step into depression but then stopped herself "NO! I'm not broken anymore! I CAN FIGHT!" She punched the wall of the building next to her. "AAHH!" She yelled in pain as she dropped to her knees. "Oh man..." she groaned with a sigh while she looked at her hand seeing that it was fine as the pain went away. After a moment she began to relax while closing her eyes, took a deep breath and in instinct began to pray. "Lord... you changed my life, helped me find myself again and reclaim my sanity... I thank you... but, What should I do now?... I just don't know what to do anymore, I feel stuck-"

"HELP MEEE!!!" a woman cried out nearby.

"What?" Sheena knew what she heard as her instincts kicked in. She ran towards the screams.

"SOMEBODY HELP ME!!!" The woman screamed again as Sheena continued running down the street and saw an ally. The screams sounded like they were coming from there. She turned right into the ally and saw a man on top of a woman.

At reflexive speed she opened her purse, grabbed her USOD Modified M76 service pistol, drew it out of her purse at reflexive speed and immediately aimed it at the man. While advancing steadily, she yelled in a commanding voice "USOD! GET OFF OF HER NOW!" The man stopped and looked at Sheena. He saw the gun and immediately complied by putting his hands up with a knife in his right hand. "DROP THE KNIFE!" Sheena commanded with the man throwing it back behind him further down the ally. "Stand up, turn around and walk backwards towards me!" The man complied while he moving backwards towards her. "Stop where you are and get on your knees!" He complied. "Place your hands on the back of your head and interlock your fingers!" The man paused. "DO IT!" He did as she commanded. "Don't move!" She advanced towards the man, grabbed his fingers firmly with her left hand as she kept her gun aimed at him with her right hand making sure the weapon wasn't too close to the subject. "Are you okay miss?" She asked the victim to her left. In Shock she nodded yes. "Good, call the police and tell them what's happened he-" Suddenly the subject violently twisted his upper body right. Knocking the gun off target. By the time Sheena reacted by trying to squeeze the man's fingers together, it was already too late. She lost her grip on the man's fingers due to the rain making her grip slippery. The man continued to twist around and pulled Sheena to the ground than began to move on top of her. Immediately Sheena's combative training kicked in, while keeping her weapon away from the subject, she tried to violently shrimp out of the man's hold. As she shrimped, her skirt tore along her right leg allowing better mobility to fight. She shrimped again than pushed his lower torso down with her feet and grabbed his left arm with her left hand and pulled him to the left of her body while pushing his lower body back with her feet locking him in that position away from her gun than pointed the gun directly at his head. He looked up in shock. "Gotcha!" She said to him with pride as she smiled and pulled the trigger. There was a gunshot as a flash of electricity flashed around his head than immediately went numb. Sheena shrimped out from underneath the man's numb body and stood back up in a shooting stance, charged the slide of the pistol back readying it for another round than aimed at the man making sure he was down. Her black dress was covered in dirt and grime due to the struggle. While keeping her eyes on the subject, she talked to the victim. "You okay?"

"Is he dead?" The woman was scared.

"No, he's not."

"How's that possible? You just shot him in the head."

"With taser rounds. Although shooting someone in the head at that close range could kill someone, I didn't have much choice at that point. He's breathing so I think he'll be alright, I'm just lucky that one round to his head was enough to knock him out so easily." Sheena lowered her weapon and backed away from the subject as the two woman looked at each other. "You called the police?"

"No, not yet."

"Okay, I'll do it. You just wait here and relax for a moment."

"All right." The woman agreed.

Sheena picked up her purse from the floor and looked inside it for her Taclet. As she looked, she was surprised to find her old disc case of face paint. "Raymond?..." She remembered giving it to Raymond long ago. She took it as a sign from him that he still believed in her fighting spirit. "I…" She tried to hold back her tears. "I still got it." Sheena smiled as she now knew what to do. She found her Taclet and called the police. Fifteen minutes later, the police arrived, took the man into custody, and questioned the victim and Sheena. It was a half hour later by the time she was free to leave.

"You sure you don't want a ride home ma'am?" The young NYPD police officer kindly asked her. "I know you're USOD and all so I can't force you but it looks like the rain is gonna get worse soon."

"Don't worry," She chuckled, "I'm only going a couple of blocks away from here, thanks though."

"Okay than, have a safe evening."

"You too officer." The officer closed the driver door to his patrol car and drove away. Once out of site, Sheena immediately started running back towards the Lounge with excitement. Her intent was to pass the lounge and go towards the hotel where Raymond was staying. As she was running it began to rain harder. "Oh great..." She said to herself in annoyance and began to run faster. By the time she reached the bar she was soaked but didn't stop. She knew the hotel was only a block away from the bar so she began to run at a full sprint. Once she reached the front door of the hotel, she slowed down, walked through the door and began to catch her breath as she was still soaked from the rain. She walked closer to the lobby desk with a man behind the desk wearing a black suit professionally representing the hotel.

The man was surprised to see Sheena coming in this late at night from the pouring rain. "Can I help you miss?" he asked in concern seeing her dress dirty, soaked, and torn skirt.

"Yes" Breathing. "You can." Breathing. "Sorry, I was just running like crazy to get out of the rain."

"It's perfectly fine miss, I understand. What do you need?" He asked with an awkward expression.

"I'm looking for a Raymond Reynolds? He told me he was at this Hotel in room 595? Is he here at the moment?"

"Yes he is."

"Thank you." Sheena smiled and began to walk towards the elevator.

"But miss, he's not in his room."

"He's not? Where is he?" She was puzzled.

"At the hotel's gym in the basement."

"The gym?" She had a curious expression. "Why would he be at the gym this late at night?"

"That's what I said when he came through earlier, he asked me what time is the gym usually clear. I told him around this time of night."

"That's strange… mind if I?"

"Not at all miss, I can tell you have some important business with him."

"Sure do." She smiled. "Thank you."

"Your very welcome miss, have a goodnight."

Sheena pressed the elevator control panel button for the basement. As the doors closed she responded to the man at the desk. "You to." Once the doors closed her upper body leaned forward in exhaustion with her hands on her knees. "Okay Sheena," She spoke to herself. "Maybe it's time you start doing PT more seriously again... whew..."

As the elevator went down, she stood back up and started to think of what to say to Raymond. Should she start about how she felt about him? Or how she changed her mind about the job? Or what happened in the ally and how that lead to her changing her decision? Or maybe with a thank you for giving back the face paint she gave him so long ago? Before she could figure out what to say, the elevator stopped with the doors sliding open. "Here we go..." she whispered to herself as she walked out of the elevator. She was now in a short hallway with small signs along the wall in front of her. She saw a sign that said "Gym" on it pointing to her right. She followed the hallway to the right a few meters and saw a door with a sign next to it that also said "Gym". "This is it," She said as she took a deep breath and poised to open the door. She was just about to open the door when she heard something like strange high pitch thumping noises coming from inside the room. "What is that?" she asked herself.

She opened the door and walked through as she saw Raymond training in the Flow System wearing jeans, a black compression shirt, and his plate carrier with plates inside. He was on the other side of the room in an open area where visitors would normally do calisthenics. He had his German Long Sword in his hands with a scabbard on the left side of his waist for the sword connected to a belt. With the sword, he made diagonal cut's while moving his body forward in a diagonal motion. Each cut he made was different in its direction of movement. The first cut Sheena saw was from upper right to lower left, he twisted the sword up and cut from low left to upper right ending in a guard stance with the sword above his head and the tip facing forward threatening his imaginary target. Every cut he made sent out a high pitch thumb. He was moving so fast, it looked inhuman. He pushed the sword forward in a stabbing motion while moving his body forward in a diagonal motion than pulled the sword back into the same stance he was in earlier but mirrored, "Ha!" He than thrust the sword forward again in the same motion ending in his original high sword stance, "Ha!" Then he brought the sword down to his mid-section. "HRAAA!!!" He immediately spun his body around twice almost looking like a top as the sword cut through the air at mid height sending out two high pitch thumbs then ending the movement with the sword down on his left side and the point facing behind him. His body leaned forward in perfect form after the cut was finished. He had an expression of vicious determination. "Perfect..." He said to himself as he smiled.

Sheena stood there in shock as she had never seen anything like that before. She knew that Raymond had taken German long sword classes ever since he was a child but never had the chance to see him fight with a sword. She snapped out of it and said something. "Raymond?"

Raymond's head snapped left as he reacted to Sheena calling him. His eyes shot wide open in surprise. "SHEENA!?" He responded in embarrassment. "Um, hi!" He quickly sheathed his sword back into its scabbard, powered down the flow system than walked up to Sheena. "What are you-?" He immediately noticed her dress was dirty and skirt torn. "Oh my god, what happened? Are you okay?" He said in genuine concern.

Sheena looked down at herself and realized that her cloths were so wet they were sticking to her body shaping out her athletic figure in more detail than she was comfortable with. She looked back up at Raymond blushing and feeling embarrassed. She nervously responded as she began to fold her arms around herself trying to awkwardly cover herself up. "Uh, yea, I'm fine, I just- ah, ACHOO!" She sneezed and started to tremble.

Raymond couldn't tell if she was trembling from embarrassment or if she was cold. But he could tell she was coming down with something judging by her cute sneeze. "Feeling cold?"

"Yes," She looked at Raymond innocently as she began to lightly shiver.

"Man, I knew I should have walked you home. You can stay here with me if you want, let's go back up to my room and get you some dry clothes or something."

"Thanks Raymond." She smiled. They left the gym together, went through the hallway, and stepped into the elevator. Raymond pressed the button to the fifth floor while the doors to the elevator closed.

When the elevator began to ascend, Raymond felt his stomach move down as the elevator quickly moved up. "Eh, don't you hate it when an elevator moves so fast it makes butter fly's in your stomach?" Sheena giggled. Raymond smiled at her. "So, what happened to you anyway? Why is your dress all dirty and torn?"

"It's a long story, I'll tell you about it later but I came here to tell you... that I changed my mind."

"Huh? About the job offer?"

"Yes, I want to help. Something happened and it made me realize that I don't need to be afraid anymore. I still have what it takes."

"What about your father? How do you think he'll react if he found out you where joining me and my group?"

"Don't worry, my father always understood that I'm very independent. He knows I'll just end up doing it anyway no matter how much he's with or against it."

Raymond laughed "No wonder why we get along so well." They both laughed. Raymond felt proud of her and was happy she changed her mind. "I'm glad you decided to join us. Like I said earlier, we can start you off slowly with you just helping out where we need you."

"That's fine, I would like to take it slow at first."

"Good."

"By the way" Sheena reached into her purse, took out the face paint case and showed it to Raymond. "Thanks for giving this back to me." She smiled.

Raymond smiled back. "Your very welcome but I'll admit, I was tempted to just keep it for myself, it proved to be quite useful for me." He teased.

"Hey, I only let you barrow it." Sheena pouted. "Now that I'm back, this one is mine, go buy you own." Raymond laughed at her cute pout.

The elevator stopped as the doors opened. Sheena and Raymond walked out of the elevator into the hallway and looked for Raymond's room while walking passed other doors to other rooms.

"So, what exactly are those things on your hands and fore-arms?" She asked.

"This is the Flow System, one of the new pieces of technology this new organization gave me. These things change everything we know about how to fight, it's seriously some next level stuff."

"Wow... cool." She looked at the gauntlets in astonishment hoping she would get a chance to try them herself. "How do they work?"

"Well, it's kinda complicated to explain however, the maker of these things is also on leave so, maybe I can introduce you to him and he can tell you all about it."

"Sounds great." She smiled. They turned right at the corner in the hall than Sheena continued. "So now that I think about it, assuming those sword moves were from German long sword fighting that you told me about once, you never actually told me who taught you how to fight like that."

"Oh, Yabin did when he took me and Lucas in... after both our parents were killed."

"Oh... Sorry."

"It's okay, you should feel more sorry for Yabin. This ancient martial art has no use in today's modern battlefield. I was just curious to what would happen if I used the Flow System with it."

"I see." Sheena smiled

"Here we are, 595." He took out his Key card and slid it through the reader. The red light on the knob changed from red to green with the door lock snapping just before he twisted the knob and walked through the door with Sheena. "Make yourself at home." Sheena looked around the standard room with a TV, a bathroom close to the exit on her left, and one bed in the center of the room. She blushed a little as she stared at the bed.

"There is only one bed but if you want I'm willing to sleep on the floor." Raymond said with perfect timing as he knelled down on the floor taking off and putting away the flow system, his sword, and his plate carrier than placing them in his bag.

Sheena felt guilty. "No, it's okay," she hesitated in embarrassment, "We can... both sleep on the bed." Raymond head shot up and looked at her in surprise. Sheena rolled her eyes than gave him a smirk. "Don't get any funny idea's."

"Uh, of course not." He nervously laughed than went back into his bag. "I figured I can give you some of my clothes for tonight than I can get you something to wear from your apartment tomorrow."

"Sounds good." She smiled as Raymond gave her a pair of red shorts and a black T-Shirt. "Thanks. I'm just gonna take a quick shower and change."

"Okay, Your welcome." Raymond responded. Sheena walked into the restroom and closed the door. Raymond thought to himself thinking this would normally be awkward but, they knew each other so well, he didn't feel weird about it at all. He just hoped she didn't feel weird. "But if she did, she wouldn't be here now would she?" He thought out loud.

"What was that?" Sheena asked from the bathroom.

Raymond was caught off guard. "Uh, nothing. Hey Sheena, if you want you can leave your wet clothes at the door, I can put them in the dryer for you in the laundry room."

"Well, my dress is ruined unfortunately but everything else would be great, thanks." The bathroom door cracked open as Sheena's hand snaked through, letting go of her wet clothes with the door closing at the exact moment they splatted on the ground. Raymond picked up the cloths and immediately saw her laced underwear. He blushed at the sight as he quickly looked away keeping his thoughts in check. He left his room, hastily went down the hall to his left, swiped into the laundry room, put Sheena's cloths into the dryer and turned it on. He planned to pick them back up in the morning as he made his way back to his room. He entered and immediately noticed Sheena laying down on the bed face down reading Raymond's study guide dressed in the black shirt and red shorts he had gave her earlier. Raymond couldn't help but check her out as he saw her beautifully athletic legs, and her wet shiny brunette hair while her elegant fingers turned the pages of his study guide.

"What is this your studying?" She asked as she read the book.

Raymond snapped himself out of it. "Uh, you got comfortable pretty fast." He commented. Sheena giggled. "Stuff for leadership training." He said as he went to the restroom to change into shorts to sleep in.

"Leadership training huh? This looks like some officer level stuff."

"Yea, I know. Let's just say my new boss is a little," Raymond looked for the word. "Unorthodox."

"Huh, weird." She continued to skim through the book. "Well, with your experience and what you're learning, I'm sure you got this."

Raymond came out of the restroom wearing the same shirt but with black shorts. "Yea, I'm feeling confident in this."

"That's good." She yawned.

"Tired?"

"Very..." She said with a groggy voice as she lifted the sheets.

Raymond crawled into the bed next to her as they both covered themselves. Once under, Raymond reached out to his right with his right hand turning off the light, then laid down next to Sheena. "You don't feel awkward about this at all?" He asked.

"Nope, it's not like we haven't literally JUST slept together before."

Raymond laughed at how she emphasized the word "just." "Right, even though it was only once."

"Yea." Sheena agreed. Raymond gazed into her eyes, they were as mesmerizing and beautiful as ever. She smiled and blushed. "What? What is it?" She giggled.

"Nothing... it's just been a while since I last saw you like this." They both smiled. She moved her hand towards his and held it. Raymond was happy she was there. So was she. He shifted his upper body toward her with their lips meeting in a kiss, then he slowly backed away. "I love you Sheena..."

"I love you to Raymond... It's been too long since I've heard you say that." She smiled

"Last time I said it was when you left... I dreamed of the day I could say it to you again in person." Raymond smiled as Sheena giggled and blushed more "What's so funny?" he asked kindly.

"Hehe, You're so sappy..." She said in laughter, "...and sweet." She continued as she softly caressed Raymond's face while moving closer to kiss him again. She then moved away from the kiss as they both closed their eyes. "Can't wait till tomorrow..."

"Why's that?..." Raymond asked almost half asleep.

"Because I get to spend it with you."

Raymond smiled. "True... Goodnight."

"Goodnight." They both dosed off to sleep knowing the next day was going to be the best day they would have in a long time.

Chapter 7: The Enidon

The rest of that Week on leave was the best leave time that Raymond ever had. In the mornings, he would train with the flow system and study. Sheena, being as curious as she was, wanted to train with Raymond with the flow system taking turns. With Izzy present to assist Raymond in Sheena's training, she past out for several minutes the first time she activated the system. Despite that, her determination pushed her to keep trying. After getting used to the system, she began to train on par with Raymond. After 1200 hours, He would spend his time with her revisiting different places in the city. He also grouped up with the rest of the team so Sheena could see everyone back together again. Kathrine was especially happy to see her come back. It felt like her long lost sister had finally returned home. They went to bars on some nights and danced the night away. Raymond, and Sheena were more responsible drinkers where Katherine, Jake, and Lucas seemed to not mind getting drunk often. The couple had to make sure their friends behaved themselves in those drunken states at times. Even though he was having the time of his life with Sheena and his friends, a part of Raymond couldn't wait to see what was next for him and the team as the week drew closer to its end.

Leave was over as the sun rose on the morning of their report in day. Raymond was in bed with Sheena as he started to wake up seeing that she was already awake and watched him as his eyes fluttered open. "Good morning..." She said with a smile.

Raymond mildly laughed and smiled back. "Hello there."

She pouted her lips together with the impersonated voice of a drill sergeant. "Ready for your first day back on duty soldier?"

Raymond laughed mildly. "Yes ma'am."

Sheena Giggled. "Then wake up, and get ready you lazy bum."

"Okay." They both sat up in the bed while still clothed in what they wore to the bar last night. Raymond wore a black polo shirt, and jeans while Sheena wore tight dark blue jeans with a red blouse. As They both finished sitting up, they heard snoring. "Wait a second." Raymond looked around the bed towards the floor of the room. Lucas was on the floor to the right of the bed still wearing his black jeans with white dress shirt and white shoes from the last night while Jake and Kathrine were on the left on the floor sleeping next to each other.

"Oh great..." Raymond said sarcastically as he brought the right palm of his hand to his head and shook his head in disbelief. He put his hand down and sounded off "GUYS!!!" The whole team woke up immediately and looked at Raymond. "Come on, time to get up."

Lucas responded in a groggy fashion. "That's my line... and he's right, we gotta go." Raymond, Sheena, and Lucas got up and began to get their things together.

Jake woke up still wearing his gray Polo shirt from last night but awkwardly found his black dress pants unbuttoned and unzipped. Not remembering what happened last night, He looked up at Katherine next to him wearing a tight blue one-piece dress. They both stared at each other for a moment. In disbelief, Jake broke the silence. "We didn't-?"

"No! No we didn't!" Katherine interrupted.

Jake continued as he slowly buttoned and zipped his pants back up. "Are you sure w-?"

"Trust me," Sheena cut in with her red high heels in hand. "You guys didn't, now come on." Jake and Katherine stood up and got their things together.

By the time they left and checked out of the hotel it was already 0812. They squeezed into a taxi and took it to the Port Authority shuttle terminal. In route, another driver had cut off their vehicle in an unsafe manner. "What the fuck!" The taxi driver yelled with a New York accent as the other vehicle honked its horn. "Yea, fuck you too guy!" The team starred at the driver awkwardly. "Oh, sorry. I just hate driving in this city." The driver said to his concerned passengers.

"You sure do..." Sheena commented while sitting in the rear right seat of the vehicle squeezed next to Raymond on her left and the door on her right realizing the taxi drivers contradicting choice of work.

Comfortably sitting in the front passenger's seat, Lucas asked Raymond, "What's our report time exactly?"

Raymond, who was sitting in the rear middle seat squeezed next to Sheena on his right and Jake on his left, responded. "1500 hours"

Lucas checked his watch trying to adjust his vision due to his vision being slightly blurry. His watch said 0823. "That's hours from now, why are we rushing?"

"I would actually like to look around the ship a little, plus Sheena

118

wants to make a good impression. Especially since she wants to work in the TOC according to what Gehnarne had messaged me."

"Don't worry Ms. Over achiever," Lucas said to Sheena. "Gehnarne didn't seem like the stick up his ass type. I'm sure he'll be okay at whatever time we show up or whatever kind of impression you make." Lucas was clearly hungover and getting worse.

Jake, who was squeezed between Raymond on his right and Kathrine on his left, was staring at her. Kathrine, who was already frustrated at being squeezed up against the door was slowly getting annoyed at Jake than finally snapped at him. "Why are you staring at me?!" She seemed angry.

Jake responded. "Are you sure we didn't-"

"NOO!" Everyone in the back seats yelled at Jake so loud that even the taxi driver flinched.

"Ah, loud noises..." Lucas grunted in pain due to a growing headache.

"Okay, okay, we didn't!" Jake put an end to the matter.

The taxi stopped in front of the terminal. The whole team got out, grabbed their bags, and walked into the station. They took the elevator up to the roof where a shuttle was waiting. They boarded the shuttle, fastened their seat belts and the shuttle took off. Once the shuttle was at a high enough altitude, it used boosters to break free of earth's gravity. The g-force dampeners inside the shuttle kept the crew and passengers from feeling too much shock from the boost in speed. Once the shuttle was clear of earth's gravity, the pilots activated artificial gravity.

"Ugh..." Lucas seemed deathly ill with the palm of his hand against his face.

"You okay?" Raymond asked.

"No..." He mumbled. "So which dry dock are we reporting to anyway?"

Raymond barely understood what he said. "The southernmost dry dock. It should be in a lower orbit to the south of the earth."

"I'm assuming these pilots know where we're going?" Jake asked Raymond.

"Of course, I gave them our orders."

The shuttle moved towards the south pole with the pilot speaking on the intercom. "Here we are guys. South station. You should be able to see it on the right." The team moved towards the right side of the shuttle looking out the windows. Lucas was already on the right side still with his hands to his face looking miserable.

The whole team was in awe at the sight of their new ship. "Lucas." Raymond said.

"What?..." He groaned.

"You gotta see this."

Lucas felt so sick he didn't want to look, but he didn't want to miss the sight from a distance either so he looked anyway. The ship was a Carrier class Star ship similar to the Recluses with noticeably advanced features. It was shaped almost like a long oval cylinder with rectangular boxes running along the hull, multiple hangers and docking bay's, defensive and offensive weapons systems, and most likely FTL capable. Unlike the recluses, the weapons systems seemed like a more advanced design and had more hangers and docking bays. Lucas was astonished that they would be working on a newer model ship. "Wow... I mean, she's not that much different from the Recluses but... Ugh... Bag!"

Raymond didn't understand. "What?"

"BAAAG!"

"Oh crap!" Raymond grabbed a barf bag from the pouch in front of him on the back of the seat next to Lucas and handed it to him. Immediately Lucas grabbed it and ran to the small restroom at the back of the shuttles cabin and closed the door behind him. From a distance the team could hear Lucas barfing loudly.

"I told him to take it easy on the drinks last night." Sheena commented.

The shuttle docked with the dry dock station with the team immediately walking out of the docking bay with their bags. Lucas was the last one off drinking a bottle of water. "Much better..." He said to himself. The team continued to walk down the corridor with a long pressurized window along the wall showing the outside of where the new ship was docked. Raymond couldn't take his eyes off of it as he and the team continued to walk down the corridor to reach the ships entrance.

"Excited?" Sheena asked.

"In static." Raymond smiled at Sheena than looked back at the ship. "This is gonna be amazing, from what I can tell it's gonna be a whole new experience compared to being on the Recluses." While the team approached the gangway, Raymond noticed Gehnarne as he also noticed them. Instead of his usual business attire, he was now wearing a green military jump suit with the name tag reading "Gehnarne" on his right chest and black military grade boots.

"Alpha team! Glad you can make it." Gehnarne said cheerfully.

"Good to see you again Gehnarne, looking different from usual."

"Well, as Captain of this ship and head of SMO, I have to look the part right?" He said in excitement.

"Indeed," Raymond agreed while he looked around for a moment. "Where's Izzy and Gia?"

"They're already on board." Gehnarne answered. "Along with our crew, consisting of a few dozen scientist working with Izzy in R&D and Exploration sciences, a crew complement of four thousand in total, I know, a lot of people right, and lastly a combat group of two hundred and fifty, all well trained and well paid Private Military Contractors ready for action."

"What about fighter support?" Lucas asked.

"That's one of the reasons why the Recluses will be our QRF, unfortunately the council could not spare any fighter squadrons for our endeavor."

"I see,"

"Getting all those PMCs is pretty Awesome though," Raymond complimented. "and here I thought I was great for recruiting two people."

"Two?" Gehnarne asked?

"Sheena, and my intelligence source."

"Oh yes! Forgot about him. Speaking of recruits, I'm assuming this is Sheena?"

"Oh yes, of course, Sorry. Sheena, this is Gehnarne, our new boss."

"Hello, Nice to finally meet you." Sheena politely introduced herself and held her hand out for a hand shake.

"Pleasure to finally meet you as well Ms. Vial, "The Morrigan." Gehnarne took her hand and shook it while slightly bowing his head to her in respect. Sheena was surprised he had called her by the legendary name the rebels gave her on Kalista. "It will be an honor to see your skills in action again one day, that is if you're willing?"

Sheena seemed a bit shy. "Well, I guess it depends on the timing and the situation at hand."

"Of course." He let her hand go. "Now that we are all reunited, shall we board our vessel?"

"Yes sir." Raymond couldn't wait anymore.

"Follow me please!" Gehnarne lead the team through the gangway with enthusiasm. "As you may have noticed, this ship is a bit more advanced than the Recluses."

"How did you convince the Counsel to give you such an advanced ship?" Lucas said recovering well from his hang over. "I was expecting an old Junker."

"It wasn't easy at first but after our successful mission in Universe 1112 the counsel was so pleased they finally decided to bend to my will and gave us whatever we needed. Besides, we'll never know what's out there waiting for us. We need the most advanced technology available."

"Well that makes me feel better." Jake said.

"So what's the name of this ship anyway?" Kathrine asked.

"It's right here." Gehnarne pointed at a gold metal plaque on the inside of the hull just at the entrance to the ship. "Welcome aboard the Enidon." He said with pride.

"Enidon?" Jake asked. "What does that mean?"

"It means "Our Home" in the language of my people."

"Your people?" Lucas questioned. "Where do you come from anyway?" Raymond had a shocked look on his face knowing that Gehnarne wanted to keep that a secret. Raymond even saw that Gehnarne was caught off guard with that question however, he quickly recovered.

"Uh, from my people on the colony Ezra from the planet Malay." He responded as naturally as possible. "As we all know, many colony's throughout the years have adopted their own languages to portray a certain uniqueness of their colonized worlds."

"Oh, cool." Lucas smiled in agreement. "Nice name."

"Thank you. Now, I will show you to your quarters so you may settle in." They continued walking as Gehnarne continued talking.

"Whenever you're ready, contact my assistant Gia. She will give you guys the Grand tour of the ship."

"I bet you'll be embarrassed to see her again after last night huh Lucas?" Raymond joked.

"Oh come on Raymond, I wasn't that drunk in front of her." Lucas responded.

"No, but she still noticed." Raymond mildly laughed.

"Whatever man," Lucas chuckled. "If you weren't babysitting me, she probably would have never noticed."

Gehnarne and the team continued walking down the hall and entered an elevator. "Crew quarters one." The doors closed and the elevator started moving.

"Voice command? Fancy." Katherine commented.

"And there's a lot more where that came from, both for convenience and strategic value." Gehnarne said with pride.

"I'm just happy my stomach didn't get butterflies." Raymond commented happily. Everyone in the elevator slowly turned around looking at him with an awkward expression. "What? I'm sure you know what I'm talking about right?" Sheena giggled since she was the only one who knew what he was talking about. Gehnarne smirked than everyone turned around.

The doors from the elevator slid open as the group stepped out on to the crew quarters deck. The hallway seemed to curve off to the right with doors lining the hallway on the left. "Since your Alpha team, you'll be the first door here on the left." Gehnarne explained. "The second door is Bravo, the third Charlie, and so on. First you'll need to sign into your Quarters Access."

"How does that work?" Lucas asked.

"Just stand in front of the door and verbally say an access code. Recommend keeping it short. Raymond, give it a try."

Raymond stepped up to the door. "Okay." He cleared his throat. "Gunslinger 184"

A female voice spoke through a speaker hidden above the door. "Welcome group commander Reynolds. Would you like to save "Gunslinger 184" as your access key?"

Raymond was impressed and smiled. "Yes I would, thank you."

"You are very welcome sir." The door to the next room opened.

"Welcome to Alpha team's quarters. Please be sure to download the Quarters Access app on your Taclet through the ships servers."

Raymond and the team walked through the door as the computer voice continued. "This app will allow you to access other features of Quarters Access." Raymond and his companions walked through the door. The room was a perfect rectangle with a couch in the center facing toward a holovision monitor that was positioned on the wall about ten meters in front of the couch. The monitor was about seventy inches diagonally. Ten meters behind the couch was a small kitchen along the back wall. To the right were three doors, one directly to the right closer to the entrance to the room, another further down near the far right wall on the other side of the holovision monitor, and another on the far wall against the other side of the room between the right corner of the room and a door on its left at the center of the wall that had a sign on it saying "shower and restroom". To the left there were three more doors mirroring the other three doors to the right.

"These are your living Qaurters." Gehnarne said. "In each one of these doors is your own specific bed room."

"Compared to Military standards, this is beautiful!" Sheena said out loud.

"Well the idea is that the team that works together should also learn to live together." Gehnarne explained.

"Works for me." Lucas agreed smiling.

"Well, this is where I leave you all. Take your time settling in and preparing for the grand tour. When you're ready, call Gia and she'll meet you guys here. Just make sure you all sign into Quarters Access before you leave so you can get an access key. Don't want any of you getting locked out now." Gehnarne mildly laughed. "And don't forget to download that app as well, it will be very useful."

"Don't worry, we won't." Raymond responded. "Thanks."

"See you later Alpha." The door closed after Gehnarne walked through it.

"All right, let's settle in." Jake said.

Each team member picked their bed rooms. Jake picked immediate right, Kathrine, immediate left, Sheena far right, Raymond, the right next to the shower and restroom, and Lucas, the left next to the shower and restroom. The room to the far left remained empty. The rooms were big enough for a bed and dresser with a closet integrated into the wall. Once the team finished unpacking, they decided to look their best for the tour. They put on their United Earth Military dress blues representing each of the branches of the military they originally enlisted with and walked out to the living area.

"Sheena, why aren't you wearing your uniform?" Raymond asked.

"Sorry but… I think the red hair dye might be a little out of regs so I figured I'd wear something that looked professional at least." She wore business attire with a black skirt, a black blouse that conformed to her body figure in an elegant fashion with low heeled black shoes "What do you think?"

"Beautiful as always." He smiled

Sheena smiled and blushed. "You look quite handsome as well, it's been a while since I saw you in uniform."

"Thanks." Raymond smiled. The uniform was all black with dress shoes, slacks, a jacket covering a white shirt with a black tie. The shoulders of the jacket had a gold rank insignia of a Sergeant First Class and a few other decorations on the lower sleeves and ribbons on the left side of his chest. He wore a Green Beret with the 3rd USOD insignia at the front representing the legendary origins of the US Army Special Forces and their influence on the future in special operations with the USOD, and the Army's Special Forces Insignia that had the Latin words "De Eppreso Libre" on the right side of his chest.

"Okay you love birds." Kathrine interrupted wearing a decorated blue colored uniform representing the United Earth Military's Air Force with heeled shoes and a knee high skirt. "You ready?"

"Yup." Raymond responded. "Did everyone get an access key?"

"Yea, just finished getting mine." Lucas said as he walked through the door wearing his decorated dress blues with the rank of captain on his shoulders. His uniformed was all black with red outlines with the MARSOC insignia above an assortment of ribbons on the left side of his chest and eagle, globe and anchors on his high collar representing the United Earth Military's Marines."

"Call Gia yet?" Raymond asked.

"I called her about a minute ago." Jake responded looking sharp in his all white decorated uniform with a Navy SEAL Insignia over an assortment of ribbons on the left side of his chest representing United Earths Military's Navy. "She should be here in a moment."

"Good. Can't wait to see this ship in its entirety."

Suddenly there was three audible beeping sounds coming from the front door. The team looked at the front door wondering what that was. "I'm gonna assume that was the doorbell." Raymond guessed. "Come in!"

The door opened with Gia walking through wearing similar business attire to when Raymond first met her. "Hello Alpha team," She looked directly at Lucas with a smirk. "Lucas." She greeted him.

Lucas awkwardly smiled and greeted her. "Gia."

She looked back towards the team. "You guys ready for the tour?"

"Definitely." Raymond answered.

"Okay then." Gia smiled. "Follow me." The team followed her out the door and into the Hall way. "As you may already know, this is Crew Quarters one or crew Quarters deck one. There are many more decks of crew Quarters above this deck."

"How many in total?" Sheena asked.

"Ten, each deck houses 500 personnel. Although we have a crew of a little over 4,000 now, we can house up to over 5,000 personnel."

"That's more than the Recluses." Lucas said looking at her in astonishment.

She looked back at him smiling. "Indeed." Than looked away as they boarded the elevator. "Now down to engineering." The doors closed.

Gia guided the group through each critical area of the Enidon starting with Engineering, then R&D, sciences, docking and hanger bays, briefing room, sick bay, supply and logistics, the armory, the mess hall, combat training area that also included a firing range, then finally the bridge.

The doors to the bridge elevator opened as Gia began to step on to the Bridge deck. "Last on our tour is the bridge." The group stepped out of the elevator and looked around. "Please feel free to look around, I have some matters to attend to at Navigation." Gia walked away as Alpha team and Raymond continued looking around in astonishment.

The bridge was a large area that seemed reminiscent to a movie theater auditorium with the walls painted gray. It had a very large monitor to the front of the room about the size of a movie projector screen. A few meters just before and under the screen was a large table with holographic projectors at each corner projecting a hologram of earth into the center of the table. The table's surface was like a giant touch screen displaying a star chart of the solar system. The table also had a metal laser engraved label that said "Navigation" on it. A few meters behind the table at an elevated position lining up with the center of the giant sized monitor were two control consoles with chairs connected to them. Those consoles were laser engraved with "Helm Control". A few meters to the right and left of the helm control consoles were more control consoles, three left, and three right. They were position diagonally at the edge of each set of ramps leading down to navigation. Each console was laser engraved with every critical area of the ship. These stations, including the helm, were manned by different crew members in green jump suites per station. Another few meters behind those stations was a chair that looked almost like a throne with two small control consoles. One connected to the right arm, another connected to the left arm. To Raymond and his group, this obviously looked like the Captain's Chair. Gehnarne was currently occupying it while typing something on the left control console. Several meters behind the Captain's Chair was a large area surrounded with what looked like clear bullet proof panels sounding a table just like the one from navigation. There was no hologram being projected however the touch screen table surface was displaying a live overhead feed of Manhattan. You can see the cars driving through the streets and people walking the sidewalks like little ants. The table was laser engraved with "Tactical Operations Center" on it or TOC. Encircling the table were monitors and control consoles mounted along the bullet proof panels. In front of the consoles were more crew members sitting on roller chairs monitoring the TOC's network.

"Wow…" Raymond said out loud awe-inspired. "This place is huge…"

"The most advanced bridge setup ever created." Gehnarne said proudly as he got out of the Captain's chair.

"Very impressive Gehnarne." Lucas complimented.

"Why thank you. The departure ceremony will begin in a few moments so feel free to look around. Raymond, may I speak with you for a moment?"

"Sure, what's up?" Raymond responded as he walked with Gehnarne.

As Gehnarne and Raymond walked away, Lucas spoke to the team. "I have to admit, after that whole Rift thing, I don't like them talking together like that."

"Lucas, you and Raymond are best friends," Sheena said in disappointment towards Lucas. "If he trusts Gehnarne, maybe you should too."

"I know but, with Raymond's mindset how would he even know if he's just being used by Gehnarne for something devious or whatever?"

Jake interrupted. "Lucas, that's a highly unlikely scenario, now your just being paranoid."

"Maybe..." Lucas walked away towards the large monitor at the front of the bridge currently showing endless space in front of the ship and stared out into it.

"Strange," Sheena said. "I've never seen him like that before."

"Me neither." Katherine agreed.

"He's just worried that Raymond could be easily manipulated." Jake continued. "I have no doubt that Raymond could see when things aren't right, we don't need to worry. As for Lucas, he has to learn to trust Raymond's judgment. Especially now that he is technically working under Raymond for now on."

"Yea," Sheena agreed "Your right."

Gehnarne spoke to Raymond as they entered the TOC. "Now that we have completed the current phase of tasks, it's time to start the next phase."

"What does the next phase consist of?" Raymond asked.

"We need a pilot, an engineer, and a type of assault ship for more aggressive space combat and away missions."

"I thought Izzy was our engineer?"

"An engineer in R&D, not for Engineering. R&D is for weapons and tech development. Engineering is ship maintenance and specific ship tech. Almost two different departments. Izzy is currently managing both departments however he can't handle that kind of work load forever."

"I see, sounds like it's gonna be a while before we can explore the unreached worlds." Raymond elaborated.

"Not if we kill three birds with one stone. Your next mission will accomplish just that."

"How's so?" Raymond was curious.

Gehnarne pulled out a data card and showed it to Raymond. "This card contains the mission profile." He inserted it into a slot on the center TOC table. A window opened up on the table's display. Inside the window was a folder that said "Operation Red Nova". Gehnarne double tapped on the folder opening it revealing multiple files. From a quick glance, Raymond saw what he thought were blueprints to a building and maps of the mission area. "This mission will take place in universe 1211, the universe located beyond the rift found here in the Solar System."

"A level two Universe?" Raymond asked.

Gehnarne looked at Raymond and smiled. "Precisely." than double tapped the folder that said "Red Nova Crew" on it. It revealed three different files each with a different name. "Let's start with our pilot." He double tapped on the file with the pilots name, opening it to reveal a mug shot picture of a man a little older than Raymond. He had short jet black hair and a small scare on his right cheek. "This is our pilot, Jason Lennes, call sign, "Star".

"He's human?"

"Of course he is, why so surprised?"

"Well, since level two universes are just other parts of space at insanely unreachable distances, I figured he might have been an alien of some kind."

"Humans never solely existed just on earth you know."

"Well, I know now." Raymond responded in embarrassment.

"You think that's weird? They even speak English like we do."

"You're kidding?" Raymond was surprised.

"Nope. It's not called English to them however, it's pretty much the same dialect, weird huh?"Gehnarne smiled with a chuckle. "Anyway, I had the liberty to work with him a little while back. I offered him the job to be the Enidon's official pilot but he went off the grid so I lost contact with him for a while. However, I was able to do some digging. He disappeared due to some trouble he ran into with the pirates in that universe.

"Pirates?" Raymond was curious.

"Yes, Pirates. I was able to find this out through their networks. I was even able to dig up his exact location However, if I was able to find him through the pirate's network, that means it's only a matter of time before they find him as well. We have to get to him first."

"Understood, the engineer and the ship?"

"I'm getting to that." Gehnarne closed Jason's file than opened another with mug shots. "Timothy Doyle, call sign "Hawk", one of the best ship engineers I ever met. He works with Jason on the Red Nova."

Raymond looked at the picture and saw a young man with short blond hair and high tech looking glasses with different attachments on them. He also noticed that Tim seemed strangely young. "How old is this guy?"

With hesitation, Gehnarne answered. "Uh… fourteen."

"A kid, are you nuts?!" Raymond was shocked.

"That kid is a genius, I never seen someone more qualified to be a ships engineer."

"Earth gov is not gonna like this."

"I have permission from the council."

Once Raymond heard that, he stopped arguing despite how he still disagreed with Gehnarne. "Okay fine, what's next?"

Gehnarne closed Tim's file and opened another. "This is Sarah, call sign "Phoenix". She's also a crew member of the Red Nova." Raymond looked at her picture. She was a young woman with gold innocent looking eyes, and neon blue hair that looked strangely natural. "She is very important to the ship so make sure you secure her along with everyone else."

"What's a beautiful girl like her doing with a group of guys like this?"

"That part is kinda personal for her so I can't say. Don't let anything happened to her."

"Understood, the ship?"

"Right here." Gehnarne closed Sarah's file then closed the crew folder and opened the ship file. "The Red Nova, a highly advanced and extremely fast combat ready cruiser that surpasses any of the ships in her class from that universe."

Raymond saw six pictures of the Red Nova with different angles of the ship from the top, bottom, left, right, front, and back. The ship was shaped like an oval with a more arrow pointed nose with five large engines protruding out the back, one at each corner on the aft of the ship, and the fifth right in the center of the four engines. The hull was perfectly smooth and was painted the same neon blue as Sarah's hair. Raymond noticed something strange. "Wait, why is the ship called the "RED Nova" when it's colored blue?"

Gehnarne smiled. "Don't worry, you'll find out." He then winked at Raymond.

Raymond looked at Gehnarne with an odd expression. "Okay, fine. So how did this rag tag bunch get their hands on this high tech ship?"

"They stole it."

"Stole it? From who?"

"The pirates."

"Well that explains why they're looking for them."

"Yea, they really want that ship back."

"I'll be honest Gehnarne, I'm not too comfortable with having thieves in our organization, especially ones that have crime organizations looking for them."

"When you meet Jason talk to him, then you'll see why he had to steal that ship." Gehnarne reassured.

Raymond was now curious. "If you say so."

Gehnarne pulled the data card out of the table socket. "Take this and use it to brief and train your team accordingly. The Rift is only two hours away from here at maximum sub FTL speed, I'm giving you at least twenty-four hours to train and rehearse for any possible scenario."

Raymond looked worried as he took the data card. "Gehnarne, that's not much time to prepare."

"My apologies but we have no choice, remember, we have to get to them first before the pirates do. Also, I'm adding Izzy to your team Roster."

"Why's that?"

"That Flow system of yours is still new and could go down at any possible moment. We need a combat capable tech expert with you encase that happens."

"Izzy helped out a bit on our previous mission but I'm not sure what he can do in a more direct action situation."

"He would have been able to run with you guys with no problem if you let him. All those little things he did on your last mission he learned from SCTG, Special Combat Tasks Group. His universes equivalent of USOD. Unfortunately, because of how that universe is, he is the last of his kind."

Raymond seemed surprised. "Now that all makes sense. I guess we'll see his true skills during mission rehearsals."

"Good, now that's out of the way let's get back out to the bridge, I have a speech to give for the launch ceremony."

"Got it." Raymond and Gehnarne walked out of the TOC to the bridge. As they walked passed the Captain's chair, Gehnarne broke off and stood in front of the chair facing the large monitor at the front of the bridge. Raymond continued to walk to Sheena and Alpha team.

"Everything okay?" Sheena asked Raymond

"Yea, I got something to pass down," Raymond looked around for the members of Alpha team. "Alpha!" He said mildly enough to get their attention but not too loud to cause a disturbance. Katherine, Jake, and Lucas's heads snapped towards Raymond. "On me." They all quickly walked and circled around Raymond. "All right, here's what's going on. We just got a mission passed down to us."

"Already? We just got here." Kathrine said.

"I know Kat but this organization needs to be at one hundred percent before we reach the unreached worlds, we were bound to get a mission at the last second like this eventually. After these formalities are finished, get into gear, and meet me in the briefing room understood?"

The whole team acknowledge with "Roger."

"Good, Gehnarne's speech is about to start. I'll be right back." Raymond walked away from the group as they started to look towards Gehnarne. Raymond continued walking towards Izzy. Once he was close enough, he tapped Izzy on the shoulder and quietly told him, "Izzy, after the speech, meet me and Alpha team in the briefing room."

"What's up?" Izzy asked.

"We got a mission."

"Alright." Just as Izzy Acknowledged Raymond, Gehnarne began his speech.

"Good afternoon crew of the Enidon, this is your Captain speaking." Throughout the ship you can hear Gehnarne's voice echoing through all the speakers on each deck. "In a few moments we will be launching this fine ship on its first deployment into colony space. As you all know, our travels will not stop there. We will be the first ship in fifty years to officially cross over the border into the unreached worlds and claim them in the name of humanity. Unfortunately, there have been rumors that remnants of rebel forces might have beaten us to those planets first. However, our mission is not only one of exploration, but also of combat. If we do meat any rebel forces stationed on those planets, we will meet them head on and destroy them. I for one hope that this will not be the case, for this is a great moment for humanity. This is our manifest destiny, to expand and explore the universe and learn of what else is out there besides us. Take pride in this mission, and in yourselves for the willingness to move forward into the unknown and embrace it as your own. God bless. Rifter out." Gehnarne sat back into the Captain's chair as all the crew on the bridge began to clap in support to his speech. Raymond and Alpha team also clapped however Lucas clapped slowly in displeasure.

"Helm," Gehnarne said. "Begin exiting dry dock at five percent throttle, nice and slow. Once we are clear, increase throttle to ten percent."

"Aye, sir." The crew member at the helm responded.

The Enidon began to move forward out of the dry dock station as the bridge crew stayed at their stations watching the Enidon move out of the dry dock corridor through the monitor with Raymond and Alpha team also witnessing this moment. As the Enidon finished exiting dry dock, Raymond stood up straight with pride with the biggest smile of excitement in his expression.

You know that saying, "Practice Makes Perfect"? Same thing in the military. When we rehearse, we train our asses off for any possible scenario and set up a make shift shoot house matching the same layout of the Area of Operations where the mission will take place. He run the mission over, and over, and over again with multiple different factors and possibilities. By the end we will have ran the mission so many times, that not only we will know the layout by heart, but we can practically read each others mind during the mission, we automatically know each others jobs and tasks before they are executed. That's probably one of the reasons why USOD teams become so close. Not only do you learn about your own strengths and weakness, but the strengths and weakness of your teammates as well, and knowing those secrets about each other kinda brings you closer together as a family.

Chapter 8: Star

The Enidon moved at maximum sub FTL speeds to make it within range of the Universal Rift in the solar system leading to universe 1211. Within the twenty-four hours Gehnarne gave them, Alpha team made mission plans for all possible scenarios, rehearsed, refined the mission plans, then rehearsed again. After several refinements, Alpha felt ready. On the day of the mission, they walked out of the briefing room into the hall with confidence. The team was armed with a similar load out from the previous mission wearing all black civilian clothes with black bandannas around their necks. Sheena however was clothed in a green jump suit issued to crew personnel and not armed as she was tasked with supporting the team from the TOC. Since Izzy didn't have an SDT like the rest of the team, he was issued an ear piece variant of a similar design.

"Feeling ready Izzy?" Lucas asked wearing jeans, boots, and a hoodie being the only team member with a skull patterned bandanna hanging from his neck.

"Definitely, it has been a while since I actually used a weapon like this in combat." He was holding an AR30 in his right hand configured to a CQB setup. He wore the same cloths as Lucas with a black beanie on his head. "Although these weapons are a little primitive compared to what I'm used to, it will do."

"Primitive?" Katherine responded in surprise wearing a zipped up half glove hoodie with tight fabric paints made out of a thick durable material and boots. "Last I checked, those thugs we killed in your universe had similar weapons to ours."

As Katherine spoke, the team turned right into the elevator as Raymond said "Science Deck," while wearing dark blue Jeans, t-shirt, and a leather jacket. The Flow System Gauntlets were exposed but blended nicely with his outfit. The elevator doors closed as Izzy continued while the elevator moved.

"On the contrary, my former unit with SCTG had highly advanced weapons systems. Our primary weapon was a PR38."

"PR38?" Jake asked wearing a leather vest with a short sleeve T-shirt underneath showing off his bi-ceps and cargo pants.

"Pulse Repeater thirty-eight, a compact rifle capable of firing up to thirty rounds per second of ultra-high frequency pulses capable of penetrating through human like flesh."

"Nice." Raymond was intrigued. "We could use something like that for our organization."

Izzy gladly answered. "I can get to work on a prototype model if you want?"

"You can seriously build one of those?" Sheena asked.

"Yea, my grandfather built the very first one." Izzy said with pride. "He taught me how to build my own."

"If you built your own, where is it?" Lucas asked.

With a somber expression, Izzy answered. "Someone took it from me..."

"What happened?" Katherine asked with sympathy noticing his depressed demeanor.

"Sorry... I'd rather keep that to myself..." Izzy said not making eye contact.

"Oh..." Katherine was apologetic. "I'm sorry."

Izzy looked at her with a smile of reassurance. "It's okay, don't worry about it." Kathrine smiled back and seem to blush a little. Jake saw this and rolled his eyes in jealousy.

The elevator came to a halt at its destination with the door sliding open. The team walked down the hall of the science deck till they reached the UTS room on the left several doors down and entered. The Dimensional Teleport was in the middle of the room in the same configuration as it was on the Recluses. There were several people walking around the room conducting different tasks of work with Gia in the control room on the second floor typing information into her computer. She looked down at Alpha team from her position, grabbed a nearby headset, and switched it to room intercom.

"Good morning Alpha." She said with a smile. "You guys ready?"

"Yes ma'am." Lucas said smiling at her.

Gia's expression melted to a frown. "Please don't call me that... Before we send you off, Izzy has a couple of things for you, Izzy?"

"Yes," Izzy continued. "Step this way."

"She didn't like that very much." Raymond whispered his comment to Lucas while walking with the team in the direction Izzy instructed.

"Don't worry," Lucas responded. "She's just one of those civi's who don't know that saying ma'am or sir is a sign of respect."

Sheena stated. "I get the feeling you say ma'am to her for reasons other than just respect."

Lucas looked at Sheena and said, "Your right, it's her looks," he looked at Gia again at a distance. "and that accent of hers... uh... so sexy." Katherine slapped the back of Lucas's head. "Ow! Really?" Sheena giggled.

The team stopped in front of a table as Izzy began to speak. "These are your TC's, Tactical Contacts."

"Like, contact lenses?" Jake asked.

"Yes, but with a twist." Izzy took a nearby bottle of hand sanitizer, squeezed it into his hand and rubbed his hands together. Than he took one of the contact cases, opened it, plucked his finger into the case pulling out one of the contacts and carefully placed it into his right eye. He did the same thing for the other eye with the other contact lens, then looked back at the team. "These lenses give you a Heads Up Display. They also have a built in camera so command and your fellow team mates can see what's going on from your perspective, and they also have night vision and thermal vision modes that can be activated via voice command. I also took the liberty of installing the TC app or Tactical Contacts app on your Taclets so you can control what you see on your HUD."

"Nice work Izzy." Raymond complimented as he put his contacts in his own eyes.

"You know it's against Reg's to wear contacts during a deployment for a reason right?" Jake commented while putting the contacts in his eyes. "They are a hassle to put in, they can cause eyes infections, and they feel completely uncomfor-" Jake paused as he blinked a couple of times. His eyes comfortably adjusted to the contacts as he saw a HUD appear in front of his vision. The upper left showed each of his teammates perspectives in four small squares with a heart rate and pulse monitor colored green below each square with each teammates name under it, up center showed his own heart rate and pulse monitor also colored green, upper right showed a motion sensor ranging out twenty-five meters. On the motion sensor he saw several blurry white dots and four solid blue dots. The white dots would disappear in and out but the blue dots stayed constant and never disappeared. The lower left corner said "No Flow Connected". "Wo... These are actually pretty cool, and comfortable." Jake said in awe.

"I knew you would like them." Izzy said happily. "This technology was perfected by the SCTG, my old unit from my home universe. I was able to copy the technology from a pair of contacts I had left over. You guys see the motion sensor on the upper right?" the team nodded. "The white blurs are unconfirmed personnel movement. The solid blue dots are Confirmed friendly's. Solid red dots are marked enemy targets."

"What's this "No Flow Connected" thing about on the lower left?" Kathrine asked.

"I don't have that." Raymond said. "I have some kind of battery indicator."

Izzy explained. "That's for the flow system, the contacts app syncs up to your FS app to notify you of important information about your flow system. Last time you used it, it was only for a moment so battery power wasn't an issue, same for training. However, you could be in the field for a prolonged period of time. I felt it would be best to have a way to keep track of the battery in situations like this. It should last up to twenty-four hours of constant use but let's face it, you're not gonna use it constantly so give or take two to three days of average use."

"Understood." Raymond acknowledge. "Everyone ready?"

"Roger." The team acknowledged in unison.

"Then let's hit it." The team moved towards the Universal Teleport stepping onto the platform with Sheena staying behind looking at Raymond. He turned around looking back at her while she began to laugh. "What's so funny?" He asked.

"You guys look like some goth band going to a concert." Laughing louder.

Raymond chuckled. "Well, according to the mission profile, this universe does have a..." Raymond paused to find the word. "Unique style of fashion."

"Right, blend in with the locals." Sheena stated one of the rules of unconventional warfare as her expression began to show worry. "Be careful." She said to Raymond in concern.

"Don't worry," he kissed her than backed away. "Your gonna help me do that from the TOC remember?" Raymond smiled, Sheena smiled back. "Besides, if all goes well, we'll be in and out without firing a single round."

"Well, just encase you do, take this." She gave him her face paint case.

Raymond chuckled as he stopped her. "It's okay." He reached into his right pocket and pulled out his own case of face paint. "You did say to get my own remember?"

Sheena laughed. "Yea, I did."

"I'll see you when I get back." He put the face paint back in his pocket than stepped further back on the platform.

"See you." She took several steps backwards.

When the team was assembled on the platform, Lucas gave the thumbs up to Gia in the control room. Gia nodded back at Lucas in confirmation and began the teleportation sequence. The teleport began to hum louder with blue waves of electricity encircling the team into a spherical shape as they began to levitate.

"Here we go again." Lucas commented nervously.

Gia began talking over the intercom. "Beginning five-way coordinate sequence. As planned, you guys will be split up in five different locations within a one block radius of the night club. Also just in from the TOC, our techs were able to wirelessly hack into the night club's security systems. We are using their surveillance network to support you on this op."

"Roger that!" Raymond responded. "Strike us in!"

"Roger, striking in three... Two... One..." Gia pressed the enter key. Suddenly the team disappeared at a thunder like sound.

Universe 1211 - Planet Roesha
August 20th, 2238
2331 Standard Earth Time

There were multiple thunder like sounds around a one block radius of where Raymond had landed on his hands and left knee. His body rocked forward grunting from the impact than slowly stood up as he conducted SLLS, Stop Look Listen Smell, taking in his surroundings. He looked around seeing that he was in an ally between two buildings. One end of the ally was a dead end with a brick wall. The other end was open to the streets as he saw people walking by and another building across the street. He heard people talking, cars

139

driving and honking, other noises of the city, and the base thumping from the nearby club. The ally smelled like urine and alcohol combined. He was definitely in the right place.

"All units, this is Slinger. Check in."

Lucas. "*White, up.*"

Izzy. "*Digit, up.*"

Jake. "*Rophe, up.*"

Katherine. "*Cat-Eye, up.*"

Raymond acknowledged. "Roger. Command, all units up." He said while walking down the ally to the sidewalk.

"*Roger that Slinger.*" Gehnarne said over the radio as he saw Sheena walking into the bridge heading towards the TOC. "*Alpha Team, welcome to planet Roesha of universe 1211. Unlike 1112 this universe is not in a state of total anarchy however, it's like the wild west. No one here will kill you unless you give them a legitimate reason to. Good luck and godspeed. Switching you over to Crimson at the TOC. Rifter out.*"

Raymond reached the sidewalk as he saw hundreds of people and oddly shaped cars in the streets driving by.

"*Crimson here,*" Sheena spoke. "*Slinger, the club is a couple of buildings down to your right.*"

Raymond looked to his right and saw a big vertical neon sign that said "Dark Essence". "Roger Crimson, Oscar mike." He casually walked down the street to the club blending in nicely with the civilians around him. Just like Gehnarne's reports had stated, this universe had a dark theme to it, almost gothic. Everyone seemed to wear black and other accessories that would normally seem off in style from universe 1111. Raymond respected the unique look of this universe as he continued down the street noticing a strange life form he had never seen before. The creature seemed to peacefully interact with the humans from this universe. In surprise, Raymond called it in. "Uh command, what are-"

Gehnarne cut him off as he looked through Raymond's point of view from his captain's chair's left arm control panel screen.. "*They're called the Sethra. A reptilian based species, they are one of many Alien races that the humans in this universe had discovered. Female Sethra are quite friendly but male Sethra could be very hostile if you trigger them the wrong way."*

As Raymond continued walking and listening to Gehnarne, he almost bumped into a male Sethra who yelled at him in an unknown language while pushing Raymond out of his way. Raymond looked at him in surprise. He had a head like a lizard with snake looking eyes. Rudely passing Raymond, the Sethra hissed while sticking his snake like tongue at Raymond than continued walking

"Wo..." Raymond shivered as he continued towards the club. "That was creepy."

Gehnarne laughed. *"Don't worry, you'll get used to it. You'll run into other alien species out there besides just the Sethra. We might even find other races and species in our own universe."*

"Right, All units in position?" He asked as he looked at the camera feeds of all of his teammates on the upper left corner of his HUD. Each feed showed someone in front of a different entrance to the club. Two were at the fire exits, Kathrine at the North exit and Jake at the south exit. The other two perspectives were from the main entrance. Lucas on the left, Izzy on the right. The team acknowledged with a *"Roger"*.

"Check, hold your positions till I need you." Raymond walked up to the club placing his right hand on the door. He looked right and saw Izzy giving him a thumbs up while leaning against the wall of the building casually. He smiled at him than looked left towards Lucas who was also leaning against the wall with his black bandanna covering his face revealing the bottom half of a painted skull on the bandanna. He looked back at Raymond calmly and nodded. Raymond nodded back then faced the door pushing through it. As he walked through the door way, he heard slightly muffled music. He recognized the style of music that was playing knowing that this type of music existed in his universe as well. It had a violent, dark electronic beat with someone singing in a distorted voice. "Huh, doesn't this sound familiar." He said to himself as his killer instinct began to build up on its own, craving for combat. "Who needs face paint," He smiled with a dark sense of motivation, "with music like this?" He opened the second set of doors as he heard the music perfectly loud and clear walking through the doorway seeing what was on the other side.

He saw hundreds of humans, Sethra, and other Alien races he had never seen before all looking completely different from each other, dancing and jumping extremely close to each other to the dark beat. Lights flashed everywhere at random patterns and colors around the large dimly lit room with two floors. He moved through the room casually as he observed every detail. He looked right and saw more people and aliens. Behind them was a bar packed with clubbers waiting for drinks. He looked left and saw even more clubbers. Behind them were some small tables where groups of people were sitting, having drinks, and talking. Behind the tables against the walls were circular shaped booths where some individuals looked like they were taking drugs and doing other obscene things. He looked up and saw cages hanging from the ceiling scattered evenly at different elevations. Some were empty, others had dancers of different genders and races dancing inside them. He also noticed a second floor mezzanine going around the large room with rooms on the second floor. Raymond looked forward and continued to make his way through the crowd. As he started to see the back wall, he continued to scan left and right noticing what looked like an empty VIP booth in front of him. "Rophe, I think I found the perfect spot for your future bachelor party."

Jake responded. "*Yea, if I ever get married, Now I wish I was in there instead of you.*" He said with a laugh.

Kathrine said under her breath forgetting the channel was open. "*Doubt that will happen.*"

"*What was that?*" Jake quickly responded to Kathrine.

"*Nothing, nothing.*" She responded being caught off guard.

The TOC personnel on the Enidon chuckled. However, Lucas was not amused.

"*Alpha, White. Cut the chatter, over.*" He said with harshness in his voice.

"*Roger.*" Jake could tell he was annoyed.

"Sheesh Lucas," Sheena said to herself in the TOC. "Lighten up a little will ya?"

Raymond turned left and saw something familiar. "Hold on," He looked at the last circular shaped booth and saw all three Red Nova crew members. Timothy Doyle was on the left with a look of disappointment wearing a dark green jacket, black shirt, cargo pants and boots. Jason was in the center with a black compression short sleeve shirt showing off his arm muscles and a couple of tattoos. He also wore black jeans, boots and gloves as he seemed to be enjoying himself while taking a swig from his drink. Sarah was on the right motionless and quiet with a knee high black skirt, a tucked in black blouse and short heeled black shoes who seemed very shy as she tried to cover herself with a brown leather jacket that looked too large for her. "I have visual contact on the Red Nova crew, moving in to interact, standby."

"Roger that Slinger." Sheena responded.

As Raymond approached the booth, Jason had noticed him getting closer and moved into a cautious posture. Raymond grabbed a chair from one of the tables he passed and placed it at the open end of the booth with the back piece of the chair facing away from the booth sitting down on the chair in a reversed fashion leaning forward against the back piece.

"Jason Lennes?" Raymond asked in a very relaxed manner.

"Who's asking?" Jason responded with a serious tone and expression.

"Raymond "The Gunslinger" Reynolds of SMO, at your service." He introduced himself with a smile and light bow. "I'm here to get you and your crew out of here."

Sheena and the TOC technicians observed Raymond from the club's cameras. One of the TOC technicians spoke up. "Is it just me or does he seem to have a certain... swagger going on right now?"

"Yea," Sheena agreed. "Your right." She had never seen Raymond act so smooth before. He almost seemed like a different person altogether.

Back at the booth. "Ah I see," Jason said as he relaxed. "All right then, let me buy you a drink!"

Raymond was surprised. "Wait, what? We have to go, like now."

"Relax, relax, how can I trust someone I never had a drink with before?"

Suddenly Gehnarne cut in on the radio. *"It's okay Slinger, he's always like this. Have a drink with him, you'll be fine."*

"All right then." Raymond smiled.

"Great!" Jason signaled over a waitress. The waitress was an alien with violet colored skin and bald head who wore a short black skirt with fishnet stockings, long black combat boots, a black skin tight t-shirt.

"What are you having?" Jason asked Raymond.

"Well unlike a certain friend of mine," Raymond said in a way to make sure his communications app picked up what he said. "I'm gonna be smart to assume that the drinks in this universe are different, so I'll have whatever you're drinking."

Lucas sighed loudly over the channel *"Shut up Raymond."* Followed by the whole team chuckling along with a few of the TOC technicians and Sheena.

"Good point." Jason chuckled as he looked at the waitress and gave her the order. "Just a bottle of Westen for my guest".

"Gotcha." The waitress smiled and walked away.

Jason looked back at Raymond. "So... Gunslinger huh? How did you get a dumb call sign like that?"

Raymond chuckled. "I don't know, why is your ship Called the Red Nova when it's blue? You color blind or somethin?"

Timothy mildly laughed at Raymond's timely insult. "I like this guy." He said with a childish voice. Jason looked at Timothy in way of none verbally telling him to "shut up." In response he rolled his eyes at Jason while shaking his head and looked away. Jason than turned towards Sarah with a caring look as she looked back with an innocent expression and nodded. Jason nodded back in agreement than looked back at Raymond smiling.

"Okay smart ass, I didn't pick the color, but just because my buddy Tim here likes ya, how about we do this. You tell me how you got that lame call sign of yours and I'll prove to you I'm not color blind. Sound good?"

The waitress came back with the beer. "Here you go hun." She placed the drink in front of Raymond while smiling and checking him out.

Sheena saw what the waitress did on the camera's and got a little annoyed.

"Fair enough." He responded to Jason. "Thanks." He said to the waitress as she walked away. He grabbed the beer and took a swig. It had a familiar alcoholic taste that he never got used to. He placed the beer back on the table. "Not bad. Now how did this story go?..." He thought for a moment. "Oh yea! Now I remember." Raymond began his story. "When I first joined the USOD, one of my team's first missions was a black op. to assassinate a colonial senator who was working with the rebels. Our team was assigned to provide security for the assault team."

Sheena listened to Raymond telling the story as she remembered being on that mission as well.

Raymond continued. "The assault team was tasked to attack the senator's home while my team was tasked with containment. However, the assault team met heavy resistance and was almost wiped out. The mission was about to be aborted until a surviving member of the assault teamed named Crow called in."

Jake listened as he remembered the horrific image of Crow's amputated leg with a tourniquet and blood everywhere as he tried to stop the bleeding from other wounds on his body.

Raymond continued. "He said there was a group of rebels already in the house who flipped on the senator and killed him. With that, command called mission complete, RTB. However, knowing it was a black op. The rebels couldn't know there was a second team. We were ordered to leave the survivor to die or be a prisoner. There was no way I was gonna leave him behind."

Lucas listened and remembered arguing with Raymond on following commands specific orders. They all got in trouble after that mission but a part of him was glad that they saved Crow. He still felt guilty that he was trying to force Raymond to leave him behind.

Tim, Jason, and Sarah looked at Raymond with heavy interest as he continued the story. "Against commands orders we moved in anyway engaging multiple Rebels. When we finally reached Crow, we were almost out of ammo. Reflexively, I grabbed one of the dead rebel's side arms along with my own already drawn, turned around, and began shooting down the hall with both pistols killing quite a few rebels while moving down the hall. The rest of the team instinctively backed me up clearing the rooms as I moved forward down the hall."

Katherine listened and remembered a detail that Raymond left out. She remembered the horrific image of a woman and a child dead on the floor near Crow. It looked like they were killed in some kind of explosion that Crow was clearly caught in. It was the senator's family. The team's orders were to kill the senator only. Clearly the rebels had other plans or didn't care. She remembers Raymond going into a state of combat rage over the loss of the other team, that woman, the child, and Crow getting hurt. He grabbed the enemy's pistol off the floor along with his own, aimed down the hall and immediately started shooting at any hostiles that came down the hall with vicious intent.

Continuing to tell the story, "When we reached the last room at the end of the hall I kicked in the door, extended both arms towards both corners and fired. I didn't even know if there were enemy's there or not, I just did it. Just so happens there were enemies in both those corners and I was lucky enough to shoot both of them in the head, it was crazy." As Raymond remembered the events to the story as he told it, he left out a gruesome detail. After killing those two rebels in the corners, he pointed both guns down center at a rebel who just threw his weapon down and begged not to be killed. Raymond didn't care. He fired both guns savagely as the rebel fell backwards out of a window behind him. Raymond remembered the rage he felt in that moment, the sense of satisfaction in payback for the Rebels killing his friends on the assault team and many others they have massacred throughout the years this war has been waged. He also remembered the guilt he felt for letting his rage reach that level of hatred and losing control in satisfaction. Since that moment, he tried his best never to go to that dark place again.

Jason looked at Raymond with intrigue wondering why he took a long pause in his story. "Then what?" He asked

"Huh?" Raymond snapped out of it. "Oh! Sorry, just trying to remember the details. So after killing those two, the team went around me and cleared the room. Since that day, they called me Gunslinger as a joke, then it became my call sign. Of course "Gunslinger" has three syllables so people just started calling me Slinger for short since it only has two. Plus, I actually prefer to be called Slinger. It flows better when talking on a radio which is the whole point of a call sign in the first place. However, I do use Gunslinger at times when I introduce myself formally."

Sheena remembers seeing Raymond directly after shooting that last rebel out the window that he left out of the story. When he turned around towards her at the end of the hall, she saw pure rage in his eyes. A side of him she thought never existed till then. That was the day she started to respect Raymond. Thinking back at it now however, she should have felt concerned for him, for doing something she now understood was so wrong. Guilt crept into her heart realizing how wrong she was.

"Ma'am!" One of the TOC technicians called out to Sheena.

She snapped out of her memory and turned around. "What is it?"

"We're detecting an energy signature in the vicinity of the club on the Taclet sensors."

Sheena walked towards the adviser. "Can you track and see where it's coming from?"

"I can try."

"Good." Sheena said hoping that the energy signature was nothing significant.

Jason was quiet for a moment then responded to Raymond's story. "Bullshit."

"You can ask my teammates about it," Raymond said. "They were all there."

"Really?" Jason was surprised.

"Really, really." Raymond confirmed.

"Wow, that's a pretty impressive story! Cheers to the Gunslinger!" Raymond and Jason laughed as they lifted their beers, tapped them together then drank.

"So, why is your ship called The Red Nova anyway?"

Jason looked at Sarah. She smiled and nodded. Then he looked at Timothy. With a smirk he also nodded, then Jason looked back at Raymond. "Okay Raymond, you seem like a pretty cool guy, I trust you. I named my ship that becau-"

"Slinger, this is Crimson, over."

"Hold on a sec Jason." Raymond interrupted.

"Sure, take your time."

"What's up Crimson?"

"We're detecting a strange energy signature in your area, check your Taclets. We're getting a fix on it now."

"Ma'am!" A TOC technician spoke up to Sheena. "It's coming from inside the club and it seems to be mobile!"

Sheena now knew this was not normal. "Be advised, that energy signature is in the club and is on the move!" She said urgently.

Raymond became very concerned. "Team, did you see any suspicious personnel walk in?"

"Negative," Lucas said. *"Nothing from our end."*

"Oh shit," Jason said in disbelief.

Raymond looked at Jason. "What's wrong?"

"Pirates."

"Pirates?" Raymond looked around. "Where?"

"Behind you to your left, the group of guys in the black suits and the tats on their hands."

Raymond turned around to his left and saw a group of five matching Jason's description. "Huh, and here I was expecting eye patches and peg legs."

"What?" Jason didn't understand.

Raymond realized Jason probably didn't get the reference due to universal differences. "Ugh, never mind let's move." Raymond said while The four of them stood up. Jason took the leather jacket from Sarah and put it on himself fitting perfectly than took Sarah's hand and guided her out of the booth. The group tried to sneak around the pirates. Unfortunately, the pirates had already spotted Raymond and the Red Nova crew and walked towards them with haste.

"Team, the pirates have spotted us, standby for possible hostile response." Raymond put out to the team as he took the black bandanna on his neck and covered his lower face with it.

"Roger." The team acknowledged in unison as they readied they're weapons. Kathrine and Jake set breach charges on their assigned doors than put their black bandanna's on.

"Hope it doesn't get hot in their." Izzy commented at the front entrance to Lucas while putting on his black bandanna

"Trust me," Lucas responded coldly, "With our team, things always get hot."

Back inside the club, "Hey!" One of the pirates yelled out as he stepped in front of the Red Nova crew cutting them off. The Pirate was another Alien race with a very brutish body and face. As the pirate began to talk, Raymond couldn't help but notice the music in the club change to something that sounded like a slower, darker beat.

"What do you want?" Jason asked. Sarah seemed scared. Timothy looked angry as he hid behind Jason ready to draw his weapon from his belt holster.

"You of course," The pirate responded harshly. "Asrin wants to see you."

"Sorry but he's with me." Raymond interrupted. "Excuse us," He tried to push past the pirate as he suddenly grabbed Raymond by the collar of his shirt and slowly lifted him off the floor.

"And you are?" The pirate asked in anger. The slower darker beat of the music sounded like it was building up to a beat drop.

"Team, Crimson. We looked through the live security footage and found multiple hostiles in the club. We have marked targets for you, check mail."

Lucas responded on channel. "Roger Crimson, good mail." He said as he noticed Raymond's pulse increasing on his HUD. "Come on Raymond." Lucas said to himself eagerly waiting for Raymond to give the go order.

The pirate holding Raymond had a red outline appear on Raymond's HUD. He quickly looked around and saw multiple humanoid shaped silhouette's with red outlines throughout the club all representing hostile pirates. He counted between thirty to forty. Raymond knew the only way out now is to fight their way out. "I said, who are you?!" The pirate yelled in anger while still holding Raymond with one hand.

The pirate than snatched off Raymond's bandanna with his other hand, revealing Raymond's sadistic smile as his killer instinct began to scream in the back of his head saying *"KILL THIS PUNK!!!"* Grunting in sadistic laughter responding to the pirate's question, "The wrong guy, remember this face when I send you to THE AFTERLIFE!!!" Raymond quickly tapped his wrists together twice as the discs spun up creating a flash and sending out a bass like shock wave at the exact moment the music in the club beat dropped. The beat turned fast, dark, and violent while Raymond grabbed both of his M76 pistols set to automatic under his leather jacket as he lifted his legs and kicked the pirate square in the chest so hard the pirate slammed into the floor with Raymond launching himself off to the cage hanging over him. He grabbed the bottom of the empty cage with his legs, his body hanging upside down as he drew his weapons in a dual wield fashion and fired two three round bursts from both pistols. The rounds smashed into the pirates face and upper torso as his body juddered and went numb with purple blood spraying the floor.

Raymond looked at the Red Nova crew. "TAKE COVER NOW!!!"

Sarah and Timothy were staring at Raymond in disbelief. Jason hesitated for a moment then snapped out of it. He grabbed Timothy with his right hand while still holding Sarah's hand with his left, pulling them to run while yelling "Let's move!"

"TEAM, EXECUTE!" Raymond ordered on the radio.

Jake and Kathrine detonated hinge breach charges on the doors to prevent civilian casualties. The doors fell off the hinges as they went through the doorways with their black bandannas on their faces and their AR30's up clearing their sectors of fire. Lucas and Izzy moved through the second set of doors in the front of the club. Gunfire erupted throughout the club as Alpha team and the pirates exchanged fire on the first floor. Raymond began moving from cage to cage supporting Alpha team's movement throughout the club killing two to three pirates with each displacement. The Red Nova crew took cover behind the VIP booth. "Now What!?" Timothy asked with a childlike voice and his gun drawn.

"Stay here and shoot any pirate that gets too close!" Jason said while drawing his pistol.

"Got it!"

Sarah poked her head out of cover for a moment to look around, suddenly there was a loud crack as Jason pushed Sarah's head down with force "Sarah, stay down!" He yelled. Sarah curled herself into an upright ball holding her legs close. With every cracking bullet that passed over her, she flinched and whimpered in fear. Jason and Timothy aimed their guns at the pirates shooting at them and began returning fire as a team.

Despite the gunfight, the club's music continued to play as civilians ran out of the club for their lives. Alpha continued to clear the first floor as Raymond supported them. "*Check your fire, watch out for civilians!*" Sheena advised on the channel.

Suddenly Raymond felt a bullet graze off his gravity field on his right. He reflexively turned and immediately opened fired while yelling "SECOND FLOOR, RIGHT SIDE!!!" He fired while holding on to the cage from the side with one hand while shooting with the other killing two pirates out of the three he had spotted. The third was shot from the lower level by Lucas reacting to Raymond's call out. "Tango down! Alpha, I'm gonna start clearing out the second floor!" He said while reloading his weapon with a one handed quick reload mod on his holster. "Let me know when the first floor is clear!"

"Roger that Slinger!" Lucas responded. "Be careful!"

Raymond chuckled in enjoyment and smiled as he just finished reloading. "As always!" He said as he pushed himself off the cage using the gravity field as a boost and spun his body like a vortex towards a window while shooting a pirate on the other side. He busted through the window while moving his body right side up. He turned left with his left gun up and fired at two pirates near the corner of the room while throwing a small breach charge set for impact at the wall behind him leading to the next room with his right hand. Just after killing the two pirates in the corner, the breach charge impacted and detonated destroying the wall. Raymond back flipped into the breach while drawing his right hand gun, outstretched his arms with both guns in both hands and fired them in midair killing two more pirates in opposite corners of the next room, then landed on his feet. As he turned to his right towards the door in the new room, Sheena called in.

"Slinger, Crimson. We narrowed down the location of that energy signature." Raymond opened the door knowing there was a pirate behind it and kicked him so hard he flew past the second floor banister and fell to his death down to the first floor almost falling on Jake.

"Oh shit!" Jake jumped in surprise than immediately looked up at Raymond. "Hey watch it!"

Raymond looked down at him and responded. "Sorry Jake!"

Sheena continued. *"It's coming from the DJ booth on your level."* Raymond looked forward and saw the DJ booth directly ahead on the other side of the mezzanine.

"Kill the bastard!" Raymond heard and turned to his right as a small group of pirate's readied their weapons just after running up a set of stairs on the right side of the mezzanine. He turned around and sprinted while shooting at the pirates only killing one and suppressing the other two, than took cover behind a table halfway to the DJ booth's left entrance.

"Explains why the music is still going." Raymond commented.

"Slinger, White! We cleared the first floor and are moving to the second floor now!" Lucas reported on channel.

"Roger White, I'm heading to the DJ booth, finish off these punks!" He ordered as he just finished reloading and began sprinting towards the DJ booth again while the pirates opposite from him were still in cover.

"Check!" Lucas responded just as Alpha reached the top of the stairs to the second floor behind the pirates that Raymond suppressed earlier. Alpha finished them off while Raymond kicked in the DJ booth door but was caught off guard when an unmarked human pirate grabbed him by the neck. Raymond tried to counter with punches and jabs with no effect. He fired a burst from his pistol also with no effect as the rounds immediately deflected off and slammed into the nearby walls. In shock, Raymond looked down and noticed this pirate had flow system gauntlets similar to his own. He was unsure of what to do as the pirate spoke.

"So you're the one killing all my men." The pirate said with a deep, dark voice.

"Who the hell are you!?" Raymond grunted struggling to breath while looking into the pirate's pale white eyes, scared up face, and tattooed body with combat pants and boots.

"I'm Asrin, pleasure to meet you."

Asrin's grip started to get tighter just as Lucas came through the right side entrance behind Asrin with his AR30 up and yelled. "LET HIM GO NOW!!!" Asrin looked at Lucas and smiled

"As you wish." He threw Raymond out the window of the DJ booth. Glass shattered everywhere while Raymond fell all the way down to the first floor.

"Raymond!" Sheena gasped over the channel.

"NO!" Lucas yelled as he began to shoot on full auto at Asrin just as the whole club went dark. All Lucas could see were the muzzle flashes of his weapon as he fired. He stopped and said "NODs up!"

His contacts went into night vision mode as he saw that Asrin was no longer in the room. Everything was quiet except for the club's music that was still playing at a slow, dark, beat again. "Slinger! You okay?!" Lucas asked on the radio

Raymond sat straight up while grunting recovering from the fall after landing on his back safely. "Ugh... Yea... I'm good..." Sheena and Lucas sighed in relief as Raymond slowly got back on his feet. "The gravity field cushioned the impact more softly than I thought." He looked around while switching into NOD mode with his contacts. "Anyone got a visual on Asrin?"

Izzy. "Negative."

Kathrine. "Nothing here."

Jake. "I got nothing."

Lucas. "I don't see him either, let's find this guy before-"

"I was told there would be someone else with the flow system like me." Asrin said at an unknown location in the club on the loud speakers while the music continued to play at a slow dark beat. "I've been training for this encounter for weeks."

"Crap, he's still here." Raymond said while slowly moving into stance with his weapons drawn.

"Tell me, what is your name... before you die!"

"Alright." Raymond responded as he began reloading both of his pistols at the same time using the one handed reload mod on his leg magazine holsters. "The name is Slinger," He said as he finished reloading. "Gunslinger," He finished as he spun his guns once on his fingers while moving into stance. "I already sent one of your boys to the afterlife remembering my face, now you'll remember my name." He said with vicious motivation in his voice.

Asrin laughed "We'll see." Suddenly, Asrin dropped from the ceiling behind Raymond while he turned around just in time to see Asrin swing a sword that looked like a Japanese Katana at him Vertically. Raymond dodged right, Asrin followed up with an upward vertical cut, Raymond dodged left, horizontal cut, dodged by moving his hips back, another horizontal cut, dodged by leaning back as Raymond followed up with a kicking back flip hitting the pommel of the sword launching it up into the ceiling of the club. When Raymond landed on his feet after completing the back flip, he launched himself backwards with his feet while shooting at Asrin. He flew backwards several meters, landed on his feet and stopped himself at a grinding halt while still firing. All of Raymond's rounds deflected left and right as Asrin smiled.

"What the hell?!" Raymond said in frustration as he stopped shooting and began to reload. Suddenly Asrin pulled a shot gun out from his lower back that was connected to his belt. "WO!" Raymond said in shock as he dove right just barely dodging the shot gun blast and took cover behind the bar. "Digit! I thought I was the only one with the flow system?!" He asked in frustration.

Izzy was in shock. *"I-I don't know! Maybe someone else picked up the design somehow?!!"*

"Alright, whatever!" He said as Asrin got closer while still shooting his shotgun. "How do I kill this guy!?"

Izzy quickly thought out loud. *"Seems like his flow system was configured to use the gravity field at maximum output."*

A shotgun blast screeched over Raymond's head. "English dammit!"

Izzy groaned in annoyance for a second. *"He's Pretty much, bullet proof, your gonna have to hit him with anything that has constantly controlled thrust like an object in your hand or something!"*

Raymond thought for a second. Than he looked up towards the ceiling and saw Asrin's sword. He had an idea. "White."

"Yea!?" Lucas responded.

"Light this guy up, I'm moving."

"Roger that! Team, suppressing fire!" everyone on Alpha team began firing from their current positions on the second floor just as the music in the club intensified back to a dark, violent fast beat. Jason and Timothy caught on and began to fire as well. Immediately Asrin's attention shifted away from Raymond as he turned around and began shooting his shotgun at Alpha on the second floor missing his shots due to so many rounds pelting him all at once. At that moment, Raymond sprinted out of the bar from the right. Once he was in the open he jumped on a table to a cage, then to the second floor, then to a ceiling rafter. Alpha, Jason, and Timothy took turns engaging Asrin to help conserve ammo and keep him confused and unaware of what Raymond was doing. "Aim for his face! Blind him!" Lucas ordered

out loud.

Raymond climbed the rafters finally reaching the sword stabbed into the ceiling and pulled it free. This was not the type of sword he was used to but, "It'll do." He said as he looked back down and saw Asrin. He pointed the sword directly at him then let go of the rafter, letting himself fall while keeping the sword straight as he fell at such a velocity that the flow system detected it as a strike and consistently boosted him down faster. As soon as Raymond felt the boost of speed, he couldn't help but key up with a "HRAAAA!!!". Asrin heard the yell from Raymond and looked up.

At that same moment, Lucas saw Raymond coming down and yelled "HOLD FIRE!!!" with the team instantly stopping their engagement. By the time Asrin saw Raymond, it was already too late.

The sword penetrated through his mouth and exited out his lower back forcing Asrin's body to arch backwards a bit. Raymond balanced himself on the pommel of the sword upside down as he looked at Asrin's dyeing expression. He looked into his eyes with vicious intent as he said to Asrin "When you join your men, don't EVER forget WHO KILLED ALL OF YOU!" Asrin's face spiked in disbelief for a moment then went numb, he was dead. Raymond forced his balance towards the front of Asrin's body, forcing the carcass to its knee's while pulling out the sword. Once Raymond landed on his feet and the sword was pulled all the way out of Asrin's body, covered in blood, he spun at an inhuman speed, cutting off Asrin's head with a clean cut. The body fell as the head fell on top of it. Alpha team starred in shock as Sheena in the Enidon's TOC starred at the monitors in disbelief that Raymond could have done something so vicious again. "Are we clear?" Raymond asked while standing in the middle of the club empty with bullet holes riddling the walls and tables destroyed.

Lucas snapped out of it. "Yea, we're clear." He responded as he and the rest of the team took off their bandannas.

"Good." Raymond said dropping Asrin's sword next to his dead headless body. "Everyone okay?" He asked.

Sheena pushed her concerns about Raymond's actions to the side, *"Green status across the board."*

"Well that was the craziest bar fight I've ever been a part of." Lucas commented. "Jason, you guys good?" He asked.

"Yea!" Jason responded as the Red Nova crew stood up out of cover. "We're good." He began to guide Sarah down from the VIP booth.

"Man that was insane." Timothy said while looking around and brushing himself off from small dirt and debris on his jacket.

"How did you do that?" Jason asked as Raymond walked closer.

Raymond stopped than smiled with pride as he shut down the Flow System. "That's an even longer story."

Sheena spoke on the radio. *"Alpha, be advised, we have what appears to be local law enforcement surrounding the club building."*

"Roger Crimson." Raymond responded.

"Hold up." Jason interrupted. "Law enforcement? Can you get a visual on them?"

Raymond was curious to how Jason heard what Sheena said. "...Okay, sure. Crimson, get me a visual on the police outside on my Taclet."

"Roger." Sheena transferred the club's exterior camera imagine to Raymond's Taclet. Raymond lifted his left arm up as both him and Jason looked at the small screen. They both saw what looked like an armored truck parked across the street from the club with the double doors on the back of the vehicle swinging open as eight unknown armed men in full combat gear rushed out of it towards the club. They set up portable barriers as cover just outside the entrance.

"Hell no, those aren't cops." Jason said in worry.

"Who are they?" Raymond asked.

"I don't know but I have seen them before, they work with the pirates. We gotta get out of here now."

"We still need the Nova." Lucas informed Jason.

"Don't worry, we're already on it." Jason said as he began to look towards Sarah. Curiously Raymond looked at Sarah as well and saw something he had never seen before. He saw her looking up towards the ceiling peacefully as a blue aura surrounded her body and her blue hair glowed while stretching outward like flowing water.

"Jason... what is she doing?" Raymond asked as the rest of Alpha team couldn't help but stare in wonder of what Sarah was up to.

"You'll see in a moment." Jason answered while smiling as a

distant roaring sound drew closer to the club. The unidentified armed men outside heard the roaring sound as well and wondered what was happening. Alpha team looked around in wonder as the roar reached its peak volume from above the club.

"What is that?!" Jake asked.

"Just stay close to us!" Jason informed. "We're getting out of here!"

Raymond saw Izzy running towards Asrin's body. "Digit!?"

"Hold on, I'm collecting intel!" He disconnected the flow module from Asrin's body and took it with him. Alpha team created a circle around Sarah as her blue glow faded away and her blue hair falling back down to her shoulders.

Jason looked at Sarah and said "Do it." she nodded back at him than looked straight ahead. Her right gold eye suddenly flashed red than back to gold just as a loud explosion went off above the group. Alpha team flinched as they heard the explosion and looked up flinching again as they saw debris from the ceiling falling towards them. Suddenly a bright beaming light shown down on the groups position halting the debris just above them. It floated for a second, then was thrown to the side throughout the club by an unknown force. As Raymond looked up towards the light, he saw what looked like the Red Nova hovering over the club.

"FREEZE!" A man said as he and other soldiers next to him pointed their rifles at the group. Alpha and the Red Nova crew held their ground as sharp red beams of light came crashing down from above the ceiling on the hostile soldiers. They were immediately cut to pieces while screaming in pain. Alpha was shocked by what they saw while a sudden sensation of zero-g was felt around their body's as they began to float up towards the light. Alpha looked around in wonder as the Red Nova crew seem to not react at all like this was the norm. Shortly after they began to float, the group found themselves inside a bay of the Red Nova. The floor slid closed underneath them as they slowly floated back down one-meter landing on their feet softly. Raymond and Alpha team looked around the bay that was lined with white walls. Raymond looked at Jason, and the Red Nova crew. Jason smirked at Raymond and said. "Welcome aboard the Red Nova."

My home universe can be described as a kind of space western,

whatever the hell that means, Raymond described it that way once.

Basically there are three factions that exist there. The Krelis Empire,

The Pirates, and the Mercenaries. The Empire is the main governing

faction that controls most of occupied space. The Pirates are clans of

crime syndicates that have grown over time due to there massive

influence in the underworld. The Mercenaries are free willed, free

minded souls who are just trying to make a living any way possible

while trying to steer clear of both the Empire and the Pirates. For a

while, me and my crew lived as Mercenaries living aboard the Red

Nova and taking any job we could find. However, after working as a

Merc for so long, my past was bound to catch up with me eventually.

That's one of the reasons why I joined Lightning, so me and my crew

can have a better future.

Chapter 9: The Red Nova

The Red Nova blasted off into the sky sending debris from around the club flying into the streets. While the ship began to break through the atmosphere into orbit, Alpha team followed Jason and his crew to the bridge. As the automatic sliding doors to the bridge opened, Raymond saw a room several meters long and wide with a giant spherical monitor surrounding the room that was currently blackened, two seats lined up with each other half way into the floor in the center of the room with the rear seat's front touching the back of the front seat surrounded by piloting controls. Directly to Raymond's right and left were two more seats with small monitors and control consoles facing towards the front on the bridge. Raymond asked in enthusiasm while visually scanning the bridge, "How the heck did you do that?!"

"You can thank Sarah." Jason said while jumping into the pilot seat positioned behind the second seat. "She has a neural connection to the ship that allows her to control it remotely."

"Neural network based technology?" Izzy was intrigued. "Impressive, how did she get that kind of tech? And this ship... it truly looks amazing!"

"It's kind of a personal story their buddy so maybe we could talk about that later," Timothy said with an attitude then jumped into the copilot seat located in front of Jason's seat while looking at the smaller monitors along the sides of his station. "We got hostile bogies intercepting us on our port and starboard bow!"

"No way they could scramble fighters that fast." Jason commented while powering up the pilot display.

"Maybe there is a ship out there somewhere." Sheena suggested through the comm channel.

"Try using long range scanners." Lucas suggested.

"Yea, already on it." Jason activated the sphere monitor on the bridge so he can see what was outside the ship. When turned on, it created the illusion that the pilot and co-pilot seats where floating in the middle of space. Alpha team was becoming more intrigued by this ship's advanced features. At the same time Jason activated the long range scanners, it sent out a visible pulse that was seen traveling outward on the monitors. After two seconds of traveling outward, the pulse marked six enemy fighters inbound. Three Port side and three starboard side. They looked very similar to United Earth Military

F-93 Fighters but highly modified with unknown technology. Five seconds later the pulse detected a ship directly ahead of them. It looked three fourths the size of the Enidon with a similar ship design. "Found it, it's directly ahead of us at about five clicks."

"A Mid-Carrier from our universe?" Lucas surprised. "Who are these guys?"

"What's a Mid-Carrier?" Jason asked

"A Mid-Carrier is similar to a full Carrier except it's smaller and holds a smaller compliment of fighters, maybe between Twenty-Five to Thirty. It also has missile launchers and defensive turrets.

Gehnarne heard what Jason said about the Mid-Carrier's position and thought that position sounded familiar judging from the Red Nova's current location. *"Slinger, can you connect your Taclet to the Nova's navigation computer?"*

"Jason, Gehnarne wants me to-" Raymond asked as he was interrupted.

"Yea I heard him, the port is right there." He pointed to a connection on his pilot display. "It should be compatible with your tech."

Raymond was once again puzzled at how Jason heard what was happening on the team's secure communications. "...Uh, okay."

As Raymond knelled down to connect his Taclet, Izzy became curious as well. "Wait a second, how did you know what Gehnarne said?"

Timothy explained. "We've been monitoring your comms ever since Jason and Raymond had drinks together. Let's just say that the toast was a distraction while I hacked in."

Izzy felt insulted. "How the hell did you manage to do that?"

"It was quite simple actually," Timothy pulled out what looked similar to a Taclet but different in its manufacturing design. "My device here was set to auto decryption to hack into your secured frequencies."

Izzy felt even more insulted that someone managed to crack his communications decryption so easily. With a calm voice he tried to compliment Timothy. "Well, I guess you are as good as Gehnarne says."

"Thanks, although I have to admit, it was really not that hard I mean it was set to auto decryption so it's not like I actually had to do anything. If anything I probably could have done it even faster myself on manual if I would have known how weak the decryption protocols we-"

"Okay, kid I get it-!" Izzy lashed out at him feeling insulted.

"*Jason,*" Gehnarne interrupted over the channel. "*We got a problem, According to our navigational data compared to what we're getting from the Nova's Navigational computer, we have determined that the enemy ship is blocking your path to the universal rift.*"

"How could that ship know exactly where the Rift would be?" Kathrine asked

"*I don't know, the only way they could know that is if they had prior knowledge of it being there. Judging from the ships design and White's observation, it's not from that universe. Neither are those fighters.*"

"Figures," Jason commented. "Must be that other group working with the pirates."

"So what do we do now?" Jake asked.

"*The only thing you can do is punch through. Your objective now is to get past that ship and get to the Rift. After that I can stabilize the Rift using the beacon on our end.*"

"Wouldn't they just follow us in?" Timothy asked.

"*Our Rift control system through the beacon is designed to lock out hostiles with an IFF. If they do happen to go through that Rift, they will be destroyed the moment they reach the other side due to destabilization of the Rift.*"

"Nice." Katherine said.

"Those fighters out there will crush us before we get anywhere close to that ship." Lucas commented.

"Hey," Jason looked back at Lucas and Alpha. "Don't underestimate my ship." He said while smiling. "I have four turret guns that can be controlled on auto and manual. Since you guys are here, take manual control and destroy those fighters."

"What about that Carrier?" Izzy asked.

"Leave it to me. Just listen for when I tell you to set the guns back to auto control okay?"

"Roger that." Raymond said while disconnecting his Taclet from the Navigational computer. "Lucas, you get the bottom gun, Kat, starboard, Jake, port, I got top gun. Izzy, you stay here on the bridge and help where you can, let's move!" Alpha team stormed back through the sliding doors and down the hall to the ship's turrets.

"When you get to your turrets just press the red "Arm" button on the right side of your controls!" Timothy yelled as they ran out.

"Got it!" Raymond responded. Everyone jumped into their turret seats that were in small alcoves along the walls, floor, and ceiling of the passage way leading back to the bay where they first came aboard. When they pressed the arming buttons, the turrets automatically locked and loaded and were ready to fire.

"Unlocking throttle control, climbing to full throttle." Timothy said to Jason. "Jason, why not just use... well," He looked at Sarah while she walked to her seat on the right side of the bridge. "You know. The sooner we use her to fight, the less chance of us getting killed."

"Say what?" Izzy asked as he buckled himself into the seat on the left side of the bridge.

Sarah buckled into her seat opposite from Izzy while she looked at Jason as if she was asking permission to do something. Jason looked back at her and shook his head with a no gesture. She nodded in understanding. As Jason looked forward, "The art of war is deception Tim. I want to surprise those bastards as we just zoom right passed them while flipping them off. Make them think we're some ordinary ship with basic defensive turrets."

"Oh, I see." Timothy responded. "Sounds like a plan to me. I just hope those gunners back there are good enough to keep us alive till we reach that carrier."

"Okay, I get the deception part," Izzy spoke up, "but, can someone please explain to me what the hell your talking about with Sarah?"

"Sheesh buddy, mind your own business will ya?!" Timothy rudely snapped at Izzy as payback for him lashing out earlier.

"What!? Listen you little shi-!"

Suddenly a warning alarm went off. "We've been locked, going evasive! HANG ON!" Jason dropped throttle, jerked the controls to the left while pressing the left foot petal under his feat then engaged full throttle while pulling up on the controls slightly to the left making the ship barrel role.

"Targets acquired and locked!" Lucas reported.

"ENGAGE!" Raymond ordered while pulling the trigger as an automatic volley of red beams shot out of his turret at almost thirty shots per second immediately destroying one enemy fighter. The remaining enemy fighters fired back at the Red Nova with missiles and energy weapons similar to the Red Nova's guns. The energy beams missed due to Jason's evasive piloting, the missiles were quickly shot down by Lucas. "Nice shooting Lucas!" Raymond complimented while firing.

"Thanks brotha!" Lucas responded to Raymond holding down the trigger.

Katherine fired her turret, shooting down two of three, missing the third. "Jake, one bogie heading your way!" She yelled.

Jake sat there frozen while space spun around him as Jason continued to pull evasive maneuvers making him dizzy.

"Jake!?"

The fighter just started crossing his path.

"JAKE!?"

"Crap!" He snapped out of it and fired his weapon destroying the fighter.

"Solid shot, you alright?!" Kathrine asked while trying to engage another two incoming fighters.

"How the hell do you guys do this?! I can't focus with all the turning and spinning!" He shoots at another fighter and misses.

Raymond spoke just after destroying another fighter. "Think of it as a roller coaster ride or something!"

"Leave it to Raymond to say something like that." Katherine commented while destroying more enemy missiles.

"More fighters incoming Port side!" Lucas reported while shooting.

"Okay, okay... like a roller coaster." Jake said to himself as he got ready for the fighters to come into his line of sight while the Red Nova continued to move evasively. As soon as the fighters crossed his path, he fired just when the Red Nova maneuvered along the same path as the fighters giving Jake the perfect shot to kill all three in his sight. He continued to fire until all three of the fighters were destroyed. "Yea, that's right, get some!" Jake shouted in excitement.

Everyone on the guns laughed hearing him yell in motivation.

"Nice work Jake!" Raymond said while still engaging.

"Not bad," Jason said. "Not bad at all" He was still jerking around the controls trying to pull every maneuver he knew. "We might just survive this after all."

"More fighters inbound!" Timothy reported.

"Don't worry Tim, I think our guests can handle it."

"Yea, but we're getting pretty close to that ship now. Maybe now would be a good time to use our secret weapon?"

"And break up their fun back there? I can't do that to them." Jason joked.

"Dammit Jason!" Timothy grew aggravated.

"Okay, okay, fine. Sarah, you're up."

Sarah nodded, unbuckled herself from the chair, stood up and walked behind Jason's pilot seat.

"Oh here we go." Izzy commented in anticipation.

"Engaging Advance Neural Control now." Timothy pressed a button on his control console activating a metal beam that shot out from the floor behind Jason's seat. The Top of the beam shot out handle bars from the side as if Sarah was supposed to grab them.

"Gunners, engage auto control now!" Jason announced on the intercom to Alpha team in the back.

"Roger!" Raymond acknowledged. "Engaging auto control." All of the guns switched into auto. "Guys, stay on the guns, I'll be right back." Raymond climbed out of his seat and ran straight down the passage to the bridge.

"Where are you going?" Lucas asked.

"To see what Jason has planned next." Raymond ran through the sliding bridge doors and stopped just as he saw Sarah reaching out to the handlebars. "What the?" He said to himself as Sarah was inches away from touching the bars.

"Raymond, strap yourself in now!" Jason ordered.

Sarah grasped the handlebars sending out a powerful surge of red energy that flashed and pulsed out from her throughout the ship. "The heck is going on?!" Raymond demanded as he saw the pulse pass him along the walls of the bridge.

"Now Raymond!" Jason demanded.

"Okay!" Raymond acknowledged with a worried expression while moving to where Sarah was previously sitting and strapped himself in knowing something crazy was about to happen.

Sarah looked forward with her gold innocent eyes silently, then closed them. Her blue hair began to glow and float like water again. After a moment, her eyes snapped open full of rage with her left eye still gold but her right eye filled with a violent red glow. Her blue floating hair changed to the same violent red with a flash, then spread throughout the rest of the ship turning the white walls and the blue outer hull of the ship the same violent red. Raymond and Alpha team witnessed this in astonishment. Suddenly, Sarah spoke for the first time with a solid emotionless voice "ANC activated." She looked at the enemy carrier. "Engaging enemy target." She said as her red eye flashed. At that moment, the Red Nova boosted to an even faster speed than before beyond full throttle. Jason held on to the controls to make more precise course corrections. "Engaging weapon systems." Sarah said as the turrets snapped to the twelve o'clock position.

"The hell?!" Lucas was surprised by how the ship had changed so dramatically as we saw his turret automatically snap to the front. "Raymond, what's going on up there?!" He asked.

"It's Sarah, she's taken direct control of the ship somehow!"

"Not completely," Jason interrupted. "I'm still piloting this ship alongside her. She makes the calls based on theoretical actions while I take hands on control based on actual combat experience. Combine the two together and the real time movements become more dynamic and have faster reaction time." Jason looked right at the same time Sarah did observing a flight of three enemy fighters. Immediately Sarah reacted by making the ship flip over them while Jason targeted and fired on the enemy fighters while still in the invert, destroying all three of them just before the Red Nova completed the maneuver returning to its upright vertical position. "If it was just her controlling the ship alone, you lose the human aspect of hands on combat experience. The ship would just move around all clunky like a machine, we work together as a team to maintain the ships combat flow."

"This is genius!" Izzy said. "Who made this ship?!"

"My father." Jason said while grunting as he and Sarah pulled another maneuver. The ship went into an extremely high speed role while pulling to the right dodging and shooting incoming missiles as it fired its own set of missiles to another group of fighters. The fighters pulled evasively but failed as they were obliterated by the missiles.

"Wait, your father?" Raymond was surprised. "I thought it was the pirates who built this ship?"

"Hate to interrupt but, we got L2 missiles incoming!" Timothy interrupted.

"Launching counter measures." Sarah reported coldly.

The counter measures were launched towards the bow of the ship as the Red Nova went invert, thrusted under the counter measures as the enemy missiles impacted them, than continued its flip back into vertical and pulled up getting back on course towards the cruiser.

"Good work Sarah!" Jason complimented.

"They are not stopping us." Sarah responded in a cold tone.

"Got that right, Tim, prep the package for these dirt bags, we're almost on top of them."

"Got it!" Timothy punched in some keys on his controls.

"Package?" Raymond ask.

"Just a parting gift to cover our exit." Jason informed.

"Sounds good."

"Hostile ship is charging weapons and are preparing to fire." Timothy reported.

"Roger, okay Sarah bow shield output at max power and prepare for some serious maneuvers." Jason ordered.

"Understood." Sarah responded coldly.

"Let's show our new friends how fast we really are!" Jason said with motivation in his voice.

The four engines on the Red Nova surrounding the center engine began to expand out ward away from the ship than locked into place.

"Enhanced Evasion System active." Sarah reported coldly.

The enemy Carrier opened fired with missiles and energy turrets.

"They've opened fired! Incoming Missiles!" Timothy reported.

"Brace yourselves guys!" Jason announced on the intercom. "You're about to feel some serious G's!"

"Oh no." Jake said out loud with a worried voice.

The energy beams were meters away from the ship.

"LET'S DANCE!!!" Jason shouted as he began to jerk the controls in many different directions at once. The Red Nova's four outer engines snapped up and down literally pushing the ship in multiple different directions dodging energy beams and missiles while the fifth center engine kept the ship moving forward on course. Some of the dodging maneuvers even flipped the ship at times.

"AAAHHH!!!" Jake screamed in ectreme discomfort.

"WHAT THE FUUUUUCK!!!" Lucas felt more uncomfortable than getting hang overs.

"HOLY SHIIIIIT!?" Kathrine hated every second of this.

"HAHAHA!!!" Raymond was loving this.

"THIS IS AMAZING!" Izzy shouted.

"I always hate this part!" Timothy said grunting while bracing himself.

Sarah stared forward with a rage filled expression while Jason stayed focused and continued to maneuver the ship with Sarah's precise assistance. The Red Nova was just about to pass the enemy ship. "TIM, NOW!" Jason ordered.

"Launching package!" Timothy slammed down a button on his control console launching a pod out of the Red Nova's port side missile tube.

As the Red Nova zoomed by, the crew on the unknown hostile ship reacted in fear. They were all wearing similar gear to the armed men back at the club. They looked out the windows watching the Universal Rift open to the Red Nova. Unlike the Rift the Endeavor encountered five years ago, the stabilized Rift was clearly visible to the human eye. It looked like a black hole with a glowing blue rim but with no gravitational pull. The moment the Red Nova Entered the rift, it immediately closed. The crew of the enemy Mid-Carrier scanned out the windows and saw the pod that was left behind by the Red Nova. They became fearful thinking it was some kind of explosive device. After a moment of hesitation, the pod flashed and projected a hologram of a hand holding up the middle finger. The crew reacted in relief knowing for certain that was not some kind of bomb. After five seconds of getting flipped off by the pod, the hologram changed from the middle finger to the words saying "Bye,

Bye". The crew saw this and became shocked knowing that their initial assumption was incorrect. Suddenly there was a large explosion that cut through the ships armor severely damaging and disabling the ship.

Universe 1111 - The Red Nova
August 20th, 2238
2330 Standard Earth Time

The Red Nova zoomed out of the Rift from the other side. Alpha team was now back in universe 1111. The Enidon was waiting for them three kilometers away from the Rift.

"Tim, power down, we're clear." Jason ordered while stepping out of his seat.

"Aye, powering down." Timothy began shutting down the Red Nova's combat systems as the ships engines began to re-position to the center engine and the inner and outer hull changed back to their previous colors.

"Well that was fun." Jason said as he began to move behind Sarah.

"Sure was," Raymond responded with joy while getting out of his seat. "Glad we could help keep your ship alive."

"I appreciate it." Jason thanked Raymond while holding his arms out behind Sarah as her face was still filled with rage, her right eye and hair still glowing red with her hair floating. "Tim, deactivate ANC."

"Gotcha." Timothy flipped a switch. At that same moment Sarah's hair shot to black, her right eye went back to gold as her eyes closed while she fell backwards fainting. Jason was ready to catch her as she fell back into his arms going numb with the ANC beam descending back into the floor.

"Wo!" Raymond was concerned. "Is she okay?"

"Yea, she's just fine." Jason said in displeasure. "Believe it or not, this is normal. I think my father had plans to make disconnection a smoother transition but, that's what happens when you steal a ship that's not entirely complete." Jason looked at Sarah respectfully admiring her innocence despite what she had just participated in.

"Maybe I can help?" Izzy said while standing up from his seat.

"Trust me," Timothy said with an attitude. "I tried. As far as I know, the only person that could figure this out was his father."

"Maybe a perspective from someone else might help?" Izzy suggested earnestly.

"You really like sticking your nose into other people's business don't you?" Timothy responded rudely.

Izzy was on fire with anger. "Kid, you're really starting to piss me off you know that!"

"Both of you, Shut up!" Jason shouted. "You two haven't had the best first impressions of each other today huh?" Jason looked at Timothy angrily as he looked back in a pout.

"Raymond?" Izzy asked in concern.

"He's right Izzy." Raymond acknowledge. "Play nice, you and him are gonna be working together for now on so get used to it."

"Okay..." Izzy sighed in agreement while looking away.

"Now that's taken care of, Raymond, think you can help me bring Sarah to her room?" Jason kindly asked as Raymond gave him an awkward look. Jason chuckled at his expression. "Don't worry, all I need you to do is press a button, we can discuss some things as we go."

"Okay sure."

Jason cradled Sarah's limp body then lifted her off the ground while standing up using his legs. "Tim," He said while grunting. "Contact the Enidon and prep for docking."

"Aye, aye." Timothy responded as Jason left the bridge holding Sarah in his arms with Raymond following closely behind. Timothy than looked at Izzy. "Well?"

"Well what?" Izzy asked.

"You gonna help?"

"Oh! Sure." Izzy was happy at the chance to learn how this ship worked even though it was from someone he already disliked.

Jason carried Sarah down the hall with Raymond following as the rest of Alpha team climbed out of the turret control areas. Lucas saw what Jason was doing and was concerned. "Is she okay?" he asked.

"Yea, she's fine." Raymond responded while passing Alpha team. "We're just bringing her to her room." Alpha team stared as Jason and Raymond continuing down the hall wondering what had happened.

"Soooo..." Katherine tried to break the silence. "What do you think about this new bunch?" she asked looking at Lucas.

"I think things just got a whole lot weirder." He said turning around towards the bridge and began walking towards it.

"Okay... How about you Jake?" She asked.

In a frightened voice. "I never want to do that shit again..." He said while also walking towards the bridge.

"Puh, men." She said as she began walking towards the bridge herself.

Jason and Raymond were in the cargo bay where they initially entered the ship with doors encircling the bay along the walls. "I'm assuming one of these doors is her room?" Raymond asked Jason.

"Yea that third one on the right."

"Okay, so earlier you said your father built this ship, I thought you stole it from the pirates?"

"I did, think you can press that button on the right there?" Jason asked just as they reached the front door to Sarah's quarters.

"Sure." Raymond pressed the button making the door to the left of it slide open. Jason carefully moved into the room trying not to bump Sarah's head on anything.

"Thanks, So, the pirates kidnapped my father, he was a renowned ship builder that was forced to build many ships like this." The room was very small, barely able to fit the three of them. Sarah's bed was against the wall on the right. "This was the last one he made, and the most powerful." He grunted as he bore Sarah's full weight on his arms carefully laying her down on the bed facing towards the wall in a resting position. She laid there peacefully as Jason took a seat at the end of the bed.

"What happened to your father?" Raymond asked while leaning against the wall facing Jason.

Jason looked at Sarah for a moment as he remembered what happen to his father than looked away from her. "The Pirates killed him."

"Oh... I'm sorry."

"It's okay," He said looking at Raymond. "They killed him after he finished building this ship. This was their ultimate goal, to build the most powerful combat star ship ever conceived. He hid this ship away in an asteroid field without them knowing, ruining their plans. He sent me the coordinates to that asteroid field hoping I would find it."

"Why you?"

"At the time I was a part of the Krelis's Imperial Navy."

"Krelis?" Raymond was curious.

"Yea, the home world of my universe's humans. Last time I saw Gehnarne, a couple of years back, he told me your humans come from a similar planet from your universe called Earth?"

"Yes." Raymond was even more intrigued. "Would you mind sharing data on your universe's history?"

"Sure, I can transfer this ships archival records to the Enidon. You can transfer your universe's history to my ship as well if you'd like, I'm up for learning more about your people."

"Sure, that would be great." Raymond smiled than continued where they left off. "So your father contacted you while you were still in the Imperial Navy?"

"Yes. I was a pilot, one of the best. When I received the coordinates I took a leave of absence and tracked down the ship. However, I was being tracked that whole time. You see, the Krelis Empire knew who my father was and how much of a threat he could be if his expertise fell into the wrong hands so when they saw me leave, they knew this was out of the ordinary. I made it to the location, found this ship and another message from my father. He warned me that the pirates will start to look for me and to also not trust the Empire."

"Why not?"

"He feared they would want to use this ship to their own gain. Enforce their will on whoever would threaten their government. The moment I finished the message the Pirates and the Empire found me but, they were so busy with fighting each other, I slipped past them. After escaping I searched the ship and saw a stasis pod in the cargo bay. That's how me and Sarah met. My father stored her in there with a message saying that she was very important to the ship and to keep her safe. So that's what I did. After that I traveled off the grid as best I could as a mercenary. Been that way ever since."

"I see. So, what's up with Tim?"

Jason laughed. "Tim was a stow away. I landed on a station to refuel my ship when he snuck aboard. If he didn't prove how smart he was and how much Sarah liked him, I would have given him the boot a long time ago."

"Mhm, speaking of Sarah," Raymond said while looking at her. "She's not much of a talker unless in combat huh?"

"Yea, there's a reason for that."

"What happened?"

Jason hesitated to say. "She..." He mournfully looked at her. "She went through a lot. you see that small tattoo on the back of her neck?"

Raymond looked at Sarah's neck more closely. He saw a very small square of numbers and dots like some kind of coding. "Oh man, that's not what I think it is, is it?"

"Yea, it is, a slave brand. She was involved in human trafficking against her will, not sure how long she was there for, I'm not even sure how old she is. I guess she stood out in some way leading the pirates to buy her for their sick experiments with neural networking technology in an attempt to create a neural connection with the ship. My father made a deal with the pirates that he would only work on the ship if she was with him at all times. He did that to protect her from any sexual deviants among the pirates. He saved her life."

"I can't believe they do something like that to such an innocent girl... our universe eliminated human trafficking a long time ago,"

"How was that possible?" Jason asked in curiously.

Raymond looked at Jason firmly, "With extreme prejudice, we have zero tolerance for sick crap like that. The council, the leaders in my universe, sent out a kill order on all buyers and sellers of human slaves. Probably one of the few decisions I actually agree with them on."

"Damn," Jason chuckled. "That's zero tolerance all right. From what you've probably noticed, she has no tolerance for that either. Her rage towards what happen to her is unleashed in combat. A side effect not even the Pirates expected. Goes to show how much they really knew about this shit. Like kids playing with fire, I swear." Jason sighed with anger towards his feelings about the pirates.

"Well, makes sense now why that ANC thing you guys use isn't complete."

"Yea, with all my father had to do to hide her and the ship, he never had a chance to complete the process. As for why she doesn't talk, at first I thought there was something physically wrong with her brain due to the experiments. However, after bringing her to many different underground doctors, they all said that despite the obvious signs of tampering, her brain was functioning normally... they believe her silence is due to her dramatic experiences, not a physical ailment."

"Man..." Raymond began to pity Sarah.

Timothy called on the intercom. "Jason, Raymond, We're about to land in hanger one of the Enidon."

"Want to see it?" Raymond asked.

"Of course." Jason responded walking to the door.

Raymond stopped at the door and looked back at Sarah. "Will she be okay like that?"

"She'll be fine, she just needs some rest." Jason responded while closing the door.

Sarah laid in bed with her eyes closed while her hair slowly began to change from black too blue. Her eyes opened as she became aware of what had happened. In that moment she began to cry feeling bad that she had to unleash her rage again, calmly sobbing in isolation.

Jason and Raymond walked through the cargo bay towards the hall. "So how did you meet Gehnarne?" Raymond asked.

"At one point in our travels the Empire found me. He personally gave me a heads up on a ship that was sent out to get me. For those few weeks he helped and told me he was looking for a pilot that could help him with his organization. At first I refused but after seeing the kind of man he was, I figured I'd give it a shot. He wasn't a pirate or a dictator so why not right? Unfortunately, due to my situation I couldn't join right away but, I'm here now right?" They reached the passage way and continued on towards the bridge. "How about you?"

Raymond laughed a little. "He found me at a very strange time in my universes history. We were just starting to wrap up a war."

"That does sound interesting."

"Yea, he probably bailed me out of a possible court martial too."

Jason chuckled. "Sounds like you're a trouble maker like me."

Raymond mildly laughed. "Something like that. That's just what happens when your military's moral values get thrown out the window." As they entered through the bridge sliding doors, they saw the Enidon in front of the pilot seats on the spherical monitor. Alpha team was looking at the monitor's front watching as the Red Nova got closer.

"Good timing," Lucas said. "We were half way through final approach."

"Tim, give us a real eye's view will ya?" Jason ordered.

"Got it." Timothy pressed a button on his control console. Shortly after the Spherical monitor turned off and began to slide apart down the center in front of the pilot seats. Behind the separating monitor was a spherical window that gave the bridge a clear view outside. The Enidon was in front of the Red Nova as it moved closer to the Enidons hanger on its starboard side.

"Beautiful huh?" Raymond asked Jason.

"Very." Jason said. "Can't wait to see the rest of her."

Chapter 10: Debrief

The Red Nova entered the hanger slowly penetrating the shield covering the entrance. Once inside, the landing gear extended as the ship slowly descended to the floor than touched down softly. Once settled, a ramp extended out from the cargo bay of the ship to the bow. As it extended, Alpha team and the Red Nova crew walked down the ramp. Sarah was behind everyone walking faster trying to catch up. Once caught up, Jason noticed her. "Oh! Sarah, your awake." He was happy she felt better.

Sarah looked at him and nodded.

"Glad you're up." He said as they continued to walk beside each other.

As they walked down the Ramp, Gia entered the hanger walking towards the Red Nova to greet them. She stopped and smiled as she greeted. "Welcome aboard the Enidon. I'll be escorting you to the TOC for a debrief."

"Got it." Raymond acknowledge.

"Is Gehnarne there?" Jason asked.

"Yes, he'll be at the debrief as well." Gia responded

"Alright, let's go." He said to his crew as the group followed Gia to the TOC. While proceeding to the bridge, the Red Nova crew looked around astonished at how advanced and roomy the Enidon was on the inside. They asked Gia questions about the ships specs, weapons, crew, and much more.

Once the elevator reached the bridge, the doors slid open as Alpha team and the Red Nova crew walked onto the bridge. "Gehnarne is in the Captains seat," Gia said while staying in the elevator. "You can just report to him, I have some work to attend to." She said while smiling as the elevator doors slid closed.

The group walked towards Gehnarne with Raymond taking the lead. "Gehnarne," Raymond said. "Alpha team reporting to the TOC for debrief."

"Good, good." Gehnarne responded. "I'll meet you guys back there in a moment."

"Gehnarne!" Jason said loudly. "It's good to see you again!"

Gehnarne happily reacted as he turned to face him. "Jason!" he got out of the Captain's chair and approached him. "It's been to long, how are you!?"

"Seen better days," He hugged Gehnarne than let go. "but hanging in there."

"Glad to hear." He looked right and saw Timothy. "Little Timothy, you sure have grown."

"Yea, yea, just please don't call me little." He said in embarrassment.

"Hey, don't grow up to fast kid."

Timothy whispered to himself. "Kinda late for that..."

Gehnarne looked and walked towards Sarah. "And Sarah."

She lightly bowed her head in greeting.

Gehnarne chuckled "Still the quiet type huh?"

Sarah made a sad face as she looked back up towards him.

Gehnarne felt bad and placed his hand on her shoulder. "It's okay, you're with us now."

She smiled back in response.

"Alright, let's get in on this debrief." Gehnarne said as the group walked into the TOC. As Raymond entered he saw Sheena and smiled at her. She smiled back, walked up to him and stood by his side holding his hand. Sarah noticed this and seemed curious.

"I'm gonna patch in Yabin on the monitor." Raymond said as he pulled up the communications app on his Taclet and selected Yabin in his contacts list. "We have a lot to share with him."

Yabin answered the call. "Is this line secure?" He asked.

"Yes, it is." Raymond said. "Good to see you again Yabin."

"Like wise." He looked at Lucas. "Lucas." He greeted.

"Yabin." Lucas greeted back with no emotion.

"So, what do you guys have for me? How did the mission go?"

Gehnarne stepped forward. "The mission went well but there were many unexpected factors. Ones that we think might link with the intel you have on Carnivore. Raymond?"

Raymond stepped forward. "Here is footage from my perspective of the mission." He plugged his Taclet into the TOC table, uploaded the footage taken from his contact's camera and skipped to when he met Asrin. "As you can see, Asrin has a flow system like I do. It was configured differently but it is the same technology. Also," Raymond fast forward. "After defeating Asrin, an unknown group of combatants came to the club to stop us just before we left," Footage of the unknown group of armed men storming out of the armored vehicle outside the club played. "Lastly," He fast forward again. "A heavily modified Mid-Carrier with modified F-93's attacked us while moving the Red Nova to the Universal Rift. The ship attempted to block our exit as if they already knew where the Rift was located."

"I see," Yabin analyzed, "Those fighters and that ship must have been Carnivore. Were there any identifying marks on that ship or fighters?"

"Negative," Raymond confirmed. "They were completely clean."

"So we can't say for sure than. About that other Flow System, can you confirm it was actually a flow system similar to yours?"

"Yes." Izzy said as he placed the flow module on the table. "This is Asrin's flow module. It's an almost identical design to Raymond's before I created the Flow System app for his Taclet."

"I see," Yabin was intrigued

"Has there been anything from Carnivore that could tell us how these pirates got this technology?" Gehnarne asked.

"Not exactly however, that next day after Raymond saw me, my sources reported back that they lost track of another one of Carnivore's shipments. This shipment was quite small unlike that jamming device and turrets so I didn't think much of it. Seeing how small these flow modules are... I think I need to rethink my strategy on what to track."

"You think that small shipment was the flow system Asrin used?" Jake asked.

"Can't say for sure but with all this Intel, it's highly probable."

"I see," Gehnarne said. "Thank you Yabin. From now on inform us immediately if another shipment connected to Carnivore go's missing no matter how big or small."

"With that said," Yabin interrupted Gehnarne. "I just received word this morning that another shipment about the same size as the previous one went missing. I'm gonna try to have my sources track these shipments in more detail for now on but assuming that Carnivore is selling this stuff to people in other universes, I'm gonna need access to some of your technological resources related to the rifts."

Gehnarne seemed disappointed. "I'm sorry Yabin but our

technology hasn't reached a level of open access yet. Your gonna have to try the best you can for now."

"I understand."

Gehnarne smiled. "Thanks for the help Yabin. Keep doing your best."

"Thank you, Yabin out." Yabin disconnect from communications.

"Okay," Gehnarne turned towards Alpha team and the Red Nova Crew. "let's piece this together. So judging from Yabin's intel, it seems that this flow system was the first missing shipment and most likely the second missing shipment is another flow system, under the circumstances, we're gonna have to develop a counter measure for the possibility of another flow system being out there."

"We already have one," Raymond smiled. "The only thing that was able to penetrate Asrin's configuration was his sword, I can add my German Long Sword to my load out as a contingency. Like Izzy said during the fight, the only way to penetrate through the gravity field effectively is with an object in a constant state of thrust. Luckily for me I trained in German long sword fighting so hopefully that helps."

"Good idea." Gehnarne complimented.

"What I don't understand is why would Carnivore be doing this?" Jake questioned. "You would think we did something to piss them off in the first place or something."

"Even better question," Izzy jumped in, "How the hell did they get the design to the flow system? Spy's maybe?"

"Izzy, I had you work on the flow system in another universe for those exact reasons despite the dangers," Gehnarne said. "I highly doubt it was a spy."

"I'm sure more will be revealed in time." Raymond said. "But we should focus on our current objective."

"Right," Gehnarne agreed. "Speaking of our current objective, we are now ready to go beyond the boarder to the unreached worlds. Our long range observers on Croza recently launched a probe to this new world in preparation for this expedition. Our first planet is a highly habitable world with lots of vegetation, wild life, and water sources. So far no intelligent life has been reported. At FTL nine we should be there in six days."

"Sounds interesting," Katherine said. "Could use a break from combat missions."

"I figured you'd say as much." Gehnarne responded. "With that said, your dismissed. Gia," Gehnarne called Gia on the ships internal communications. "Could you please show the Red Nova crew to their quarters?"

"*On the way.*" Gia responded.

"See you Alpha," Gehnarne said as alpha team began to leave the bridge. "Jason, you and your crew can stay here till Gia arrives."

"Thanks." Jason said. Everyone walked out of the TOC to the bridge.

As Alpha team left the bridge, Sheena walked beside Raymond. After walking a few feet down the hall, Sheena nudged Raymond to the side. "What's wrong?" He asked.

"We need to talk." Sheena seemed very concerned.

"Okay." Raymond was curious to what Sheena wanted to talk about. The rest of Alpha kept moving while Sheena and Raymond talked privately in the hall. "What's up?" He asked.

"It's about your last mission,"

"What about it?"

"I don't want to sound like I'm judging you but... don't you think what you did to Asrin and his men was... too extreme?"

"Like what exactly?"

"Like Cutting his head off... I mean using a sword okay, you had to because of the flow system but the head cutting off thing... He was already dead. And those comments you made about the afterlife and remember who killed them? What was that all about? It just seemed so unnecessary and extreme that's all."

Raymond thought back at those moments feeling a ping of guilt. "Yea... your right. I didn't think about what was too much or too little, I just did. That was extreme of me though... sorry."

"You don't have to apologize it's just that I'm worried about you. When I saw what you did to those pirates it reminded me of that time when-"

"When I shot that unarmed rebel through the window... Yea... It did kinda remind me of that too but... this was different, those pirates had every intent to kill us."

"Trust me, I understand... Just... Be careful with this flow system okay, you're a good man Raymond, I just don't want this power to change you."

Raymond felt comfort knowing that Sheena thought of him as a good person "Thanks Sheena." He hugged her in reassurance "You have nothing to worry about, I promise." He backed away from the hug and smiled at her looking into her eyes. She looked at his feeling reassured and smiled back.

"Okay." She said while moving closer to him and kissed.

Sarah was nearby around the corner watching them in secret as they kissed. She couldn't help but wonder what that meant and what they were doing. However, she knew it meant something special between Sheena and Raymond. The same way she felt that Jason was special to her but wasn't sure how to express those feelings to him. As Raymond and Sheena stopped kissing, they walked away holding hands. Sarah looked at her own hand realizing she had held Jason's hands many times before in the past. Could that have meant some kind of sign of affection this whole time and never realized it? She began to blush at the thought as she was interrupted.

"Sarah?" Jason called from behind her as she quickly turned around in surprise. She suddenly felt embarrassed. "Why are you spying on them?" Jason asked with a chuckle.

Suddenly Sarah's face turned red as she blushed even harder in embarrassment looking away from Jason.

Jason laughed. "It's okay, I don't think our new friends would mind if you were a little curious about them."

Sarah looked back at Jason as her face went back to a normal skin color.

"Come on, Gia wants to show us to our quarters." Jason turned away and began walking back into the bridge. Sarah paused and thought for a moment at what she saw from Raymond and Sheena. She knew how she felt about Jason but felt that now wasn't the time to express those feelings yet. "Sarah? Come on." Jason called her again. That time she ran to catch up and followed him.

Chapter 11: Down Time

Three days later, Katherine decided to take a walk through the ship. Her first stop was R&D, Izzy's department of expertise. She walked through the sliding door wearing her camouflage uniform as she looked around observing a large bay with smaller rooms and offices along the walls. Many people were walking about conducting tasks as others repaired and worked on current and new technology. "Wow," She said to herself in astonishment.

Izzy was walking toward Katherine looking down at his tablet reading his notes. He wore a white lab coat with jeans, and a blue t-shirt. He looked up from his tablet for a moment quickly noticing her. "Katherine?"

"Izzy, hi." She responded politely with a smile.

"Hey, is there something I could do for you?" he asked politely.

"Well, I was just exploring around the ship a little more. Gia took us here briefly for the tour but didn't get too detailed on what you guys are working on here."

"Ah, I see. Well, as you know, we are working around the clock to advance our technology for our organization."

"Okay, is there anything in particular your working on now?"

"Yes actually, here I'll show you, follow me." Izzy walked towards one of the offices along the wall in excitement. They both walked through the doorway as Katherine observed what looked like a giant metallic ball with a pointed cone on one end, and connections along the surface of the ball. "Here it is."

"What is it?"

"It's a Mark II Beacon. It works the same way as the Beacons we already have deployed near the rifts for the universes we have discovered so far, except it doesn't just teleport personnel through the UTS on board our ship, it can also teleport entire ships. Here, let me show you a simulation."

"Okay." Katherine was curious to see how it worked. She followed Izzy to a small computer in the corner of the room as he opened the simulation file.

A video of the Enidon flying through virtual space was displayed on the screen. Izzy began to explain as the video played. "So this whole time in order to bring a ship from one universe to another, you need to find the Universal Rift, use a Beacon to open it and presto, you just go through." The video mimicked the actions that Izzy described. "The problem here is, what if the universe your trying to reach is only accessible through a rift that's hundreds of light years away from your current position? You'll have to travel for days to get to that Rift in order to get to your final destination. The Mark II Beacon makes this process easier by actually teleporting the ship from that beacon at that ship's current location to another beacon light years away." The video showed a new simulation mimicking what he was explaining. "We can even tell that beacon at that ship's current location to send that ship immediately through that other beacon's rift the moment that ship arrives so they won't even have to fly through the rift. The ship will just be sent to that other universe instantly." The simulation ended in the video as he finished explaining.

"That's amazing!" Katherine complimented. "This technology could change space travel as we know it!"

"Thank Gehnarne for that, he's the one who gave me the plans on how to build these things. He said that him and the council assigned scientists to help make the first beacon models during their initial experiments with the Rifts. This Mark II is just a prototype still in its experimental phase however, the complete version should be finished within the year or so. Than we can mass produce them."

"Awesome," She said while turning towards Izzy. "You and your team are really getting things done quickly."

"Of course, we are way ahead of schedule." Izzy said while he began to turn towards her. "Our mission here is very-" as he turned he noticed she was looking at him first in a flirtatious manner. He suddenly became nervous. "...Important."

"Yea," She said as she continued to look into his eyes. "It is." Izzy and Katherine paused while looking at each other for a moment. Than Katherine felt awkward and tried to break the silence. "So, how does a combat specialist like yourself go from stacking body's to becoming an engineer?"

"A lot of schooling." Izzy responded with a chuckle. "A part of me was starting to think that retaliation and conflict on an equal level wasn't fixing our world, it was making it worse. So I redirected my focus into engineering science to create technology to give my government an edge. To create things no one else had. Unfortunately, just as I finished my schooling at some of the best engineering schools, the Anarchists had committed to a full scale rebellion that threw our universe into chaos. We had to end this once and for all, and I knew I had the smarts to do it thanks to my technological expertise and my Grandfathers inspiration."

"What was he like?" Katherine asked.

"He was a great man, one of the best scientific minds of his generation. He taught me everything he knew." Izzy suddenly grew sad. "Then one day, I found him dead..."

"What?" Katherine was surprised. "What happened?"

"According to the investigation, someone shot him with my PR38, almost as if someone was trying to frame me for murder. You see, each PR38 has a specific pulse frequency. The wound patterns matched the frequency of my PR38, that's how the investigators knew it was mine. I haven't seen it in years after that. If it wasn't for the rise of the anarchists, I could have been in prison right now for a crime I didn't commit." Izzy looked at Katherine as she grew sad from the story. "Oh, I'm Sorry, didn't mean to upset you with that story." Izzy smiled at Katherine.

"No, it's okay. I guess I was just concerned about you." She responded in a smile.

Izzy was beginning to like Katherine with every moment he spent with her. He decided to muster up the courage and asked her a question. "Katherine, I'm sorry if this may seem awkward but I was wondering if maybe you and I could have lu-" Suddenly Izzy was interrupted as Sheena walked through the doors of the room. "Oh! Miss Vial!" Izzy acknowledge her presence.

Immediately Katherine felt annoyed by Sheena's interruption knowing how close Izzy was to asking her out on some kind of date.

Sheena responded to Izzy while politely smiling. "Please Izzy, you can just call me Sheena."

Izzy still felt a bit off guard. "Uh, yes, of course! Can I help you with something?" He asked her as he walked away from Katherine.

"Actually yes," Sheena responded. "But first I need to talk to Katherine?" Katherine was surprised as she wondered what Sheena needed to talk to her about.

"Of course," Izzy responded, "I can wait, I'm here all day."

"Thanks, Katherine?"

"Sure, coming." Katherine said with an annoyed tone. "We'll talk later okay Izzy?" she politely remarked while smiling at him.

"Of course, have a great day." Izzy smiled back.

Katherine and Sheena left the room as Izzy got back to work. They walked out of the R&D lab, moved off to the side of the entrance then began to talk.

"Sheena," Katherine started in an annoyed fashion. "Do you not realize how close he was to asking me out?"

"I'm sure he was close but since we're on the topic, what about Jake?

"Jake? What about him?"

Sheena made an implied facial expression towards Katherine.

"Oh come on, we're just friends."

"Your telling me you haven't noticed his advances over the past couple of years?" Sheena responded.

"Oh I've noticed, I just don't look at him as more than a friend that's all."

"Yet your willing to date jerks that whole time you friend zoned him?"

"Ugh," Katherine was getting aggravated. "You had to bring that up.

"Someone had to, I mean you have a perfectly good guy standing right in front of you for years and you pick someone you just recently met? I mean, Izzy is a good guy, he's part of our team now but still, why him and not Jake."

"Have you seen the way Jake has been acting lately? Like some hotshot asking if my date had any female friends he could take out? It's a total turn off. I'll admit, there was a time that I had feelings for him but then he seemed to have changed at some point, I don't know."

"Have you ever thought that maybe he changed to try to impress you?"

"Yea, I figured that, but that was the biggest part of the turn off. He shouldn't have had to change himself just to get to me, I liked him for who he was. Maybe it wasn't right for me to choose all those jerks over him but, him changing jeopardized his integrity to me and I don't know if I could trust that sort of mentality in a relationship. Hell, at this point... I don't know if I can trust myself with being in a relationship after what I did..."

"What are you talking about?" Sheena was curios. "What did you do?"

"I..." Katherine debated in her head whether to tell Sheena what she did or not. "I'm sorry Sheena... I can't talk about it... not yet at least."

"Okay." Sheena moved close to Katherine and gave her a hug "If you ever want to talk about it, I'm here."

"I know." Katherine smiled and hugged her back. "Thanks."

"Anytime." They moved away from each other. "I should get back in there, Izzy's probably wondering why I'm taking so long."

"Yea, I should go too."

"I'll talk to you later." Sheena said as she moved through the R&D Lab doors.

"See ya." Katherine looked away from Sheena and walked down the hall ready to see more details of the ship she missed during the grand tour. After they parted, Jake came out from around the corner of the hall next to the R&D lab entrance wearing his camouflage uniform. He seemed concerned after just eavesdropping on what happened between Sheena and Katherine. He always cared about Katherine romantically but never realized she felt the same way at any point during their friendship. Now he felt it was too late to fix things. He walked away pondering as to how he could fix this and was also concerned about what Katherine was hiding that she didn't want to tell Sheena.

Sheena walked back into the room where she had left Izzy. "Hey, sorry about that."

"It's fine Miss Via-" Izzy stopped himself. "I mean Sheena. So what did you need?"

"Well, I was wondering if you had any other Flow system models available? You see, I have been training with Raymond and I thought it would make more sense to have one of my own, If there is one available of course."

"Well I have been building another one but it's not complete yet and this is supposed to be the one I'm handing off to my government."

"I see." Sheena looked disappointed.

"I'll tell you what, when it's complete, I'll let you run the final checks on it before I send it to my home universe, then I'll build another specifically just for you. What do you think?"

Sheena smiled "Yes, that would be great, Thank you."

"Your welcome, just make sure you explain to Raymond about our arrangement. I initially told him he would conduct the final checks on this one but there was no way I could resist you asking."

Sheena laughed. "Don't worry, if it's me, he won't mind at all."

"Good," Izzy smiled. "Oh, and could you do me a favor aswell?"

"Sure, what's up?"

"I've been making some modifications to Raymond's flow system ever since we came back from universe 1211. I was wondering if you could give it back to him for me?"

"What kind of modifications?" Sheena was curious

"Well, I was very intrigued by the Red Nova's special ability's. More specifically how Sarah can affect the ship in such a way. After..." Izzy annoyingly hesitated. "kindly asking for Tim and Jason's permission to look at Jason's father's research, I found a way to integrate a similar combat mode into the flow system."

"You and Tim playing nice?" Sheena chuckled. "This must be good."

"Don't get me started..." displeased. "Anyway, this new mode for the Flow System is very impressive. I simply call it... Rage Mode."

"Rage Mode?" Sheena was concerned.

"Yes, you see, what we witnessed on the Red Nova was Sarah's inner rage being expressed through the ship in combat. The ship was faster, more powerful, and overall deadlier. She was able to do this because of her neural implants, however, with the flow system we can do the same thing by using the magnetic gravity field to sense the users stress levels. Kinda like one of those mood stones this universe used a hundred years ago except it's actually designed to sense your emotional state."

Sheena started having flashbacks to when Raymond mercilessly killed the unarmed rebel in the past and how he viciously killed Asrin and his men on the last mission. This Rage Mode made her deeply concerned "Izzy, is this safe? I mean... what if the user... Raymond, losses control?"

"Ah, I understand your concern. Well, the Rage Mode is designed to unleash the full energy of one's rage and turn it into action, however, it does not deny the user control over the flow system when activated. With that said, it is still up to the user's free will on how to use or concentrate that energy from that inner rage. If Raymond is a strong willed and disciplined warrior, he should be fine. It's all up to his free will like it's always been."

"I see..." Sheena's worry dwindled to an extent. "Okay, I'll bring it to him."

"Thanks." Izzy smiled as he grabbed a sealed case on his desk, walked towards Sheena and handed her the case. As Sheena reached for the case and grabbed it, Izzy continued, "Don't worry about Raymond, he'll be fine with this new tech, I know it." He smiled at her in reassurance.

Sheena smiled back. "Thanks Izzy"

"Your welcome, I better get back to work." Izzy turned around and walked towards the Mark II Beacon. "Say hello to Raymond for me okay."

"I will, bye Izzy." She turned around and went out the door with the Flow System safely stowed in the sealed case.

Later that night in Alpha team's quarters, Raymond was sitting on the couch in the living area in front of the holovision monitor wearing his multi-camouflage uniform without his jacket exposing his tan compression t-shirt. He had just finished cleaning his AR30 and began to perform a functions check when Jake walked in through the main door. "Hey Jake." Raymond looked at him walking through the door. His posture seemed more slouched than his usual prideful stance. Raymond could tell something was wrong. "You okay?"

"Yea... I guess." He said with no confidence walking towards the kitchen.

Raymond knew him too well. "Come on man, pull up a seat, what's up?"

Jake grabbed a beer from the refrigerator than took a seat at the kitchen table facing Raymond. "It's Katherine." Jake answered. He popped the cap open on his beer then took a drink.

"What's up with her this time?" Raymond asked with a chuckle as he leaned back and relaxed on the couch looking at Jake.

"You know how she's had me friend zoned for the longest right?" Raymond nodded. "I'll admit; I was never really sure how to get her attention as more than a friend and... now I realize my newest strategy just made me look like a jerk, she's totally not into me anymore. She used to be but... I ruined it." He took another swig as he just remembered the detail of Katherine not wanting to tell Sheena something, but decided not to tell Raymond out of loving respect for her.

"Dude, I told you acting like that wouldn't work, you should have just kept being yourself."

"Yea your right man, I was never really good at this crap. I can patch up gunshot wounds but I can't talk to a woman, weird huh?" He sipped on his beer again.

"Tell me about, it took me and Sheena a while before we started becoming friends."

"Right, I remember. She hated your guts thinking you were some naive idiot and you thought she was some feminazi trying to prove that woman are better than men. It's crazy how things can turn around so unexpectedly." He took another drink of his beer.

"Yea, once she found out about my past with my parents she started to understand me better, and when I found out she was just trying to prove herself under her father's shadow I started to understand her better as well. From there things just got better and we started to jell in unexpected ways. After that experience I realized that half of this stuff is about pushing your pride and arrogance aside and just choosing to try and understand where the other person is coming from."

"I see."

"Just a word of advice though, until the day you and Katherine get together, if you ever get together, you should guard your heart man."

"What's that supposed to mean?" Jake asked.

"It means care and be kind but, don't allow yourself to care too much. Hold back a little, your still just technically friends at the end of the day. The more you put your heart into it, the worse it's gonna hurt if she denies you."

"You got a point." He sipped again. "Where did you get that from anyway?"

"I..." The words Raymond had spoken earlier just flowed out of his mouth as if he said them a million times over. But for some odd reason he couldn't seem to remember where he got them from. "...I don't know."

"Well, wherever you got that from, must have been one heck of a good book."

As soon as Jake mentioned a book, Raymond suddenly remembered where he got the advice from. Proverbs 4:23, The Holy Bible. He was surprised that he remembered such a detail although he had lost his faith in such things. "Yea..." He responded to Jake nervously. "It was..." He shook the thought out of his mind. "Say, what were you doing down there at R&D anyway?"

"Well," Jake placed his beer on the table, took out his Taclet and showed Raymond an image on the screen. "I wanted to show this to Izzy." The image was an insignia with a silver sword piercing through a gold infinity symbol all surrounded by a blue circle. "It's an idea I had for our new organization's insignia, I feel like it's missing something though, I thought Izzy may be able to help with this since he's head of R&D."

"Looks cool Jake but your right, something is missing... You wanted Izzy's advice on that? I thought you hated him?"

"I don't hate, we all know he's a good guy-"

"But you are jealous-."

"Oh would you look at that!" Jake chuckled nervously while looking at his Taclet trying to interrupt Raymond to avoid talking about his feelings. "It's time for chow."

"Already?" Raymond checked his Taclet's clock. "Man, the day flew by. I'll get Lucas."

"Okay." Jake took one last swig of his beer than threw the empty bottle in the garbage pail as he walked towards the exit. "See you guys down there."

"Alright, See ya." Raymond responded getting up from the couch while grabbing his multi-camouflage jacket than walked towards the front door of Lucas's room as he put on the jacket. He stopped at the door than knocked three times. "Lucas?" Raymond called.

Surprised, Lucas immediately minimized the communications window on his Taclet and almost jumped out of his bed. "Who is it?"

"It's Raymond. Chow time, you coming?"

"Yea sure, I'll meet you guys down there in a few."

"Okay, don't take too long now."

Hearing Raymond's footsteps moving away from the door, Lucas sighed in relief as he enlarged the communications window on his Taclet with his camouflage uniform on with no top exposing his tan compression t-shirt. He was talking to Yabin privately before Raymond interrupted. "So how much longer till your people finish hacking into the personnel files?"

"We're already in the servers, however, there might be some errors due to the incomplete encryption keys, this was a pretty hasty hack after all. We managed to extract most of the information if you want to view some of it now?"

"Sure, just send it to my-"

"Wait," Yabin interrupted. "Don't jump to conclusions after you finish reading this okay? I know how you feel about secrets and I get it, but not all secrets get people killed."

Lucas grew aggravated at Yabin's statement but kept it in check. With an Attitude Lucas said, "Noted, now send the file to my email."

Yabin was saddened by Lucas's reaction. "Okay kid, I'm sending it to you now, standby." Yabin typed on his computer. "Check mail."

A new email notification popped up on Lucas's Taclet. "Good mail." Lucas acknowledged.

"Okay, the rest of it will come in later tonight."

"Alright." Lucas said as he was about to cut communications with Yabin.

"Lucas," Lucas stopped and looked at Yabin. "We, uh... really should talk."

"I didn't call to talk, all I wanted were those files. Thanks for doing this but, we have nothing more to talk about."

"Luca-" Yabin was cut off.

Back on earth, Yabin was in his home office sitting at his desk with his computer's Holo Monitor saying "Transmission Terminated". Yabin was disappointed. He sighed as he looked left and saw a picture of his younger self and Lucas's father David next to each other wearing advanced combat gear holding the flag of the first colonial rebellion like a trophy. The picture was taken during Operation Valhalla, the first full engagement against Rebel Forces on the planet Shauno. Yabin remembered the days they fought side by side to help bring order back to Shauno's government. This was before David Walker became a pastor. "I'm sorry my old friend," He said taking the picture in his hands. "I tried the best I could...".

Back on the Enidon, Lucas ended the call with Yabin than selected the Email App on his Taclet. He opened the Email Yabin had sent him and immediately began to read the information attached to it. Like Yabin stated, there were errors in the files. However, Lucas was able to make due with what wasn't jumbled in code fragments. "..... What the hell?" Lucas was surprised as he stopped to think of the complexity of the attachment he just read. As he continued reading he spoke to himself in astonishment. "He's been lying to us this whole time..."

When the colony on planet Shauno began an armed rebellion against

it's own colonial government, the UEM had stepped in. Naval forces

blockaded the planet and deployed Marine and Air forces to maintain

order. Once planet side however, things quickly changed from a

peace keeping mission to a combat operation. My team of SEALs in

close cooperation with a team of Delta operators as part of a new

JSOC initiative that would later be called the USOD were sent to kill

or capture key rebel leaders. Our operations were successful however,

as our actions got bolder, other rebel factions on other planets began

to grow in power and became more aggressive. Soon enough, the

fires of rebellion spread like wild fire through out the colonies. This

marked the beginning of The Colonial Wars.

Chapter 12: Planet Side

Three days after Lucas's discovery, The Enidon reached its first planet to explore beyond the border of the unreached worlds. The Enidon entered orbit as the away team, commanded by Raymond, was sent down to the surface on the Red Nova. The away team consisted of Lucas, Katherine, and Jake. Sheena and Izzy stayed aboard the Enidon for tactical and technical support. As advised by Lucas, Raymond had his team equipped for combat just in case Rebels could have ventured beyond Croza to this world. He also brought his newly modified Flow System gauntlets and his German Long Sword. He planned to use the sword as an enemy Flow System user contingency. The sheathed sword was tide tightly to the left side of Raymond's waist on a tactical belt by the scabbard.

The Red Nova vibrated harshly as it broke through the planet's atmosphere. "So we go in, drop them off, get to low orbit, and wait?" Timothy said to Jason on the bridge. "Well this is gonna be exciting." Sarcastically expressing himself while rolling his eyes.

"Enjoy it while it lasts Tim," Jason responded. "You never know when crap will suddenly hit the fan."

"Yea yea, sure, just wake me up when the mission is over." Timothy said as he leaned back in his co-pilot seat closing his eyes.

"Seriously Tim?" Jason said to himself as Sarah giggled while monitoring the ships status on her screen to Jason's left. When Jason heard Sarah giggle, he was surprised and looked at her. "Huh? never heard you laugh before." He said with a surprised expression. Sarah looked back at him equally surprised as she began to blush than immediately turned back to her screen seemingly working faster trying to hide her face. "Man I got the weirdest crew." Jason commented looking forward.

Alpha team was seated in the circular cargo bay on seats integrated against the walls waiting for touchdown. From the aft of the ship, Raymond and Lucas sat next to each other on the left while Katherine and Jake sat next to each other on the right. Jake looked at Katherine as she started to check her weapon and gear making sure everything was okay.

"Hey Kat," Jake said. "Everything alright? You seem nervous."

"Me? Well, it is the first time we'll step on a whole new world that has never been colonized before, so yea, a little nervous."

"Same." Jake responded then paused as he quickly reconsidered what he was going to say next. He then decided to continue. "Kat,"

"Yup?" She acknowledges while finishing her final gear checks.

"I know this might seem weird to say now but... I'm sorry."

Katherine immediately stopped checking her gear and looked at him wondering what he was talking about. "You didn't steal my food from the fridge again did you?"

"What?! No, I..." Jake mustered up his courage to tell her the truth. "I... overheard you and Sheena talking about me the other day and-"

"You heard what?!" Katehrine was shocked and embarrassed.

"I-uh-"

"Oh no..." Katherine put her face into her right hand's palm in embarrassment. "You weren't supposed to hear that."

"I know, and that's why I'm saying you were right."

"Huh?" Katherine was surprised. "Right about what exactly?"

"About the way I was acting. I was being a jerk, making it look like I was focusing on others instead of you the whole time, trying to impress you... not being myself." He said while looking at her. "I know this doesn't change anything over night but I just wanted you to know I'm sorry, and if you can't look at me romantically anymore because of things I did, then that's fine, I get it. But as a friend and your team mate, I'll always be here for you." He said smiling at her. "And even if you like Izzy-

"Oh my god." she said in embarrassment

"I support you." He said trying his best not to show any indifference.

"Really?" She responded in surprise.

"Of course."

Katherine smiled at him knowing that the awkwardness between them might have finally come to an end as she recognized that very same personality she used to love from Jake. "Wow... thanks Jake."

"Your welcome." He said moving back into his seat comfortably.

Katherine thought for a moment. She cared for Jake very much, definitely more than just a friend. However, this whole time she waited on him to change back to who he used to be and finally gave up when she saw Izzy. Now, after hearing what Jake had to say, she decided to take Sheena's advice and give him one more chance. "Ja-"

"So what was that thing you did that you weren't willing to tell Shee-"

Katherine's head snapped at lightning speed facing Jake with an angry expression. "Don't push it!"

"Okay, okay!" He reacted in shock immediately turning away from her concluding their conversation as he started to nervously check his gear as well.

"What's up with those two?" Lucas said while watching Jake and Katherine check their gear nervously.

"Eh, who knows," Raymond responded as he checked out the new discs installed on his Flow System gauntlets he was wearing. They were now the same blue color as Sarah's hair and the Red Nova when not in combat state. "Those two have always been awkward around each other."

"Gotta point." For a moment there was silence as the Red Nova stopped vibrating, breaking through the planet's atmosphere. "Raymond?"

"What's up?" He put his arms down and looked at Lucas.

"You trust Gehnarne right?"

"Of course I do." Raymond promptly responded.

"Why?"

Raymond was puzzled to why he was asking a question like that. "I..." Lucas looked at him waiting for the answer. "I just do, he seems like an honorable man and has good intentions for this organization."

Lucas thought for a moment than responded to Raymond's Answer. "Mmm... naive as always... but despite that, you never let me down. I trust you, and if you say he's trust worthy then... I'm gonna try."

"Try?"

"Yea try, trust takes time, you know that."

"Ye but your usually hard with trusting others even with time." Raymond said with a chuckle.

"True."

Jason spoke on the ship's intercom. "Touchdown in ten seconds, alpha up?"

Raymond responded. "Roger, we're up." Raymond and Alpha Team unbuckled their seat belts, moved to the ramp promptly, and stood by waiting for it to open. "Alright guys, we already know their isn't any intelligent life forms on this planet but just in case, get out slowly. We don't want to look like an invasion force coming in with violence of action."

"Check." Alpha said in unison. The Red Nova smoothly jerked downward as it made contact with the planet surface. The cargo ramp opened as Alpha team began to slowly move down the ramp with their weapons at the low ready.

They slowly moved down the ramp, visually scanning the area. As they looked, all they saw was a thick jungle with dense vegetation, trees, and bushes. "Wow," Katherine said.

"We knew we were gonna be dropped in a jungle but I didn't think it would look this." Lucas said.

"It's beautiful, completely untouched by human hands." Jake said.

"Yea, sure is something." Raymond commented while looking at a bush with what appeared to be many flowers colored red like rose's with thin violet outlines.

"That looks beautiful." Sheena said over the channel.

Raymond chuckled. "You want one?" He asked her.

She giggled. *"As long as quarantine doesn't have a problem?"* She said while looking at Jakes status screen waiting for a response.

Jake walked up to the bush, visually examined it from all angles than began to scan it with his Taclet that was equipped with a new device that sent out a small blue laser light that moved up and down on the flower. "Doesn't appear to be poisonous, scans aren't detecting anything unusual. Looks just like another type of flower to me, just be careful."

"Okay, let's hope Izzy's new scanner attachment is accurate enough to detect these sort of things." Raymond took out a pair of scissors and a containment capsule from his assault pack. "While I'm taking this sample, you guys proceed to your objective areas. Kat, Jake, you guys start moving to the top of the hill a half a click to the north and scout out the area to the North West. Let us know what you see when you get there."

"Understood." Jake and Katherine said simultaneously.

Raymond placed the containment capsule underneath the plant to catch its fall. "Lucas and I will move North West to our points of interest as you guys provide over watch for us."

"Right." Lucas agreed.

Raymond snipped the plant free from the bush with the scissors. It fell into the containment capsule as Raymond immediately closed it to preserve the specimen. He packed it in his assault pack than faced the team. "Lets move out."

"Right behind you brotha." Lucas said while Katherine and Jake began their movement towards the hill.

"Star, as soon as my team is clear, move the Nova into low orbit and stay on station."

"Roger that Slinger," Jason answered. *"Have fun, Star out."* Raymond and Lucas proceeded as planned moving further away from the landing site. Once clear, the Red Nova boosted its vertical thrusters gaining altitude than fired it's main engines sending it out of the planets atmosphere into low orbit.

As Lucas and Raymond walked together, Lucas asked. "So, what are we gonna name this planet?"

"Good question," Raymond responded. "I didn't even think about that. Command, what do you think?"

Sheena looked at Gehnarne. "Tell him it's his choice." Gehnarne said while smiling.

Sheena looked back at the TOC's map screen. "Slinger, it's your call. What would you like to name our newly claimed planet?"

"Okay, mmm..." Raymond thought for a moment. "How about Selva?"

"Selva?" Lucas questioned.

"It means "Jungle" in Spanish, and this place is clearly a jungle so, yea." Raymond and Sheena laughed as he walked.

"Okay, Selva it is I guess." Lucas said.

"Command, planet's new designation is Selva, confirm?"

Sheena responded while looking at one of the techs in the TOC. "Roger that Slinger, planet designation Selva is confirmed." She nodded to the tech as the tech looked back and nodded as well. He looked away from her and typed Selva into the planetary records for review by the council back on earth.

"Roger that command," Raymond said. "Proceeding with the expedition." Him and Lucas continued to walk between bushes and dense vegetation dodging branches and brush with every step.

fifteen minutes later, Katherine and Jake were halfway to their objective area. "Wow," Katherine said to Jake. "I would love to come back here on vacation and just explore."

"Maybe we could request some shore leave here after this mission is over, this planet is perfect. Breathable atmosphere, amazing sights, and interesting wild life," Jake said while he looked left watching what looked like a pack of white furred squirrels with large ears running up a tree. "You don't see that every day."

"You don't see that every day either, look." Katherine pointed to a waterfall with a pond glowing blue like a bio luminescent lake back from earth except it was visibly glowing during the day. "Amazing."

"Definitely." Jake agreed with a smile.

Lucas and Raymond continued walking North West as Lucas seemed to be on edge. "Relax Lucas, you look tense. This isn't a combat Recon, it's an expedition." He looked up seeing an extremely large tree in height and width, bigger than any he's seen before. "Enjoy the sights will ya?."

"Last I checked you and Gehnarne said that there could be Rebel forces on the unreached worlds. As long as that's a possibility, I'm treating this like a combat Recon." Lucas looked towards Raymond's sword as they walked. "Besides, at least I don't look like a goofball with a sword strapped to my waist," he said jokingly.

"Hey, don't be dissin on the sword bro, this is the only thing standing between you and another Flow System User like Asrin from tearing you apart."

Asrin's image flashed in Lucas's mind. "God I hated that guy, he creeped me out."

"Yea, me too. I will admit though, swords like this were designed almost a thousand years ago and became obsolete with the invention of the gun so carrying it around like this isn't exactly practical. I was thinking of asking Izzy to make a sword specifically designed to today's standards of combat. After discovering its usefulness against hostile Flow System users, maybe something smaller and more compact would be more practical. What do you think?"

"Now that's a pretty cool idea."

Shortly afterwards, Jake and Katherine reached the base of the hill and began to climb it at a steady pace. Ten minutes later after moving halfway up the hill, Jake noticed something strange off to his left at about 500 meters away. "Wait a second." He said to Katherine.

"What's up?"

"What is that?" He said as he squinted to see in better detail.

"I..." Katherine noticed what Jake was talking about. She saw sparks of electricity flaring in midair. "I don't know..." Katherine stated.

The sparks seemed to have disappeared as if they were being sucked in by an invisible force. "What the hell was that?" Jake started to get a little worried as things seemed quiet, too quiet. Suddenly there was some rustling sounds to their right. Jake and Katherine reacted as they slowly turned towards the sounds while they slowly lifted their AR30's. "...I get the feeling we're not alone on this planet." Jake said.

"I'll call this in." Katherine agreed. "Sli-" Just as she tapped her SDT, she heard a suppressed weapon fire. Everything suddenly went black.

Lucas and Raymond weren't far from their first point of interest as they both heard a quick chirp over the channel. Assuming it was Katherine and Jake, Raymond called them by holding down on his SDT. "Cat-eye, Slinger, was that you guys just now?" Raymond waited for a response... there was nothing. "Cat-eye, Slinger, you copy?" Waited again... nothing. "Cat-eye? Do you copy? Over." Nothing.

"What's wrong?" Lucas asked.

"Katherine and Jake aren't responding on comms."

"Let me try." Lucas said. "Rophe, White. Do you copy? Over." Nothing. "The heck is going on?"

Raymond called command. "Command, Slinger, are you tracking Rophe and Cat-eye?"

Sheena responded. *"Yes, we are, they are halted about 113 meters from their designated over watch position."*

"Ma'am!" one of the TOC technicians got Sheena's attention. "You better see this, transferring image to your screen now!"

Sheena saw a satellite style image of the area where Jake and Katherine were halted and saw multiple men with combat gear and weapons preparing to move Jake and Katherine's unconscious body's. "Oh my god." Sheena reacted. "Slinger! We have a problem!"

"What's wrong?" Raymond asked.

"Transferring visual to your Taclets now!"

Raymond and Lucas looked at their Taclets watching an unknown group of men carrying Jake and Katherine while another group took and smashed their Taclets. Then moved into a more concealed area with heavy vegetation and disappeared.

Lucas recognized their gear and uniforms. "Rebels." Lucas said with Anger.

"This isn't good." Raymond commented in concern. "Command, can you track their movements?"

"Roger, their SDT's are still active." Sheena reported.

"Good, keep tracking their movements and send their locations to our Taclets, we're going after them." Lucas and Raymond began to run in the direction Jake and Katherine were last seen.

Gehnarne jumped in on the channel. *"You don't plan on taking them on by yourselves do you?"*

"Negative, they must have some kind of base, we're gonna follow them there, get eyes on it and figure out what to do from there. In the meantime, I want all combat teams on stand by for immediate operations."

"All of them?" Gehnarne asked in surprise.

"All of them, we have no idea what these guys are capable of, we need to prepare for the worst."

"Digit, White." Lucas called in while running next to Raymond. "Can you do an orbital scan of the planet?"

"Roger but we already did that before you guys landed." Digit responded.

"Than do it again, we must have missed something."

Izzy thought for a moment than spoke. *"Okay, I'll run another scan, and I'll look for any anomalies on the previous scans as well."*

"Good." Lucas said.

Raymond contacted the Red Nova. "Star, did you get all that?"

Jason slapped the back of Timothy's head. "Wake up you idiot!"

"OW! What the hell man?!"

"Two of our guys are MIA!"

Timothy had a scared expression. "Oh shit,"

"Get your station up!"

"Alright, Alright!" Timothy said as he quickly powered up his control panel.

"Slinger, Star. Yea, we got that. What do you need from us?"

"I want the Nova to launch a mini drone than send the controls to my Taclet. Than I want you to move back to the Enidon and pick up teams Bravo through Foxtrot. We'll brief them on your way back to the surface once we get a plan together based on our recon."

"Roger that." Jason acknowledge. "Sarah, get a drone ready for launch." Sarah immediately got to work on her terminal without saying anything to Jason. For a moment, Jason thought Sarah didn't hear him due to her silence. "Sarah?!" Jason said aggressively as he turned his head to face her. He saw a shocked look on her face as he just remembered she was mute. "Oh, sorry I forgot." Upset with him, Sarah made an innocent looking pout. "Just, continue what you were doing." He said facing back towards the front. Sarah nodded her head in forgiveness as she returned to her terminal. Jason spoke to himself. "Relax Jason, this isn't the first time you've been in a situation like this."

"Course is set, drone launched." Timothy report.

"Put the drones imaging on the monitor and start moving the Nova back to the Enidon." Jason ordered.

"Aye." Timothy acknowledged. The spherical monitor showed a window with Raymond and Lucas running as the camera view from the drone followed them from an overhead angle. The camera kept them in the center while zoomed out so the Red Nova crew could see Raymond and Lucas's surroundings for early enemy detection. Behind the window, the spherical monitors image moved as the Red Nova moved away from the planet back to the Enidon.

"Slinger, Crimson." Sheena called Raymond. *"Cat-Eye and Rophe's SDT signals stopped moving about 156 meters north west from their last known location. Sending you the way point now."*

A white blip showed up just to the left of Raymond and Lucas's vision through their contacts with a count-down starting at 345 meters as they got closer to that location. "Roger Crimson, intercepting." Raymond responded while him and Lucas slightly changed the direction they were running towards the blip, centering it in their vision.

"*Slinger?*" Sheena sounded concerned.

"Crimson?"

"*Get them back... and be careful.*"

"We will." Raymond picked up the pace as he stopped talking on the channel. Lucas stayed next to him keeping pace. Together they ran through areas with less vegetation at top speed and bulldozing through areas with thick brushes trying to maintain the pace.

Chapter 13: Hostages

Meanwhile, at an unknown location on Selva, Jake began to wake up. However, as he opened his eyes, all he saw was darkness and felt a fabric bag over his head. He remained calm as he heard nearby voices talking.

"So these are our two trespassers." A familiar sounding male voice spoke as Jake tried to remember where he had heard that voice before.

"Yes sir," Another man spoke. "We found them just outside our parameter. I believe they saw the breakdown in our field's camouflage."

"Was it fixed?"

"Yes sir."

The man with the familiar voice had paused his response, then answered. "For your sake, I hope so." Suddenly, everything became bright as the fabric bag was pulled off of Jake's head. His eyes ached while they adjusted to the overhead light as a man stood in front of him with the man slowly leaning forward towards him. Once Jake's eyes completely adjusted, he immediately recognized who the man was. "Assuming from your Taclets and other equipment, you must be USOD?" The man was Garza Liankos, the supposedly deceased leader of the Rebel forces. "Am I right?" Despite his shock in seeing Garza still alive, Jake maintained his solid composure like he was taught in SERE training, Survival Evasion Resistance Escape. "Nothing?" Jake looked straight ahead with Garza just out of his center of view. He noticed Garza wearing combat gear, Gauntlets looking similar to the flow system, and a type of sword sheathed in a scabbard on his left hip. "Of course nothing, you USOD types are all the same. So rude." Garza said as he looked at Jakes neck expecting to see something there but didn't. He immediately grew angry and walked with rage in his step towards the man he was talking to earlier. "Why weren't their SDT's removed!" While Garza looked away, Jake looked around seeing Katherine to his right with a black fabric bag over her head. He looked at her chest, she was breathing, leaving him relieved.

"Sir?" The man wondered what Garza was talking about.

"Their Sub-dermals you ass, every USOD Operator has one, why weren't theirs removed!"

"Sir, I swear, I had no idea they even h-" Suddenly, at almost inhuman speed, Garza drew his sword out from its scabbard and thrust it half way into the man's gut. "AAHH!!!" The man screamed in pain as blood spurted out from the exit wound and slowly oozed out the entry wound. The sword was a rapier of an elegant design. Jake had never seen one used in such a way before.

"Your incompetence has failed me for the last time, and yourself." Garza said looking straight into the dying man's eye's. "May you be released of this shame." He violently ripped the rapier out of the man's gut as the man fell to his knees, then to his side uncontrollably. "Guards!" Immediately, three guards in combat gear walked in through the door shocked at the dead body. "You!" Garza pointed at the guard in the middle with his rapier "Take care of your former lieutenants remains." The guard immediately grabbed the body of the man Garza had killed and dragged it out the door. "And you two," The other two guards payed close attention. "Relieve our guests of their Sub-Dermals before they attract any more attention." The guards nodded and immediately started moving. One stood behind Katherine and removed the black bag from her head. She squinted in pain as her eyes adjusted just as the guard behind her grabbed her head forcefully and pulled it to her left. She didn't resist as she cringed preparing to bear the coming pain. The second guard came up behind Jake grabbing his head the same way. Both of the guards drew their knives and slowly began to dig the blades into the necks of Jake and Katherine trying to dig out their sub-dermals. Katherine shrieked as she tried her best to resist her reaction to the unquantifiable pain. Jake also shouted in pain as he felt the blade digging into his neck prying on the small circuitry of his SDT.

Back on the Red Nova currently docked with the Enidon, Jason and his crew continued tracking Lucas and Raymond's position through the drone's camera as they began to load teams Bravo through Foxtrot on board. Suddenly, Jake and Katherine's SDT markers disappeared from the Red Nova's spherical monitor. "What the?" Jason said in surprise. "Uh Command, Star, we just lost Rophe and Cat-Eye's SDT signals."

"*Roger that Star,*" Sheena responded. "*We saw it too. Slinger, you tracking?*"

Back on the surface of Selva, Raymond had his assault pack off to the side with his AR30 on top of it inside a thicket next to Lucas in a prone position. "Roger that Crimson, we saw it." He responded. "We're about 100 meters away in dense vegetation just east of that position. We're about to send in the drone with manual control."

"*Roger,*" Crimson responded.

"*White, Digit.*" Izzy spoke up on the channel. "*I looked at the video stream monitoring Cat-Eye and Rophe where they were taken.*" Lucas responded. "What did you find Digit?"

Izzy continued. "*It seems that just before Cat Eye and Rophe were taken, there was some kind of visual anomaly just north of their position, if anything I think they might have saw it. That anomaly happened right on top of where their SDT's signals were lost, there has to be something that we're not seeing. I recommend using your drone on that area at a low altitude.*"

Lucas and Raymond looked at each other in agreement to what Izzy recommended. "Roger that Digit."

"I have control of the drone." Raymond used his Taclet's touch screen controls as he piloted the small drone seeing through its camera point of view with his contacts. The drone was high enough in the air to see the valley and all of its plant life. "Strange," Raymond said. "There's nothing out here but nature."

Lucas was watching the same image Raymond was seeing through the drone on his own Taclet. By this point, the drone was seventy-five meters from the position where Katherine and Jake's SDT's died. "Digit said there has to be something out there, let's get closer." Lucas suggested.

"Okay." Raymond agreed while focusing on his piloting. Suddenly there was a flash of light as the drone seemed to have passed through something. "What the?" Raymond and Lucas said simultaneously. After the drone settled to a stop, Raymond saw what the drone had found through the camera. "Wo!" Raymond said in surprise as he realized that a patch of the valleys vegetation was replaced by an advanced outpost of some kind surrounded by concrete barriers and a small runway in the middle surrounded by small buildings and tents. "What is this place?"

"I don't know." Lucas responded.

Izzy, and Sheena, saw the drone image from their stations. As Izzy scanned the image, he noticed a strange light beaming out towards the sky from a small building to the right of the runway. "Slinger, Digit, could you have the camera focus on the building with light coming out of it?"

"I see it, Standby." Raymond answered as he centered the drone's camera on the building.

Upon closer examination, Izzy had a theory. "That's gotta be some kind of camouflage projection field. That would explain the strange anomaly we saw, it must have malfunction at some point. This is the reason why we couldn't see this outpost from our initial scans, it was blending in with the planet's surface."

As Izzy finished, Raymond noticed some Guards roaming the base, they were using the same gear the Rebels that Lucas spotted earlier. "Definitely Rebels. Where the heck did they get this kind of technology from?" Raymond expressed.

"Doesn't that seem to be the most asked question of the month." Lucas commented.

"Your telling me," Raymond thought for a moment. "Command, Slinger. May I suggest a plan of action?"

"*What do you got Slinger?*" Gehnarne asked while stepping into the TOC on the Enidon.

"This place seems pretty vulnerable from what I can see with the drone." He said while scanning the area with the drone. "I suggest deploying a platoon sized element of about five teams. One to assault through from the North East, the second from the North West. The other two will take up containment positions from the South East and South West to cut off the enemy's retreat. The Red Nova can land just to the North behind the two teams to set up a rally point, Foxtrot team can provide Aid and Litter, and Security for the nova. As for that camouflage field, we can use the drones EMP to disable the projector's electronics allowing us to see the outpost from long range, maybe get some accurate orbital strike fire after Cat-Eye and Rophe are rescued."

As Raymond continued to scan, Sheena noticed something on the drones imaging. "*Slinger, Crimson. That hill with the large tree to the East.*"

"What about it Crimson?"

Sheena was nervous in answering Raymond because she knew what it would mean for herself. However, the fear of losing Katherine and Jake overpowered the fear of her past. *"That position would be a good spot to provide Sniper support once that camouflage field is down."* Sheena recommended.

"Sounds good Crimson, any recommendations on who to position there?"

Crimson was puzzled that he asked that question. *"Yes, me."* All the TOC technicians and Izzy looked at Sheena wondering what she was planning. Even Gehnarne paused when he heard this on the channel.

"What? You?" Raymond was surprised.

"Uh, Crimson, Star." Jason called in on the channel. *"Sorry to disappoint you but we just detached from the Enidon, we can't transport you down to the surface with the rest of the teams."*

Sheena was disappointed she missed her chance to help her friends more directly. "Understood Star..."

"Crimson, Slinger. Private Channel."

Sheena switched over to private channel as she walked away from the TOC's monitors. With disappointment in her voice she responded. "Slinger?"

As Sheena walked away, one of the TOC technicians noticed a change with the open channel active user manifest on his screen. "What the?" He reacted.

"Hey, it's okay," Raymond said with care. *"We're gonna save them."*

"I know, it's just... I can't just sit here doing nothing while our friends need our help."

"Uh, ma'am!" The TOC technician called Sheena just as Katherine's call sign "Cat-Eye" chimed in on the private channel with an unknown voice speaking on the channel both on open and private.

"Aw, isn't that sweet, wanting to save your comrades."

"What?!" Sheena and Raymond said in surprise simultaneously.

Gehnarne heard the man's voice on the open channel. "Who is this?! Identify yourself?!"

"Encase you don't believe me, I suggest you begin a voice recognition program to confirm who I am." As the man continued,

Gehnarne nodded at Izzy who immediately began his own voice recognition software as Sheena and Raymond switched back to the open channel while Raymond suddenly recognized the voice. "*My name is,*" The man said in unison with Raymond saying the man's name to himself in shock. "Garza Liankos!"

Immediately after saying his name, the bridge and TOC crew spoke in a dull mummer asking questions like "I thought he was dead?" and "Did he use a double?"

"Settle down everyone!" Gehnarne ordered with a calm yet firm voice. "Alright Mr. Liankos, what do you want from us?"

"*I want you and your forces to fall back to your ship and leave this planet immediately, if you do not comply within fifteen minutes, I will kill your two operatives.*"

Gehnarne looked back at Izzy to get confirmation on the voice. Izzy looked back in concern and nodded, it was definitely Garza Liankos. "Alright Mr. Liankos, Standby."

"*Don't keep me waiting.*" Garza said with a serious tone.

Gehnarne cut from the channel. "How the hell did he get access to our comms?" Gehnarne asked.

"He used Cat-Eye's SDT some how." The TOC technician who noticed the strange occurrence earlier confirmed. "Her call sign just logged back into the open channel when Ms. Vial stepped away for a moment so our Operational Security shouldn't have been compromised."

"How did he manage to get a hold of her SDT?"

Sheena's expression grew pale. "The SDT is inside her neck so... I don't even want to imagine how he got that thing out of her." Heavy concern began to build for her friend.

"My God," Gehnarne couldn't imagine how painful that must have been.

"Brandon," Sheena called the name of the TOC technician involved in the communications breach. "Did you block her SDT from our comms systems?"

"Yes ma'am, I just did."

"*Command, Slinger!*" Raymond called in on the channel. "*Is this channel secured?!*"

"Channel is secured Slinger, go ahead."

"We got movement on the Runway! I see Rophe and Cat Eye with them!" Gehnarne, Sheena, and Izzy looked back at the bridge monitor watching the footage from the drone controlled by Raymond. They saw Jake and Katherine with blood on their necks from the wounds made during the removal of their SDT's. Their hands were tied behind their backs as they were pushed towards the middle of the runway, forced to their knees with pistols put to their heads by their captors. Garza was behind them with a pistol in his right hand and a radio in the other with a blood soaked SDT attached to the radio with an auxiliary cable. He lifted the radio preparing to speak.

"Brandon!" Sheena ordered. "Unblock Katherine's SDT now!"

"Yes ma'am!" Brandon worked his station allowing everyone to hear Garza's voice again.

"Knowing you USOD types, I know you are watching somewhere from someplace. With that said, you have fifteen minutes starting now. There will be no negotiations." Garza unplugged the SDT from the radio, threw it to the ground and smashed it with his foot.

"Oh man..." Izzy commented. "He's pretty serious about this."

"Indeed." Gehnarne said in concern.

Sheena looked at the monitor watching Jake and Katherine on their knees. She became extremely worried and desperate, wondering how she could help her friends. As she thought for a moment, she had an idea. "Izzy?" Sheena called him.

Izzy turned around. "What is it?"

"Is it possible to set the UTS for a local universe teleport?" She asked while moving closer to him.

Izzy was surprised she asked that. "Uh, yea but it's extremely risky. The UTS wasn't designed for local universe teleportation. It could cause a kind of feedback loop in the system. Plus, without Beacon support, we can lose your bio data."

Sheena was not understanding what he meant by that. "Meaning?..."

"You could die." Izzy said bluntly.

Sheena's expression went grim. She looked back at the monitor watching Katherine and Jake still on their knees. She didn't care about the risks anymore. "Can it still be done?"

Izzy was getting concerned "Listen Sheena, Raymond and Lucas have the situations under cont-"

"Can it be done!?" Sheena asked again aggressively.

Izzy was now annoyed "If I can trick the system into thinking the planet surface is a beacon and monitor the teleport stream to correct any anomalies in real time than yes, I can do it. I'm going to need Gia's help with this."

"Okay, Gehnarne," Sheena called out to him. "Permission to-"

Gehnarne interrupted. "You don't need my permission." He turned to Sheena. "Good luck." He smiled at her.

Sheena smiled back. "Thank you, let's go Izzy." She said while turning towards the elevator than walking in. As the elevator doors began to close, she contacted Gia on her Taclet. "Gia, report to the UTS Chamber immediately."

"*On the way.*" Gia respond back on the Taclet as the elevator doors shut.

Back in the TOC, Brandon looked back at Gehnarne and asked, "Sir, shouldn't we tell Raymond of what Sheena is doing?"

Gehnarne looked at him and said, "If we do that, he'll only try to stop her and with the mood she's in It will only complicate things."

"Right." He agreed as he looked back to his station.

While the elevator moved, Sheena opened her Quarters Access app and spoke to the Quarters Access computer. "Crimson131"

A female computer voice responded "How may I help you Sheena?"

"Please send my Sniper load out and kit from my locker to the UTS Chamber immediately."

"Yes ma'am." The voice responded. "Load out and kit sent."

"My lab is on the way to the UTS chamber." Izzy spoke. "While you inform Gia of the situation, I'm going to stop there for a moment to get something for you."

"For me?" Sheena asked. "What?"

"The final Flow System model, it's ready, I want you to use it."

Sheena smiled. "Perfect timing."

"You could say that again, I stood up all night trying to finish the final touches on that thing. Thank goodness I did. I tested everything on it, so it's ready for combat."

"Good." Sheena said as the elevator moved closer to its

destination.

While Sheena, Izzy, and Gia conducted their tasks, The Red Nova flew along Selva's surface at a low altitude to a designated landing zone. "Tim, lower the engines thrust output." Jason ordered. "We don't want that outpost to hear us from all the way out here."

"Aye, Aye." Timothy responded. The Red Nova slowly came to a stop with the circular cargo bay, as a whole, opened downward with a hydraulic system controlling it from four points around the circular bay. The sides of the circle where exposed to the outside as Bravo, Charlie, Delta, and Echo teams attached magnetic repel hookups to the floor of the bay and repelled out the sides of the opening into the thick jungle below. Once the teams were on the ground and began to move to their way points, Raymond and Lucas briefed the combat teams of the situation. As head of the Combat Group, Raymond assigned more specific tasks for each team based on the initial plan. The whole process in Raymond's head was like conducting an orchestra of violence. It was stressful knowing his friends lives were at stake. However, Raymond enjoyed the challenge conducting such a task. The feeling of so many moving parts of a strategic operation working together to accomplish success was always satisfying to him.

Back on the Enidon, "You want to do what?!" Gia was shocked. "Do you realize how dangerous this is right?!"

"Izzy already explained it to me," Sheena responded while she finished putting on her combat gear over her green jumpsuit. Her load out consisted of a plate carrier with multiple 7.62 millimeter magazines, a sniper rifle of the same model and set up she used on Kalista, one M76 side arm, and a combat knife. "He said he needed your help with the UTS to prevent a feedback loop." She moved to the open gear conveyor to her left along the wall, placed her empty gear bag onto the conveyor and closed it as it was immediately taken away through the conveyor system back to Sheena's locker in her Quarters. "He should be here momentari-" Sheena was cut off by the sound of sliding doors opening as Izzy walked through them.

"Here they are," He said as he walked straight towards Sheena with a silk cloth in his hands that seemed to be wrapped around something. He stopped in front of Sheena unwrapping the silk revealing the new flow system he had built.

"Wow..." Sheena Starred at the gauntlets in amazement.

"Beautiful huh?" Izzy said with pride. "I made a few improvements over the prototype that Raymond is using. Instead of just a finger less glove, Raymond preferred a removable half glove design with rubber palms so he can have a better grip with his sword and have the ability to use different choices of gloves, the Gauntlet's outer forearms are also reinforced with titanium alloy for impact absorption, a Taclet compatible locking slot on the inside of both gauntlet forearms so he didn't have to strap his Taclet on top of the Gauntlet itself anymore, the slot is also compatible with Taclet attachments like the scanner and other future attachments I have in mind, and I was able to tuck the wires under the gauntlet so they wouldn't be exposed making a sleeker looking design,"

Sheena smiled. "Very nice Izzy." She complimented as she took the Gauntlets in her hands and began putting them on. "I can tell that Raymond would love these." She slid on and locked the left gauntlet. "Too bad I'm the first to try them and not him." Then she slid on and locked the right gauntlet.

"Don't worry, I'm sure he won't mind however, just so you know, I didn't install the Rage Mode on this. As you can see, these are the silver discs." He tapped on the plexi glass cover protecting the disc on one of the gauntlet's. "The same discs that used to be installed on the prototype Raymond is using."

"Okay, I understand."

Gia interrupted. "Sorry but, we don't have much time, we have to get her down there quickly." She began to walk towards the stairs leading to the control room as Izzy and Sheena looked at her. "Safely, I might add!" She continued as she walked up the stairs.

"She's right," Izzy agreed. "I better get up there." Izzy looked back at Sheena and patted her on the shoulder. "Godspeed."

"Thanks." Sheena smiled, turned around than stepped on to the UTS's platform as Izzy walked away to the control room. As Sheena waited, the UTS's humming became louder.

Izzy entered the control room and went straight to work on his monitor. "Okay, all I have to do now is override the UTS to think the planet surface is a beacon."

"Izzy, this is a really bad idea." Gia commented in protest.

"I know Gia," He responded as he continued working. 'But we can do this, just pay attention for the feedback anomalies and we should be okay."

Gia was nervous. "Okay," She pulled up a monitor on the control panel and a keyboard. "I'm ready."

"Good, so am I," As he finished the final touches on the override and tapped the enter key, "I'll Begin the start up sequence." Izzy started a new sequence of typing as the blue sphere of electricity began to form around Sheena. She began to float in the air while nervously trying to stay perfectly still. "Coordinates set." Izzy said. "Standby Gia, from this point on we will be getting feedback anomalies."

"Got it." She responded just as the blue sphere around Sheena flickered.

Sheena became very nervous. "What was that?!"

"Gia!" Izzy reacted. "You got it!?"

"Got it!" She responded nervously just as she finished working on her station.

Izzy sighed in relief. "Oh good, be ready for a lot of those."

Gia had enough. "I can't see why you can't just do this!" she yelled while looking at Izzy.

Izzy reacted in frustration. "Gia, you know how this system works! I have to maintain data integrity during the teleportation sequence, especially now with this override in place! I can't do that and correct feedback anomalies at the same time!"

Sheena also grew fustrated. "Could you two please stop arguing and get this shi-mmm..." She stopped herself realizing she was about to swear, "crap over with!"

Izzy calmed down and spoke into the intercom. "Roger that Sheena, sorry." He turned off the intercom and spoke to Gia. "Gia please, just stay focused."

Gia took a deep breath. "Alright." She looked back at her monitor and stood by.

"Good." Izzy put his pointer finger over the enter key then got back on the intercom. "Standby Sheena, we're striking, in five... four... three," The blue sphere flickered again. Sheena was scared.

Gia began working on her keyboard. "Stabilized!"

"Two... One... Striking!" Izzy pressed enter on the keyboard just as Sheena closed her eyes in fear. Immediately she disappeared with a flash and a thunder like sound. Suddenly, on Gia's monitor, there were feedback anomalies popping up on her screen one after another. "Gia?"

"Standby." Gia responded to Izzy as she worked as fast as she could. Her fingers danced across the keyboard at striking speeds as she desperately tried to clear out all the feedback anomalies before Sheena's transport sequence was completed. The thought of Sheena ending up on Selva as a blob of goo made Gia sick to her stomach.

"Gia!?" Izzy was getting worried.

"Hold on!" Gia responded aggressively while staying focused on the monitor. "Got it!"

Suddenly there was a loud thunder like noise in the jungle on Selva. Sheena had landed uncontrollably on the jungle floor face down grunting on impact. "Ah!" She reacted in pain. "Crap... that sucked."

"*Crimson!?*" Izzy called on the channel. "*Crimson, do you copy?*" With worry in his voice.

Sheena tapped on her SDT. "Crimson here, Digit, I'm okay." She said while standing to her feet and looked around. "Although the landing could have been a little better."

"*Oh thank god,*" Izzy began to speak away from the microphone through the channel. "*Gia, you can take a seat and relax now, just please don't barf.*" He spoke back into the microphone. "*Crimson, where are you, what's your location?*"

She smiled as she looked up towards a very large tree. The same one she suggested to Raymond for a good sniper perch. "Exactly where I wanted to be." She pulled out a repel launcher from her kit and fired it at a large branch. Once the hook was lodged deep into the branch, she hooked up to the launcher's rotary device and began to ascend up the tree to the branch.

"*Excellent,*" Izzy responded. "*I'll patch you into Alpha teams comms. standby.*"

"Can't wait to hear what Raymond has to say about this." Sheena said to herself. Shortly after, Sheena's SDT chirped signaling that a new communications channel was connected. She double tapped on her SDT and began to speak just as she reached the large branch and started climbing on to it. "Slinger, Crimson. I am on station and standing by to provide sniper support." She said while moving into a prone firing position near the edge of the giant branch, opened the bipod on her sniper rifle and settle it on the branch she was laying on. She was now in a perfectly steady firing position overlooking the area where the rebel base should be. As She looked through the scope, Sheena couldn't see the base itself due to the camouflage field.

Raymond was shocked. "*Crimson!? How the hell did you get down here so fast without a ride?*"

Sheena paused thinking of what to say, then responded. "I could tell you, but you're not gonna like it."

Raymond cringed at the thought. "*Okay fine, we'll talk about this later. As for now, we're about to kick this off. Sending marked targets to you now.*" Sheena's HUD on her contacts began to show red human shaped silhouettes through her scope. "*Hold fire until the field is down.*"

Sheena took a deep breath then responded with a "Roger," in a calm voice as she breathed out slowly, relaxing her body.

"You ready Lucas?" Raymond asked

"Ready when you are." Lucas responded in a serious tone.

"Okay, let's do this." Raymond got back on the channel. "All units, moving drone into position now, standby." The drone began to move towards the camouflage field projector. It was almost there. "Standby..." Raymond said nervously knowing that all hell was about to break loss. Just as Raymond was about to activate the drones EMP, a gun shot went off with the drone spinning out of control, plummeting to the ground. "What the hell!?" The drone smashed to the ground inside the base.

"Oh shit!" Lucas was shocked. "Activate the EMP now! It still might work!"

"I'm trying, it's not responding!" Raymond said in a fearful voice.

"Fuck! What happened?!"

"I don't know, but the camera is still active." Just as he said that, one of the rebels walked up to the downed drone and picked it up. Raymond and Lucas watched in fear wondering what would happen to Jake and Katherine. The rebel holding the drone walked towards

Garza's position.

"What was that gunshot just now?" Garza asked.

"I shot this down sir." The rebel presented the drone. "It was heading straight towards the projector."

Garza took the drone and smiled devilishly into the camera. "Good work, stick around, you might be useful." He said to the rebel who brought him the drone.

"Yes sir." The rebel responded.

Garza walked up to Jake as the other rebel followed. He got into Jake's face with the drone and forcefully asked. "What is this?" Jake knew what it was but stayed absolutely silent. "This is one of yours isn't it?" Jake continued to stay silent. Garza looked at the rebel that had followed him. "You, take the drone and put it in a spot where our... audience can see our guests."

"Yes sir." He said while taking the drone than re-positioned it on the floor with the camera facing Jake and Katherine.

Garza looked back at Jake then suddenly punched him. Katherine's heart sank as she was scared of what he was going to do to Jake. Garza began to yell at him. "I HAD ENOUGH OF YOUR DAMN USOD GAMES!!!" He punched Jake again, "Who else is out there?!", then again, "Who is watching us!?", then grabbed his head and kneed him in the face breaking his nose, "where are they!?" Katherine, and the rest of Alpha team including Sheena watched helplessly as Jake was being beaten. Blood spattered on the floor as Jake grunted in pain. His face was swollen, cut and bloodied. He looked back at Garza in emotionless defiance with one eye as the other was swollen shut still refusing to talk.

Garza grew even more angry and was tempted to hit Jake again. However, he knew it wouldn't work, so he decided to change his approach. He looked at Katherine seeing emotion in her face, she clearly seemed scared for Jake. Garza then figured, if she was scared for this man's life, maybe he would be scared for hers. He smiled as he pulled out his pistol and walked aggressively towards Katherine. He grabbed her hair pointing the gun at her head.

Jake saw this and immediately grew angry. "Leave her alone you bastard!"

"Oh!" Garza responded giddily. "The stone speaks, now tell me!

How many more of you are there and where are they?!"

Jake looked at Katherine, unsure of what to do. She looked at him with a scared expression but still shook her head with a no gesture. Jake gained his composure back and stayed silent.

Garza was now furious. He pistol whipped Katherine on the cheek cutting her, as she whelped in pain with blood trickling from her cheek down to her chin. Garza than grabbed her hair tighter than cocked the pistols hammer back making the weapon all the more ready to fire on a hair trigger. "DO YOU THINK THIS IS A GAME!? I will kill her if you don't tell me everything I want to know!" He pressed the pistol's barrel tip against Katherine's temple forcefully as she was feeling pain from the metal pressing against her skull. Jake looked at Katherine with her looking back scared for her life.

"Oh God," Raymond said to himself as he continued to watch the drone's camera feed. "He's gonna crack."

Garza continued. "This is your last chance! How many more of you are there and where are they!?"

"Raymond," Lucas said. "What do we do?"

"Crimson," Raymond said through the channel. "Do you have a clear shot?"

"With the red silhouette markers I might be able to make a shot through the camouflage field," Sheena reported. "However-"

"What?" Raymond asked cutting her off.

"If I shoot now, they will just kill them both anyway, we need some kind of distraction."

Lucas continued, "And the EMP would have been that perfect distraction when shutting down the camouflage field."

"Exactly." Sheena regretfully confirmed.

"Dammit!" Raymond said in frustration.

Garza looked straight into Jake's eyes intently. Jake looked back. He knew there was nothing he could do. So he looked at Katherine and spoke. "Katherine..." He said just barely able to pronounce her name correctly with his face swollen in pain. As he spoke, Garza's expression changed thinking he was about to win. Katherine was in shock with tears flowing down her face wondering what Jake would say. "For-" Jake grunted in pain from his beaten face but fought through it to speak. "For as long as I've known you, I've tried to protect you." Katherine was surprised. "Even from some things you didn't know about..." Garza was starting to wonder where this was going. "I did this because I cared for you and wanted you to be safe." Katherine's expression began to cringe as her crying slowly intensified. "But now... this is something I know I can't protect you from... I'm so sorry..." Garza was once again furious understanding that Jake would not talk.

Believing this would be her last moment alive, Katherine felt guilt for all the times she mistreated Jake, pushed him away, and even used him. Before she would die, she had to tell him how she felt. "Jake... I'm so, so-" Suddenly a loud gun shot went off. The loudest that Alpha team had ever or will ever hear.

Chapter 14: Good Times

"So a priest, a Rabi, and an Atheist walk into a bar," Lucas said while sitting at the bar with his friends wearing black jeans with white dress shirt and white shoes dressed to impress. The name of this bar was Daniel's Pub. A bar that Yabin and his friend Daniels co-owned together. Although similar to the Velvet Star, this bar did not cater to live performances.

"The hell is this? A joke?"Jake responded in annoyance to Lucas's lame set up for a joke wearing a gray Polo shirt and black dress pants with black material shoes.

"Obviously!" Lucas say's as he laughs drunkenly. The rest of his friends look at him awkwardly as he is the only one laughing.

"Dude, your drunk." Raymond said with a straight face wearing all black polo shirt, jeans and sneakers while Sheena, who was wearing tight dark blue jeans with a red blouse and red high heels, giggled at Raymond's cringed expression.

"I'm not drunk, I'm just getting started!" Lucas say's while taking another drink from his beer.

"Take it easy Lucas." Sheena said in mild laughter.

Lucas finished his beer and noticed a familiar woman across the room ahead of him reading a book with a small drink to the side of her table. She was wearing a black dress with a knee high skirt with legs crossed leaning over the table wearing glasses. "Is that Gia?" Lucas asked.

Raymond looked forward to see what Lucas was talking about and saw her too. "Yea, I think that is Gia."

Lucas smiled. "I'm gonna have a chat with her." He began to stand up unevenly from his bar stool.

"Lucas, be nice." Sheena spoke in concern.

"Ah don't worry, I'm just gonna have a friendly conversation with her that's all. See ya." Lucas walked away towards Gia with unbalanced steps.

Sheena sighed. "Yea, you better go with him." She said giving Raymond a concerned look.

Raymond rolled his eyes. "I know, and here I thought we were on leave, not babysitting." Sheena smiled at his comment. He got out of his stool and walked the same path Lucas took. "Be back soon."

Sheena looked back at Jake and noticed he was slumped over the bar table looking depressed. "Why so down Jake?" She was concerned.

"Katherine is on a date with that guy she met on social media."

"Oh, I see." She thought for a moment. "A nice guy like you could really use a nice girl you know. I mean, I love Katherine but I realize now that maybe she really isn't the one for you."

"Yea... maybe." He said turning around with his beer in his hand feeling buzzed. He was about to drink it until he looked towards the entrance of the bar and saw Katherine with her date walking through the door. "Oh shit!" He was momentarily stunned by Katherine's beauty as she was wearing a beautiful short one-piece blue dress. He quickly snapped out of it and turned back around towards the bar.

"What's wrong now?" Sheena asked.

"It's Katherine, she's here!" He said with a nervous voice trying to keep his head low.

"Really, where?" She began to look around and spotted her and her date walking towards a table. "Oh there she is."

"Dammit, what if she sees me? She'll think I'm stalking her or something."

Sheena looked at him with an annoyed expression. "Relax, you're with us and that's all she needs to know."

Meanwhile, Lucas continued to walk closer to Gia's lonesome table as Raymond took a seat at a distant table to observe knowing how much Lucas would hate it if he cramped his style.

"Hello Gia." Lucas said with a smile once he reached her table.

"Oh!" Gia was surprised to see Lucas. "Hello Lucas, what are you doing here?"

"Was just having a drink with the rest of the team, enjoying our leave."

Gia looked behind Lucas and saw Raymond at a nearby table waiving at her making hand gestures trying to tell Gia that Lucas was a little tipsy. She made an awkward look at Raymond while saying to Lucas, "I see."

She looked back at Lucas just as he asked "Mind if I sit with you?" Against her better judgment, she didn't want to seem rude. "Sure, why not." She gestures for Lucas to sit with her. He takes the seat opposite from her, putting his drink on the table.

"So," Lucas asked. "How does a beautiful woman like you end up with a guy like Gehnarne?"

Gia blushed as she prepared to answer.

Back at the Bar table, "I don't get it," Jake said to Sheena while looking at Katherine and her date as she laughed at something her date had said. "What does he have that I don't?"

"Oh come on Jake, just let it go." Sheena said while turning back towards the bar.

Jake continued to observe as he witnessed Katherine getting up from her seat and walking towards the restroom. Once she was out of site, he looked back at her date and observed something disturbing. The date had carefully pulled out a small pill from his jacket pocket, grabbed Katherine's drink than cracked open the small pill releasing a powdery substance into her drink in such a way that anyone not directly observing him wouldn't see his actions. He then tried to dissolve the powder quickly by swirling the glass carefully. He placed the drink back in the spot that Katherine had left it, then quickly stuffed the small pieces to the pill in his jacket pocket.

"What the hell?" Jake said in disgust.

"What?" Sheena asked looking at Jake. "What's wrong?"

Meanwhile, with Lucas and Gia, "Just partners?" Lucas said in surprise.

"Yes," Gia happily answered. "He shows me the secrets of the multi universe, I show others how to mathematically get there."

"Wow," Lucas was amazed. "You must really be a genius."

"Thank you, I'm flattered. However, I've studied into other things as well before I became a mathematician."

"Like what?" Lucas asked as he was very interested in the conversation while taking a swig of his beer.

"I have a degree in psychology and am a licensed psychologist."

Immediately Lucas choked on his beer and forcefully swallowed it down. "You're a-" He coughed. "You're a shrink!?"

In concern, "Are you alright?" Gia asked.

"Yea, I'm fine." Lucas found his composure. "I'm just not very good around... Shrinks."

Gia was a little offended. "Well, sorry to hear that. You see, my mathematician and psychiatric skills are a couple of the reasons why Gehnarne handpicked me for this organization."

Lucas felt guilty for offending Gia. "Sorry Gia, I didn't mean to-

"What did you put in her drink!?" Jake yelled at Katherine's date so loudly, the whole bar can hear him.

"The fuck man, relax!" Katherine's date said.

"Screw that!" Sheena said backing up Jake. "You spiked our friends drink, we saw you!"

Lucas looked back at Gia in worry. "Would you, excuse me minute?" He got up and walked towards Raymond. "What's going on?" He asked Raymond.

"I don't know, they both just started yelling at that guy." He said in concern as they both walked towards the commotion. Gia stood up in concern to see what was going on.

"What's the problem here?" A big muscular bouncer with jeans and a tight black shirt asked.

Jake answered. "This piece of shit spiked my friends drink. He had a pill, cracked it open and poured the contents into her drink."

"Fuck you man you don't know shit! I didn't do nothin!" Katherine's date answered.

"Everyone relax!" The bouncer said loudly. "I have a quick solution to this." The bouncer reached into his pocket and pulled out a small baggy of white powder. "This is what I call the Spike Test. This powdery chemical will turn the drink black if it has a chemical reaction to any other substance that is not usually used in alcoholic drinks, such as a type of drug like what you guys are claiming." He grabbed Katherine's drink, poured in the white powder and stirred it with a spoon he picked up from the table next to him. The drink immediately turned black.

"Oh that's some bullshit man!" Katherine's date reacted.

"Alright buddy, time to go," The bouncer said aggressively as the he attempted to escort Katherine's date to the door when the man suddenly turned violent and lunged after Jake. When this happened, Jake, Raymond, Sheena, and Lucas were ready to react. However, from out of nowhere a man with black hair and gray streaks along the side wearing black slacks, a gray button down shirt and black leather shoes jumped in front of the group, grabbed Katherine's date by the shoulders and kneed him so hard in the stomach that the date immediately collapsed gasping for air. "Attacking my daughter and her friends?" The man said viciously, "Not a smart idea, even if I wasn't here to save their asses!" The man than finished off Katherine's date with a kick to the face, knocking him out on his back. The whole bar cheered at the man's heroic act while the bouncer forcefully grabbed the defenseless date, dragging him out of the bar as the heroic defender turned around to face the group.

Immediately Sheena recognized him. "Dad!?"

"Hey honey!" Colonel Vial smiled. "Reynolds, Walker, Morgan,... Luma." He nodded at each one of them in greeting as he said their names.

"Luma?" the team was puzzled as they turned around and saw Katherine standing behind them with a look of disappointment. "Katherine!" They all said in surprise.

"Oh shit," Jake spoke, "I'm so sorry, I didn't mean to ruin your-"

"It's, okay Jake..." Katherine interrupted him leading to an awkward silence between the members of Alpha team.

"Well, I guess I should probably head out now." Colonel Vial broke the silence.

"Wait, dad!" Sheena stopped him. "Raymond, I'm gonna stay with my dad for a bit so you can head back to the hotel if you want, I'll meet you there."

"Sure that's fine, I'll see you later than." He looked at Colonel Vial with a smile. "Thanks for the help sir."

"Don't mention it Reynolds." Colonel Vial and Sheena began to walk out of the bar together.

Lucas tried to slip away as Raymond noticed him. "Where do you think your going you drunkard!? I can't leave you alone for five minutes in the state you're in!"

Lucas groaned in annoyance. "Fine, just give me a moment!" He said as he walked back towards Gia.

Jake continued to look at Katherine with remorse as her disappointment seem to turn to sadness. "I think..." Katherine said.

"...I think I'll just head back too."

She turned around as Jake softly grasped her shoulder. "Wait," He said as Katherine turned around sadly looking at Jake. "Care to have a drink with me?" He smiled. "I'm sure after that incident, the bar would probably give us a couple on the house right?" He winked at her.

Although Katherine didn't want to give Jake false hope about the boundaries of their relationship, she couldn't help but want to seek comfort from a friend. She smiled back and responded. "Sure." They turned around and walked to the bar together.

Lucas approached Gia as she seemed impressed by his loyalty to his friends. "I see you and your mates handled that pretty well."

"Why thank you." Lucas responded with a bow.

"Unfortunately I'll be leaving now as well. I have to report to Gehnarne early tomorrow to inspect the new ship."

Lucas looked disappointed. "Aw, I thought we could talk some more."

"Last I heard you didn't like talking to shrinks remember?" Gia said flirtatiously smiling.

"That may be true but I do like talking to you." He responded to her flirtatious gesture.

Gia giggled and blushed. "Well, next time we're off, I'll be sure to keep that in mind. Have a good evening." She smiled at him.

Lucas smiled back at her for being so kind and polite. "You have a good evening as well." Gia than walked away hoping the next time she saw Lucas he would be in a more sober state.

Lucas regrouped with Raymond outside leaving Jake and Katherine alone together at the bar while Sheena and her father went for a late night walk down the street. There was an awkward silence between them until Sheena decided to break the ice. "So, why did you take so long to see me?"

"I'm sorry honey." Colonel Vial humbly apologized.

"Sorry? I don't mean to sound disrespectful dad but, I think I'm owed a bit more of an explanation then just a sorry."

"Your right..."

"Huh?" Sheena was surprised that her father was being so humble. Normally this kind of conversation would lead into an argument.

Colonel Vial stopped as Sheena moved in front of him looking up at her father. "Dad?"

"I felt guilty."

"Guilty? About what?"

"About what happened to you. Sheena, I've been a military man my whole life, I love it but... if I knew that my life as a soldier was going to influence you to join yourself and get you involved in such terrible things like that incident with those child soldiers... I would have never joined. I blame myself for influencing you. Than on top of that, once you were in, I feel like I pushed you too hard. I'm so sorry honey..."

"Dad," She hugged her father. "I did look up to you and there were times I felt like I was under your shadow in the USOD, but none of this is your fault. You taught me how to live and survive in this world but, not once did you influence or discourage me from joining the Army in the first place. This was my choice alone, you have no reason to blame yourself."

Colonel Vial hugged her back with a smile. "I love you honey."

"I love you too dad." She smiled back feeling her father's warm loving embrace.

They slowly stopped hugging as Colonel Vial made a suggestion. "Say, how about we get some ice cream together?"

"Ice cream? Don't you think we're both a little too old for a father and daughter ice cream date?"

"Oh come on," He laughed. "No one is too old for that."

Sheena sighed playfully. "Okay, okay." Than giggled.

"Good." He smiled as they continued to walk together.

"What places are open this late at night anyway?"

"Trust me, I know a few. Me and your mother used to stay out late all the time getting deserts."

"Really?" She laughed. "Didn't think you had a sweet tooth like that."

He chuckled, "Only when I was with your mother." He paused in thought. "Speaking of things like that, how is Raymond? Does he treat you okay?"

Sheena couldn't help but blush at the question. "Well... I love him dad."

Colonel Vial felt a small sense of shock hit his heart as he was reminded that his little girl was all grown up. "Yea... I figured that... and he loves you too, very much."

"I know dad..."

"He told me you sing now, is that true?"

"Yes I do, I love it. Maybe next time we come back to earth you can hear me sing at Yabin's lounge."

"Definitely, how is that old geezer doing anyway?"

Sheena laughed "Well..." they continued to walk down the street into the night in deep conversation eventually finding the perfect desert shop for their father and daughter date.

Back at the bar, Katherine and Jake talked, drank, and even danced together like no tomorrow. By 0317 hours, Katherine and Jake opened the door to the hotel room as they laughed and giggled loudly and drunkenly. Once the door was open, Katherine made an audible, "Shhh!" while laughing mildly, trying not to wake the others in the room. They both stepped through the door stumbling in a drunken state trying not to trip over bags and suitcases in preparation for tomorrow when the team's leave would come to an end. Jake closed the door behind them. They looked around the cluttered room and saw Lucas sleeping on the floor on the left side of the bed with an empty beer bottle on the ground. The both of them chuckled at the sight knowing that Lucas was going to feel it tomorrow.

As Jake continued to chuckle at Lucas, Katherine's attention was drawn towards Raymond and Sheena in bed together. She looked at how perfect of a couple they seemed to be while they slept with their hands held together and Sheena's head resting on Raymond's left arm like a pillow. Although she loved them both like family, she couldn't help but feel jealous at the sight. She always wanted the perfect relationship but never got it. "What about me?..." She asked herself.

"What was that?" Jake asked while still chuckling when suddenly, Katherine kissed him. Jake was caught off guard as she pulled away a second later. He looked at her in a way he thought would never come. He moved closer to kiss her back. She let it happen as their lips touched passionately. They guided each other to the floor as they continued to make out passionately and quietly, trying not to wake the others.

Jake began to touch Katherine sensually as her neck arched back slowly in pleasure. At that moment, Jake started kissing and nibbling on her neck leading her to moan lustfully. Her legs began to spread as Jake's lower body sunk in between her blue dress's short skirt. Once his lower body touched hers, Katherine moaned in satisfaction.

Later that night, Jake was asleep while holding Katherine by her waist from behind with his pants and underwear down. Katherine began to wake up with the short skirt of her dress lifted above her waist with a smile of contentment from what had happened moments ago. She turned around to face Jake and calmly caressed his face with a loving touch feeling satisfied. Reality set in as she began to realize what she had done. Her smile turned into panic with emotions of guilt flooding her mind. She pushed her skirt back down, pulled up Jake's pants trying not to wake him, slowly stood up than walked quietly to the rest room and closed the door.

Katherine immediately felt the need to throw up. She rushed to the toilet holding her hair back and barfed into the toilet. She took her time and slowly stood up still feeling dazed and drunk. She walked towards the mirror and checked her neck for hickey's than splashed her face with water. She took a towel drying her face and wiping off her make up. She than looked straight into the mirror above the sink putting the towel down, beginning to assess what could happen after this. Remembering that Jake usually forgets the night prior if he's drunk enough, Katherine hoped that would be the case by tomorrow. She left the restroom looking for a spot to sleep. With the room so cluttered with bags and suitcases, the only comfortable spot for her was next to Jake. Katherine sighed in embarrassment and decided to risk sleeping next to Jake again facing away from him. "I can never tell him..." she whispered to herself as the guilt from using Jake in such a way haunted her. "You can never tell-"

Lightning Archival Records
The Legend Of "Taps" Explained
By Sheena "Crimson" Vial
AKA The Morrigan Of Kalista

Just before the American Civil War broke out, A college student

from the North was studying music in the South. Unfortunately he

was drafted into the confederate army and fought. Around that time,

his father, a Captain in the US Army from the North, had also fought.

One night, the Captain heard grunts of pain out in the battlefield.

Wanting to help, he found the wounded soldier and brought him back

to his camp. Once in the medical tent, not only did he find out that the

soldier was a confederate but also his own son who had died of his

wounds. Saddened by the death of his son, he searched his pockets

and found a sheet of music with lyrics. It would later be used at

military funerals without the lyrics and be named Taps.

Chapter 15: Battle Of Selva

"JAAAAAKE!!!!" Katherine shrieked as she watched Jake's lifeless body fall backwards in a pool of his own blood and brain matter. Katherine's emotions went rabid in her mind as she slowly slipped into shock while starring into Jake's cold dead eyes.

As she knelled there frozen, Garza aimed his pistol with a smoking barrel tip away from Jake's body and pointed it back at Katherine. "The only reason your still alive is because you have more use to me than he did." Katherine's hands began to shake with anger, "The way I see it, even if you don't talk, we can at least have our way with you, then sell you." Her rage screamed for Garza's blood. "Either way, you'll definitely be more fun and profitable then him." Garza chuckled devilishly. Katherine wanted Garza dead without any concern for her own safety.

Suddenly, a loud engine roar zoomed overhead at low altitude catching Garza and his two guards completely off guard. Garza looked up as he saw the Red Nova launch missiles towards the camouflage field projector. The missiles impacted, sending shutters and shock waves throughout the outpost as the camouflage field surrounding it flickered then shut down. The Red Nova continued on its course at top speed then began its descent down into the distant trees about half a click away from the outpost.

"What the Fu-!?"

"AAHH!!!" Kathrine screamed as she interrupted Garza by lunging and pouncing on top of him. She fought back with everything she had with no fear of death as her hands were still tied behind her back. She bit, and kneed Garza as his men jumped in trying to get her off of him.

During the struggle, Raymond spoke over the communications channel as he began to stand. "Crimson." He said with a rage filled voice as his flow system Gauntlet's discs began to spin on their own flickering back and forth from blue to red making a high pitch whining sound every time it turned red due to the higher speeds of the red disc's spinning. "On my order, kill the guards, leave Garza to me."

"Understood." Sheena responded with a cold voice while she lined up her shots waiting for the order as she tried her best not to cry over the loss of her friend Jake.

"Raymond?" Lucas asked in concern and fear as he saw the red and blue discs flickering. "What's happening to you?"

Raymond ignored him as he continued. "All units, standby for my order." The frequency of the disc's color flickering was increasing.

"Raymond?!" Lucas yelled to get his attention.

Raymond looked towards Lucas menacingly with rage in his eyes. Lucas recognized that look. He was never scared of it however, it always meant trouble. Raymond spoke to Lucas. "When I've lured Garza away from Katherine, save her." Suddenly the disc stabilized on red as they made a constant high pitch whining sound. The invisible gravity field's outline was now visible with a red glow as Raymond's right brown eye immediately began to glow red, just like Sarah on board the Red Nova in combat mode.

"Holy shit..." Lucas was frozen as he felt like he just saw Raymond's raw hatred in physical form. Raymond looked back towards Garza's position keeping his eyes locked on his prey than suddenly shot off sprinting at inhuman speeds towards the outpost, even faster than that time he ran on the edge of the roof the first time he used the flow system. Lucas quickly got up, attached Raymond's AR30 and assault pack together, slung the pack onto his back and ran as first as he could, impossibly trying to catch up with Raymond.

"CRIMSON, FIRE!" Raymond ordered in mid sprint.

Sheena slowly exhaled as she saw Garza punching Katherine while mounting her with his guards stepping back realizing Garza had her under control. Sheena moved her weapon towards the guard on Garza's right and began to squeeze the trigger. The guard turned towards Sheena's direction making Sheena unexpectedly stop due to her seeing what looked like a child soldier in her cross hairs instead of one of Garza's guards. She flinched and blinked in fear as the guard reappeared in her sight. "NO!" She said to herself out loud "Not this time, no holding back!" She readied to fire again as she took one deep breath and exhaled. She slowly squeezed the trigger making a loud gunshot. The 7.62 millimeter-round flew out of the barrel at supersonic speeds flying past brush and trees. The round began to drop which Sheena had already compensated for as it penetrated through the guard's skull turning his brain into mush than explosively exited out the other side.

The second guard was shocked by his comrades sudden death as he immediately met the same fate dropping to the ground with an explosive gaping hole through his head.

Garza flinched in surprise seeing both of his guards dead on the floor. He stood up from the mount he had over Katherine and activated his flow system expecting more trouble. "The fuck is going on here!" He said as he heard someone at a great distance quickly running up behind him.

"hraaaAAAH!!!" Raymond yelled viciously as he swung his sword down colliding into Garza's just barely drawn rapier blocking Raymond's attack causing Garza to fly back uncontrollably from the force of the swing. Garza's back skid across the floor several meters while he used the flow system to bring his legs up towards his head, bringing his body back to a right side up standing position grinding to a halt on his feet. Garza looked up and saw Raymond in a Guard position with his blade pointing behind him from the follow through after his previous strike on Garza.

"And who might you be I wonder?" Garza was intrigued as he admired how Raymond looked with his flow system's rage mode active.

"All units, EXECUTE!" Raymond ordered with a vicious tone in his voice. At an instant, all hell broke loose as Bravo, Charlie, Delta, and Echo teams began firing at their designated attack points killing many rebels in the initial engagement. Garza jumped in surprise from the initial attack and looked around to see what was happening. While Garza looked away, time seemed to move slowly in Raymond's mind as he knelled down next to Jake's body. Explosions, sparks, and debris glistened nearby as he wanted to pay tribute to his fallen comrade. Refusing to look directly at Jake's body knowing he would lose focus, he took his right hand's pointer and middle finger, scooped up some of Jake's blood, and swiped it across his face from ear to ear in the same ritualistic manner he would always do with the black face paint. Time began to move back to normal as Garza turned around and saw Raymond standing back up with a blood strip across his eyes matching the same color of his gravity field's outline and his right red eye. Some of the blood trickled down his cheeks and dried in place. "I swear on the blood of my friend, my family, and all the innocent people you have massacred over the years, I WILL KILL YOU!!!"

With a smile, Garza was impressed. "You truly are something different... amazing... I also see you are a student of the arts judging by that sword." He looked directly into Raymond's red eye intrigued at what else he can do. "So am I."

"SHUT UP AND FIGHT YOU BASTARD!!! HRAAAAA!!!" Raymond lunged forward with a one handed stab as Garza's rapier just barely parried the attack. Raymond then spun quickly following the momentum of Garzas parry trying to perform a vertical down ward cut now holding his sword with both hands, Garza blocked desperately, Raymond parried then thrust, Garza parried almost uncontrollably and backed away at a great distance with the help of his Flow System.

"Damn he's fast!" Garza thought to himself enthusiastically. "So fast that I can barely block and parry his attacks, let alone be able to attack without giving him an opening. I'd better play defensively for now." He grinned devilishly as Raymond advanced towards him at excessive speed.

"HRA!" Raymond yelled as he attacked. Garza and Raymond moved further away from Katherine and Jake's body as they continued to fight.

Katherine lay next to Jake on the floor in shock feeling numb and out of place. She had a bloodied lip, a left black eye, and a cut on her cheek. Her eye's were wide open in hysteria as she stared at Jake feeling more lifeless along with him.

"Katherine..." She heard someone yelling at a distance and getting closer. "Katherine..." She heard it again as her head began to slowly turn instinctively on its own reacting to the voice. "KATHERINE!" Lucas yelled at her while taking a knee next to her grabbing her arm. "Are you okay!" She stayed silent and stared at Lucas motionless. "Come on, we have to go!" He yelled over the loud nearby gun fire and explosions. "Help me with Jake's body!" She continued to lay there as she slowly looked back at Jake's body. "Katherine!?" Lucas was growing frustrated that she was in this state.

"There they are!" A rebel with four others yelled as they readied their weapons to fire while running towards Lucas and Katherine.

"Oh shit!" Lucas readied his weapon just as the rebels were cut down by a combination of machine gun fire, sniper fire from Sheena and his own AR30. As the rebels lifelessly dropped, Lucas looked right in surprise as he saw the source of the Machine Gun fire. It was from an LMG mounted on a ATLV, All Terrain Light Vehicle, with three occupants, a driver, a passenger, and a gunner. Its body was mostly exposed due to a lightweight aluminum frame design and had four seats with a top gunner hatch.

The ATLV pulled up to Lucas. "Sir, you okay?!" The passenger asked as he jumped out of the vehicle wearing full combat gear and holding an AR30 running towards Lucas.

"Who the hell are you guys!" Lucas asked as a stray bullet cracked nearby.

"Fox team, on orders from Star to pick you guys up and get you to the Rally point!"

"Jason?" Lucas was surprised at how well Jason was taking initiative. First destroying the camouflage field, now this. "You got a medic?!" He yelled as the LMG on the ATLV began to fire at enemy targets.

"I'm a medic!"

"Take care of her, she's hurt! Driver!"

"Yes sir!"

"Help me with the body!"

"Moving!" The driver jumped out and helped Lucas lift Jake's body to the back cargo area of the vehicle. The medic grabbed Katherine's arm as she instinctively stood up and was guided by the medic. Lucas and the driver strapped down Jake's body so it wouldn't fall off, then seated themselves in the vehicle as the medic sat Katherine in her seat next to Lucas. The medic took his seat, turned around and began to clean Katherine's cut on her cheek as the vehicle turned around and drove back in the direction it came from as the gunner continued to lay down fire maintaining fire supiority. The medic also wiped the blood off her face then put a sticky gaw on the wound just as the gunner ceased fire. She starred forward the whole time barely moving a muscle.

"How is she?" Lucas asked in a normal toned voice as the vehicle exited the battle space.

The medic already had his pupil dilation light out and began to shine the light in her eyes. Her pupils didn't react. "I think she's going into neurological shock." He reported in concern.

"Dammit." Lucas said as he turned to Katherine, held her hand and tried to help her out of shock. "Katherine, you're gonna be okay now, just stay with us." Katherine slowly looked towards Lucas with a blank stare. Lucas was shocked at the state she was in. He'd never seen her like this before.

"Lucas...?" She spoke quietly.

Lucas was happy to hear her voice. "Yea," He smiled. "It's me." She slowly started to look behind herself where Jake's body was secured when Lucas stopped her by gently using his right hand to push her face back towards him. "No, no, no, don't look back there, look at me. We're getting you out of here okay?"

Katherine than realized she didn't need to look back for she already knew what was there. She began to cry as her blank stare turned to sadness. She leaned forward into Lucas's chest and sobbed. Lucas wasn't sure what to do, so he followed his instincts and embraced her in comfort, trying not to cry himself.

"How-" Lucas sniffed back his tears. "-how much further to the rally point?"

"Not much longer sir." The driver stated.

"How is the fight progressing?"

"All teams are effectively engaging the enemy sir. The objective should be taken within the hour."

"Good." Lucas said in confidence while trying to breath normally holding back his tears.

The battle continued as teams Bravo through Echo assaulted the outpost from the North. All teams coordinated together as they laid down bases of fire, flanked the enemy, and cleared buildings taking intel and killing the rebels. In some areas of the outpost, orbital strikes were called in from the Enidon as loud explosions decimated enemy structures. In the middle of this controlled chaos, Raymond and Garza were viciously fighting each other.

Raymond thrust with his sword, Garza narrowly blocked with a steadier posture as he thought to himself "He used this move before, if I keep analyzing his movements, it could help me defend myself better, maybe even try to go on the offensive if I can start to read his movements." Raymond parried Garza's block and cut up, Garza dodged back several meters and began to run towards a burning hanger. Raymond ran to catch up as a rebel tried to shoot Raymond but was immediately put down by Sheena from her sniper support. Garza saw this as he looked back realizing that sniper was a serious threat. "Judging from how all of my men had died so far, the sniper has to be somewhere to the west." He grabbed his radio attached to his chest rig to call in the sniper position as he noticed Raymond running next to him from the other side of the burning hanger starring down Garza not once taking his eyes off of him as pieces of the hanger blocked his visual at moments. Garza began to use the radio contacting a team he knew was patrolling the western woods. "Long shire, this is Rezno! Do you copy?!"

"Long Shire here sir." The man said as him and his team patrolled their assigned area near Sheena's position.

"I need you to find a sniper in your area of patrol."

Raymond looked at Garza wondering, "What is he up too?"

"Roger sir, we're already on it, we've heard gun fire in this area. Shouldn't be long till we find them."

"Good," Garza approved with a smile. "When you find them, let me know first than proceed with whatever means necessary. Rezno ou-" Suddenly, Raymond disappeared from the other side of the hanger. "Huh?!" Garza was puzzled.

"HRA!!!" Raymond was now above Garza ready to cut down.

"Shit!" Garza was caught off guard as he let go of the radio, leaned back with his rapier up and slid under Raymond backwards while blocking his attack with his rapier. Garza used the momentum from the slide to get back up and continued running. Raymond was now behind Garza trying to catch up. Garza plowed through the burning building and was now across from Raymond on the other side again. "Is that all you've got kid?!"

Raymond grew even more angry. "RAAH!!!" He plowed through the burning hanger by launching himself into a vortex aimed directly at Garza. Garza was impressed at his technique as he readied his rapier to block the attack. The tip of Raymond's sword slammed into the tip of Garza's as Raymond spun in a vortex for two more rotations and stopped, landing on his feet with both tips of their swords glowing red from heat.

"Such aggression!" Garza said. "I compliment you on your technique!"

"SHUT UP!!!" Raymond thrust his sword forward into Garza's Rapier so hard, Garza launched back several meters.

When Garza came to a grinding stop on his feet, he spoke. "That's the spirit, come at me again, show me what you can really do!" Although Garza liked the challenge, he was also trying to distract Raymond and learn all of his moves. With pure ferocity, Raymond lunged forward at an incredible speed to make a downward cut.

Long shire and his team slowly scouted the area hearing another gunshot. This time it was almost right on top of them. Long shire took out a thermal sight and looked toward the large tree just in front of him at fifty-three meters. At ninety-seven meters off the ground, he found a heat silhouette of a woman in the tree as she was shooting at another target. "Gotcha." Long Shire called it in. "Rezno,"

"*Rezno, do you copy?*" Garza's radio squawked as Garza and Raymond's swords where locked.

Garza smiled as he heard the radio go off. Raymond angrily asked. "The hell you smiling about!?"

"I think you should let them take this." Garza responded calmly.

"Screw you!" Raymond put more pressure forward on the swords.

"Fine, if you really want another one of your friends to die, be my guest."

"What!?" Raymond was puzzled.

"You know, your little sniper friend?" He said to Raymond with a devilish gaze. Raymond stopped putting forward pressure as he was now interested.

Garza's radio squawked again. "*Rezno? Do you copy? We have located a female sniper, I say again, we have located a female sniper.*" Raymond was shocked.

"OOOoohh!" Garza said in surprise. "More than a friend perhaps?"

Raymond was unsure of what to do. He jumped backwards away

from Garza unlocking their swords and landed on his feet several meters away with his guard down. "What do you want?" Raymond asked viciously.

"Simple, you go and save your friend while I get off this planet."

"You won't get far befor-"

"I have my ways." Garza interrupted.

"And if I don't let you go?"

"My men will kill your friend." He looked at Raymond with deadly seriousness. "Plain and simple, what is your choice?"

Raymond looked away from Garza and thought for a moment. The perfect chance to end the Colonial Wars, avenge Jake, and avenge his parents was right there in front of him. However, his love for Sheena exceeded that thirst for revenge, he would never be willing to sacrifice her. He looked back at Garza vengefully and pointed his sword at him, threatening him with the razor sharp tip and said, "Next time I see you... You die."

Garza grinned and chuckled. "I look forward to the challenge."

Raymond sheathed his sword and immediately began running to the west as the flow system gave him a boost in speed.

"*Rezno?*" Garza's radio squawked. "*Do you copy?*"

Garza grabbed his radio and spoke. "You have your orders, proceed."

Long Shire and his team were ready. "Yes sir." He responded as he attached the thermal sight to his rifle.

As Raymond ran, a warning beep went off as his battery indicator on his contacts HUD flashed saying twenty percent. "Crap." He said as he pressed his gauntlet wrists together for three seconds, deactivating Rage Mode to save Battery power as the red outline of the gravity field dissipated and his right eye's red glow turned blue with his flow system now in standard mode. Although still faster than normal sprinting speed, he immediately slowed down compared to how much faster Rage mode allowed him to move. "Crimson, this is Slinger!" Raymond said as he ran as fast as he could in standard Flow System state.

Sheena heard Raymond's transmission and responded. "Crimson here."

"*Crimson, you've been compromised!*" Raymond said as Long shire lifted his rifle. "*Get the hell out of there now!*" Raymond yelled frantically.

"What!?" Sheena said in shock as Long Shire looked through the scope and lined up his shot. Just as Sheena began moving to displace, Long Shire squeezed the trigger. A loud gunshot was heard as the 7.62 millimeter-round cut through the leaves of the tree and hit Sheena's right shoulder, penetrating through her shoulder Kevlar plate. "AAHH!!!" She shrieked in pain while the channel was still open as she fell off the large tree branch.

"*SHEENA!*" Raymond yelled in fear of the worst.

As Sheena fell, she hit two smaller branches on her way down, than landed on a large branch face down, stopping her fall. Her right arm hung over the side as it bled.

Back on the Enidon. "Sir!" A TOC technician yelled to Gehnarne. "Crimson's been hit!"

"Oh no," Gehnarne said out loud as he contacted Raymond. "Slinger, Rifter, be advised, Crimson's been hit."

"Oh God no," Raymond said out loud as he tried contacting Sheena again. "Crimson, Slinger, do you copy!?" With worry in his voice. Sheena slowly rolled left as she felt her right arm soaked in her own blood and in excruciating pain coming from her right shoulder. "Come on Sheena, talk to me!" Raymond called on the channel again.

She grunted in pain as she double tapped her SDT. "Slinger... Crimson." She spoke quietly and slowly. "I'm still in this fight..." She opened her medical kit as she tried to relax her breathing.

"Thank god," Raymond sighed in relief. "Crimson, stay there and be still, I'm on my way."

Sheena heard repel launchers go off as she looked around to find the enemy. She saw them already climbing up the repels to confirm the kill. "Negative Slinger... they are moving in on my position." She said as she took the foam injector from her med kit and readied it near her wound. "You won't make it in time..." She pushed the injector deep into her wound as she cringed her teeth in pain trying to suffer in silence. She cried as she pressed the injector releasing the foam balls into the wound, instantly stopping the bleeding. "I'll have no choice but to fight them..." She pulled the injector out of the wound. "Digit gave me the final version of the flow system." She pulled out a pressure dressing. "I can use it to fight." She wrapped it tightly than began to get up to her knees.

Raymond didn't like that she would have to fight wounded and on her own but also knew she had no choice. "Crimson, can you hold them off long enough till I get there?"

Sheena closed her eyes, took a deep breath and exhaled trying to regain focus. She opened her eyes in confidence and responded. "Yes, I can..." She grabbed her pistol and her combat knife, one in each hand as she prepared for combat. "and I will." She was ready and focused for the fight.

Raymond was worried but had confidence in her ability's. He knew she would give it everything she had to survive. "Sheena, you still remember what they called you back on Kalista right?"

"I do."

"Remind them of how you got that name!" Raymond said viciously to motivate her.

"I will," She responded with motivation. "I am, the Morrigan!" She ran towards the tree trunk, double tapped the gauntlets together activating the Flow System with a bass like sound. She jumped on the tree and wall ran for several steps around the right side of the tree. In the first couple of steps, she fired her pistol downward hitting one of the rebels in the head. As he fell dead, Sheena holstered her pistol, grabbed the rope the dead rebel was hooked up to as his body fell, jumped off the tree and swung towards another repel rope. Another rebel fired at her but missed due to her speed. She passed by his rope, cutting it with her knife. He screamed as he fell to his death. The other rebels on Long Shire's team on the ground looked up, saw what was happening and opened fire at Sheena.

She planted her feet on the tree trunk and began to wall run while holding on to the rope with her left hand. With her right hand she drew and reloaded her pistol using a holster mod, switched the weapon to full auto, and began to return fire. Her right shoulder ached in pain with every shot as she struggled to maintain accuracy. She hit two out of the ten rebels on the ground. "Come on!" She grunted knowing she could do better.

As she ran out of slack on the rope, she swung off it with a back flip to the next rope shooting the rebel who was on it in midair. She then grabbed the new rope with her legs in an upside down posture as she extended her arms down, ready to shoot. Her left arm accidentally hit a small branch, sending her body into a spin while she fired her pistol on full auto. Although unplanned, the spin proved useful allowing her to dodge the incoming ground fire. Once again she struggled to maintain accuracy killing three more rebels on the ground. After losing so many men in that short amount of time, Long Shire did what he had to do. "Command, this is Long Shire, requesting reinforcements!"

The ATLV pulled up to the Red Nova entrance ramp as Jason walked down the ramp quickly to help the medic get Katherine out of her seat. "I got her sir, help out Captain Walker." The medic told him. Jason moved quickly to the back of the vehicle as Lucas starred at Jake's body.

Because of the trauma to Jake's head, Jason couldn't recognize him immediately. With a disturbed expression, "Fuck, is that really-?"

"Just help me Jason." Lucas asked somberly.

"...Sorry" Jason said as he grabbed Jake's arms while Lucas grabbed his legs. They hobbled up the ramp and into the cargo bay.

The medic helped Katherine take a seat on the floor in the cargo area. "I have to go back with my team to get more casualties, I'll check on you later when I get back."

"Thank you..." Katherine quietly responded.

The medic stood up and left Katherine, walking past Sarah who was observing the whole situation from behind a large crate of ammo. She continued looking at the medic leaving as he passed Lucas and Jason carrying in Jake's body. They moved it to the left of the cargo bay, opposite from where Katherine was to avoid her from seeing the body. They respectfully placed Jake's body on the floor and stood up. "Thanks Jason..." Lucas said.

"Your welcome..."

"Could you-?"

"Of course." Jason interrupted. "If you need anything, let me know."

"Thank you..." Lucas said. Jason than walked away.

As Jason continued walking through the middle of the cargo bay towards the bridge, he noticed Sarah observing Lucas. He walked up to her and spoke. "You okay?"

She looked at him and nodded.

"Good," He looked back towards Lucas while still speaking to Sarah. "I don't mind you observing them but... they're in a lot of pain right now... keep your distance a bit alright?"

She nodded slowly with a somber expression.

"Good." He turned back towards the bridge and continued walking as Sarah looked back towards Lucas.

Lucas starred quietly at Jake's body for a moment. He then glanced right and saw a cargo blanket covering a large crate of cargo. He walked towards it, grabbed the cargo blanket, and walked back towards Jake's body. He then knelt down next to the body, softly closed Jakes's eye's while saying "Till Valhalla brother..." He then draped the blanket over Jake's body, covering him. Lucas knelt there for a moment longer, unsure what to do next.

"Was it always that simple?" Katherine said as she walked closer to Lucas from behind surprising him. He turned to look at her. "I mean," She continued with a trembling voice. "people have died around us before but, never one of us..." Lucas was growing concerned for her. "I mean, if it was always that simple, then what's the point of all this?" She was slowly getting more frantic.

"Stop." Lucas said. However, she continued.

"Why do we struggle so hard for something we're all going to lose anyway?"

"Don't go there Kat." Lucas stood up facing her in anger.

"Why do we all struggle to survive if we're all gonna die anyway?!" She said hysterically.

"ENOUGH!" Lucas yelled loudly sending an echo throughout the cargo bay. Katherine froze in shock as Sarah who was still hiding behind the cargo jumped in fear. "He loved us! He died for us!" Lucas slowly calmed down as he walked towards Katherine. "He was willing to die to make sure the rest of us had a future." He stopped in front of Katherine as he began to cry himself. "Don't..." Lucas choked as tears began to flow out of his eyes while he tried to hold them back failing. "Don't make it seem like his sacrifice was in vein..."

Katherine then remembered that she wasn't the only one who loved Jake. She hugged Lucas in comfort. Lucas hesitated then did the same as they both mourned together for the loss of their beloved friend.

Sarah continued to observe without being noticed. She stood up and walked back to the bridge learning an important lesson about love. She now knew what she had to do with her feelings for Jason.

Lucas and Katherine hugged for a moment longer when a thought came to Katherine making her concerned. "Where is Raymond and Sheena?..." Lucas eyes shot open wide in concern as he just remembered they were still out there fighting.

Sheena was still using the repelling lines in her strategy as she swung across the side of the tree shooting at rebels on the ground. However, she was unaware of Long Shire's plan. "NOW, Shoot the rope!" The rebels switched targets from Sheena to the rope she swung on and opened fired.

The rope suddenly broke at a point above from where Sheena was grabbing it as she unexpectedly lost control and went into free fall. Because the flow system detected the swing as a forward thrust, she didn't fall straight down, Instead continued to move forward out of control as her torso slammed into another tree branch. "AH!" She grunted in pain as she heard a crack from her right rib. She than fell several meters to the ground with enough time for the flow system to detect it as an uncontrolled fall. She screamed as she fell thinking she was falling to her death when suddenly the system's gravity field cushioned the impact than released her to the floor.

"GO, Kill her!" Long Shire ordered as the last of his men moved in with weapons up shooting.

Sheena quickly crawled up to a boulder struggling to breath due to the pain from the cracked rib. She looked around for her pistol as she lost it in the fall however found a dead rebel next to her with his weapon. She pried the dead rebels older model M16 out of his dead hands. She than reflexively ejected the magazine, saw it was loaded, slightly pulled back the charging handle of the weapon while looking in the chamber and saw a round loaded. She quickly slammed the magazine back in, set the weapon to full auto, leaned out the right side of the boulder and fired two-five rounds bursts hitting one rebel. She moved back into cover with bullets cracking all around her. She then switched firing hands, leaned left out of cover and fired another five round burst than moved back into cover. The rebels were almost on top of her, outnumbered, out gunned, and no effective flow strategy due to being too far away from walls or other useful objects. She knew, "This is it..." She thought of Raymond one last time thinking she would never see him again. She mustard up her courage into one last move. She jumped up high in the air using the flow system as a boost with her M16 up and ready to fire. "AAAHHH!!!"

"HRAH!" Raymond came out of nowhere to the right of Sheena catching the rebels off guard instantly cutting two of them in half at the waist with blood spattering in the direction of the blade's movement.

"Raymond!?" Sheena said in shock as if everything moved in slow motion at Raymond's arrival with a glowing blue right eye, and blood stripe still on his face.

Carrying through with the momentum of the cut, Raymond turned around while grabbing what looked like an old rebel AK-47 with a one-hundred rounds drum magazine on his back, than threw it towards Sheena while yelling "COVER ME!!!"

Sheena caught it, immediately readied and fired on the rebels on full auto while landing on her feet killing and suppressing the nearby rebels as Raymond aggressively dodged and cut down other rebels near him.

"Another one!?" Long Shire said in fear, unsure what to do.

Raymond cut down two more rebels as he, came close to Sheena with a spin, passed her the sword and quickly took the AK-47 from her while saying, "Switch up! Go clutch!"

"Gotcha!" Sheena acknowledge as she thrust forward stabbing a rebel, "HA!" then cutting him in half while Raymond maintained the suppressing fire with the AK-47.

With the mental shock of facing two flow system users, their fellow fighters literally being cut to shreds, and being suppressed by heavy incoming fire rendered the rebels efforts useless, turning the tables against them. "Fall back!" Long Shire ordered. "Move!" as he and others began to run for their lives frantically.

Raymond shot three more rebels as he noticed the rest fleeing. "Assault through! Finish them off!" he ordered to Sheena.

"Roger!" Sheena responded as she pulled the sword out of another rebel while grabbing his weapon then threw the sword back towards

Raymond who quickly caught and sheathed it. With weapons up, they both stayed on line next to each other while running forward at an incredible speed finishing off the remaining rebels. Once the field was clear, Raymond stopped and drew his pistol at reflexive speed, pointed it to his left without bothering to aim, than fired. The nine millimeter-round flew straight into the back of Long Shire's head as he was running several meters away. He fell forward to the ground dead.

"Clear!" Raymond barked.

"Clear..." Sheena said with a gasp as she began to faint, falling backwards against a tree.

While Raymond turned to face her, he heard a thud just seeing Sheena collapsing to the floor. "Sheena!?" He yelled in fear as he powered down the flow system with his blue right eye turning back to its natural brown while he ran to Sheena. "Sheena, you okay!?" He asked as he knelt by her side and began to carefully assess her injury's

"I- I can barely breath." She gasped for air.

Raymond looked down and noticed the front of her plate carrier was imploded inward. He immediately pulled on her plate carrier rip cord causing the vest system to fall apart in pieces. Sheena gasped for air getting more adequate amount of oxygen but kept her breathing restricted due to the pain from her cracked rib. Raymond pulled the pieces of the plate carrier away as her green jump suit became exposed, splattered in her own blood. "The hell did this?" He asked as he looked at the front half of the vest feeling the plate inside was horizontally snapped in half.

Sheena weakly laughed in pain and said "I had a run in with a tree."

"A tree?" Raymond was puzzled.

"I'll explain later." She said weakly

Raymond looked at her right arm. It was covered in fresh blood as he noticed the pressure dressing on her shoulder had come undone "Oh no," He said as he double tapped his SDT. "Star, this is Slinger, requesting immediate MEDEVAC at my location, over."

Jason responded from the bridge as him and Timothy were in the pilot and co-pilot seats. "Roger that Slinger, all casualties are aboard and are in-route to your position." The Red Nova lifted off the surface and hovered at a low altitude to Raymond and Sheena's position. "So much for a boring mission huh Tim?" Timothy didn't respond making Jason concerned. "Tim? You alright?"

"Huh?" Timothy snapped out of it. "Oh, sorry I uh... I just wasn't expecting us to... lose anybody... Now I kinda regret saying what I said earlier..."

Jason understood. "Always be careful what you wish for Tim."

"Yea..." Timothy sadly agreed.

Back on the ground with Raymond and Sheena, Raymond had unzipped her jump suit exposing her upper torso with her black sports bra also covered in blood. As he tried to peel back the jump suit down to her waste, he realized the new flow system gauntlet's were in the way. Not caring about the new tech at the moment, he quickly took them off Sheena's arms, placed them next to the rest of her gear, then immediately focused back on Sheena. "Hang in there Sheena, help is on the way." Raymond said trying to comfort her as he redressed her shoulder wound stopping the bleeding again.

"Raymond," Sheena spoke weakly "There's something I have to tell you."

"Relax Sheena," He urged her as he checked for more wounds. "Save your strength."

"No, I-I have to tell you this now."

"Sheena, don't be pulling that last word bullshit on me okay, you're gonna be fine!" He said aggressively.

"Would you shut up and listen to me!" She yelled at him desperately with anger in her voice. Raymond froze in surprise as she felt bad for yelling, "Sorry... I-" she got to the point. "Remember when we talked about what you did to Asrin and those pirates?"

Raymond was now paying close attention. "Yea, I remember"

"I had more to say about that but, at the time I figured Garza was dead so it didn't matter... but now that he's alive, I have to say it."

"What is it?"

"You..." She built up the courage to speak knowing Raymond would most likely disagree. "You have to forgive him and move on."

"What!?" He said in surprise.

"This hate you have towards him, it's luring you down a dark path. One that will surely destroy you... That rage, vengeance, it will consume you even after you've killed him." Raymond disagreed with her but kept it to himself in this moment and let her talk. "God gave us freewill so we can freely choose to love him and others. However, free will is like-" As Sheena continued speaking, Raymond heard Sheena and Pastor Walker's voice in the same statement. "-a double edged sword..." Raymond was now shocked as he remembered the dream he had a couple of weeks ago. He now had confirmation that it meant something important. "Men like Garza, they use God's gift of free will for hate... and it has to be stopped with love... love of family, friends, to protect them, and whenever possible, use that same love for mercy on those who wronged us in the first place. If you continue to fight with hate, the hatred will only continue." Her lips began to tremble. "The v-vicious cycle of h-hate has to stop." She began to shiver.

"Sheena, what's wrong?" Raymond was worried.

"I f-feel cold" She began to shiver more. Raymond immediately recognized the symptom, she was going into shock due to blood lose. He elevated her legs with a nearby rock than embraced her from behind to keep her warm, feeling her body shiver in his arms. He held her hands as they felt cold holding his composer trying not to panic. "Come on Sheena, hang on, stay with me," He whispered in her ear.

"Raymond..." She said softly trying to stay awake just as the Red Nova arrived, hovering overhead with the circular cargo bay opening up and dropping rescue lines connected to a litter off the side down to Raymond and Sheena. The Fox team medic repelled down another line to assess the situation as the hovering engines roared loudly overhead.

"Sir! Step aside please!"

"She's going into shock!" Raymond said while standing up and stepping away from Sheena.

"She's gonna be okay sir!" He said while taking out a space blanket from his medical bag and wrapped it around Sheena to keep her warm. "I could use your help in hooking her up to the rescue litter!"

"You got it!" Raymond acknowledged. He helped the medic lift Sheena into position and strapped her to the litter.

The medic gave a thumbs up to the crew above while Raymond gave Sheena a kiss on the forehead as she was lifted away. She looked at him one last moment before she was lifted up towards the ship.

"Hook up sir!" The medic said to Raymond while they both grabbed all of Sheena's consolidated gear including the new flow system, and hooked up to the rescue line. The medic gave a thumbs up to the crew above. The crew hoisted them up, lifting Raymond and the medic into the air. As Raymond was lifted higher, he looked to the east with the sun almost set. He saw what was left of the rebel out post after the battle. Rebel bodies littered the base grounds, buildings destroyed, bullet holes everywhere and friendly teams maintaining security around what was left of the outpost. The PMCs of Bravo through Foxtrot teams were extremely effective. He looked up seeing Sheena being carefully pulled into the cargo bay. She was safe.

A moment later, Raymond reached the top with the medic. He carefully stepped into the cargo bay and unhooked himself from the rescue line. Just as the medic stepped into the cargo bay, Raymond noticed the other Fox team members carefully lifting a stretcher with Sheena on it with a blood bag of O Positive blood connected to her arm through a small hose and an oxygen mask due to Sheena's difficulty with breathing. Katherine was next to Sheena's stretcher and stood up from kneeling just as they lifted up Sheena. They carried her to a designated casualty area where Raymond saw two other wounded PMCs with various injuries being treated. As Sheena was carried away, Katherine turned and ran towards Raymond. "I just saw Sheena." Katherine said, stopping in front of him in worry. "She didn't look so good."

"She'll be okay." Raymond responded. "Are you okay?"

Katherine looked down as Lucas took a step out of the shadows of the cargo bay behind her to see Raymond. Katherine spoke. "Jake... he didn't-"

"I know..." Raymond said somberly. He looked at Lucas behind Katherine and walked towards him as Selva's sun had set.

"Good to see you in one-piece brotha." Lucas said.

"Good to see you're okay as well." They clasped hands and hugged. As they hugged, Raymond looked behind Lucas and saw a body covered with a cargo blanket. They let go of each other as Raymond asked, "Is that-?"

"Yea..." Lucas interrupted mournfully. "...It is."

Raymond sighed in sorrow. "I can't believe he's gone..."

"Neither can I..."

Katherine looked at Raymond and Lucas as they talked. She began walking towards them while the circular cargo bay slowly began to shut. The battle of Selva was now over.

Chapter 16: After Math

Gehnarne stared at the monitor in the TOC observing the destruction of the rebel base, and the status of everyone who came back from the surface. "Gehnarne," Gia said as she handed him a tablet. "Here are the casualty reports."

He took the tablet and made his assessment. "Three WIA... one KIA."

"Yes..." Gia regretfully reported.

"Despite the loss of Jake, we can't deny that our forces operated very effectively on the ground."

"Yes, and speaking of effective," She scrolled through her tablet and found what she was looking for. "If you look at section seven of the report, you'll see that Bravo team found a very valuable piece of intel we should look into immediatly."

Gehnarne was curious. He scrolled to section seven and saw it himself. "Plans for a battle station?" He was surprised.

"Yes, according to the rest of the intel Bravo found, that outpost was an early warning post meant to inform the battle station of incoming hostiles."

"I see, and where is this station now?" Gehnarne asked as he looked for the answer on the tablet.

"According to the intel we have on the stations orbital flight path listed under section eight, category B, it should be in the exact opposite orbit as ours."

Gehnarne was shocked. "You mean it's here?"

"Yes." Gia confirmed.

"Walk with me." He said to her as they both walked out of the TOC. "What happened to Garza after Raymond let him escape?" He asked while walking into the bridge elevator following up with a voice command to the elevator. "Sick bay." The doors closed just after Gia walked in with the elevator imediately moving to the sick bay.

"We tracked him to a shuttle and followed. However, once he left the atmosphere, he activated some kind of camo field similar to what the outpost used but on a smaller scale."

"I see, there's no doubt he was on his way to that station." The elevator doors slid open as they walked out of the elevator.

"I wouldn't be surprised if that station uses a camo field as well." Gia assessed as they walked down the hall towards sick bay.

"Which could explain why we haven't detected it on our initial scans when we first arrived here. Gia?"

"Yes?" They both stopped at the entrance to sick bay.

"I want you to have Izzy re-scan the orbital space around Selva and look for any small anomalies to find that station. Also, I want you to contact the council, send them our reports and set up a meeting."

"Understood." Gia responded. "What will you be doing in the mean time?"

Gehnarne looked through the glass door into sick bay and saw Raymond sitting in a chair in the waiting room still in his combat gear without his flow system gauntlets looking down at his Taclet no longer wearing a blood stripe across his face. "Giving our friend my condolences."

"I see," Gia said somberly while looking at Raymond than looked back to Gehnarne. "I'll get to work right away."

"Thank you." Gia walked away to conduct her tasks just when Gehnarne faced the glass door and slowly walked through it as it automatically opened.

"If it were anyone else that you were trying to save by letting Garza go, I would have scolded the shit out of you," Colonel Vial said through the speakers on Raymond's Taclet *"But knowing it was my daughter… Thank you son… thank you for saving her."* Gehnarne leaned against the wall waiting for Raymond to finish his conversation with Colonel Vial.

"There's no way I was gonna leave her or anyone else for dead sir." Raymond responded.

"I know, if anyone gives you any flak on that decision, I'll back you." The Colonel thought for a moment. *"You know, ever since Sheena was a kid she always held herself to a higher standard like I do. So much pride in her. So much that she felt all the boys in school were beneath her."* Raymond's expression changed to curiosity as he wondered where the Colonel was going with this. *"As you know she*

joined the Army at a young age of sixteen like you did so, she had never been in any kind of romantic relationship before you came along. When she told me she had fallen in love with you, I was skeptical but then I remembered that higher standard... that pride of her's. I knew long before she met you that if she ever fell in love, it would be with someone that even I would probably feel proud to call a son." Colonel Vial smiled at Raymond as he felt proud understanding what Colonel Vial was trying to say although it was in a very indirect way. *"If you and Sheena ever tie the knot, which I hope you do one day, you have my blessing."*

Raymond felt overwhelmed as he tried not to cry. "Th-thank you sir."

"Sir" someone said outside of Raymond's Taclet's field of view to Colonel Vial. *"We just received orders from the council."*

"Understood." Colonel Vial responded to them. *"Duty calls Raymond, Good luck out there."*

Raymond sniffed back a tear and responded. "You too sir."

"Thank you, Watchman out." The transmission ended

Raymond put down his Taclet and looked at Gehnarne as he spoke. "Wow, never thought I'd see Colonel Vial being so nice" Gehnarne commented.

"He's honestly not a bad guy once you get to know him, he was just stressed out and frustrated by what happened with Sheena back on Kalista."

"I see." Gehnarne said while he took a seat next to Raymond as his expression turned somber. "I'm sorry about Jake."

"...He was a good man... he will be missed..." Raymond seemed sad.

Gehnarne agreed with a mild nod to Raymond's statement. "How is Sheena doing?"

"She was shot in the shoulder, just barely missed an artery. The doctor said she was lucky, if the artery was severed, she would have definitely died from blood loss. The MEDEVAC came just in time although the blood loss was so severe they had to conduct a blood cell regeneration treatment along with blood transfusion. She also has a cracked rib but the doctor said they can repair it easily, nothing too serious. With all that, she should be out by late tonight."

"And Katherine?"

"All of her injuries were superficial, she was quickly treated and fitted with a new SDT, she's as good as new." Raymond reported.

"I'm still amazed at how advanced medical technology has gotten in this universe."

"Definitely." Raymond still had a concerned expression despite agreeing with Gehnarne.

Gehnarne looked at Raymond wondering what else was wrong. "You feeling alright? Looks like you're still pondering about something."

Raymond hesitated to answer than sighed with a response. "It's about something Sheena had said to me... you'll probably think it's stupid."

Gehnarne chuckled. "Raymond, I'm an inter universal traveler," He looked straight at Raymond. "Try me."

Raymond chuckled at Gehnarne's reaction than answered. "Well that's just it, you are an inter universal traveler. I would think that you of all people would know with all certainty that there is no God."

Gehnarne was surprised. "Wait, you think that because I've traveled to different universes, or the simple act of inter universal travel proves there isn't a God?"

Raymond was surprised at Gehnarne's answer. "Uh... yea something like that, why?"

"On the contrary, me being an inter universal traveler has solidified my faith."

Raymond was shocked and curious. "You have a faith?"

"Yes, you see, my people believed in the Great Entity. In ancient times, before we evolved to the powers of the Nexiose, we believed that he and he alone created us and our universe. Thousands of years later when we discovered the multiverse and inter universal travel with our powers, we began to believe in more than one God. One God per universe. However, after years of studying the ancient texts and scriptures of each universe we visited, we discovered a pattern."

"What pattern?" Raymond asked in intrigue.

Gehnarne looked forward as he tried to remember. "That in every one of those ancient writings from all those different universes, God described himself as "I Am." Raymond's mind hadn't been blown like this since watching a twist ending to a horror movie he saw with Sheena during leave. Gehnarne continued. "Even in the book of Exodus your God describes himself in this way. With that discovery, my people went back to the ancient ways of worshiping one God, because we now believed that the same God that created our universe, also created all the other universes in the Multiverse." Gehnarne looked back at Raymond. "Including yours."

Raymond was speechless with his eyes wide open. "Wo... Gehanarne, that changes everything. Have you ever told anyone from my universe about this? This is some revolutionary stuff!"

Gehnarne chuckled. "No, I haven't because of two reasons. One, even in my universe and others that we had partnered with, despite that information, there were still people who couldn't believe there is such thing as the Great Entity or God or even still believed there were multiple Gods, one per universe as we initially believed. Sure we could preach my people's discovery in this universe but nothing will change with the current doctrine of how faith in God is already properly taught and preached so whats the point? However, one big difference between my universe and yours is that despite my people's differences in beliefs, it never interfered with our unity. With love, we coexisted with each other in peace... and even fought side by side to the very last man against The Darkness that I told you about. If only this universe had the same willingness to love regardless of our differences."

"Wow... that sounds beautiful." Raymond complimented.

"Yes," Gehnarne had a peaceful sense of nostalgia come over him. "Yes it was... which brings me to the second reason." Raymond continued to pay attention as Gehnarne seemed to become more serious about what he would say next. "I was never blessed with the dream to be a preacher." Gehnarne looked directly at Raymond. "My dream, is this organization. An organization that will be a guiding light for other universes currently shrouded in darkness and war, to help them achieve everlasting peace, love and coexistence. With mercy by our side, we will be a dangerously destructive force against those willing to disrupt those ideals of peace. Our actions will echo throughout the multiverse like a clash of thunder as we strive forward into the unknown... This is my God given dream Raymond, this is what I was made for."

Raymond looked away from Gehnarne as he was honored that Gehnarne was so honest with him, finding purpose for himself in his words. In return, Raymond became honest with him as well. "Gehnarne... after my parents were killed, I lost my faith in God... However, after hearing what you and Sheena have told me, I am considering to reconnect with my faith. But one thing is certain," He looked at Gehnarne with respectful seriousness. "I promise to do everything in my power to help you build, maintain and solidify the ideals of this organization forever." Gehnarne was surprised at Raymond's dedication. "You have my word."

Gehnarne felt honored that he had gained such a loyal companion. "Thank you my friend." He smiled at Raymond just as his Taclet suddenly vibrated. He checked it and saw that he had received a message from Gia. Gehnarne stood up. "Well, duty calls, I need you to come with me."

"What's up?" Raymond asked while standing up.

"We're going to talk to the council."

"The Council?!" Raymond suddenly grew nervous since he had never talked to the council directly before.

"Yup, follow me, I'll explain along the way." Gehnarne turned around and walked out the door. Still nervous, Raymond stumbled to keep up as he followed Gehnarne.

Raymond and Gehanarne walked into the conference room on deck two where Gia was waiting at the end of the table closest to the entrance. The room was set up like it was ready for a holographic conference with holographic projectors on the walls and a silver metal conference desk in the middle of the room. "The meeting is set and ready." Gia said.

"Thank you Gia." Gehnarne smiled at her as she began to leave the room. Raymond and Gehnarne both stepped closer to the edge of the table as Gehnarne's hand reached for the conference call controls. "You ready?"

Raymond took a deep breath trying to iron out his nervousness. "Yea."

Gehnarne chuckled. "Don't be so nervous, just be respectful and truthful." Gehnarne pressed the call button on the controls. The line began to ring as the holographic projectors showed the word "Connecting..." floating on the other side of the conference desk. After two rings, the projector's holographic image suddenly showed the council of seven. Two males and one female on the left with the female sitting in between the two men, two males and one female on the right seated in the same fashion, and one male in the middle between the two groups. "Good evening councilors." Gehnarne greeted them. "I apologize for such a late meeting however, we have very important matters to discuss."

Councilor Soller spoke. "Yes Gehnarne, judging from your reports, we do." He looked to his right allowing councilor Quince to speak.

"First of all, we are highly disturbed to hear that Garza Liankos is still alive."

Gehnarne answered. "Yes councilor, we were just as disturbed by this."

Councilor Lock spoke with an Australian accent. "Despite that, we are pleased to hear of how effective your PMC's were against the rebels. However, we are not pleased with how," The councilor briefly looked back at his notes. "Raymond Reynolds let Garza escape." Raymond now grew more nervous.

Councilor Soller spoke. "Is this man next to you Raymond Reynolds?"

Gehnarne softly nudged Raymond forward. He spoke as he moved forward almost tripping. "Y-yes! Yes councilors."

Councilor Grant spoke with a French accent. "Please explain yourself."

Raymond chose his words carefully. "Well, councilors uh, as you have most likely read in the report, we had already lost one of my men by the hands of Garza." Raymond began to relax as he continued. "When the moment came, I couldn't allow another one of my people to die, so I chose to let him go. I take full responsibility for my actions." Raymond lightly bowed, "I am gravely sorry."

Councilor Stratus spoke with an African accent. "Mr. Reynolds, we accept however, this is not a hearing."

Councilor Greaves spoke with a Spanish accent. "The purpose of this meeting is to review the prior mission and to state our next move."

Councilor Sven spoke. "Due to Raymond Reynolds failure to place the mission first, we feel more confident in having the Recluses go after Garza and destroy or capture this battle station that was written in your reports."

Gehnarne was shocked at the decision. "Wait a minute councilors, from what we can tell, that station is highly advanced with some of the most advanced tech we have ever seen." The council patiently listened to Gehnarne. "From what we can gather, there is no way rebels could have gotten any of this technology without some kind of assistance. I have reason to believe that Carnivore might be involved. With the most up to date and advanced technology from our travels at our disposal, I Think the Enidon would be the best choice for this mission."

The councilors looked at each other, then back at Gehnarne and Raymond. Councilor Soller Spoke. "I regret to inform you Mr. Gehnarne that this decision was already made. As we speak, the Recluses is already in route to immediately attack the station. They will arrive in six hours at FTL ten."

"What!?" Raymond and Gehnarne both said in shock.

"Your ship is ordered to hold position in orbit around Selva and wait for the recluses to complete its mission. Once the objective is captured or destroyed, you will rendezvous at the objective area."

Raymond grew angry. "Councilors! You can't-" Gehnarne stopped him from speaking up as he Looked at Raymond and shook his head. Raymond couldn't believe Gehnarne was going with the councils decision.

Gehnarne turned back to the councilors and spoke. "Yes councilors, as ordered we will hold position here."

"Good, this meeting is adjourned." The holographic image of the council faded away as the call ended.

Raymond turned back to Gehnarne. "Gehnarne, you can't be serious about going along with this?"

Gehnarne looked back at Raymond smiling while Raymond looked back at him wondering why he was smiling. "You see Raymond," Gehnarne said as he grasped Raymond's right shoulder. "This is why I picked you." He then let go of Raymond's shoulder, pulled out his Taclet and made a call. "Izzy, this Gehnarne, I want you to prep the

Mark II Beacon for launch than report to the bridge immediately with the Mark II Beacon schematics."

Izzy responded. "The Mark II? Gehnarne, not sure what your planning but it's still in its prototype stage, hell it hasn't even been tested yet."

"Besides testing, should the Beacon work?

Izzy paused than answered. "Theoretically yes, it should work."

"Good, I'll explain everything when you reach the bridge."

"Understood." Izzy acknowledged.

Raymond began to smirk. "You're not going to obey the council's orders are you?"

"Nope." Gehnarne said giddily. "We have other plans." He began to walk out of the conference room with Raymond following him.

"Wait a minute!" Raymond caught up to Gehnarne in the hall. "What are we doing with the Mark II beacon?"

With a smile Gehnarne responded. "It's a part of my marvelous plan Raymond, I'll tell you along the way." They both walked into the elevator and headed towards the bridge.

The elevator doors on the bridge opened as Gehnarne and Raymond walked out. "You can really do that?" Raymond asked Gehnarne.

"It has been a while but yes, I can." Gehnarne responded as they walked towards the Captains seat.

"That's great but... wouldn't this reveal your secret?"

"I was planning to reveal my true background in the near future anyway." Gehnarne sat down in the Captain's chair. "Guess it's gonna happen sooner than I thought, desperate times call for desperate measures right?"

"Yea." Raymond understood. "I'll inform the team leads."

"Thank you." Gehnarne smiled as Raymond walked to the back of the bridge to the TOC. Around the corner from the Captain's chair, Raymond saw Lucas waiting for him at the entrance of the TOC.

"What did the council say?" Lucas asked Raymond.

"They want us to hold position here."

"Really, why?" He asked while both of them walked into the TOC.

"They don't believe we have the resolve to take on an assault against that station, so they sent the Recluses instead."

"Well that doesn't make any sense."

"It does when you factor in what I did."

"I guess, what does Gehnarne think?"

"He plans to disobey the council and support the Recluses."

"What?!" Lucas was shocked. "We're defying the council?!"

"Unfortunately yes." Raymond said calmly as he activated the intercom system and called the combat team leads. "All combat team leads, please report to the briefing room."

Lucas continued in concerned protest. "The council will hang us from the tallest tree on the highest mountain if we do this."

"I know Lucas." Raymond said as he walked back towards the bridge. "But I trust Gehnarne's judgment." As Raymond finished that statement, he saw Katherine and Gia walk off the bridge elevator left of the TOC. Katherine was still in combat gear with a black left eye no longer swollen, right bruised cheek, and a scare on her left cheek. He was happy to see Katherine was well and moved to greet her when out of anger Lucas suddenly spoke his mind.

"Why do you trust him so much?!" Lucas yelled.

Raymond, Katherine, and Gia were surprised at Lucas's tone. Others on the bridge including Gehnarne and Jason, who were at the helm, heard Lucas's loud question and drew their attention towards him.

"Lucas?" Raymond responded in shock.

"Tell me Raymond," Lucas continued. "Do you even know what he really is?"

Raymond now understood where Lucas was going with his argument. "Lucas, don't." He pleaded.

"He's not even Human," Lucas grew angry as he continued to confront Raymond. "Hell, he's not even from this damn universe!"

The TOC technicians and the Bridge crew looked at Gehnarne puzzled, wondering if what Lucas said was true.

"Oh no..." Jason said to himself as he heard this, knowing what Lucas was talking about.

"This whole time he kept this from us, why would he do that unless he planned to use us like pawns or worse yet, betray us!"

"Lucas! Stop!" Raymond ordered.

"Knowing you, even after what I just said," Lucas began to walk up to Raymond aggressively. "You still trust him, don't you?!"

"Lucas! Stand down!" Jason yelled at Lucas while standing up as he slowly reached closer to his side arm in his leg holster, hoping he didn't have to draw it on Lucas. However, Lucas ignored Jason's warning and continued to aggressively walk towards Raymond.

"We already lost Jake, I'm not gonna lose someone else because of your fucking naive mentality!" Lucas yelled as Raymond was starting to feel threatened by Lucas while he got in Raymond's face. "So tell me Raymond! Why the FUCK do you trust him so much!?"

"BECAUSE HE TOLD ME!" Suddenly a bass like hum sounded with an invisible force pushing Lucas and Raymond away from each other like an expanding bubble. While being pushed back In forceful surprise, they both took several steps backward as everyone on the bridge gasped at the mysterious event, unsure what was happening. Once they were around five meters apart, out of each others faces, the invisible force stopped. They both looked at Gehnarne with his right hand extended out and his right green eye's glow just starting to dim while he slowly lowered his hand. Lucas was in shock that Gehnarne was capable of such power with that small demonstration. Raymond however was not surprised at all. Lucas than quickly looked at Raymond and saw how casual he seemed to react from the mysterious force confirming what Raymond had yelled just a moment ago. Lucas's expression shifted from shock, to heartbreak from a sense of betrayal just as the bridge elevator door's suddenly opened with Izzy walking in with a tablet in his right hand and a hard plastic case in the other.

"Gehnarne!" He said as he looked around. "Sorry I took so-... long?" He than paused as he realized something had just happened judging from the awkward silence. "Okay... what did I miss?" He asked out loud in awkward curiosity.

"...You knew?" Lucas asked while Raymond turned to face him.

"Yes," He responded with a regretful expression towards Lucas. "I did."

Lucas felt an over whelming anger towards Raymond but kept it under control. He turned towards the opened bridge elevator doors and walked through them with the doors closing immediately behind him.

Gia saw this and took pity on Lucas. "I'll talk to him." She said to Raymond while she quickly moved to the opposite end of the bridge to use the second elevator. The elevator doors quickly opened as she entered than closed behind her.

Raymond took a deep breath, calming himself, then turned towards Gehnarne. "Gehnarne, I'm so sorry that happened the way it did."

"It's okay Raymond." Gehnarne humbly assured him, then began to speak to the bridge crew as they starred at him in confusion and wonder. "I'm sure all of you have the same concerns as Captain Walker. However, please allow me to explain." Gehnarne stood up from his Captains chair and slowly walked towards the helm near Jason as he looked at each member of the bridge staff.

"We have been ordered by the council to stay here while the Recluses engages the rebel station," Gehnarne said. "However, we all know from our intel that the rebel station is highly advanced. The Recluses won't stand a chance. With that, I have a plan to support the Recluses. However,... this plan will also confirm Captain Walker's statements concerning my origins." The bridge crew softly gasped at the confirmation as Gehnarne stopped in front of the helm while Jason stood up and gave Gehnarne space to talk. "Yes, I am not human, I am from another universe. Unlike our most recent recruits however, I am an inter universal being with powers unlike any of you have ever seen before, and those powers are critical to the success of this plan, with that being said," Gehnarne slowly and softly grasped the head rest of the helm stations chair sadly humbling himself before the crew with a slightly bowed head. "I am sorry for withholding this information and humbly ask that you forgive my insecurity and doubts towards all of you, for I should've had none." He said as he looked back up towards the crew with confidence. "I realize now that this organization is everything it needed to be." He said with a joyful smile. "You discovered new universe's, new planets, new technology, and have even successfully fought," Gehnarnes expression turned firm, "and destroyed those who threaten to keep you from these discoveries." The bridge crew began to feel a sense of motivation in Gehnarnes words. "If you give me this chance, I promise you," He looked directly ahead to make sure he could see everyone from the bridge crew as possible, even crew members that were just in range of his peripheral vision. "I will not let you down."

The bridge was silent for a moment. "Gehnarne?" Katherine spoke as Gehnarne, Raymond and the rest of the bridge crew looked at her, "I would hope I'm speaking for the rest of the crew by saying, anyone willing to risk it all to save our comrades on the Recluses is worth trusting." Katherine finished with a smile.

Gehnarne smiled back and responded. "Thank you Katherine." He looked around the bridge and asked with a smile, "Does anyone object?"

"No sir!" Everyone on the bridge said in unison.

"Then let's back up our friends on the Recluses!"

"AYE, AYE SIR!" Everyone sounded off as they all immediately returned to their duties with a sense of urgency.

"Katherine, Izzy, Jason your with me, we gotta a briefing to prepare." Raymond ordered while walking to the elevator.

"On the way!" Katherine quickly followed him.

With the Mark II Beacon schematics in hand on his Tablet, Izzy marched towards the elevator with pride while talking to the weapons station. "Weapons! Make sure the Mark II beacon is on standby to launch!"

"Aye sir!" The crewmen at weapons responded to Izzy.

Jason was relieved at the helm as he quickly walked towards the elevator while calling the Red Nova crew on his Taclet. "Tim, Sarah, report to the briefing room immediately."

"*On our way!*" Timothy responded on the Taclet.

Back in Alpha Team's quarters, Lucas sat on the couch while he looked at a picture of Alpha team back when they used to be Charlie team with the USOD during the invasion of Kalista. Everyone in the picture was wearing multi-camouflage combat gear. From left to right, Jake was standing, slightly turned to his left while smiling with his AR30 in his hands at the low ready and a Medical bag on his back. Katherine was also standing, facing straight towards the camera with a smile exposing her perfectly white teeth also with her AR30 in hand and a communications bag on her back with a small antenna sticking out over the top of her shoulder wearing a baseball cap with her short blonde hair lightly blowing in the wind. Sheena was casually smiling while kneeling in the middle of the picture holding on to the barrel of her sniper rifle with the butt of the weapons stock touching the ground with her brunette hair in a ponytail, before she cut it short and dyed it red, with a multi-camouflage boonie cap. Raymond was standing, slightly turned to his right while smirking with his AR30 clipped to his back, pistol in his right hand and a knife in his left in a low back hand stabbing position. Lastly, Lucas stood straight towards the camera with a straight professional look also with an AR30 in his hands and an assault pack on his back. They were all standing at the top of a fortress with a ranging valley behind them.

Lucas looked at it, reminiscing about the past when him and Raymond treated each other like brothers, Katherine and Jake were the best of friends, and Sheena was just starting to fall for Raymond. Although some things had stayed the same, "Too much has changed," Lucas said to himself. The doorbell for Alpha team's quarters had rang. "Come in." Lucas said in annoyance.

Gia walked in the moment the door slid open. "Hello Lucas." She said with a smile while looking at him.

"Gia? What are you doing here?" He said while putting the picture down and sat up straighter on the couch.

"Well, you and Raymond did create quite a stir on the bridge."

Lucas groaned in annoyance.

"Are you sure you're not drunk this time?"

"You know, for a shrink, you really do suck at making your patients feel comfortable."

"Well, I never said I was a good psychiatrist." She smiled playfully.

"What do you want?" Lucas said firmly, trying to get to the point.

Gia seemed a little disappointed. "Last time we talked you said you liked talking to me," Lucas seemed to relax as he looked at her apologetically while she put her hand on his. "Please talk to me," Lucas was unsure of what to do. "Your friends are worried about you and so am I, what's wrong?" Gia was sincere in her words, leading Lucas to be honest about his feelings.

He sighed, "I just can't believe that Raymond never told me about Gehnarne, who he is, what he's truly capable of, he's usually honest with me about that sort of stuff."

"I see." Gia was curious. "You weren't the only one he kept that secret from you know but I'm sure it hurts more for you since he's like a brother to you. Why is it that you feel so resentful towards people with secrets? I remember a similar reaction happened when you first met Izzy, when he mentioned the rifts back in his home universe?"

"Yea," Lucas felt embarrassed. "I kinda flipped on him to." Lucas thought for a moment trying to think of why he felt this way. Deep in himself he already knew why. "I guess it all started when me and Raymond were kids. We were best friends. My father was a pastor of the church me, him and his parents went to." Lucas's expression went sad. "Then one day... the rebels killed our parents in a bombing at the church."

"I remember reading about that in Raymond's personal file." Gia was saddened by the story thus far.

"Yea, it's in mine too. After we were orphaned, my father's best friend Yabin took us both in. He raised us to be strong and taught us how to survive in this relentless world." Lucas's expression became resentful. "Then, when I was sixteen and wanted to join the marines, he told me the truth about my father." Gia's curiosity grew. "Turns out that church wasn't targeted randomly, the rebels were targeting my father and in the process, wanted to kill as many people as possible."

"What?" Gia was curious. "Why did they target him?"

"Him and Yabin were in JSOC together. JSOC or Joint Special Operations Command was the foundation of the USOD before the world unification summit. My father was a member of First Special Forces Operations Detachment Delta. Also known as Delta Force, CAG or Combat Applications Group, all those fancy shmancy names. Yabin was a SEAL for SEAL Team Six. Two of the best Teir One operators and their teams worked closely together despite the different branches of service."

"Wo." Gia was impressed.

"They fought the first five years of the Colonial wars before JSOC was disbanded and reformed into the USOD."

"So, your father was targeted for what he did at the beginning of the Colonial wars?"

"Yabin believed so, although he was never really sure of the exact reason. They probably just wanted an easy target to hit while also sending a message. For years that secret was kept by my father as he led his congregation, getting himself and hundreds of others killed. I never wanted anything like that to happen again. That's why I'm so cautious about those sort of things. Once I actually joined Special Operations, my aggression towards those things only got worse as I felt like I was a pawn to the council's will at times, not being told the whole truth or facts about certain missions and operations. Those sort of things would get my friends from other teams killed. I would speak up about it but I know at the end of the day, my loyalty is to earth and I would do whatever it took to keep her safe, despite how angry I would get at the council at times."

"I see," Gia understood. "That does seem unfair. Tell me, how were you able to get the truth about Gehnarne?"

"I unfortunately had to request Yabin's help."

"Unfortunately? Do you resent Yabin for keeping the truth about your father from you for so long?"

"Well, yea, I do I'll admit but, it's not like I hate him for it, I'm just not friendly with him."

"I see, when you got the information about Gehnarne, were you aware that his whole universe was destroyed?"

Lucas was shocked. "What, really?"

"Yes, the official yet classified reports you read only mentions who he really is, where he's from and what he can do but it isn't a profile about his home. At the age of two hundred fifty-three, he witnessed the destruction of everything he ever knew."

"Wait a minute," Lucas was confused. "Two hundred fifty-three, that doesn't make sense."

"His race develops slower than ours in compensation to their vastly longer life span."

Lucas was very curious. "How vastly longer are we talking about here?"

"He told me once that the longest living person of his race lived all the way up to two thousand, five hundred and fifty-three years old."

"What!?" Lucas tried to think while trying to ignore his own shock. "Wait... so he was like-"

"A child when it happened... it seems that you and him might have something in common."

Lucas didn't know what to say now feeling guilt and remorse for what he had done. "I'm assuming Raymond knew this as well?"

"He trusted Raymond enough to tell him so that he can understand Geharne's intentions better, gain his trust. Raymond also understood why Gehnarne didn't want him to tell anyone about his past. It was very personal to him."

Lucas looked down in regret. "Man I'm such an idiot..."

Gia smiled. "You're not an idiot." Lucas looked at her. "You just have some issues like everyone does which is normal. However, it doesn't mean they can't be worked out."

Lucas smiled at Gia. "Thanks Gia." He said while touching the top of her hand. "Even when I was drunk, I knew you would be a good person to talk to." Lucas said with a chuckle.

Gia laughed. "I guess you were right, just make sure you make a check out to me later."

They both laughed together. Than Lucas let go of her hand, stood up and began walking to the door while saying, "Well, I better get to the breifing, my brother needs me."

"Good," Gia smiled as she quickly got up and walked past Lucas through the door. "Let me brief you on the plan Gehnarne sent me on my Tablet along the way."

Lucas was surprised at how fast she moved past him through the door. "Yes ma'am." He said to her trying to catch up.

Gia grew annoyed. "I told you to stop calling me that!" She said loudly down the hall as Lucas walked through the door and closed behind him.

Although Izzy may disagree, there does seem to be some psychology

involved in using the Flow System according to Raymond. He'd

described to me on occasion that he felt an almost overwhelming

sense of confidence that he must keep under constant control

whenever he would use the system. He also mentioned that it would

get more powerful as the subject uses the system over time however it

does cap at a certain point. Whether this reckless boost in confidence

is truly an effect of the flow system or just Raymond's inner psyche

can't be determined however I truly believe it takes a mentally strong

individual to harness the power of the flow system and avoid being

over confident in combat, especially in Rage mode. If not, the user

may loss control and execute actions beyond the Rules of

Engagement or put him or herself and their team in greater danger.

This is why our organization has only deemed our most trusted and

highly trained members with such powerful technology.

Chapter 17: Orbital Battle Of Selva

"Lady's, gentlemen," Gehnarne started. "Here's the brief." As Gehnarne talked, Raymond was leaning against the wall in the right corner of a dimly lit steal wall room with chairs and a holographic projector at the front in full combat gear while admiring the craftsmanship of his new flow system gauntlets with the blue discs installed, his AR30 on his back and his German Long Sword sheathed to the left side of his waist. The team leaders were gathered in the room in seats ready to receive the brief. The holographic projection behind Gehnarne, showed the battle space around the rebel station as Raymond put his arms down and began to pay attention. "The Recluses," an image of the Recluses appeared with the station at a distance in front of it, "will exit here, about one to two clicks away from the station. Judging from our Intel, the station should have the ability to detect incoming ships from FTL which means the Recluses will most likely sustain heavy fire the moment it enters the battle space. The Recluses may plan to use evasive maneuvers, however, I'm certain the enemy will be ready for this as well. The Enidon, will take a different approach. This will be a three phase operation. Izzy?"

Gehnarne stepped to the right as Izzy, who was in full combat gear, took the center from the left for the brief while the image changed to the Enidon in its current position facing towards a Mark II beacon. Izzy continued the brief. "Phase one, the Enidon will use the prototype Mark II beacon to Teleport from our current position in orbit above Selva, back to the Mark I beacon Orbiting Croza."

Just as Izzy finished his statement, Bravo team leader asked a question. "Sir, I don't understand, how is the Mark II beacon going to Teleport us back to a Mark I beacon? Aren't they incompatible?"

Raymond spoke, answering his question. "The two beacons are incompatible however, Mark I beacons were designed to work with future Beacon models. The Mark I cannot send Teleport signals to other Mark II beacons; however, they can receive them."

Izzy smiled at Raymond. "Thank you Raymond," then continued his brief. "Once we are back in position near the Mark I beacon in orbit around Croza close to the universe 1112 rift, we will begin phase two of our movement. Gehnarne?"

Izzy moved back to the side while Gehnarne took the center for the brief again. "Phase two, we will use the universe 1112 rift to position ourselves opposite from the Recluses position from the enemy station."

The crew seemed confused while Lucas and Gia stepped off the elevator into the briefing room just as Katherine asked a question. "Wait, the rift to universe 1112 leads to Izzy's home universe, how is that rift supposed to get us all the way back to Selva behind that station?"

Gehnarne was about to answer when Lucas interrupted as he just heard the question while entering. "That's because Gehnarne has the ability to manipulate rifts to send us where ever we want in the universe that rift is active as long as it's a position he's familiar with, which I must say, is pretty bad ass." Lucas than smiled at Gehnarne.

Raymond was happy to see Lucas. Gehnarne was also pleased. "Yes Lucas, that is precisely correct, nice of you to join us." He said with a smile than continued his brief. "Because we are not coming out of FTL there is no way the station will detect us coming into the battle space, allowing us to take them by surprise. Now for Phase Three and the combat strategy. Raymond?"

Gehnarne moved to the side again as Raymond took center for the brief. "Phase Three, we arrive in position in the battle space and launch combat operations. The Enidon will immediately launch Assault Boarding Pods with the Red Nova leading the way as an escort. The station will eventually detect the Enidon and the Red Nova however, during that time the station is reacting to the new contacts, it will give our ABP's a window of safety. Once the station begins to engage the new contacts, the pods should still be safe due to the ABP's small form factor. As the ABP's get closer however, the enemy will be able to make visual contact which is why the Red Nova will cover our pods from incoming enemy fire."

"We'll do our best." Jason spoke up from the back of the room with a grin while Timothy gave a thumbs up with a smirk on Jason's right and Sarah on his left smiling.

Raymond responded with a respectful nod. "I know you will. Teams Alpha through Delta will be the first wave of boarding teams in the ABP's. Each team will hit a different primary area of the station. Delta will attack weapons, Charlie, engineering, Bravo, crew courtiers, Alpha, the control center. Once those primary areas have been secured and weapon systems are shut down, we will launch the second wave of ABP's with teams Echo through Hotel to secure the rest of the station and assist with aid and litter. After that, the station should be secured."

"And Garza killed or captured." A familiar female voice said from the back right entrance to the briefing room. Raymond couldn't believe who's voice he just heard as that person stepped out of the dimly lit entrance and into the light as they continued. "Officially putting an end to the colonial wars." It was Sheena. She smiled at Raymond with motivation. Raymond's heart jumped as he looked at her. She seemed ready to fight by his side again wearing full multi-camouflage combat gear and had a black stripe across her face from ear to ear.

Raymond began to walk towards her as Gehnarne moved back to the center of the brief. "Any questions?" He asked. There were none. "Good, you are dismissed, God speed."

As the Combat Team Leaders left the room, Raymond hugged Sheena. She mildly grunted in pain as she grabbed her right shoulder. "Oh, sorry." Raymond said as he immediately stopped hugging her. "You Okay? You sure you can go out there like this?"

"The doctor cleared me," Sheena responded. "Even though it still feels a little tender, the internal damage has been repaired and the scarring can be repaired over time with treatments. Besides that, he and I both agreed that we've seen people in worse conditions go out on mission."

"I don't know Sheena you lost a lot of blood before-"

"Hey," Sheena interrupted him with a soft touch to his face. "I'll be okay, let's just focus on stopping Garza."

Raymond trusted her judgment. "Okay." They both smiled at each other.

"Sheena!" Katherine said walking up to her, "I'm so glad you're okay!" She tried to hug her.

"Wo, easy!" Sheena said giggling, stopping Katherine from hugging her.

"Oh, sorry." Katherine reacted.

"Glad to see your all in this fight." Gehnarne said walking up to the group and stopped. "Including you Lucas." He said while turning left to face Lucas as he walked up to the rest of the team.

Lucas didn't know what to say but spoke the best he could. "Gehnarne... I'm sorry, I was out of line and didn't understand the full background of your situation. Please forgive me."

Gehnarne smirked. "Tell me truthfully Lucas, do you trust me?"

Lucas looked straight into his eyes and spoke with confidence. "Yes, I do."

Gehnarne smiled. "Then there is nothing to forgive. All of you, win this fight together." He looked back at Raymond and than walked out of the briefing room.

As Gehnarne walked away, Lucas faced Raymond. "Raymond, I-"

"It's okay Lucas," Raymond interrupted with a smile. "You don't have to apologize."

"I was out of line with you too, you're the leader now not me."

"There is no designated leader between you and me Lucas, we're brothers, a team." Raymond held out his hand.

Lucas saw this and smiled as he clasped his own hand with Raymond's. "Unity?"

"Is victory." Raymond answered.

"Let's end this war." Lucas said in motivation letting go of Raymond's hand as the whole team walked out of the briefing room.

Izzy was waiting for them outside the room in the hall. "Raymond hold up!"

Raymond and the team turned around to face Izzy. "What's wrong Izzy?" He asked.

"I have something for you!" Izzy responded with excitement as he reached into his pocket and handed Raymond what looked to be a new small case of black face paint.

"Uh, Thanks Izzy but, I already have face paint."

"Not this kind you don't, this one contains a substance that goes through a chemical reaction with the energy given off by the magnetic gravity field based on your current flow system state."

Raymond was confused. "Meaning-"

"Meaning, it changes color depending on what state of flow system you're in. With the Flow System off, it looks naturally black, on, it turns blue, rage mode, it turns red, tell me that's not awesome!"

Raymond immediately became excited to use it "That's really

awesome Izzy, thanks!" he put the small case in his right shoulder pocket.

"Your welcome, we better start getting to our pods now."

"We? Your coming with us this time?" Raymond asked.

"Hell Yea," Izzy said as he bent down, grabbed the AR30 against the wall and stood back up. "Why else would I be in full combat gear?"

"Of course, let's get going guys." Raymond said as the team began to walk towards the ABP bay next to the briefing room with Izzy following.

As the team began to enter the bay, Izzy caught Katherine's attention "Hey Kat?"

"What's up?"

Izzy's expression became somber. "I'm deeply sorry about Jake..."

Katherine's expression grew sad. "...Thank you Izzy..."

"You gonna be okay?"

"No..." Katherine said depressingly. "...but I will be... once this war is over."

"If you need anything at all... I'm here for you." Izzy said with sincerity.

"Thanks." Katherine said with a small smile.

"Your welcome," Izzy said humbly. "Let's go."

"Yea." Katherine and Izzy went through the bay doors and caught up with the rest of the team.

Back on the bridge, "Weapons, Launch the Mark II beacon on my mark." Gehnarne ordered from his Captain chair.

The weapons officer responded. "Standing by."

"Launch." Gehnarne ordered. A missile launched out of a bow missile tube of the Enidon. Once it was one Kilometer away, it split into multiple pieces like it was shedding its skin, revealing The Mark II beacon inside. The beacon immediately used thrusters to halt its position.

"Mark II beacon is in position." Weapons reported.

"Good," Gehnarne said. "Navigation, initiate teleport synchronization."

"Beginning synchronization now sir," a crewman from navigation reported.

"Uh, sir?" The helmsmen got Gehnarnes attention. "This teleport thing..." he seemed nervous. "Is it safe?"

Gehnarne answered him. "This particular beacon was never tested before," The helmsmen seemed worried. "However," Gehnarne continued while smiling in reassurance, "The technology has been proven to work over the past couple of thousand years, is perfectly safe I assure you."

"Aye sir." The helmsmen nodded still seeming worried as he turned back towards the helm.

"Synchronization complete." Navigation reported.

"Initiate teleportation sequence." Gehnarne ordered. The beacon shot out a blue beam towards the Enidon, surrounding it in blue waves of electricity in a spherical shape very similar to how the UTS initiated teleportation. "Execute in three, two, one." The Enidon suddenly flashed and disappeared out of space at a muffled thunder like sound.

The Recluses
August 26th, 2238
2259 Standard Earth Time

"Sir," the navigational officer of the Recluses spoke. "We will be exiting FTL in one minute."

"Well done navigation." Captain Michael Cross said. He tapped on his right captain's seat display opening ship wide communications. "All hands, this is the Captain, standby for engagement."

The Recluses bridge was similar to the Enidon's except the TOC for ground operations was located on the secondary bridge making the primary bridge smaller compared to the Enidon's.

As soon as the Recluses exited FTL the ship was immediately pelted with red energy beams and missiles coming from the station that looked like a giant metallic ring with four struts connecting to a metallic sphere about half the diameter of the ring surrounding it. The station's overall size was twice the size of the Recluses. The incoming missiles slammed into the Recluses's Armor plating.

"Helm!" Captain Cross ordered. "Go Evasive, forty-five degrees down, 180-degree role to starboard! Weapons, fire everything we've got, we're taking a beating here!"

"Aye sir!" Helm and Weapons sounded off simultaneously. The Recluses fired missile volleys and heavy gun rounds with little to no effect as the energy beams blocked all the Recluses attacks.

"Launch all fighters, get them close to the station and attack their defenses!" All the fighters the Recluses had launched out of the hanger dodging energy beams the moment they left the hanger. Some fighters were immediately shot down upon exit.

"All fighters!" Captain Cross ordered. "Get close to the station and destroy those turrets!"

"Roger that sir." Spectra Squadron Leader Lieutenant Danial Sykes acknowledge as he tried to dodge incoming enemy fire. "You heard the man, let's get in there!" Sykes went full throttle with his squadron following close behind towards the station.

"Spectra one, this Spectra five" one of his wing man informed. "We've been locked!"

"All fighters, break formation and go evasive!" Sykes ordered as the fighters immediately spread out while continuing to push forward with evasive maneuvers. The fighters pulled extremely high G-force maneuvers pushing the pilot's physical limits.

"Spectra one, Spectra three," Another pilot called in. "We can't keep this up for much longer, there's just too much cross fir- AH!" Static filled the channel as the pilot was shot down.

"Shit," Sykes looked around and saw three more pilots being killed. "This isn't gonna work," He got on the channel. "All fighters, pull back!" He ordered.

"What?!" Captain Cross was in shock. "If you don't push forward we'll all die!"

Sykes responded. "If my pilots keep pushing forward like that, we'll all die anyway! Sir, I advise an immediate withdraw!"

Captain Cross thought for a moment and knew that Sykes was right. "All fighters pull back and-" Suddenly the whole ship violently shook as the lights on the bridge flickered. "The hell was that!?"

"Sir," A female engineer officer advised. "Our engines have been severely damaged, we're dead in the water!"

Captain Cross immediately grew scared for the lives of his crew and himself. He knew it was over. "We're taking heavy damage!" The operations officer advised. "Multiple hull breaches!"

Captain Cross knew what call he had to make. "All hands, abandon ship-!" Suddenly the ship rocked again. "Report!"

"The bridge armor's hall integrity is compromised!" Operations reported.

"Oh no, Everyone, evacuate the bridge n- AAHH!!!" Captain Cross tried to give his final order as the bridge was destroyed with all the bridge crew on deck.

The Enidon
August 26th, 2238
2305 Standard Earth Time

With a muffled thunder like noise, the Enidon suddenly appeared in orbit above Croza near the Mark I beacon. "Report." Gehnarne ordered.

"All systems normal sir." The crewmen at the operations station informed.

Gehnarne sighed in relief. "Good."

"Sir!" The communications officer said getting Gehnarne's attention. "We've intercepted reports about the Recluses through the UEG communications network."

"What's the word?" Gehnarne asked.

"Not good, they've taking a serious beating. Their bridge is gone and the crew has begun to abandon ship. There are now reports of rebel shuttles already attaching and boarding the Recluses."

"We have to get in this fight now, helm, move towards the rift." Gehnarne ordered.

"Aye." The helmsman confirmed as the Enidon immediately began to move.

Gehnarne continued to command. "Red Nova, Combat teams, as soon as we're on the other side of the rift, launch."

"*Roger*." Jason and Raymond responded simultaneously.

"Sir," The helmsman reported. "we're on a direct course to the rift, would you like me to pull up the thermal image for you?"

Gehnarne stood up out of his seat and said. "I can see it just fine helm, hold your course."

The helmsman was curious to how Gehnarne could see the rift without thermal imaging while trying to focus back on his job. "Aye sir."

Back in the ABP bay, all the combat teams were strapped inside their pods, ready for launch. In Raymond's pod, he started to feel nervous as he began to remember how dangerous ABP method of boarding action was. How his instructors said that the slightest miscalculation could send him off into infinite space. "*Slinger?*" or if the pod was damaged, he would be exposed to open space and burn from the inside out, the worst possible way to die. "*Slinger!*" Sheena called him again, this time getting his attention.

Raymond snapped out of it as he looked at the small monitor to his left with Sheena's face, immediately calming him. "Shee- I mean, Crimson?"

"*You okay?*" She was concerned. "*Your heart rate monitor cranked up a notch.*"

"Oh, yea I'll be okay." He tried to hide his fear.

Sheena was still concerned. "*I remember how scared you used to be of this ABP thing during training, you'll be okay.*" She smiled at him. "*I'll see you on the other side.*"

"Well, let's just hope the other side is that station and not some random planet out there somewhere a million years from now." He nervously smiled back in a joke.

Sheena chuckled. "*We'll make it, you'll see. Crimson out.*" The monitor shut down while Raymond looked towards the ceiling trying to relax.

Meanwhile, on the bridge, Gehnarne closed his eyes as he lifted his right hand with his fingers spread out like he was holding something. An unnatural humming could be heard through-out the bridge as a teal outline began to surround Gehnarne. The bridge crew began to whisper among themselves, wondering what was going on.

Back in his pod, Raymond was still looking at the ceiling while he took a deep breath as everything around him seem to move in slow motion. The stale oxygen of the pod flooded his nostrils as he felt the coolness of the air conditioning blow through his freshly cut black hair. He looked forward again as he grabbed Izzy's new face paint and ritualistically painted a black stripe across his face from ear to ear across his eyes perfectly.

Back on the bridge, Gehnarne's eye's opened with his right green eye glowing intensely while the rift opened in front of the Enidon with a green outline. "NOW!" Gehnarne ordered. "PUNCH THROUGH!"

"Aye, Aye sir!" The helmsman said with motivation as he increased the ships speed to full throttle. The Enidon entered the rift than immediately appeared on the other side near the hostile station.

Still in his pod, Raymond put the face paint disc back in his pocket as he exhaled while closing his eyes, focusing, meditating into battle mind, preparing for a fight. He opened his eyes as his situational awareness was on point and his killer instinct was ready to decimate anyone who got in his way for this final battle. Time seemed to go back to normal while he clearly heard Gehnarne order on the channel "All units, launch!"

The Red Nova boosted out of the hanger taking point while at the same time twenty-three ABP's shot out of the Enidons ABP launchers all heading straight towards the station. "Alpha team is away!" Raymond informed on the communications channel.

"Bravo team away!" Bravo leader reported.

"Charlie team launched!" Charlie lead.

"Delta is clear!" Delta leader.

"Red Nova, on station!" Jason reported.

"All teams," Raymond said. "Stay on course and standby for evasive action and course corrections!"

"Roger!" All the team leads acknowledge.

As the pods moved closer to the station, Sheena looked at her monitor connected to the camera on the right side of her pod showing the Recluses with rebel shuttles connected to it's hull and severe damage riddling the ship. Her heart sank in concern for her father. "Lord… please let my dad be okay."

Raymond heard her on the channel. "Don't worry Crimson, I'm sure your father is fine."

"Of course he is!" Lucas interrupted. "He's probably kicking rebel ass and taking names right now." He finished with a chuckle.

Sheena smiled in reassurance. "Yea, you're probably right."

Meanwhile in the control center of the hostile station, "Sir!" a rebel operations technician got Garza's attention. "We have multiple new contacts in sector five!"

In the large two floor square room with multiple windows on the second floor and multiple stations in a large circle on the first floor with monitors and control consoles, Garza, who was clothed in all black military grade cloths with a brown leather jacket, his flow system gauntlets and his rapier, stood in the center of the circle turning left towards the operations station. "Display sector five on the main monitor." Garza ordered.

"Yes sir." The technician pressed a combination of controls switching the Main monitor to the camera image looking towards sector five.

Garza looked at the image and saw the Enidon moving around the station towards the Recluses, and the Red Nova with multiple smaller craft behind it moving closer to the station at high speed. "ABP's, all guns, shift fire towards sector five now!" He said while turning right towards the weapons station.

"Yes sir!" The rebel at the weapons station acknowledge.

The stations Turrets shifted towards sector five as the Red Nova came within their firing Range. "Jason," Timothy informed. "We're almost in range of the enemy's defenses."

"Roger Tim," Jason responded. "Sarah, standby for ANC activation,"

Sarah nodded as she stood up and walked towards the ANC beam slowly rising out of the deck behind Jason's seat.

"Tim, do not activate ANC until I tell you," Jason ordered. "We'll pull some basic maneuvers in the meantime."

Sarah grabbed the beams handlebars standing by for ANC activation.

"And those turrets?" Timothy asked.

"Those Turrets use the same focused energy weaponry as us, once we're in range of them, they'll be in range of us as well, our advantage is that we can move." Jason said with motivation and a determined smile.

The Red Nova and the ABP's came into range of the stations turrets as they immediately fired both energy beams and missiles. The Red Nova fired on the incoming missiles with one pair of its own weapons while the other pair fired upon the turrets on the station at long range with the Red Nova dodging incoming fire.

Raymond noticed the incoming barrage of fire that missed the Red Nova on his main monitor in his ABP. "All units, incoming, go evasive!"

"Roger!" All team leads acknowledge.

"Dammit!" Lucas twitched his thruster controls just barely dodging a missile. "That was close," He sighed. "Thank goodness we're too small of targets to lock on to."

"AH!-Static." Lucas heard someone scream over the channel.

"Bravo six is down! Bravo six is down!" Bravo lead notified on the channel.

"This is Charlie leader! We lost Charlie two!"

"Slinger, White!" Lucas notified Raymond. "We're losing guys out here!"

"Roger that White!" Raymond responded. "Star, Slinger! Can you take out those turrets any faster!?"

Jason responded. "Slinger, I'm already doing the best I can! There's just too many turrets for me to handle all at once!"

"This is Delta leader! I'm hit! I-" Static.

"Crap!" Raymond said in frustration.

Sheena Notified. "If this keeps up we'll be combat ineffective before we reach the station!"

"Red Nova, this is Spectra one from the Recluses!" Lieutenant Sykes called in on the channel. *"My squadron is on station and op-com to you."*

Jason looked left and saw a flight of thirteen F-93 fighters moving quickly towards the station. "Roger that Spectra one, good to see your still in this fight." Jason looked straight as he gave orders. "I need your squadron to get close and destroy any turrets in our flight path. They think we're the biggest threat now so they shouldn't notice you moving in."

"Roger that Star, we're on it." Sykes said as his squadron just made it in range to fire. *"Spectra one, Fox two!"*

"Spectra two, Fox two" All the spectra squadron fighters fired their weapons. Their volley of missiles impacted and destroyed many of the turrets at once.

"Spectra one to all fighters, break formation and proceed with your own discretion, stay close to the deck to avoid being targeted by the remaining turrets!" Sykes ordered.

"Roger!" all the pilots of spectra squadron acknowledge as they broke formation and destroyed more turrets at random.

"Good work Spectra squadron!" Raymond complimented. "Keep them busy!"

"This is Delta two, the enemy fire seems to be letting up." Raymond heard on the channel.

"This is Digit!" Izzy called in frantically. "I've been hit, I've lost control and straying off course, at this rate I'll miss the station!"

"This is Cat-Eye, Digit I'm going to attempt an early pod link to get you back on course, standby!"

"Be careful Cat-Eye!" Raymond informed Katherine.

Katherine's pod carefully moved closer to Izzy's. "Come on," Katherine carefully flicked the thruster controls. "Easy," The pods were perfectly aligned. "Got it!" She pressed the link up button as high powered electromagnets snapped the two pods together.

Izzy's pod shook violently as Izzy braced himself. Katherine than corrected her course along with Izzy with a long thruster burn. Izzy sighed in relief. "Thanks Cat-Eye, I owe you."

Katherine smiled. "Your welcome Digit."

"All units!" Raymond said on the channel. "Begin link up procedures!" What was left of Bravo, Charlie, and Delta teams linked up into their teams, aiming their linked pods to their assigned target areas on the station. Alpha team was the last to link up.

"Alpha, linked!" Raymond notified.

"Bravo, hooked up!"

"Charlie, ready!"

"Delta, attached!"

The Red Nova was headed straight into the station. "NOW TIM, ACTIVATE ANC!"

"Roger!" Timothy pressed the ANC activation switch just as the Red Nova performed a barrel role while the inner and outer hull turned red with both Sarah's long blue hair and right gold eye instantly flashing to red. The Red Nova pulled up with a high G-Force maneuver, just barely avoiding the station with the ABP's not too far behind.

"All teams," Raymond warned. "Impact in three, two, one!"

Alpha team's pods slammed into the station penetrating its armor and stopping on the first deck they encountered. The rebels on the station were sucked out into space as the pods shot sealing foam back towards the hull breaches to maintain air pressure on the deck while at the same time shot flash bangs and spewed smoke out the sides of the pods to disrupt the enemy from firing on the team as they exited the pods. The remaining rebels staggered as they got back up on their feet when suddenly gun fire erupted out of the smoke, killing the remaining rebels.

"Clear!" Lucas reported as him and the rest of Alpha Team walked out of the smoke with their AR30's up, scanning the hallway in front of them with their contacts on thermal mode.

"No we're not." Izzy said as he pointed his AR30 up towards the ceiling and fired a single shot at a surviving rebel's head who was stuck between the foam of the hull breech. "Now we're clear."

Alpha team looked around. The halls looked silver with LED lights illuminating overhead and thick ballistic windows along the walls allowing the team to see outside towards the Enidon. "All teams, status?" Raymond ordered on the channel as Alpha moved into formation just shy from touching the wall.

"Bravo here, one down, five up."

"Charlie, One down, five up, In contact, I say again, in contact!" Gunfire can be heard over the channel.

"Delta, two down, four up, preparing to breach objective."

"Alpha lead copy's all." Raymond responded. "Alpha team in route to objective. Let's move Lucas,"

"Roger," Lucas gave the hand signal to advance.

The Red Nova continued to move evasively destroying the station's defensive turrets with pinpoint accuracy. "Spectra squadron, what's your status?" Jason asked.

"Almost finished on our side Star." Spectra lead reported.

"Good, once all turrets are destroyed, set up a perimeter around the station."

"Roger."

Back on the Enidon, Gehnarne was pleased that the plan was getting back on track despite the casualties and the minor mishap. "Not much longer now."

"Sir!" One of the bridge staff reported. "We're receiving a message from someone on the Recluses," the crewmen double checked the sender ID "It's Colonel Vial!"

"What?!" Surprised. "Why is he still there? Patch him through."

The transmission came through on the main monitor at the front of the bridge. "This is Watchmen, Rifter, are you receiving me?"

"Well enough Watchmen."

"Good, I need to speak with Crimson, please connect me to her."

"Colonel, Crimson is on mission aboard that station with Alpha team."

Colonel Vial was shocked. "What? How did she recov-" He cut himself off. "Never mind, just patch me through to my daughter," Gehnarne grew concerned at why he wanted to talk to Sheena so badly. "Please." The Colonel asked again sincerely.

"Roger," Gehnarne performed the action on his captain's chair controls. "Connecting you now."

"Thank you." Colonel Vial said somberly.

Alpha team moved down the stations hall way in a CQB formation as the Recluses out in space came into view along the windows. Lucas was at the front on the left side of the hall with his AR30 up, Raymond also at the front on the right side of the hall with his AR30 up, Sheena behind Raymond with her weapon just over his shoulder pointing towards the inside of the hall, Katherine mirroring Sheena behind Lucas, and Izzy behind Sheena taking up rear security.

Sheena's Taclet beeped with an incoming transmission. "Hold on guy's," the team stopped as she checked her Taclet.

"What's wrong Sheena?" Lucas asked in concern.

"A priority transmission… from Watchmen?"

"Answer it, we'll hold here." Raymond said as everyone simultaneously took a knee while Sheena answered the call.

Sheena opened the channel on her communications app and connected it to the team's open channel. "Watchmen, this is Crimson, go ahead."

Colonel Vial looked somber as he spoke. "Sheena,"

Sheena and the team was surprised he didn't use her call sign and grew concerned. Puzzled, Sheena responded back "Dad?..."

"I'm glad we had a chance to talk back on earth honey... I really enjoyed our time together."

Sheena's heart slowly began to sink knowing for sure there was something wrong. "Dad, why are you bringing that up now, what's wrong?"

Colonel Vial closed his eyes for a moment, then opened them again with confidence as he admitted his plan. "The rebels on this ship know you're on board their station, they are falling back to their shuttles to redeploy to the station. With a force that size, you will surely be overwhelmed... unless someone stops them." Colonel Vial pulled out what looked like a kind of transmitter with an antenna and a trigger with his finger just off to the side of it.

Sheena immediately recognized what he was holding, it was the Recluses's manual self-destruct transmitter. She gasped and became frantic now understanding what he planned to do. "NO! Dad! don't! You don't have to do that, we'll be okay! Can't you just use the automatic sequence?!"

"The auto sequence was damage during the initial attack... Sweet heart, you know as well as I do this is the best tactical option."

The whole team grew concerned as they looked at Sheena in worry. "Dad, please, please don't do this!"

"Raymond!" Colonel Vial called him through the channel.

"Sir!?" Raymond tried his best to hold his composure.

"I have one last order for you... Take care of my daughter..."

"Dad..." Sheena began to cry.

"...With my life sir..." Raymond held back his tears.

"Good man..." Colonel Vial began to cry than sniffed holding them back with tenacity. "Lucas!" He called him next.

"Sir?" Lucas held his composure in honor of his mentor.

"Kill every single last one of those sons of bitches on that station for me, understood?"

"Understood Sir." He said with a cold emotionless voice of a killer.

"I love you honey..." Colonel Vial said to Sheena as he lifted the transmitter.

"Dad no! Please!" His finger began to squeeze tighter on the trigger. "DAD!" The trigger was pulled immediately cutting off the transmission. A flash of light became visible through a nearby window along the hall way from outside the station. The team looked at the flash and saw the Recluses breaking up into large pieces of debris.

"Oh my God..." Katherine said in shock.

Sheena looked out the window watching the Recluses break up. The fond memories of her and her father flooded her mind as she frantically cried out, "NOOOO!!!"

Gun fire erupted as Alpha team was caught off guard by rebels just coming down the hallway "CONTACT FRONT!" Lucas screamed viciously as he immediately suppressed and killed four of the rebels with a long cycle of full auto fire almost depleting his sixty round magazine. The whole team engaged the remaining rebels as Sheena snapped out of it, set her weapon to semi and waited for one of the rebels to pop his head out of cover. One did just that on the right, behind a crate and paid for it with a 5.56 millimeter round exploding out the back of his head from Sheena's deadly accuracy. Another rebel who was next to the one Sheena had killed realized he was the only one left in the group. He remembered his orders from Garza and switch to his pistol equipped with armor piercing rounds with enough power to break the station's ballistic windows. He pointed the pistol at a nearby window and fired off one round jamming the pistol. The bullet pierced through the window immediately setting off warning alarms.

"Warning! Hull breach immanent!" A female computer voice warned.

"Oh fuck!" Lucas reacted. "Everyone move NOW!" The whole team stood up, and frantically sprinted to the door leading to the next portion of the station. In mid sprint, Raymond pied the corner of the crate on his right and quickly put three shots into the rebel, two to the body, one to the head. "RAYMOND MOVE!" Lucas screamed.

Raymond sprinted as fast as he could jumping through the open pressure door flying past it just as Izzy slammed it closed behind him, sealing it just as the hall way on the other side where the team came from had exploded out into space with bodies of dead rebels flying out into the dark abyss. "Hull Stabilized." A female computer voice informed.

"Status!" Raymond ordered.

"White, up."

"Cat, up"

"Digit, up."

Sheena remained quiet. "Crimson?" Raymond turned around and saw her leaning against the wall with her head down trying to wipe her tears, Raymond quickly walked up to her, "Hey, are y-"

"He's gone..." She said mournfully. "And I never even had a chance to sing for him..." She cried, mourning the death of her dearly loved father.

"Sheena, look at me." Raymond gently touched her chin and softly moved her head to look at her in the eye. Her eyes had that same look he remembered from when he had helped her on the Recluses almost a year ago. They were red and watery as he tried to comfort her. "I promise you when this is all over you can mourn for your father as much as you want, and if you want me too, I'll be by your side the whole time. But right now, I need you to focus on the here and now. We need you, okay?"

Sheena saw hope in Raymond eye's. The same hope she saw that night he had helped her on the Recluses. She sniffed, wiped away her tears lightly smudging her face paint and took a deep breath as her expression went from sorrow, to determination. She looked back at Raymond with motivation in her eyes. "Okay, I'm ready."

"Okay," He was proud of her strength to continue as he softly kissed her on the forehead. "Let's finish this."

"Right." She lifted her weapon to a low ready as the both of them got back in formation and moved forward with the rest of the team.

"The control room is just ahead," Lucas informed.

"Center stack," Raymond ordered "Katherine, you're up." The team stacked up on the large sliding double door. Sheena and Raymond on the left with Sheena facing towards the door and Raymond facing down the hall they just came down posting security, Lucas and Izzy on the right mirroring Raymond and Sheena with Izzy looking down the hall towards a set of stairs along the left wall leading to another door. Katherine knelled in front of the door just barely able to snake in her wire camera through the thick padding under the door to see what was on the other side.

"Okay, I see two floors, the second floor looks like a balcony over looking the first." She said as she marked targets one at a time. The targets showed up on the team's contact HUD as red human shaped silhouettes. "I count nine hostiles, four on the second floor, and five on the first however, I don't have a full visual on the second floor targets, there could be more. Judging from the shape of the room, it looks like the door up the stairs down the hall from us leads to the balcony." She said while pulling out the wire camera from under the door.

"Okay," Raymond acknowledge. "Lucas, Izzy, and Katherine will breach the second floor. Me and Sheena will breach here on the first floor."

"Wilco." Lucas confirmed just as Katherine finished putting away her wire camera than followed him and Izzy to the second floor entrance. Once they moved away from the door, Sheena shifted position to the other side of the door as Raymond reached into his equipment pouch on his plate carrier grabbing a concussive breach charge. Despite its size, Raymond knew that this little guy had more than enough punch. He removed the adhesive peel and stuck the charge on the door just as Izzy did the same thing on the second floor door.

"Alpha one set." Raymond said on the channel.

"Alpha two set." Lucas responded

"Standby,"

Raymond readied the breach charge trigger and looked at Sheena. She had the eyes of a predator ready to hunt down it's pray. "Standby..."

Lucas looked at Katherine and Izzy on the opposite side of the door from where he was. They were ready.

"Execute, execute!" Raymond said as he and Izzy pulled their breach charge triggers simultaneously. Both doors blew open at a loud explosion as the rebels inside the room were stunned from the concussive force of the blast.

Sheena moved in first taking the path of least resistance on the left. Knowing exactly where her targets were thanks to Katherine's reconnaissance, Sheena immediately engaged her targets sweeping inward from the left side of the room to the right. Raymond took the opposite path of least resistance once Sheena was clear of the door way, mirroring the same movements as Sheena on the right.

On the second floor, Izzy went through the doorway first mimicking the same movements as Sheena and Raymond down on the first floor, killing his targets that consisted of marked and unmarked rebels. Lucas followed taking the opposite path, engaging the opposite targets from what Izzy was currently engaging. Than Katherine followed along the same path as Izzy engaging the last target. Just after Katherine killed the last target, two more rebels that were unmarked moved out from cover behind a set of terminals further in the room and fired at Lucas. He saw them immediately engaging, as he was shot in the left leg with a 7.62 millimeter-round passing straight through the ligament. As the round impacted causing him to lose balance with blood shooting out the back of his leg, three of Lucas's shots tore through the first rebel's chest killing him. Lucas fell backwards on the ground "AH!" he grunted in pain, trying to stay in the mode as he posted his AR30 between his legs from a ground firing posture and fired at the second rebel with five rounds, killing the second rebel.

"Status!" Raymond ordered.

"Crimson, up!"

"Digit, up!"

"Cat, up!"

"WHITE, DOWN! Fuck!" He yelled in pain.

The team grew concerned for Lucas. "Lucas!" Katherine ran to him seeing blood smeared on the floor and soaking the left side of his pants. She grabbed his med kit, took out the medical foam injector, then immediately used it on his wound instantly stopping the bleeding.

"Ah shit! How bad is it?!" He said in anguish.

"Judging from the wound and how quickly the bleeding stopped," Katherine responded as she dressed the wound with a pressure bandage. "I don't think the bullet hit any major artery's, you should still be able to walk."

"Shit, that's easy for you to say." He grunted in pain as he struggled to stand.

"Oh get up you big baby," She helped him stand.

"We're clear up here!" Izzy announced.

"No sign of Garza?" Raymond asked.

"Negative," Katherine reported. "He's not here."

"He's not down here either." Sheena reported.

Raymond spoke on the channel. "All teams report, does anyone have a positive ID on Garza?"

"Bravo here, that's a negative Alpha Lead."

"This is Charlie, negative Alpha."

"Delta, No sign of him from our end so far."

Raymond sighed in annoyance "Great..." sarcastically. "Looks like we're gonna have to search the whole station now."

"I assure you, you won't have to search far." Garza's voice said over an intercom projecting his voice in the control room's surrounding speakers.

The team was surprised as Raymond aggressively responded. "Where are you?"

"Just behind that heavily sealed door behind you." Raymond turned around towards the right wall from the main entrance and saw an armored door that was slightly larger than the control room's main entrance. *"That door leads to the stations main server room where me and you will have our final battle."*

Raymond grew angry. "If you think I'm dumb enough to go in after you alone-"

"Oh, you will come in alone, because if your team follows you in, I will flood this server room with a deadly nerve agent killing everyone without an active flow system protecting them from the effects." Raymond pondered the horrible thought as his team reassembled around him. *"You and only you will come in here, and no guns either, just your sword, besides guns aren't as effective against flow system users like us anyway, am I right? Don't keep me waiting."*

"I guess we don't have much of a choice." Lucas said limping up to Raymond.

"I'm afraid not." Raymond seemed worried.

"Don't worry, we'll wait here. Just be careful in there."

"I will."

"Raymond," Sheena walked up to him in worry.

"Sheena," He unbuckled his AR30 from his plate carrier, took off his plate carrier with his shoulder Kevlar plates connected to the shoulder straps, unbuckled his M-67 pistol and gave it all to her.

"Hold on to my gear for me will ya? I'll be getting it back from you later so don't worry." He gave her a reassuring smile.

She grabbed his gear only seeing him wearing his multi-camouflage compression combat shirt with matching combat pants, brown belt, brown boots and his sword sheathed in its scabbard on his waist. She looked at him hoping this wouldn't be the last time she sees him alive. With his gear in her hands, she moved forward and kissed him. The team normally wasn't much for public display of affection in the middle of a mission but they knew that this was going to be very dangerous for Raymond and understood Sheena's emotions. She moved away from the kiss. "I love you..." she said somberly "Now give him everything you've got." she said with aggression in her voice and fire in her eyes.

"I will, and I love you too." He said feeling more at ease after such a peaceful kiss. He turned around and walked towards the armored door. As he got closer, the door unlocked on its own, depressurized, then opened with nothing but darkness on the other side. He felt a ping of fear, but continued to march forward into the unknown. He passed the door as it automatically shut closed, locked than pressurized behind him.

After Raymond separated from the rest of the team, Gehnarne reported in. *"Alpha, team, be advised, we are detecting a very large contingent of hostiles moving towards your position on thermal scanning, they really want that control room back."*

"Shit, Roger command, setting up defensive positions now," Lucas's mind immediately went tactical thinking and planning as he gave orders. "Okay Alpha this fight isn't over yet, Sheena, start passing out what's left of Raymond's ammo, once you're done you'll join me on the second floor posting just above the main entrance getting an elevated shooting angle, Izzy, Katherine, you two post side by side in front of the main entrance behind this large circular console for cover, I'll watch our six from the stair way, lets lock this shit down alpha!"

"Roger!" The team sounded off in unison and quickly conducted their tasks. Izzy and Katherine posted their weapons on the large console facing towards the main entrance. After dropping Raymond's gear next to them, Sheena took three thirty round-magazines worth of ammo and brought it upstairs with her. Once upstairs, she took a prone firing position aiming towards the main entrance below her. She held two magazines above her head as Lucas quickly limped past her taking the magazines from her while moving to his position.

Lucas saw everyone set and ready for a fight. "Alright." He was satisfied as he posted up on the second floor entrance getting comfortable with his shooting position analyzing all of his possible shot angles down the stairs. "This is it Alpha!" Lucas sounded off. "USOD's Reaper team had their shot at Garza and blew it on a double! Now it's up to us to finish the job! This is our time to make history! Let the whole galaxy know that it was SMO's Alpha team that ended this war! UNITY!?"

"IS VICTORY!" Alpha team sounded off.

Lightning Archival Records
Intercepted transmission
During The Orbital Battle Of Selva
Possible Enemy Frequency
Transmission Fragmented
Female Voice Identification Unknown
Due To Fragmentation

Prepar-... Adavanced Com-... Drone. Let-... pilots-... do, especial-

... Red Nova. Tha-... Target. Re-... LAUNCH!-...

Transmission lost
Intelligence Interpretation
Possible Attack On Friendly Vessel Red Nova

Chapter 18: Final Engagements

Raymond walked further into the dark room as the lights suddenly turned on. The large room was about half the size of the Recluses hanger with white LED lights running along the sides and center of the ceiling. Some servers ran along the walls while others were positioned like pillars more in the center of the room in an organized grid.

"Raymond "The Gunslinger" Reynolds." Garza said as he walked out from behind a server showing himself to Raymond. He held his composure as Garza walked closer than stopped only several meters away. "That's your name and call sign right?"

"Yea," Raymond confirmed with anger in his voice. "I guess an intel source got you that much huh?"

Garza chuckled with a devilish smile. "That source got me much more than just your name. I also know that your parents were killed in a church bombing I had orchestrated many years ago as a demonstration of my resolve." Raymond grew angry. "Seems that we share something in common."

"I HIGHLY doubt that!" Raymond said furiously as he began to draw his sword.

Garza saw this and got to the point. "Like you, I have been wronged too." Raymond grew closer to attacking becoming impatient. "You see, I am really not Garza Liankos."

Raymond's anger quickly turned to confusion. "What?"

"The real Garza Liankos died a long time ago when I forcefully took power away from him. My real name... is Lusha Cralix."

"Lusha Cralix? Who the hell-"

"I was a spy for the council under the UEI, United Earth Intelligence. This is where our common issues come into play." Lusha looked at Raymond sincerely. "You see, I was a part of a highly sensitive mission, one that is partly connected to your organization I'll admit. However, in the end that mission played out poorly I'm afraid. Because of its poor outcome, the council had to cover their tracks. In doing so, they betrayed me and tried to have me killed." Raymond listened to Garza, now known as Lusha, intently. "I managed to escape thanks to the help of an acquaintance. From that point on I vowed to destroy the council by any means necessary. With help I made my way to colonial space where I made contact with the rebels and quickly rose up the ranks thanks to my combat skills and experience. The real Garza Liankos made me his right hand man however, his ambitions only sought to free the colonies from earth government. My ambitions were greater, I wanted to completely destroy the council!"

While still in a ready posture, Raymond was intrigued. "So how did you manage to make yourself look like the real Garza Liankos and take over his rebel force?"

"That acquaintance of mine helped me yet again as he inspired me to take over the rebellion. He had many connections and access to extremely advance technology. So advanced that he was able to manipulate my DNA to look like Garza. From there, I killed Garza and took control of his rebel horde."

"You said that failed mission had something to do with my organization, what did you mean by that?"

"I'm sorry Raymond, in order to protect my acquaintance, I cannot say anymore than that."

"Because your acquaintance is probably a member of Carnivore I bet, so what the hell does this pathetic story of your rise to power for revenge have to do with me?

"Do you not see the connection?!" Lusha became frustrated at how little Raymond seemed to care. "If it weren't for the council, none of this would have happened! If they had never betrayed me, I would have never committed the acts I deemed necessary to destroy them! If it weren't for the council's devious acts causing this chain reaction, you could have lived a completely different life." Lusha spoke as if he pitied Raymond. "One with your parents still in your life."

"SHUT UP!" Raymond interrupted him. "Although I do believe you in saying that the council destroyed your life, who the hell gave you the right to destroy mine!" Lusha let Raymond speak. "You had a choice! We ALL have a choice, and you made the most most-evilest one of all! For that, you will suffer the consequences for what you have done!"

"I told you all of this in hopes that you might be willing to join me against the council. With the flow system, we can destroy them easily together!"

Raymond didn't even have to think about how to answer Lusha's offer. "The council maybe wrong in their acts and will one-day answer for them... However," Raymond tapped his gauntlets together twice, activating the flow system in standard mode with a bass like hum immediately causing the blue discs inside the gauntlets to spin as Raymond's black face paint and right brown eye both turned blue at the same time matching the same blue glow of the discs. He quickly drew his sword and went into stance with his sword's blade near his shoulder. "Right now, you're my target, not them!"

Lusha was disappointed. "Very well then." He pressed a button on his flow systems control module strapped to his upper right shoulder. The servers in the center of the room descended down into the floor as Lusha doubled tapped his Guantlets together, activating his flow system also making a bass like hum. He then slowly drew his rapier while speaking. "By the end of this fight, either you will be by my side against the council... or dead. I personally hope it's the former." He went into stance, threatening Raymond with the tip of his Rapier just as the servers finished their descent and locked down into the floor below. "It would be such a shame to kill such potential."

Raymond stayed silent to Lusha's comment as he allowed his killer instinct to take control, but only to an extent as he kept in mind what Sheena had told him back on Selva. He decided to hold back this time thinking that he could beat Garza without the speed of Rage mode, that his standard mode and skill as a German long sword fighter would be enough without losing control of his killer instinct and rage.

Lusha attacked first with a thrusting one handed stab traveling at a great distance towards Raymond. Raymond riposte, deflecting his sword than thrusted, Lusha parried, pushing Raymond's sword up than cut down diagonally to the lower left towards Raymond, Raymond saw this and immediately dodged, then moved diagonally forwards with his body as he swung his sword diagonally down to the left attempting to cut Lusha who than blocked and kept Raymond's sword locked with his own as he devilishly smiled at Raymond. Raymond gritted his teeth in frustration realizing that Lusha was going to be more of the aggressor this time compared to how he was on Selva.

"CONTACT!" Lucas yelled as he opened fire on a group of rebels coming up the stairs.

Sheena heard him as she saw more rebels right at the first floor entrance. "ENGAGING!" She sounded off putting controlled pairs into each rebel she saw attempting to enter the room.

"TWELVE O'CLOCK, IN THE HALL WAY, FAR SIDE!" Izzy called out firing on full auto in short controlled bursts.

"ROGER!" Katherine acknowledge as she fired her weapon in coordination with Izzy's every time he stopped firing in order to conserve ammo.

"Rifter, White," Lucas called on the open channel. "We've made contact with the enemy attempting to retake our position," He paused his transmission to fire his weapon at two rebels coming up the stairs while two more behind them tried to lay down cover fire for them. After killing the two rebels, he went back into the doorway for cover as he reloaded and continued his transmission to Gehnarne. "We got a lot of them here, can you give us an exact estimate on their numbers?!" He finished as he snapped out of cover and fired his weapon on semi, hitting one rebel straight in the head.

"Negative white," Gehnarne reported. *"The heat signatures are too close together, we can't pinpoint individual targets."*

"Dammit," Lucas hissed off the channel.

"Alpha, this is Charlie!" Charlie lead interrupted on the channel, *"We just completed our objective and are on our way to support you, ETA, give or take fifteen minutes!"*

Lucas looked at his ammo reserves and the frequency at how the rebels were coming at them, getting a guess estimate on their possible ammo use, then responded. "Roger that Charlie, get here as fast as you can."

"Roger Alpha, hang in there."

Lucas commented to himself off the channel. "I hope we have enough ammo to last that long." He then snapped out of cover again firing a controlled pair into a rebel's center mass and one to the head just as the rebel fell forward dead.

Back on the Enidon, Gehnarne thought out loud. "Things are gonna get a whole lot worse for Alpha if Charlie doesn't get there in time."

"Sir!" A crew member from navigation got Gehnarne's attention. "We're detecting a new contact in sector two approaching the station!"

"Rifter, this is Star," Jason called on the channel. *"We just finished destroying the last of the enemy turrets, requesting permission to engage new contact in sector two!?"*

Gehnarne immediately responded. "Roger that Star, you are clear to engage!"

"Roger!" Jason said with motivation in his voice. "Spectra squadron, you guys hang back and secure a perimeter around the station, this guy is mine."

"Roger that Star, give em hell!" Sykes responded.

The Red Nova accelerated faster towards the new contact's location as it came into visual range. It was a highly advanced fighter of an unknown design with short stubby wings and energy based weapons. As the Red Nova closed in, the unknown fighter suddenly accelerated straight towards the Red Nova as if it now perceived the Red Nova as a threat. Once in range, the fighter fired missiles. "Incoming!" Timothy warned. "Firing forward counter measures!" The counter measures launch from the nose of the Red Nova impacting into the enemy missiles creating a large blinding flash of light.

When the light disappeared, the unknown fighter was no longer in its last spotted position. "What!?" Jason said in shock.

"Ninety degrees high, moving towards aft!" Sarah said with a hint of surprise in her voice. The Red Nova suddenly shook violently as it took fire from the fighter's energy weapons.

"Rear shields at seventy-three percent!" Timothy reported.

"Shit," Jason hissed in frustration. "Sarah, activate Enhanced Evasion!"

"Understood." She acknowledges. The Red Nova's four engines began to expand as Jason tried his best to maneuver around the incoming fire. The four engines locked in place, "Enhanced Evasion active." Sarah notified.

"Alright you bastard," Jason said in anger to the enemy fighter.

"Oh boy," Timothy said in fear. "Not again."

Jason continued. "SHOW ME WHAT YOU'VE GOT!" He pulled the controls back towards himself.

The Red Nova flipped upward as the enemy ship continued flying, forward. Once the nose of the Red Nova was pointed down directly at the fighter, it fired its energy cannons and missiles. The enemy fighter boosted at an unparalleled speed dodging the energy beams than immediately rolled while launching counter measures, destroying the Red Nova's missiles. Timothy and Jason both had bummed expressions while they both said in sync "You gotta be shitting me!" The Red Nova flipped back to right side up and chased after the fighter while still firing its energy cannons, attempting to shoot down the fighter.

Back on the station, Raymond and Lusha fought vigorously as their swords clashed with high pitch pings and screeches. Raymond blocked Lusha's attempt to cut him with a mid-body cut. The rapier collided with Raymond's sword leading Lusha to lift his left leg and kicked Raymond square in the chest so hard, he flew back several meters with the wind knocked out of him as Lusha shuffled away from him several meters creating distance between himself and Raymond.

"What the hell is this?" Lusha commented in frustration as Raymond began to recover from the kick. "This is not the same man I fought at Selva." Raymond listened to him as he stood back up. "What happened to that red aura of violence?! That thirst for blood?!"

Raymond also grew frustrated knowing that he couldn't beat Lusha in standard flow system state. This whole time he held back, trying to honor Sheena's words. However, he knew he couldn't do it anymore. He let his killer instinct take full control as he allowed himself to forget everything Sheena had said on Selva. Raymond mildly laughed sadistically. "Be careful what you wish for Lusha," He said with growing viciousness in his voice as the flow system's blue discs began to spin faster making a high pitch whine immediately changing the blue disc's, Raymond's right blue eye, and blue face paint to red. The red face paint looked reminiscent to the blood stripe he wore on Selva as his right eyes glowed with rage and his expression was one of a vicious animal ready to feast on the blood of his prey. "Because this is HOW YOU DIE!!!" With pure viciousness in his voice, he yelled while he ran towards Lusha at incredible speed.

Lusha smiled in satisfaction as Raymond jumped up in the air with his body shifting horizontally than spun like a bladed top at inhuman speeds towards Lusha. At matching speed, Lusha lifted his rapier and deflected all five of Raymond's blows with ease. On the final cut,

Raymond looked at Lusha in shock. "How?" he questioned in his mind as he landed on his feet and tried the same move again spinning even faster like a bladed up right top spinning on the floor with violent grace as Lusha once again deflected his attack with ten cuts. "How is he able to keep up with my speed?!" Raymond thought as the final cut of his attack bit into Lusha's rapier locking their swords together.

Lusha smiled devilishly. "I see the question in your eyes," he chuckled as Raymond's expression was puzzled. "You're wondering how I can keep up with you so perfectly this time aren't you?" He pushed back Raymond's blade as he slid back several meters gaining distance from Raymond. "Unlike our old friend Asrin, who decided to use his flow system as an overpriced piece of armor by increasing the gravity field's output, I did the opposite by increasing the fields input, increasing my overall speed just enough to match yours. Back on Selva I was already pushing a thirty-one percent increase, now in preparation for this fight, I had to push it to fifty percent despite the possibility of future physical ailments based on my sources research, but I think I'd rather die later than sooner, wouldn't you agree?" Raymond grew frustrated at this new information. "As I'm sure you already know, at these speeds, bullets are practically useless which is why I wanted you and I to fight with swords alone, guns would have only weighed us down." Raymond moved back into stance with the blade over his head threatening Lusha with the tip of the sword. "Since you are no longer holding back, neither will I," Lusha continued with obsessive motivation in his voice. "Now, show me that rage! SHOW ME THAT TENACITY!"

"HRAA!!!" Raymond yelled as he charged Lusha. Once in range he dropped to his left thigh to slide underneath Lusha's guard. With his left hand, he pushed himself to the right, getting an opening on Lusha's left side and cut with the sword in his right hand. Lusha blocked the attack as Raymond's body got back onto his feet and came at Lusha again with a barrage of stabs, all of them missing as Lusha aggressively dodged each one. Lusha had enough with the stabs, lifted his rapier stopping Raymond's sword by the tip with the flat end of his rapier.

Just outside the server room, Alpha team continued to hold off waves of rebel forces. "Ammo check!" Lucas ordered.

"Crimson, yellow!

"Cat Eye, red!"

"Digit, red!"

"White," Lucas fired one round out of his AR30 locking the bolt to the rear on his last magazine. "just went black on primary!" He informed as he switched to his M76 side arm, shooting and killing another rebel.

Sheena heard Lucas's report, grabbed an extra magazine out of her pouch and slid it backwards towards Lucas. "Make it count!" She yelled as she fired her AR30 at two rebels near the doorway killing them.

"Thanks!" Lucas complimented as he reflexively reloaded his primary weapon. "Team, switch to On Site Procurement if you have to!" He suggested.

"Roger!" Everyone acknowledged.

Izzy fired a three-round burst that immediately locked his AR30's bolt to the rear. "Changing mag-" He realized he was out of ammo after checking his pouch failing to find a fresh magazine. "Shit," he hissed, "Black on ammo! Switching to OSP!" He reported as he grabbed an old M4 model weapon off a dead rebel that was killed earlier during the initial room breach.

Next to Izzy, Katherine fired her weapon on semi trying to conserve ammo. Just after killing a rebel on her right, another rebel on her left in Izzy's sector of fire, shot at Katherine while Izzy checked the M4, making sure it was ready to fire. A 5.56 millimeter-round penetrated through Katherine's left forearm than slammed into her plate carrier spraying blood onto her chest. "AH, FUCK!" She shrieked in pain as she fell backwards to the ground wounded.

Izzy heard Katherine's shriek immediately head checking right seeing her grabbing her left arm in excruciating pain and blood splatters on her gear and cloths. "KATHERINE!" He said in worry and anger as he reflexively got his weapon up and killed the rebel who shot Katherine and another to his right in Katherine's sector of fire. "Crimson!" He barked. "Suppress that door way now!"

"Roger!" Sheena confirmed in worry as she switched her AR30 from semi to auto and fired short controlled bursts, keeping the rebels at bay from the door.

"I got you Katherine, hang on!" Izzy said to her as he grabbed her med kit, took out the medical foam injector and applied it into the wound. The entry wound on the front of her forearm was small with the exit wound larger and had small chunks of bloody meat hanging off her arm. "AAHH SSSHIT!" She screamed in pain as Izzy quickly treated her.

"Hang on, hang on!" He said as bullets cracked over head at supersonic speeds. He applied a pressure bandage to stop the bleeding. "There," He was done, "You can still shoot right?!"

"Yea!" She grunted in pain as she grabbed her AR30 with her right hand only. "I'm still in this fight!" She finished with an angry growl. With one hand she posted her weapon on the control console and began shooting. Izzy admired her strength but quickly snapped out of it and posted next to her with his M4 continuing to fire on the rebels.

Sheena ceased suppressing fire once she realized she was now out of ammo. "Black on ammo! Switching to OSP!" She picked up a nearby AK-47 and continued to fire on the rebels killing one after another. "These guys just keep coming!"

"This isn't looking good..." Lucas said to himself as he called Charlie team on the channel. "Charlie, this is Alpha, what is your ETA? Over." There was no response. "Charlie, this is Alpha, do you copy?" Still no response. "Dammit..."

"Maybe they're just under heavy fire." Izzy commented

"Or maybe they got shwacked!" Katherine said with a vicious grunt of pain trying to stay in the fight.

"Doesn't matter!" Lucas spoke up. "We hold no matter what! Understood!?"

"Roger!" Alpha acknowledged.

Back outside of the station in space, the duel between the Red Nova and the unknown fighter continued as spectra squadron watched from a distance. "*Spectra One, you seeing this?*" One of the pilots said on the channel.

Spectra One, Lieutenant Danial Sykes responded with arms crossed in his fighter's cockpit. "Yea I am, this dog fight is insane."

"*Thank God Star told us to stay out of it,*" Another pilot said on the channel. "*We probably would have gotten in the way. Despite its size, that Red Nova ship is twice as maneuverable than our fighters, and that unknown hostile fighter is keeping up with it. We would have been WAY out of our league."*

"Kinda, makes you wonder what other crazy tech they can find out there in the multiverse." Sykes said with intrigue in his voice.

The unknown fighter was on the Red Nova's six o'clock shooting energy beams as the Red Nova tried to dodge with a barrel role. One of the beams impacted.

"Rear shields down to thirty percent!" Timothy reported with a hint of aggravation in his voice.

"I had enough of this bullshit!" Jason said in anger. "Tim, get our trump card ready, but just one okay!?"

"One Nova Blade?!" Timothy disagreed. "That's a hell of a long shot Jason!"

"Just trust me, Sarah on my mark divert all power from the main engine to the pivot engines in full reverse!"

"Understood." Sarah confirmed with a solid voice.

"Nova blade one, standing by!" Timothy reported.

"Alright, three, two, one, MARK!" The Red Nova's engines went dead for less than a second as the four pivot engines snapped to the opposite direction and fired. The Red Nova instantly shot in reverse towards the enemy fighter as a linear looking projector shot out of the Red Nova's hull and activated a solid red beam of energy. "GOTCHA!" Jason said with aggression as the fighter zoomed straight into the Nova Blade immediately cutting the fighter in half down the middle than exploded as it passed into view of the Red Nova's forward monitor. Jason chuckled in motivation "How does one hundred million degrees of focused plasma energy taste?" He then set course back to the perimeter around the station, regrouping with Spectra Squadron as the Nova Blade powered down and the projector snapped back into the ship's hull.

"Regrouping with Spectra squadron now." Timothy reported than looked at Jason. "Jason, what was the deal with only activating one Nova Blade?"

"Think about it Tim, with such an advance fighter like that, why would whoever sent it to attack us only send one? Either they just wasted their one and only precious resource or there could have been more of them and our attackers only sent one to scout us. We couldn't afford to reveal all of our secret weapons to our enemy right?"

Timothy thought about Jason's wise words. "You got a point there, now that's over and done with, it's up to the guys aboard the station to wrap this up."

"Yea," Jason agreed with worry. "I hope they're alright."

Back in the server room, Raymond grew exhausted as he was barely able to keep his guard up and was kicked in the chest again so hard that he flew towards the back wall of the room with his back slamming against it. "AH!" he grunted in pain while falling to the floor.

Lusha smiled as he spoke. "You see Raymond, not only am I faster than when we last fought, allowing me to balance my offensive and defensive movements, but I've also had a chance to see most of your moves back on Selva and now I'm sure I've seen all of them during this fight. You have no hope of winning." Raymond got up on one knee growing discouraged from Lusha's words. "On top of that, the power in your gauntlets should almost be completely drained by now." Raymond checked his battery indicator on his HUD. It said thirteen percent. Lusha was right. "So, I will give you one more chance for your future." Raymond listened intently. "Either you can accept my offer and join me in destroying the council, or you can attack me one more time, however, I guarantee you will surely die after your next move if you choose to attack." Raymond had an expression of fear as his flow system's Rage mode powered down, shifting back to standard mode with his right eye, face paint, and gauntlet's discs turning back to blue. Lusha smiled believing he had broken Raymond's spirit. "Take your time to think it through," He said with confidence. "I don't want you making any rash decisions."

Raymond carefully thought of a possible solution out of this situation slowly becoming desperate. "No... all that rage... it's all useless now... If only I had killed him back on Selva where I had a better chance. If I did, none of this would have happened." He began to blame himself then stopped. "But... there's no way I was willing to let Sheena die... my love for her exceeds any amount of hate I have towards hi-" Raymond had an epiphany. "Wait..." He looked down at his sword reminiscing on what Sheena and his dream had told him.

"Free will is like a double edged sword." He twisted his sword so that the flat end of the blade faced him as he saw his own reflection on the blade. "Will I choose the side of hate?..." He remembered the sword in his dream having one side of the sword permanently stained with blood. "Or the side of love?..." and the other side perfectly silver and clean. Lusha saw him twist the sword thinking that Raymond could be planning to attack. "Love... the love for Sheena and my friends that are still out there waiting for me..." He thought about Lucas, Katherine, Izzy, and Sheena. "I must protect them with love as my strength... and everything that goes with love its self." Raymond's expression changed from fear to contentment with a smile. Lusha saw this now becoming concerned for what Raymond was doing. "Alright Lord," He thought to himself. "Let's do it your way." Raymond slowly stood up as he lifted his sword with both hands, centering the flat end of the blade in front of his face closing his eye's.

Lusha slowly went into stance preparing for what he might do. "Whatever it is your planning, you can't win."

Raymond ignored Lusha as he began to pray in his thoughts. "Lord... I give it all to you... all the hate, vengeance, and rage. Take it all from me, and in return," His gauntlet's discs began to spin faster again as if it was about to enter Rage mode.

Lusha saw the build-up in Raymond's gauntlets. "Oh please, really? Stop this nonsense, do you really want me to kill you!?"

"And in return," Raymond prayed again trying to zone out Lusha. "Grant me love to protect, justice with mercy, and lastly, right now,-!"

"Don't you get it!" Lusha warned him again. "it's over already, GIVE UP!"

Raymond had enough of Lusha's lies and spoke out loudly as if he was throwing his lies right back at him with his own voice while he opened his eyes. "GRANT ME FOCUS!!!". Immediately after he finished his prayer, the discs in the flow gauntlets whined at an even higher pitch sound than Rage mode while a pure white glowing outline of the gravity field exploded out from his body like a white shock wave. Both of his eye's, face paint and discs instantly turned to a pure white. His eyes looked none existent in the camouflage of such a pure white from the face paint. He went into stance with his sword by his left hip and the tip toward the rear. "I've made my move

Lusha." He said with a calm voice. "Now you make yours."

Lusha was shocked at the sight of Raymond's new mode, unsure what it was capable of. He pushed his shock to the side growing angry at Raymond's defiance. "FINE!" He yelled in frustration. "With this last move, YOU DIE! HIAAA!!!" Lusha charged Raymond as he kept his composure letting Lusha get closer. Once in range, Lusha jumped up in mid-air with a stab just as Raymond cut diagonally up creating a high pitch sonic boom, breaking the sound barrier with the powerful attack, cutting Lusha's rapier in two halves. The front of the blade slowly flew up as Raymond quickly adjusted his sword at another cutting angle and cut down towards Lusha's left leg, with another high pitch sonic boom, severing the leg from Lusha's body above the knee cap. Blood exploded out of the wound as the front piece of Lusha's rapier blade and his left leg flew in different directions of the room violently due to Raymond's super-sonic cuts. Lusha screamed in anguish "GAHHH!!!" He flew forward uncontrollably, slamming into the back wall of the room where Raymond was earlier. He sat up against the wall grunting in agony. "AAHH!!!" He quickly grabbed a tourniquet from his shoulder pocket with shaking hands. Blood gushed and spurted out from the wound as he slipped on the tourniquet, strapping it, then attempted to tighten the small metal pipe connected to the tourniquet strap. He cried and screamed in pain as he tried to cut off the blood flow from the wound with barely enough strength when suddenly Raymond, now in standard flow system mode, knelt down next to him and turned the tourniquet tightly for him. Still in pain, Lusha looked at Raymond in surprise as blood flow from the wound stopped. "Why?..." Lusha asked in shock. "How?..."

Raymond secured the tourniquet making sure it wouldn't come loose. "Because the love that calls me to protect my friends, is the same love that calls me to forgive you." He looked up into Lusha's eyes "You were right, you and I did have something in common, but no longer... because I chose to let it go." Raymond stood up and held out his hand. "Now I want to make you an offer Lusha Cralix. Come with me, and let me show you peace."

Lusha's expression slowly changed from shock, to confidence as he began to laugh. "hahahaHAHAHA!!!" Raymond grew worried at his laugh. "What about that promise you made!?" Raymond remembered. "The promise you made in BLOOD! You SWORE on the blood of your friend, your parents, and all those I massacred that you would KILL ME!" Raymond felt a ping of guilt. "You... You DARE go back-" he quickly extended his right hand as what looked like a small pistol that Raymond had never seen before ejected out from inside Lusha's jacket sleeve into his hand. "ON YOUR PROMISE!" He fired just as Raymond's new focus mode reactivated on its own, lifted his sword and deflected the first bullet just as a warning signal came up on his HUD saying "Flow System power at zero percent." He realized too late that this new mode used up battery power more quickly than Rage mode. He deflected the second round realizing he might not have enough power to deflect or dodge the next one, if he didn't stop Lusha now, he would be shot. Instinctively without hesitation or thinking, he crouched down dodging the third shot as the focus mode receded back into rage mode, then spun multiple times with Raymond losing his focus due to the more aggressive movement while blood and body parts spewed all over him and the room as he heard a loud agonizing scream that immediately faded into the attack and the sound of bloody splats. Raymond didn't stop spinning until the flow system shut down due to power loss which was only two seconds after Raymond began his attack.

Raymond's final spin came to a stop facing away from Lusha's remains with the flow system completely shut down with the discs and Raymond's right eye and face paint returning to their original color. He was covered in Lusha's blood from head to toe with a shocked expression. He slowly looked around the room noticing the spots of blood and body parts along the walls, the servers and the floor. He was horrified as he slowly turned around afraid of what he would see. He only saw a glimpse out of his peripheral vision of what looked like a hunk of bloody meat with one leg and a thigh from where he had severed Lusha's leg earlier with blood smeared along the back wall, then quickly snapped his head back forward away from the sight in disgust. He felt guilt for what he had done. "Lusha... I'm so sorry I made such a foolish promise... God forgive me." He was somber as he stood up to his feet, sheathed his sword and walked towards the server room's entrance, away from Lusha's remains.

Gunfire continued to echo through-out the control room as Alpha team continued to hold their ground. Lucas had switched to his M76 pistol no longer having any ammo left in his AR30 or an on-site AK47 he had just dropped on the floor. After putting five rounds into one rebel, killing him, he looked around and saw Katherine with an M16. "Izzy and Sheena are using OSP and now Katherine," Lucas thought to himself as he grew worried. "This is it..." Lucas then spoke on the open channel. "Alpha," He gave an order he thought he'd never have to give. "Switch to knifes if you have to, we're not going down without cutting some throats, understood!?"

The whole team was shocked at the order but understood they had to hold no matter what. "Roger!" they all responded just as they heard more gunfire coming from further down the hallway.

"What is that?" Sheena asked.

"What the he-" Lucas was interrupted by a transmission through the open channel.

"Alpha, this is Charlie, assaulting through the enemy position at your twelve hold your fire!"

Lucas was relieved with a smile, "Roger that Charlie! Good to hear from you!"

Four members of Charlie team aggressively assaulted through the enemy position in front of the control room main entrance. Once they reached their limit of advance, killing the last of the rebels, they regrouped with Alpha team on the lower level of the control room. "The hell took you so long?!" Lucas asked in enthusiasm as he limped down the stairs.

"Sorry to keep you waiting," Charlie lead explained. "We ran into a ton of them along the way and took a casualty, we moved as fast as we could." He looked around noticing someone from Alpha was missing. "Where's Alpha lead?"

"He's in there," Sheena responded walking up to the group while looking towards the server room door. "Fighting Garza."

"By himself?" Charlie lead asked in concern just as everyone in the control room heard the server room door depressurize.

"Someone's coming out!" Lucas said. "Weapons up!"

Everyone reflexively pointed their weapons towards the door except for Sheena as she said "Wait, what if it's Raymond!?"

"What if it's Garza?" Lucas responded.

Sheena thought quickly than said "Weapons tight!" as she lifted her weapon towards the door.

Alpha and Charlie team waited anxiously just as the doors depressurization had finished. The door quickly slid open revealing a man bathed in blood. Charlie team immediately yelled. "DON'T MOVE! GET ON THE GROUND NOW!" and other harsh warnings.

Sheena looked closely and recognized the man, "WAIT, It's Raymond, stand down!" Charlie lowered their weapons in disgust at how Raymond was soaked in blood.

"Charlie," Lucas ordered. "Clear the server room!"

"Roger, moving!" Charlie lead acknowledged.

"Raymond!" Sheena ran up to him worried about why he was covered in blood. "Raymond are you all right-"

"It's-" He interrupted her with a somber voice. "...It's not my blood..."

"What?" Sheena was confused.

"OH GOD!" One of the Charlie team members yelled in shock. Sheena looked around Raymond's shoulder curiously to see what the commotion was about. She was shocked to see what was left of Garza's diced carcass with blood and body parts scattered around the room. "Oh fuck... guah!" another member of Charlie team gagged at the site almost throwing up.

Still in shock, "Raymond... what happened?" Sheena asked.

"I tried..." Raymond spoke timidly as Sheena focused her attention back to him. "I tried to take him alive... but he wouldn't stop and I-"

"Raymond..." She hugged him in comfort.

Raymond was surprised that she would still hug him despite all the blood. "Sheena, I'm-"

"I don't care," She interrupted. "I'm just glad it's finally over." She embraced him tighter as he wrapped his arms around her.

Katherine, Izzy, and Lucas looked at Raymond and Sheena from just a few meters away. "Wow..." Katherine commented, entranced by Raymond and Sheena's embrace. "That's so romantic."

Lucas looked at the sight in disgust. "No, that's just disgusting."

Katherine's expression quickly changed to disappointed "And just like that, the moment's gone."

"Oh come on!" Lucas protested, "Who knows what nasty diseases Garza had in his system!"

Raymond and Sheena continued their quite embrace ignoring all the noise around them for a few moments longer as if they haven't been at peace in years.

Back on the Red Nova, Jason and the crew received a transmission from Gehnarne. *"Red Nova, Spectra squadron, stand down, the station is now secure, teams Echo through Hotel have been deployed."*

Both Jason and Timothy loudly sighed in relief. "It's about time!" Jason commented. "Okay Tim," he got out of the pilot seat, "Prepare to shutdown ANC."

"Aye, aye." Timothy responded. "On your mark."

Jason was about to walk behind Sarah than immediately stopped himself taking one step backwards, looking straight into her rage filled eye's with a right red eye. "Sarah," He spoke while she continued to look straight forward as if she was ignoring him. "Good work today, thank you." He said to her sincerely with a smile while she still looked straight forward with an emotionless expression. Jason than moved behind her with his arms out, ready to catch her. "Alright Tim, deactivate ANC."

"ANC," He flipped a switch immediately causing Sarah to pass out backwards into Jason's arms. "Offline." Timothy finished as Sarah's hair shot from red to black and her right eye went back to gold just as her eyelids closed.

Jason carefully eased her to the ground as he came around to face her. "There you go- huh!?" He was flustered at Sarah's expression as she laid on the floor.

"What's wrong Jason?" Timothy asked while climbing out of his co-pilot seat, walking up to Jason and also noticing Sarah's expression being surprised as well. She was smiling in her sleep.

"I've never seen her smile after ANC shutdown before..." Jason said. "Why now of all times?"

Timothy laughed at Jason. "Maybe because this was the first time you ever padded her on the back and thanked her?" He said condescendingly. "You can be a such an inconsiderate jerk at times you know that right?"

"Oh shut your trap Tim!" Jason grew annoyed at him.

"Oh come on, you know I'm right!" Timothy continued to tease him.

"Just shut up and get the ship back in order will ya!"

Despite the argument, Sarah continued to smile in content knowing that Jason expressed appreciation of her effort for the first time.

Chapter 19: God Is Nigh

"Ready." An honor Guard soldier ordered as a seven-man detail armed with perfectly polished M16s charged their weapons. "Aim." He ordered again as the soldiers pointed the weapons in the air ready to fire. "Fire." A thunderous bang echoed across the cemetery as friends and family, including Alpha team, gathered at Colonel Vial's burial. They mourned as a casket, with The United Earth Government flag draped over it, containing the Colonel's remains that were recovered in space was positioned over a freshly dug grave. "Ready." The honor guards charged again. "Aim." They aimed again, "Fire." Like thunder. "Ready." Charged. "Aim." Towards the sky. "Fire." Like a final heart piercing shot, Sheena, wearing all black with Raymond by her side in Class A uniform, had tears slowly coming down her cheeks as she remembered the ancient lyrics to the song Taps that her father had told her a story about when she was young. She remembered that the song with lyrics originated from the days of the American Civil War. Although not traditionally used at military funerals, she mournfully sang the lyrics to the first verse in her thoughts as the honor guard's bugle player began to play the gloomy melody. "...*Day is done...*" The honor guards folded the United Earth Government flag over the casket with precision and grace. "*Gone the sun...*". At one end of the casket, a lone honor guard embraced the flag. "*From the lakes, from the hills, from the sky...*" He then slowly marched towards Sheena with flag embraced. "*All is well...*" The honor guard presented the flag to Sheena. "*Safely rest...*"

The Honor guard spoke to her. "On behalf of the continental council, the United Earth Military, and a grateful world, please accept this flag as a symbol of our appreciation for your loved one's honorable and faithful service."

"Thank you..." She said trying not to cry any more than she already had as the song's lyrics continued in her thoughts. "*God is nigh...*"

The next day, Sheena and Alpha team went to another funeral for their beloved friend Jake. Once again in her thoughts, Sheena sang the lyrics to the second verse of Taps long before the bugle played.

"*Fading light...*" The sequence for the twenty one gun salute thundered across the cemetery with each gunshot vole. "*Dims the sight...*" The bugles gentle blow echoed for all to hear. "*And a star gems the sky, gleaming bright...*" Folds of Precision and grace, "*From afar...*" the flag was presented to Jake's parents. "*Drawing night...*"

The honor guard spoke. "Please accept this flag as a symbol of our appreciation for your loved one's honorable and faithful service."

"Thank you..." Jakes father took the flag respectfully as his wife, Jake's mother, cried on her husband's shoulder.

"*Falls the night...*" Sheena finished the second verse as she looked towards where she last saw Katherine in uniform. However, Katherine wasn't there. In worry, Sheena looked around for her then saw Katherine with her head against a tree several meters away behind the crowd crying. Sheena walked up and softly embraced her from behind resting her head on Katherine's shoulder trying to comfort her. Katherine wept even harder as she couldn't help but imagine Jake embracing her instead of Sheena. She tried her best not to draw attention while she gasped for air with tears flowing down her face and her legs slowly giving out as she slowly fell to the floor.

The next day after Jake's funeral, a memorial service was held on board the Enidon for all those who died on the Recluses and the battle on the station. Sheena, Raymond, all the crew and combat teams came to the service. After going to two funerals in the same week, the lyrics to Taps were still fresh in Sheena's mind as she remembered the third and final verse. "*Thanks and praise...*" Sheena in a green jump suit and Raymond in camouflage uniform marched up to the line of crewman waiting to give a final salute. "*For our days...*" pictures of the deceased lined the far side wall of the unused large bay. "*Neath the sun, Neath the stars, Neath the sky...*" Crewmen marched up to the pictures, halted, right faced, and slowly saluted with honor, paying respects to their fallen comrades. "*As we go...*" It was now Sheena, Raymond, and the rest of Alpha team's turn. "*This we know...*" Halt, right face, a slow somber yet honorable salute. "*... God is nigh...*"

Epilogue: Lightning

On the fourth day, Lucas, in camouflage uniform, was on earth visiting his father's grave at the same cemetery Colonel Vial was buried. The tomb stone said "Pastor David Walker, A man of God, a loving father, and an honorable warrior." Lucas Reminisce on the good times he had with his father when he was younger, realizing how much he missed him.

"Lucas?" A familiar female voice with an Australian accent called him.

Lucas recognized the voice and smiled as he turned around. "Gia, glad you could-" Once turned around, he saw Yabin by her side.

"Hello Lucas." Yabin greeted. Lucas was surprised she had brought him there.

"I'll leave you two alone for now," Gia smiled. "I have a meeting with Gehnarne and the council soon. See you later Lucas." She walked away towards a car down the main road of the cemetery.

Once she was far enough, Yabin looked toward Gia walking away. "Real pretty that one, and that accent-"

"Really old man?" Lucas scolded Yabin while rolling his eyes.

Yabin chuckled, "I was just being honest."

"Why are you here?" Lucas got to the point.

Yabin thought for a moment on how to start the conversation. He sighed, "I'm sorry for not telling you about your father's past sooner Lucas. When you first said you wanted to join the Marines and go into the USOD, I was afraid that you would be forced to do the same jacked up shit that me and your father were assigned to do for the council. I used his story to try to make you change your mind and instead it led you to rebel and joined the Marines anyway, I was wrong for doing that, I should have been more supportive of you joining when telling you the truth about your father. I'm very sorry." Yabin looked away, ashamed.

Lucas slowly walked up to Yabin, once close enough, Lucas hugged him. Yabin was in shock as Lucas spoke. "I'm sorry too, Although I turned out alright in the USOD, I understand that you were just trying to protect me from those bad experiences you and my father went through, and instead I was ungrateful for what you did and tried to do for me, I get it now."

Yabin embraced Lucas. "Thank you Lucas."

"Your welcome old man." They both chuckled as they backed away from the hug.

"So where the heck is Raymond? I haven't seen him all day, wanted to wish you both good luck out there."

"Yea, I spoke with him earlier, He said he had to do something before he left."

"Do what?" Yabin asked in curiosity.

Raymond, clothed in civilian attire with black sneakers, dark blue jeans, black t-shirt with a black leather jacket, stood in the middle of his empty dusty childhood bed room looking around, seeing the difference in how it looked compared to his dream. He touched the farthest wall from the entrance, closed his eyes, and remembered the peace and love that ran through the walls of this home. "Peace has returned."

"You okay?" Sheena asked while walking through the door wearing all black sneakers, tight jeans, and t-shirt with a short red hoodie. Amplifying her beauty, she also had the same red flower with thin violet outlines that Raymond had gotten for her on Selva perfectly position on the left side of her head with the stem tucked seamlessly between her hair and ear.

Raymond quickly opened his eyes and looked towards Sheena with a smile, letting go of the wall. "Just reminiscing."

She smiled back. "I understand, it's been a while since you've been here. You ready to go?"

"Not just yet," He walked towards her and held both of her hands. "If it's okay with you, could you join me in prayer for a moment?"

Sheena was delightfully surprised he asked her that. "Of course I'd join you." She smiled.

"Okay." He was also delighted as he closed his eyes and bowed his head. Sheena did the same as he began to pray. "Lord, thank you for everything you have done in our lives. I ask while we are away that you keep this home safe, fill this place with your spirit, for the next time we walk through these doors it will be a house of refuge, love and family for all those who enter." Sheena felt a warm sensation in her heart as he continued. "I also ask that you keep us and all of our friends aboard the Enidon safe as we explore your vast and infinite creation, and give us the fortitude to drive on and never quit through the harshest of situations. Lord I have faith that you will work your miracles in this prayer, in your precious all mighty name, Amen."

"Amen." Sheena looked up to Raymond seeing that his faith had truly been restored. She felt proud of him.

"Now I'm ready." He had confidence in his eyes.

"So am I." Sheena responded as they walked towards the front entrance of the apartment lovingly holding hands as they exited and closed the front door behind them leaving the apartment in peace.

On the Enidon, Gehnarne was in a meeting with the council. "After further investigation into USOD's Reaper team's mission to assassinate Garza Liankos," Councilor Soller spoke. "We have concluded that the target they had killed was clearly a double."

"I figured as much." Gehnarne spoke. "Would it be possible to review the documentation on the investigation?"

"Sorry Mr. Gehnarne," Councilor Stratus spoke. "Those files are classified to council personnel only."

Gehnarne was surprise that such a simple investigation was so heavily red taped. "I see." He spoke with a concerned expression.

"As for other matters," Councilor Sven spoke. "Despite disobeying orders, your organization did very well against the hostile threat on the station not only saving many lives from the crew of the Recluses, but even capturing the station. With such a degree of success, we have decided to push your disobedience to the side and just say you took the strategic initiative."

"Thank you for your understanding councilors." Gehnarne responded with a smile.

"In light of such successful initiative," Councilor Quince spoke. "We also have decided to officially recognize your organization as an official Earth Government based group." Gehnarne was pleased to hear such good news.

"And as a gift for everything your people have done so far," Councilor Greaves spoke. "Spectra Squadron is now under your command and the station that you had captured is now your organization's base of operations."

As Gehnarne was in static, he tried his best to control his enthusiasm while trying to remember one of the most important questions he had for the council. Now remembering, "Councilors, I can't thank you enough, Spectra Squadron and that station will prove quite valuable in future operations in exploring our universe and others, however, there is one matter I would like to discuss with you."

"And what matter would that be Gehnarne?" Councilor Soller kindly asked.

"As you can see in Raymond Reynolds report, Garza Liankos claimed that he was actually Lusha Cralix, a self proclaimed spy for you dear councilors. According to Lusha's word, for reasons unknown to me, he states that that you had betrayed him due to a failed mission that needed to remain secret." The councilors expressions grew stern. "Now please don't mistaken this as an accusation, especially when no proof of these claims exists and on top of that, the DNA testing on the remains of the man claiming to be Lusha matched Garza's DNA perfectly, also eliminating any plausible accusation. I only wish to bring this up so I may have your comments and opinions on such a heinous accusation."

The councilors looked at each other, faced back towards Gehnarne and let councilor Soller speak. "As you said yourself Gehnarne," He spoke with a friendly smile, almost fake. "There is no evidence proving such an accusation. With that said I'm sure this was just another blind piece of terrorist propaganda as he tried to continue his legacy of rebellion. Raymond Reynolds also claims this in a way judging from his reports on when Garza tried to recruit him."

"My thoughts exactly councilors, I just felt more comfortable hearing your opinion on the matter, I meant no disrespect."

"None taken, I hope that answer gives you enough comfort to focus on the expansion of humanity. Your organization is the tip of the spear in this new age of expansion Mr. Gehnarne, I hope you and your people are up to the task."

"We are councilors."

"Good!" Councilor Soller was pleased. "Carry on and good luck out there. This meeting is adjourned." The holographic transmission ended.

"That went very well." Gia said as she walked towards Gehnarne.

"It went well enough." Gehnarne was concerned.

"What's wrong?" She sensed his worry.

Gehnarne paused, then answered. "I think their hiding something."

"I see," Gia also became concerned. "Is it something we should be worried about?"

"No, I don't think so, at least not for a long time until our organization and our relationship with the council grows to a more influential level. Only then I believe this could be an issue." Gehnarne thought. "In time, I believe we should prepare for any possibility in our relationship with the council."

"Do you think that's really necessary?"

"Yes." He reassured her. "They may trust me, but I never trusted them from the start, or at least I trusted them enough to get this organization off the ground. Now that we are finally official, we have the resources and abilities to prepare for any of those possibilities." Gia became more concerned with Gehnarne's words. He smiled at her giddily in reassurance. "Don't worry about it so much Gia, it's all just a precaution, let's just stay focused on our tasks and goals and get our operations underway."

"Yes of course!" Gia snapped out of her concern in relief as her and Gehnarne walked out of the conference room.

In his quarters on the Enidon, Jason conducted maintenance on his pistol placed on top of a coffee table in the middle of the room with him seated on the couch. As he worked, the doorbell rang "Come in!" he said with a voice command allowing the door to open. Sarah walked through as Jason turned to his right to see who walked in. "Oh, hey Sarah!" He was happy to see her. She smiled back while Jason reassembled his pistol. "I'm assuming everyone is back from Earth?"

She nodded her head with a yes gesture.

"Okay," He holstered his reassembled pistol as he walked towards the door. "We better start going then." He walked past Sarah and was suddenly stopped when she had grabbed his hand lightly pulling him to stop. Surprised, Jason turned around. "Sarah, what's wrong?"

Sarah looked at Jason nervously as she opened her mouth trying to talk but nothing would come out. She tried again in embarrassment, forcing herself, still nothing.

"Sarah," He smiled at her. "I know your trying and that's great but we really need to go, we're gonna be late." Sarah looked at him somberly. "Try again next time okay." He turned back around towards the door still holding Sarah's hand.

She grew impatient as what she saw from Jake and Katherine's experience flooded her thoughts, next time was never guaranteed. Her impatience turned to frustration as she squeezed Jason's hand and pulled him back towards her yelling. "NO!"

Jason was thrown off balance from Sarah yanking him, he quickly recovered in surprise as he realized Sarah had spoken. "Sarah?!" He looked at her directly in surprise.

She mustered up the courage to try again. With trembling lips, she opened her mouth and said, "T-Th-Thank, y-you..." Jason's eyes were wide open at how her natural voice sounded so different without the assistance of the ANC. She continued, "F-For, E-E-Everything." She finished.

Jason had never heard such an innocent voice before. He proudly smiled at her as he grasped her hand with both of his hands. "Your welcome Sarah." She blushed in embarrassment afraid to look directly at him but found the courage to look anyway. "Now come on, we really gotta go, we'll talk more later okay?"

"O-Okay." She was pleased.

"Good." He continued to hold her hand as they went through the door and walked towards the bridge. Sarah was happy she was holding his hand this time now understanding it was a sign of affection judging by what she saw from Raymond and Sheena's experience. As they walked together, she felt a warm sensation building up inside her. Unnoticed to Jason, Sarah's face was flushed red the whole way to the bridge.

The bridge doors opened with Jason and Sarah walking through. They both looked around seeing that all of their friends had arrived except for Gehnarne. Jason saw Raymond in a camouflage uniform wearing Flow System Gauntlets while talking to Izzy near the TOC entrance. He turned towards Sarah and spoke. "I need to speak with Raymond, Tim is over there if you want to try talking to him next."

Sarah nodded with a smile and quickly walked towards Timothy.

Jason walked towards Raymond just overhearing the last parts of his conversation with Izzy. "Yea, I think so too." Raymond said.

"It would be interesting to see what else that new mode can do." Izzy responded proudly.

"Definitely."

"Hey Raymond, Izzy." Jason joined in on their discussion.

"Hey Jason." They both greeted.

"Raymond, I got some things I need to discuss with our new friend Sykes from Spectra Squadron" Izzy said, "I'll make sure to give my universe's officials all the information you gave me when I send them the final version of the flow system, I'm sure it will be a big help."

"Okay, see you later, and take it easy on the new guy." Raymond said as Izzy walked away. He than turned towards Jason. "So what's up Jason?"

"I read your report on what happened between you and Garza, or Lusha, whatever you guys want to call him, and it doesn't go too deep into how exactly you discovered that new flow system mode, how did you do it?"

"Yea, Izzy was just asking me the same thing. Honestly, it started with a prayer."

"A prayer?" Jason became skeptical. "So what, you're saying that God blessed you with his "Devine Wrath" or something?"

They both chuckled at Jason's cynical comment. "No, no," Raymond responded. "There's more to it than that. You see, the blue disc's that are based off the Red Nova's ANC tech senses ones inner psychological emotional state, more specifically rage, and turns it into a weapon. However, when I said that prayer, there truly was no rage left in me. I was at peace... a peace I had never felt before. In that moment it seemed like the flow system had no rage to work off of anymore but detected something more powerful. That was inner peace. With that, it turned my inner peace into an extremely powerful, but more defensive measure. I actually felt like I lost focus at one point due to the fast movement from the final blow I gave Garza causing the system to return to rage mode. Clearly this new mode is meant more for powerful precision strikes rather than high speed dynamic movement like rage mode. Plus, it uses a lot more battery power than rage mode as well."

"I see, interesting." Jason looked towards Sarah who seemed to be laughing at something that Timothy told her. "Raymond," Jason's expression grew somber. "Do you think that Sarah can ever achieve some kind of inner peace like that? Maybe even do something similar to what you did but with the Red Nova?"

"Well, she's been through a lot Jason so I can't say for sure... It's up to her really." Raymond saw discouragement in Jason's expression. "Mmm... I will say this though, although I felt like I achieved that inner peace through a kind of spiritual connection which than affected my mind, the flow system doesn't work on a spiritual level, so as long as the user has achieved inner peace at the mental or psychological level, I can see others achieving this mode as well, even Sarah. Maybe you can help her with that."

"What, me?" Jason was surprised at what Raymond said

"Of course, you two are already close friends right?"

"Um!" He felt embarrassed "Yea, of course that's what you meant, friends." He then laughed nervously.

"Yea, friends help each other through hard stuff like that," Raymond than realized something in Jason's choice of words and looked at him curiously. "What else did you think I meant?"

"Um, nothing!" Jason looked away from Raymond trying to hide his embarrassment in his expression.

"Ooookay," Raymond was now curious to how Jason really felt about Sarah.

On the other side of the bridge, Sheena, Katherine, and Lucas walked out of the elevator. "Talk to you later Katherine." Sheena said as she and Lucas walked towards Raymond.

"Yea, see ya." Katherine responded.

"Hey Katherine." Izzy greeted as he walked up to her.

"Oh, Izzy, hi." She smiled with a light blush. "About what happened on the station, you patching up my wound and all, thank you for helping me."

Izzy was pleased she was appreciative. "Your very welcome."

Katherine grew somber as she continued to talk to him. "And about a few days ago... I sensed that you were going to ask me out on a date or something I assume?"

Izzy felt nervous. "Uh, yea actually, I was."

"I figured that... Izzy, if you had asked me back than I would have surely said yes but now..."

"After what happened to Jake?..." Izzy felt bad for Katherine's loss.

"Yea... I'm sorry, I just need some time. You're a good man but, I think I just need to focus on myself for a while."

"You went through hell back on Selva, trust me, I understand. Take your time, and take care of yourself first okay."

Katherine was pleased. "Thanks for understanding Izzy."

"Of course." Izzy smiled at her just as the bridge doors opened with Gehnarne and Gia walking in.

Lucas saw Gehnarne and professionally said. "Captain on deck!" Instinctively, everyone on the bridge stood at attention.

"At ease, at ease," Gehnarne said happily as everyone relaxed while Gia walked up and stood next to Lucas while they smiled at each other.

"Well than," Gehnarne spoke standing in front of the captain's chair. "I have some good news. The council has officially recognized our organization as an official earth government sponsored para military organization." Everyone on the bridge clapped their hands in celebration. "With that said, our category of expertise is Strategic Multiverse Operations. Everything dealing with the multiverse or the advancement of any universe including our own will be our responsibility. Now to give ourselves an official name."

"How about Hawk's Reach?" Timothy suggested out loud as Jason was next to him lifting an arm, made a fist with his hand and lightly hit Timothy on the top of his head.

"Yea right." Jason said sarcastically as the bridge mildly laughed.

Gehnarne chuckled. "I appreciate the suggestion young Timothy but, I believe Raymond already had a suggestion that I liked," Everyone looked towards Raymond. "Raymond, would you care to explain and do the honors?"

"Of course." Raymond said with confidence. He paused only for a moment, allowing the anticipation to build. "...We will be a guiding light for other universes currently shrouded in darkness and war, to help them achieve everlasting peace, love and coexistence. With mercy by our side, we will be a dangerously destructive force against those willing to disrupt those ideals of peace." Raymond slowly lifted his right hand with his flow system gauntlet curling his hand into a fist. "Our actions will echo throughout the multiverse like a clash of thunder as we strive forward into the unknown." He felt a sense of pride in the name he had chosen as he let his voice echo throughout the bridge in motivation for all to hear him loud and clear. "We are Lightning!"

Everyone on the bridge clapped in approval feeling that the name matched how Raymond described their actions and ideals perfectly. Gehnarne smiled at him in approval realizing that Raymond was inspired by what he had told him in the sick bay before the battle for the station. "Lightning it is Raymond, Thank you." Raymond put his hand down and relaxed just as Sheena took that same hand and held it. Raymond looked at her lovingly as she looked back the same way. "Helm," Gehnarne sat in his captain's chair. "Set course back to Selva at FTL four, then max FTL once we're out of the Solar System.

"Aye, aye sir!"

Raymond, Sheena and all of their friends looked toward the main monitor waiting to see the ship enter FTL.

The helm reported. "Engaging FTL in five, four, three," During the count down, the engines of the Enidon revved up louder and louder while the helmsmen slowly moved up the control throttle. "Two, one." when the throttle reached full, he pressed a button at the top of the throttle that read "Launch FTL". Suddenly there was a bright flash of light as the G-force stabilizers immediately kicked in with the crew barely noticing the massive burst in speed.

Raymond looked at the main monitor with excitement, anxiously waiting for the next part of his adventure to begin. He whispered to himself with joy in his heart, "It has begun."

"So the station is under their control now?" A male voice spoke in the darkness.

"Yes sir," A female voice responded. "unfortunately."

"I see," He took a deep breath. "Lusha failed."

"What should we do now sir?"

"Take our time, let them enjoy their victory as they become complacent. When the time is right, we will set our plans in motion and overpower them."

"Understood, it will take some time to gather our resources, I believe it should take a little over a year till we're ready to strike."

"Good, very good. Proceed with your plans."

"Yes sir." Footsteps can be heard as they grew distant, fading away.

"...Of all the possible Rifters we could have run into, it had to be you Gehnarne..." Two eyes opened in the darkness, one hazel, the other green. "...My old friend."

[END OF RECORD]

Author Bio
Antonio Reyes Jr.

Antonio Reyes Jr. is a veteran citizen soldier in the US Army National Guard with overseas combat deployment experience as an Infantry Mortarmen in Afghanistan and multiple domestic deployments during hurricane Irene, New York State's increased security response after the Boston Marathon bombing with Task Force Empire Shield, and Operation COVID-19. He is a fan of anything Science Fiction, Anime, Movies, and Video Games where he draws his inspirations for creative writing and is also an avid Paintball player. Antonio has studied criminal justice at Norwich University, The Military College of Vermont, and Cinematography at The College of Staten Island where he graduated with an associates degree in Liberal Arts. In his civilian life he is an Access A Ride bus operator for MV Transportation where he assists the elderly and disabled. He currently resides at home in Staten Island New York where he continues to write the Lightning Saga.

Visit store.bookbaby.com/profile/AntonioReyesJr to learn more about this author, his latest news, and upcoming work